PET WHISPERER P.I.

BOOKS 1-3 SPECIAL COLLECTION

MOLLY FITZ

Editor: Megan Harris
Cover: TM Franklin

PO Box 873543
Wasilla, AK 99687

KITTY CONFIDENTIAL

I was just your normal twenty-something with seven associate degrees and no idea what I wanted to do with my life. That is, until I died... Well, almost.

As if a near-death experience at the hands of an old coffeemaker wasn't embarrassing enough, I woke up to find I could talk to animals. Or rather one animal in particular.

His full name is Octavius Maxwell Ricardo Edmund Frederick Fulton, but since that's way too long for anyone to remember, I've taken to calling him Octo-Cat. He talks so fast he can be difficult to understand, but seems to be telling me that his late owner didn't die of natural causes like everyone believes.

Well, now it looks like I no longer have a choice, apparently my life calling is to serve as Blueberry Bay's first ever pet whisperer P.I while maintaining my façade as a paralegal at the offices of Fulton, Thompson & Associates.

I just have one question: *How did Dr. Dolittle make this gig look so easy?*

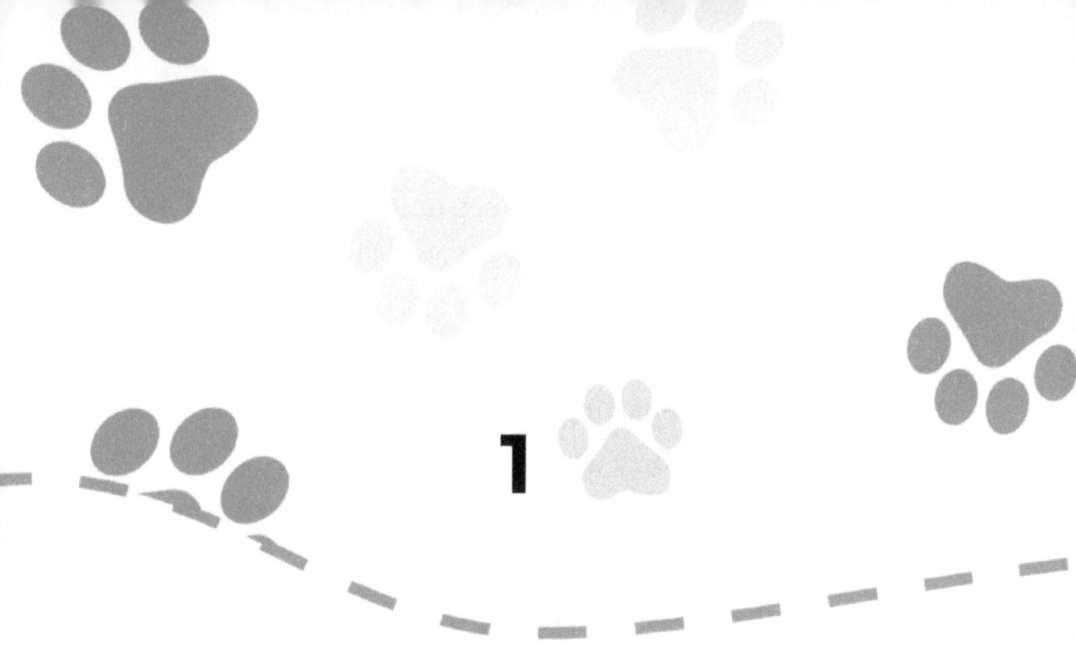

1

The first thing you should know about me is that I hate lawyers. The second is that I work for them.

I didn't plan it that way. Not one bit.

I was going to be a huge star, leave Blueberry Bay behind without so much as a farewell glance over my shoulder as I booked it the heck out of there. The problem with that plan was, well, you need talent in order to be a star—and I never had much of that. At least not that I've discovered.

Yet.

When the temp agency assigned me to work for Fulton, Thompson, and Associates as their new paralegal, I almost said no. But then I saw those dollar signs and remembered how rent is a thing that exists.

And so here I am, doing the needful to get by as I continue down that elusive path toward fame by eliminating every possible talent one at a time. Stands to reason, if I keep at it long enough, I'll eventually find my true calling. Who knows? I could be the world's best hip-hop yodeler…

Except I already tried that and I'm not.

It's fine, really. I'm enjoying the journey, although I sure do wish the destination would hurry up and get here already.

Hi, I'm Angie Russo, and one day you're going to see my name in lights.

You see, my nan used to be a celebrated Broadway actress back in the day. That is, until she quit at the peak of her career to retire to Glendale, Maine, and raise her family.

Before you ask, no, I can't sing, dance, or act, but Nan assures me that I have star power in my blood. Just like she did and just like my mom.

Oh, yeah, you probably know my mom. She's the news anchor on Channel Seven and my dad does the sports report. Seeing as they're these huge career types, it was Nan who did most of the work raising me—and that suited me just fine.

In fact, I'd still be living with her even now if she hadn't given me a gentle push out of the nest and told me it was time to fly.

That was about a year ago and happened just shortly after I collected my seventh consecutive associate degree from Blueberry Bay Community College. Yes, indeed, I've always loved learning anything I could wrap my brain around.

At least God did me a solid by making me smart, even if He made my unique talents hard to find. One of my degrees is, in fact, for paralegal studies and law administration services, which may seem like a strange thing to study for someone who hates lawyers as much as I do.

But that's a story for another time...

This is the story of how I almost died, and it's a good one.

* * *

I began my day by sniff-testing two blazers with the goal of choosing whichever was cleanest for a will reading at the office that day. Both smelled vaguely of sweat and gym shoes, meaning either would earn me a stern lecture from the partners. Then again, maybe that's precisely what I deserved for putting off that trip to the dry cleaner's for so long.

After spraying a cough-inducing fog of deodorizer into my closet, I plucked the neon pink jacket off its hanger and pushed my arms into the sleeves. A black and white polka dot blouse and stretchy leggings completed the outfit perfectly. Because I didn't have time to wash my hair that morning, I pulled my poofy shoulder-length hair into a messy bun and accented the do with a cute barrette I picked up earlier in the week from my favorite dollar store.

And before you can ask...

No, I didn't have time for dry cleaning.

And, yes, I always had time for the dollar store.

On that particular morning, I didn't have time for either one, though. In fact, I'd spent so much time agonizing over which blazer to wear that I'd pretty much run out of time altogether. I'm already not a morning person, but when you add in a manic rush to get to a job I don't even like...

Well, I could already tell just how bad this day would end up.

I raced out the door—unshowered, unfed, and uncaffeinated—hoping that I'd at least have some luck and catch all green lights on my commute that day. Instead, the longest train in the world cut me off not even two blocks from my house. The train tracks run along the only major street to serve our small coastal town, and there's absolutely no way for me to reach the firm via backroads, which meant I found myself stuck waiting in a line of angry, honking cars for a solid fifteen minutes.

By the time I actually reached the office, I was the last one through the door and we had less than ten minutes until the will reading commenced. My hope to sneak in undetected proved unfounded as well.

"Russo!" Mr. Thompson bellowed before the door even closed all the way behind me. If you pictured an old, white guy wearing boat shoes and an ascot, you'd have a pretty good idea of how Mr. Thompson looked and an even better idea of how he acted. He was a fantastic lawyer, but not a very personable boss.

A thick, meaty vein pulsed at the side of his head, and for some reason I couldn't stop staring at it. He pointed at me with a shaking finger and a scowl. "Late and dressed like you're attending an 80's themed party instead of a will reading. Nope. That's not going to fly today. Go see if Peters has a jacket you can borrow."

It took the strength of a thousand body builders not to roll my eyes as I slumped off to find the only female associate in the whole place.

We often got grouped together by nature of our shared gender, but Bethany Peters and I were nothing alike. She was blonde and pretty and *looked* like she should be sweet as pie, too—except she was actually the biggest shark of them all. I guess you have to be in order to get taken seriously in a man's world.

But what did I know?

I was just a glorified secretary who didn't even want to be there.

Bethany turned her nose up at me the second I entered her office, and I pinched my fingers over mine. See, Bethany had an obsession with essential oils and even sold them in these tacky online parties that she invited us all to about once per month. Even at that point I'd only worked at the firm for a few months but had already ordered more lavender bath salts than I could ever possibly need.

On the day of the will reading, Bethany's office reeked of juniper and lemon—definitely not one of her better combinations. Still, whatever blend of restorative girl power mojo she was trying to concoct, I sincerely hoped it would work for her.

"Let me guess," she said in that nasally, condescending tone that she always used whenever talking to me or one of the other employees without a law degree. "Fulton sent you in to borrow a jacket from me."

A smile crept across my face. "Thompson, actually." Call me a contrarian, but I loved getting the chance to prove her wrong, especially when a day started off as bad as this one had. It was a small and beautiful gift.

"Can't you pick up some more appropriate work clothes for yourself so you're not always stuck borrowing mine last minute?" She sighed before lumbering over to the other side of her office with loose arms and large, exaggerated strides. She looked like a preppy blonde gorilla, but I decided to keep that particular comparison to myself.

"Thompson... Fulton... They're both kind of freaking out today," Bethany confided in me. "Apparently the old lady that died is related to Fulton."

"How do you know?" My eyes grew wide. So, this was why everyone was making such an unusually large fuss that morning.

"Well for starters, her last name is Fulton, too." She tapped on her temple to draw my attention to her superior brain power.

I tapped on my head and shot her an ugly grimace in response. Now we were both office gorillas, and what an exhibit the pair of us made.

Bethany chuckled as she handed me the most boring navy-blue blazer God ever put on this green earth. "Try to keep it together for the reading, huh?"

I nodded while switching jackets. The blazer pinched at my armpits, but I knew better than to complain. "Thanks," I muttered, narrowly escaping Bethany's office before she could once again remind me that Goodwill or the Salvation Army were nice places to find clothes within my budget.

"I'd lose the barrette!" she shouted after me.

Aargh, so close.

But since Bethany tended to be like a dog with a bone once she had an idea, I pulled my cute little accessory out, taking a few caught hairs with it. The bun came out next, and I quickly finger combed my hair to make it semi-presentable. Hopefully that would be enough to make everyone happy.

"Angie, is that you?" Mr. Fulton, the senior most partner called from inside the conference room. For whatever reason, Thompson always uses our last names, and Fulton sticks to our firsts. Maybe that was their way of playing good lawyer, bad lawyer, or maybe they just liked to keep us on our toes.

I put on my best smile. After all, the guy did just lose a family member. "Good morning, sir. Can I help you with something?"

His eyes lingered on my face briefly before he cleared his throat and pointed to the dusty old coffeemaker in the corner of the room. "We're going to need lots of coffee, and since you're a bit late this morning, I'm afraid there's no time to make a run to the barista. You'll have to use our backup maker. As strong as you can make it, please."

"I'm on it!" We didn't use the in-house coffeemaker very often and really only kept it around for code red caffeine emergencies. The fact we needed it now was definitely not a good sign.

In fact, I'd never actually used that old thing at all. The one time I'd almost had the chance, an intern burst into the office carrying a tray of Starbucks and let me off the hook. This ancient thing shouldn't be too hard to figure out, though. After all, I had seven associate degrees.

Mr. Thompson, Bethany, and a few of the other associates entered while I was fiddling with the roast basket, which for some reason refused to line up with the necessary grooves in the machine.

Normally we'd only have one or two attorneys present at a reading, but they seemed to be pulling out all the stops for this one.

Was it just because the person who died was related to one of our partners? Or was something more going on here? My curiosity had definitely been piqued by this point.

Working in my corner, I caught a few snippets of the discussion happening around the conference room table. Our day-to-day conversations at the firm were normally pretty dry, but things sounded refreshingly juicy today.

"Admittedly, it is a somewhat unusual situation," Thompson said first.

Later, Fulton said, "Given the stipulations, I'm expecting one of the grantees to contest."

An associate named Brad set up a tape recorder—yes, another ancient relic living in our office—and Bethany shuffled a bunch of papers around.

When the coffeemaker's basket snapped into place, I let out a triumphant yip, drawing aggravated stares from my colleagues. "I'll just be right back," I promised as I rushed past the growing crowd with the empty coffee pot.

A beautiful, blonde woman wearing a matching cardigan set and a string of pink pearls stopped me before I could make it to the kitchen tap.

"Angie, I'm so glad I ran into you!" Diane Fulton—Mr. Fulton's wife—shook her head and knitted her over-plucked brow. "Did you catch last night's episode?"

Even though Diane dresses like a blue-blood snob, she was actually the coolest person in the entire place. She and I had a whole list of reality shows we liked to watch together and discuss whenever she came by the office to visit her husband for lunch.

Her eyes widened as she waited for my response. I may have been late to work, but I would never be late when it came to our shows.

"I couldn't believe Trace got eliminated," I answered with a tragic sigh as I turned on the faucet and let water fill the coffeepot. "Hopefully he'll still get a record deal out of the whole thing."

"Let's catch up later," she told me with a slight frown. "I have to..." She pointed to the conference room and knitted her brow again.

And I felt just awful for her. "I heard. My condolences. You, uh, weren't close, were you?"

She stared at me for a moment as if she hadn't heard the question. Her dangling earrings were so long, they hit her cheeks as she shook her head. "Ethel was Richard's great aunt. She was very old and had been sick for a long time. I think we were all expecting her to go sooner rather than later."

"Still, that sucks," I offered.

Diane gave me a polite smile then excused herself.

Seriously? The best I could come up with was *that sucks?* Good thing none of my degrees were in counseling. Then again, maybe it wouldn't be the worst idea in the world to go back to school. After all, school had always been my happy place. That was part of how I'd ended up with so many degrees to begin with.

I returned with a full carafe of water and a bag of coffee grounds that had expired some time last year but thankfully still smelled fresh. During my very brief absence, the meeting room had filled with even more folks. The Fultons must have been one big family. Either that, or Great Aunt Ethel had been one wealthy--and presumably generous—woman.

Mr. Fulton looked to me with one eyebrow raised in question.

"Almost ready," I assured him as I rushed past the room of people to my quiet, little coffeemaker corner.

Quick as I could, I filled up the tank with my freshly gotten water, scooped some grounds into the filter, and pressed the big red button to initiate the brewing process.

Nothing happened

So, I pushed it again... and again... and another thirteen times to no effect.

"Plugging it in would help," Bethany shouted loud enough for everyone to hear and causing them all to laugh at me and my well-meaning incompetence.

Ugh, talk about wicked embarrassing!

I groped around the back of the machine until I found the cord. Everyone was still laughing when I pushed the plug into the closest socket...

First, I felt a gentle prick on my fingertips, then my entire body lit with pain. For about two milliseconds, I became hyper-conscious of my surroundings—every smell, sound, feeling, even what the air in that room tasted like just then. The individual laughs transformed into a collective gasp that tore through the room.

Then with a sharp *zzzzztt* it all fell away.

And I fell unconscious to the floor.

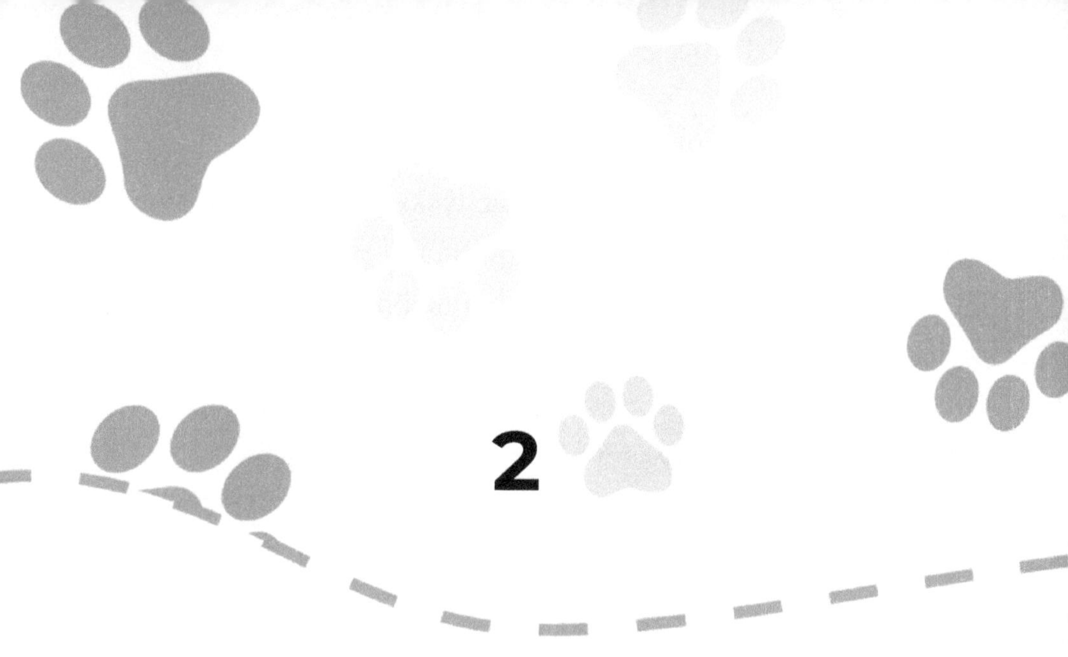

2

I woke up on the conference room floor. Funny, I couldn't remember passing out, yet there I was.

My heart womped a million miles an hour, but most of my body had become fuzzy and tingly. I tried to move my arms, but they seemed content to lay splayed out at my sides. One by one, my senses started to come back online.

Pop!

Mrs. Fulton's shriek was the first thing I heard, then others in the room began to murmur amongst themselves. Some voices I recognized, but others were completely unfamiliar.

Bethany said, "It's probably time we threw that old thing out."

Mr. Fulton ignored her as he rushed toward me. "Angie… Angie…" His panicked voice grew closer until he'd arrived right at my side. "Are you okay?"

Meanwhile, Mr. Thompson mumbled something about liabilities

and workman's compensation—exactly as anyone who knew him would expect him to do in such a situation.

I was still trying to remember what had happened when an unexpected weight pressed down onto my chest and made it quite difficult for me to breathe. The overpowering smell of tuna filled my nostrils, and the sudden intensity of it brought on a coughing fit.

A voice I'd never heard before hovered over me. "Well, how about that? This one had more than one life, after all. People, *pssh.* So fragile."

"Oh, she's breathing!" Diane shouted.

"Of course, she's breathing, honey," her husband responded with a note of relief in his previously panicked voice. "She's also coughing."

"And here I thought the car trip wouldn't be worth it," that same unfamiliar voice chimed in, pairing the words with an unkind chuckle. "That was, paws down, the best entertainment I've had all week."

Finally, my eyes flew open, and I found a gleaming amber gaze watching me from just a few inches away. Wait... Why was there a cat in the office, and why was it *on me?* I struggled to sit up, but my limbs were still too heavy to lift on my own.

"Oh, honey," that voice drawled again. "If you expect to keep walking, then you probably should have landed on your feet."

I let out a loud groan. I could feel the activity humming all around me, but the only thing I saw was the danged cat who was definitely intruding in my personal space right about then.

"What happened?" I asked before coughing again.

"I think the coffeemaker electrocuted you when you tried to plug it in," Diane revealed. Her shaky voice made it obvious she'd been crying. I felt so bad that my clumsiness put her through that.

"Oh, jeez. This one's even stupider than the first. I'm really looking forward to living with her while the rest of the family figures out where to dump me. Such a pity. They don't know greatness when it's staring them in the face."

I moaned and attempted to lift my head to get a better look around the room. "Who is that?" I demanded.

"It's me, Angie," Mrs. Fulton said, squeezing one of my hands in earnest. "You asked what happened, and I told you about the coffeemaker."

"No, the guy who just called both of us stupid." I wished I could sit up to see past this annoying cat, but he was the only thing that filled my vision in that moment. Of course, I had lots of questions about the coffeemaker and how such a tiny old appliance had managed to zap me unconscious, but the need to identify the unknown speaker weighed on me much more heavily.

A cruel snicker sounded nearby. "I called you stupid, because you *are* stupid. Honesty is the best policy, the truth will set you free, yada yada, and all that other nonsense you humans like to say."

If I hadn't known any better, I'd have sworn that strange, lilting voice was coming from the cat. Man, how hard had I hit my head when I fell?

The cat leaned in so close that his whiskers tickled my face. His unnervingly large eyes moved frantically from side to side as if stalking some kind of prey. Oh, how I hoped I wasn't that prey. I'd barely escaped the coffeemaker. If something sentient set out to hurt me today, I wouldn't even stand a chance.

"Did you... Did you really hear what I said?" the voice asked again, and again it really sounded like it was coming from the cat. Did he eat a tiny human or something? None of this made any sense.

"Yes, I hear you, and I think you're rather mean," I answered with a huff, giving the best attitude I could, considering my prone position.

"Angie, who are you talking to?" Diane asked with words that sounded unsure and just as worried as I felt myself.

"I'm not sure who it is, but he keeps insulting me." I closed my eyes tight, then slowly opened them again.

The cat seemed to smile, but not in a friendly way. Once again, I wondered if he considered me easy prey. Heck, I considered me easy prey, too.

"No one's insulting you," Mr. Fulton insisted. "We all just want to make sure you're okay."

The cat smiled again, bigger this time. "Ooh, ooh, me! I'm insulting you, you big, stupid bag of skin."

"He just called me a big, stupid bag of skin! Can you really not hear him?" I blinked half a dozen times, then pinched myself. Nothing seemed to change.

"Russo, I think maybe you should take the rest of the day off and a trip to the emergency room," Mr. Thompson commanded after clearing his throat loudly from somewhere near the door.

"Wow, you really can hear me," the voice said again. "By the way, hi, I'm Octavius Maxwell Ricardo Edmund Frederick Fulton, and I have some demands."

I was having a difficult time keeping track of all the threads of conversation. I knew the partners were worried about me and about themselves, but I still couldn't identify the mystery speaker or figure out what he wanted. "Octavius Maxwell... who?"

"Honey, are you talking about the cat?" Mrs. Fulton asked, picking the tabby off from my chest.

My straining lungs thanked her, and immediately I felt stronger.

In a cutesy baby voice, Diane held the cat up to her face and cooed, "Are you trying to help our Angie feel better? You're such a sweet fuzzy wuzzy."

The cat turned to me and narrowed his eyes into slits. *"Heeeeelp meeeee."*

Energized at last by my need to find out what the heck was going on, I managed to sit up and look around the room.

"Oh, good. Now that you can move again, Peters will take you to the hospital," Thompson decreed.

Bethany sighed but didn't argue the point.

"Wait!" The tabby cat trotted up to me the second Diane set him back on the floor. "What about my demands?"

I stared at him, dumbfounded. There was absolutely no way...

The cat flicked his tail and emitted a low growl from deep in his throat. "I know you can hear me, so how about doing the polite thing and keeping up your end of the conversation, huh?"

"What do you want?" I whispered, but still everyone in the office could see and hear the crazy lady talking to the cat she'd just met.

"My owner was murdered, and I need you to help me prove it. Also, of equal importance, I haven't been fed in hours. Maybe years."

His ears fell back against his head and his eyes widened, making me feel inexplicably fond of him despite his bad attitude.

Then the first part of what he said hit me, and I gasped. *"Murdered?"*

Bethany tittered nervously and grabbed me by the arm. "Okay, let's get you to the hospital. Hallucinations are not a good sign."

"But..." I began to argue. That argument fell away when I realized I had no sane or valid reason to resist.

"Murdered!" the cat shouted after me dramatically. "She was offed before her time, and now that I know you can hear me, you're going to help me get her the justice she deserves. It's the least I can do to thank her for all the years she spent feeding me and arranging my pillows just as I like them. Also, did you hear the part about me needing to be fed?"

Bethany and I had almost made it to the doorway. That meant it was my last chance to talk to the cat. For all I knew, we would never see each other again. Of course, I knew it was totally crazy to assume there was even a chance any of this being real, but still, I couldn't ignore the fact that the talking tabby needed my help.

"I want to help!" I bellowed back into the room just before the door closed behind us.

"No, you *need* help," Bethany growled, sounding even more like an animal than the cat had. "Thanks a lot, by the way. This was the first time they've included me in something this important to the firm. Now, thanks to your little act with the coffeemaker, I'm going to miss it."

That hurt almost as bad as the zap from the coffeemaker. "You honestly don't think I electrocuted myself just to sabotage you, do you?"

She sighed and pinched the bridge of her nose. "No, I'm sorry. I know it's not your fault. I just have to work twice as hard to get ahead since I'm the only female associate, and everyone wants to put me on the baby track instead of the partner track."

"Yeah, well... at least you're not just some glorified secretary." I honestly couldn't believe Bethany was complaining about *her* problems when I'd just had a near-death experience a few minutes earlier...

Or maybe I could. It was Bethany, after all.

She settled me into the passenger seat of her car. It was a newer model Lexus, which told me she probably didn't have things quite as bad as she thought. Still, I felt guilty for costing her what she considered to be her big shot, so I said, "For what it's worth, you're the smartest one of them all."

She laughed as she buckled her seatbelt and adjusted the rearview mirror. "Even more than Thompson and Fulton?"

I nodded, and the movement made me dizzy. "Especially more than Thompson and Fulton."

We shared a brief glance of camaraderie before she backed out of her spot and navigated onto the main road. Hopefully there would be no more trains passing through today, because despite our brief bond of sisterhood, I wasn't sure how long either of us could handle being trapped in a car together.

"Thanks for taking me, even though I know you didn't want to.

You don't have to wait around. Just drop me off and I'll call my nan to come get me when I'm done."

"Already planned on it. If I hurry, I can still make part of the reading." She tapped at her temple to once again show her superior thinking.

And just like that, we were back to normal.

As for me? I wasn't so sure.

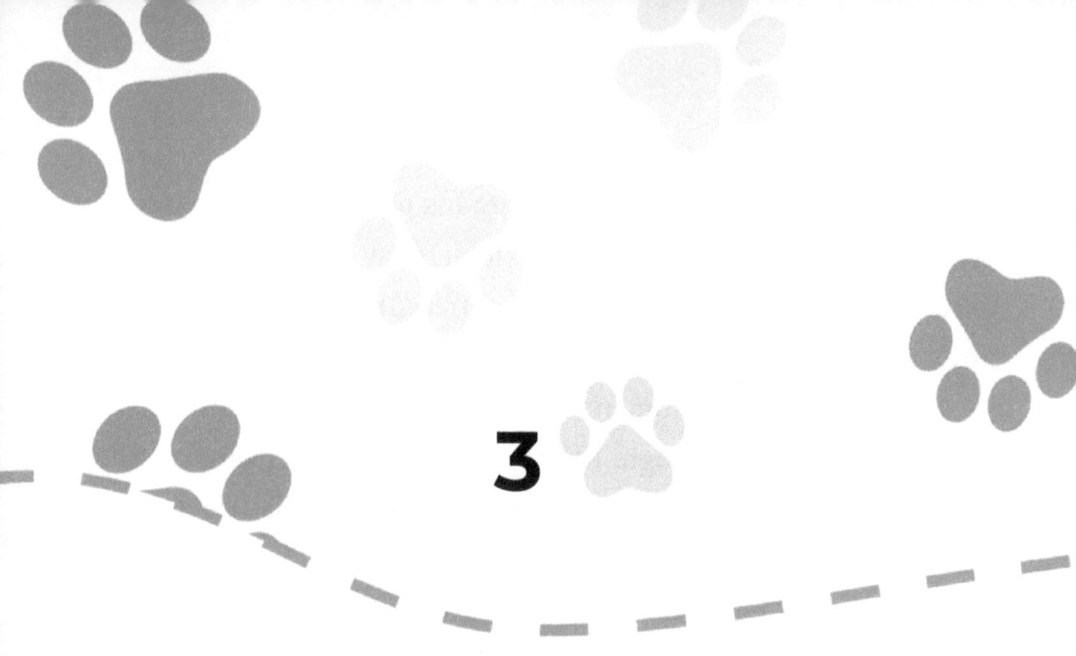

3

I sat swinging my legs off the side of a wheeled hospital bed as the emergency room doctor laughed right in my face.

"You actually got electrocuted by an old coffeemaker?" Whatever kind of reception I might have expected to get at the hospital, this definitely wasn't it.

I crossed my arms over my chest and turned away so I wouldn't have to look at his inappropriately amused expression. "Yes, I don't see why that's funny."

He finally sobered up as he twiddled his pen between his fingers like a strange tic. Studying me with a slight frown, he asked, "And it caused you to lose consciousness?"

"*Yes.*" We'd been over this before.

"Did you hit your head on the way down?"

"I don't think so." There was still plenty about my accident I couldn't quite wrap my head around, but at least I felt fine physically.

The doctor stuck his pen back into his pocket and peered into my eyes before declaring, "Well, you look okay to me. The most I'd prescribe to you is a dose of regular strength Tylenol in case there's any pain from hitting the floor like you did."

He hesitated for a moment, then shook his head and offered a wry laugh. "It's strange, though… the voltage in that coffeemaker should have only given you a light zap. I'm surprised you had such a strong reaction."

So, we were back to this. I needed to get out of there before he called in his entire staff to check out the freak on display in the ER.

"Gee, thanks," I muttered.

His vision narrowed. "Yes, *thanks* is right. Be thankful you haven't got any burns. No concussion, either. But you did manage to score a day off work, huh?" The doctor had the audacity to wink at me before letting out another chuckle and turning to walk away.

"I didn't do this to myself on purpose!" I called after him, trying not to let my frustration get the better of me. *What a jerk.*

When I was sure he wouldn't be coming back, I shot a quick text to Nan and gathered my things to go wait for her outside. The whole time I sat there waiting, I didn't see a single person come or go through those spinny glass doors. Even though Blueberry Bay wasn't the most densely populated area, I still expected the hospital to see some activity. Then again, maybe it was a good thing that clown of a doctor didn't have any actual sick people to look after.

I paced back and forth along the curb, trying my best to recall every detail of that morning. As unkind as the doctor had been, he did have a point. I'd nearly died at the hands of an old coffeemaker, and when I'd woken up again, I could talk to animals.

As a kid, I'd loved watching Eddie Murphy as the hapless Dr. Doolittle, helping his animal patients like no one else could thanks to his unique ability to talk with them. Back then, I'd thought it would be so cool to be able to understand and hold conversations with animals.

But now that I was faced with the reality?

I was scared out of my mind.

A strong gust of wind kicked up a swirl of leaves, drawing my attention to the parking lot where a pair of seagulls fought beak and talon over a fast-food hamburger wrapper that appeared to have a bit of cheese stuck to its center.

One of them held its wings out to his side and screeched. Then the other hissed and pecked at his opponent's feet. Their fight took on new vigor as they danced around the wrapper screaming and pecking at each other—and giving me the beginnings of a wicked headache.

"Oh, will you just be quiet!" I shouted at them.

If the birds could hear me, they were clearly too occupied with their impromptu battle to care.

Wait... could they hear me? Would they be able to talk to me like the cat from work did?

I tiptoed over to them, thankful I was on my own in the abandoned parking lot because I knew how crazy I looked in that moment. Still, a little crazy was a small price to pay for finally figuring out what was going on with me today.

I cleared my throat and addressed the birds. "Excuse me."

One of the seagulls cawed and nipped at the other, but neither of them gave me any credence.

"Excuse me," I called a little louder, taking several more steps forward.

One of the birds turned to look at me, and the other took the opportunity to grab the wrapper and hop away with it. The first gave chase and soon the two were locked in a tug of war, the paper wrapper twisting and crinkling between them.

I chased after them too and yelled at the top of my lungs, *"Excuse me!"*

Finally, they both gave me their attention, although neither let go of the coveted prize.

Since I at last knew they were listening, I followed up with an offer I knew they wouldn't be able to refuse. I smiled wide and told them, "I have tons of tasty food. Burgers, fries, ice cream cones... It's all yours if you just answer one question: *Can you understand me?"*

One of the gulls tilted its head as if to think about this. While he was distracted, the other yanked the wrapper free and flew off into the sky.

"Sorry about that," I told the remaining bird. "I can get you more food, better food that didn't come from the trash. What do you say?"

Before the gull could answer, a ruby red sports coupe rolled up next to me, scaring him off once and for all.

Nan rolled down the window of her favorite new toy and whistled at me. "Hop in, dearie!"

"Thanks for coming to get me." I slid onto the slippery leather seat and tugged the seatbelt across my chest.

Nan let the car idle as she lowered her cat eye sunglasses and studied me without saying a word. Her blue-gray hair was covered with a brightly patterned silk scarf, and she wore driving gloves that matched the exact same shade of red as the car's exterior. I had to admit, Nan had style. Even when she'd moved away from the spotlight of Broadway, she'd never stopped putting on a show.

I shrugged. "What? I'm fine."

Additional wrinkles formed on her forehead. "You didn't say much in your text. What happened?"

"Just a mild electric shock. Again, I'm fine."

She raised an eyebrow at me. "Then why the hospital?"

I shrugged again. "You know how the partners are. They don't want to take any risks when it comes to liabilities and whatnot."

She shook her head, then stepped on the gas pedal so hard it jerked us both back against our seats. "So where to?"

I needed to find that cat since it seemed only he had the answers I craved. If I was lucky, then this would all turn out to be one very bad dream. Either way though, I had to know—but Nan didn't. At least not until I knew how to explain what was happening to me.

"Back to the office, please," I answered, fingering my seatbelt nervously.

Nan let out a sassy little huff. "C'mon, not even going to take the full day off? You've already been excused, now let's play hooky. Maybe we could hit the beach. Or perhaps a matinee. What do you say, dear?"

Ah, playing hooky. That had always been Nan's favorite thing. Some of my favorite childhood memories involved her breaking me out of second period to go on some zany, ill-conceived adventure. As I'd grown older, our skip days had grown fewer and far between. In fact, we hadn't managed a single one since I'd moved out to get my own place.

Make no mistake, I missed my nan dearly. However…

I hated to let her down, but I had no other choice. "That sounds great, but I've got to grab my car from the office or I'll have a hard time of it tomorrow. Maybe I could meet you for dinner instead?" I offered with the biggest smile I can muster.

Nan groaned and took a sharp right turn. "This new job has changed you."

Oh, she had no idea.

* * *

Despite Nan's objections, she brought me back to the office in one piece. Hardly more than an hour had passed since I left and most everyone was still hanging around, discussing the surprise twists in Ethel Fulton's will. Could one of them really be a murderer?

Only my new cat friend had the answers, which is why it was so important that I find him without any further delays or interruptions.

I spotted Bethany chatting with the other associates and headed her way to ask that they fill me in on what I missed.

"Can you believe she left so much to the cat? What's a cat going to do with all that money?" someone I didn't recognize grumbled, taking a long pull at his take-out coffee cup.

The woman standing beside him nodded. "It's a real slap in the face."

Who are these two? Could they be the murderers? I wondered, trying not to stare as I committed their features to memory.

Diane came out of nowhere and saddled me with a giant, squishy hug. "Oh, thank goodness you're okay. We were all so worried!"

"Yup, you'll need more than an angry coffeemaker to take me out. I'm made of tougher stuff." I knocked on my collarbone to demonstrate my durability.

As much as I enjoyed my chats with Diane, I came back for one reason and one reason alone—to find that cat. Somehow, I had to figure out a way to inquire about him without raising anyone's suspicions.

"Um, did the reading go okay?" I fished, hoping she would take the bait and swim with it.

Mrs. Fulton dropped her voice to a whisper and leaned in close. "Yes, but some of the relatives are upset with their take. You know how these things are."

"At least she didn't leave it all to the cat." I tried to act casual, seeing as I'd already overheard that the dearly deceased had done exactly that.

"Well, not all of it, but it was still quite a bit. That's why he was here, you know. She required all beneficiaries be present and seeing as the cat was one of the biggest, well, there you go."

I feigned shock—not the electrocution kind this time, but the real, honest-to-goodness surprise at receiving unexpected news. "You've got to be kidding me."

Diane shook her head and made a funny face. “Never let it be said that Auntie Fulton didn’t love that cat.”

“So, what’s going to happen to him now that she’s gone?”

Mr. Fulton noticed us and crossed the office to join our conversation. “Back already, Angie? Don’t you at least want to take the rest of the day off?”

Crud. I’d been so close to getting the answer I needed from his wife. Now I had to find a way to steer the discussion back to the location of that cat without making things too awkward. Mr. Fulton was a smart guy who regularly bested the area’s top attorneys in court. Did I really think I could outmaneuver him?

I had to try.

I swallowed hard and put on the same semi-famous smile that had landed me this job in the first place. “I’m fine. I’ll probably head out early but wanted to check in first to grab my car and let you all know I’m okay.”

“Great. See you tomorrow, then. Sleep in a little if you think it will help.” Mr. Fulton patted me on the shoulder and glanced pointedly toward the door.

I knew he was just looking out for me, but I couldn’t leave without first talking to that cat, especially if there was a murderer afoot. Hopefully Mr. Fulton would thank me for my stubbornness on this matter later.

I stood my ground, twisting my hands before me. “Actually, I was wondering if the cat was still around. He seemed pretty worried, and I wanted to let him know I’m okay.”

Husband and wife exchanged a worried expression.

"It's okay, dear. We'll tell him for you," Diane informed me kindly.

I hated lying, but desperate times...

"It may not be okay," I warned then jumped with both feet straight into my lie. "I did a course on Animal Psychology back at Blueberry Bay Community College, and it would help if he could see for himself that I'm fine. Otherwise, um, behavioral problems could arise due to sublimated anxiety."

Mrs. Fulton stared at me in confused horror. "Oh, no, we don't want that!"

Mr. Fulton chuckled. "You said it, honey. Especially since he's staying with us for the foreseeable future. We don't want old Octavius taking out his sublimated anxiety on our new curtains."

And there it was. Another golden opportunity, one I was too greedy not to grab hold of.

"You know... He's probably already quite anxious. More than likely depressed, too, what with his owner dying and his whole life being uprooted."

"I hadn't thought of it like that." Diane's brow pinched with concern. "Can cats get depression?"

I almost had her.

Nodding vigorously, I dug my hooks in deeper. "Most definitely, and since they can't exactly take anti-depressants, they really need someone who knows how to recognize the signs and treat them naturally."

"What are you suggesting?" Mr. Fulton asked. Unfortunately, his face gave nothing away.

Shrugging, I try to act disinterested in the outcome to really sell it now. "I know I'm just a paralegal, but I did take that course and I've always had a way with animals, especially cats. Since you have so much going on with the family and the estate, maybe I should take him off your hands for a few days. I could keep him out of your hair and help him work through his depression, if you want."

They looked at each other, exchanging a look I couldn't quite discern. I supposed that type of thing came with being married for thirty-plus years.

Diane was the one who finally answered for both of them. "It would be a huge help to us, but are you sure?"

With a massive placating grin, I answered, "It would be my pleasure."

Yes, a pleasure—and hopefully *not* my funeral instead.

4

With the Fultons' blessing, I let myself into the senior partner's office and immediately spotted the cat. He sat right in the center of the leather desk chair like some kind of Bond villain. I half expected him to pull out a smaller, fluffier cat to stroke intimidatingly while he spoke to me.

"Took you long enough," he mumbled, obsessively licking his paw. Despite all I had been through to get back to him, he didn't even bother to look up at me. I'd known this cat for all of five minutes and could already tell that he was a major jerk.

If I'd only been grappling with the talking-to-animals problem that day, I probably would have walked away then and there. But, no, someone had been murdered—and a sweet old lady at that.

"I came as fast as I could," I hissed, wondering how he liked that little dose of his own medicine. "It's not like you had anywhere else to be."

He snorted and said something about busy schedules and important routines. I didn't exactly catch everything because he spoke incredibly fast.

Whatever the case, there I stood, conversing with a cat in a way we both mostly understood. If I was crazy, then at least I was consistent about it. Now that I'd found and confirmed my ability to talk to this cat, it was time to learn his impossibly long moniker. "What's your name again?"

He rolled his amber eyes then rose to his feet. "Weren't you paying attention? I'm Octavius Maxwell Ricardo Edmund Frederick Fulton."

No wonder he talked so fast. It was the only way for him to spit out that name without risking the other person falling asleep right in the middle of it. I tested out the strange name, hoping that if I got it right he might be a little nicer to me. "Octavius Maxwell Richard..."

"Ricardo Edmund Frederick Fulton," he corrected. "Honestly, it's not that hard."

He hopped off the chair and paced toward me, irritation flashing in his snake-like eyes. Somehow it was now my fault he had a ridiculous long name. Well, I refused to be bullied by a creature that I easily outweighed ten-to-one.

"My name's Angie. Thanks for asking, by the way."

He stopped walking and crinkled the skin above his nose. "Well, that's boring. It's got no ring to it at all."

"Sorry to disappoint you," I hissed, which made me wonder if I was speaking cat or if he was speaking human.

The tabby's voice took on a kinder tone for the first time since I'd met him. He sighed, and said, "Well, we can't all be Octavius Maxwell Ricardo Edmund Frederick Fulton, the First."

"Wait, did you just add to your name to make it longer? No, this is not going to work. Even if I could remember your string of, like, eight names, I am not saying all of them whenever I want to get your attention."

"Whatever." He widened his eyes at me and yawned. What a bratty cat. Hopefully, if I put him in his place, he'd start treating me as an equal instead of an incompetent servant.

"Since you're on board, I'm shortening your name to... to... *umm...*"

"Nice to see your mind is just as sharp as your name." He let out a mewling laugh, which I ignored.

"Shut up, Octavius... Octagon... Octopuss... Octo-Cat! That's it. From now on, I'll call you Octo-Cat." I felt so proud of myself for that cute nickname that fit him like a glove. Not even his bad attitude could bring me down now.

"Octo... Cat." He sneered and batted at the air between us. "I don't think so."

"Well, your first name is Octavius, and you have like eight names total, so—"

He padded the ground and spun in a circle. "No, my first name is Octavius Maxwell Ric—"

"Enough! Do you want me to go back to Octo-Puss? Because I can."

He began to say something, but the sound of the door creaking open stopped us both mid-conversation.

Diane's head appeared in the doorway before the rest of her. "Everything okay in here? I thought I heard voices."

I stood up straight and brushed off the knees of my pants, flashing my friend with an ingratiating smile to promise I wasn't crazy. "Totally fine. I was just introducing myself and letting him know he's going to be living with me for a few days."

She glanced toward Octo-Cat, who chose that exact moment to plop himself on his rump and start licking his kitty bits. "You're talking to the cat?" she asked, but it didn't really sound like a question.

I fixed my eyes on her to show I wasn't embarrassed, even though I most definitely was. "Of course. It helps them to forge an emotional bond which will be important even for the brief time we're living together."

She glanced from me to the cat and back again, then shrugged. "Okay, well, I just pulled his things from the car. Are you sure it's not any trouble for you to take him off our hands for a few days?"

She stopped and frowned before confiding, "I'm afraid he's not the nicest animal."

"*Positive.* Thanks for grabbing his stuff. I should probably get both of us home for some rest. Busy day, huh?" I laughed nervously, then pushed past her through the doorway.

"Here, kitty. C'mon, kitty." I clicked my tongue and patted the side of my thigh to call him over.

Octo-Cat obediently trotted after me, mumbling through gritted teeth, "If you ever call me 'kitty' again, I'm going to puke in your slippers while you sleep."

"Okay, bye now!" I yelled to Diane, quickly gathering up all of the cat's things piled by the firm's main entrance.

Once we were both safely seated in my car, Octo-Cat exploded in a litany of what I assumed were feline-specific curse words.

"Stop that," I scolded. "Didn't your mother teach you any manners?"

He paused and looked over at me with such derision, I actually recoiled. "Now you're insulting my mother? I'll have you know she did the best she could with seven kittens to feed and only six nipples to feed them with."

I shuddered and pulled the car into reverse. "Well, thank you for that visual."

Octo-Cat let out a terrible yowl and jumped onto my lap, claws extended. "Oh, my whiskers! We're going to die!" he cried. "I'm too young to die. Too pretty. And far too important."

"Aww, are you afraid?" I cooed, almost liking him in that moment, even though his claws were digging into my thigh. "That's so cute."

"I am not cute," he ground out. "Get me to safety at once, then we shall discuss your punishment."

I laughed and turned on the radio, letting the newest top forty hit flood the car and drown out some of Octo-Cat's complaints about my driving.

Despite the unnecessary drama, we managed to make it back to my house in good time, but now I had a new problem. I loved my tiny two-bedroom rental with its wide porch and tall oak tree in the front yard.

My new roommate, on the other hand…

"Where have you brought me?" he demanded, unwilling to leave the car no matter how much I begged.

"This is my house and you'll be living here, too, for a few days," I explained, even though my patience had worn so thin it was like a strand of angel hair pasta.

He turned his spoiled pink nose up at me. "No, absolutely not! This is hardly even a hovel. It's not up to the standards by which I am accustomed to living."

I had half a mind to hightail it back to the office and return him to the Fultons. Instead I took a deep, sarcastic bow and grumbled, "Well, too bad, your royal highness. This is all I can afford. Besides, you're just an ordinary tabby cat with a bad attitude and ridiculous expectations of life."

He hissed and took an honest-to-goodness swipe at me. Luckily, I managed to yank my arm out of his path before he could break skin.

"Just a tabby!" he shouted, gracing me with another diatribe full of kitty curses. "How dare you? I'll have you know that I am part Maine Coon on my grandmother's side."

I was growing really tired of this. Why did every little thing have to be a battle?

I dropped to my haunches to face him eye-to-eye, even though it put me at incredible risk given his temper coupled with those sharp claws.

"Look, do you want me to help you solve this murder or not? Because from where I'm sitting, I'm literally the only person in the entire world who can help you right now. But if you want me to actually do that, you're going to have to be a whole lot nicer."

We stared each other down, but I refused to look away first. I dealt with megalomaniac attorneys on the regular. I could handle this little, ill-tempered cat.

Finally, Octo-Cat stretched, yawned, jumped down from the car, and trotted over to my front door.

"Are you going to let me in or what?" he yowled from my porch, flicking his tail in agitation.

Well, at least it was progress.

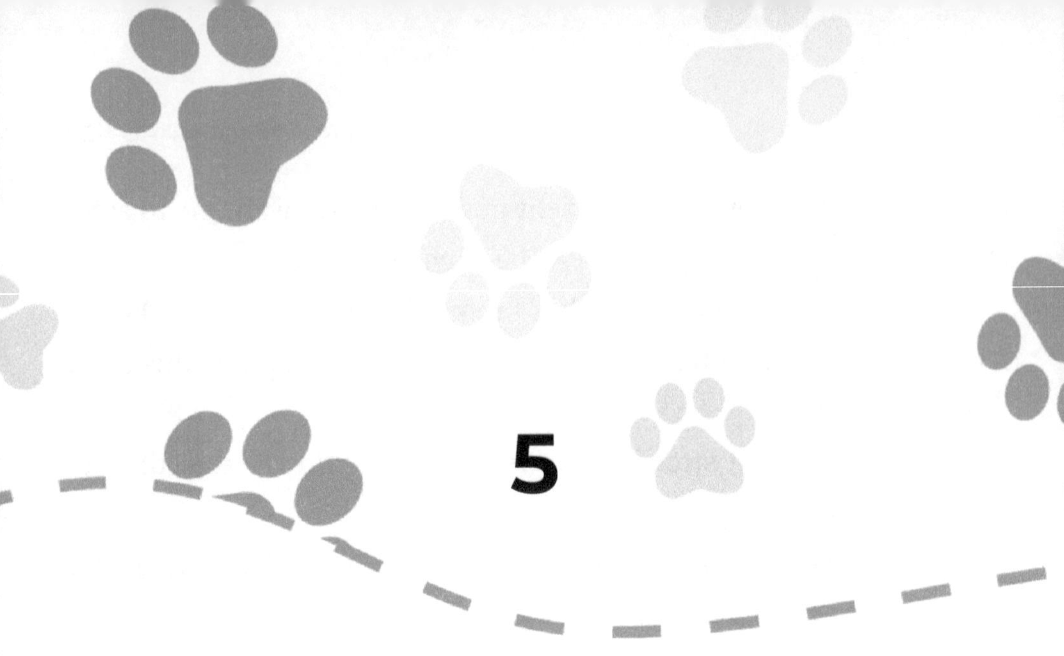

5

Once inside, Octo-Cat made a beeline for my favorite overstuffed armchair. Despite his protests only moments ago, he quickly settled in and made himself comfortable. From the state of my pants, I already knew Octo-Cat was a massive shedder. My poor cream-colored chair didn't stand a chance against his brown and black fur.

Still, he was a guest, and Nan had worked hard to teach me manners.

"Can I get you something to drink?" I asked, hesitating by the kitchen.

He perked his head up and let out a contented purr that I found just as shocking as if he'd sprouted a second tail. "Do you have any Evian?" he asked politely, crossing his paws in front of himself now.

"I have tap water and..." I glanced into the fridge and frowned at the lack of cat-friendly options. "Diet Coke and apple juice, too."

The purring abruptly stopped as Octo-Cat uncrossed and recrossed his paws. "I'll pass for now, but you're going to need to go to the store and gather the necessary supplies for my stay. I only drink Evian, and I only eat Fancy Feast. Not just any flavor, mind you. It must be fish-based, and it must come in the small metal can—not the plastic container. I can taste the difference."

I couldn't help but laugh at the audacity of this request. "Is that all?"

"No, but we need to start somewhere." He scowled at me, refusing to see the humor in the situation.

Seeing as we were getting nowhere fast, I gave up in the kitchen and returned to the living room with a can of Diet Coke for myself. I slumped on the couch with a huge sigh. If Octo-Cat was going to be melodramatic, then I would be, too.

His probing amber gaze bore into me, refusing to look away, and that danged tail began flicking wildly again. It was a wonder he hadn't learned any manners, given the circumstances in which he'd lived up until two days ago.

I cleared my throat but still, he continued to stare unabashedly. Was he waiting for me to...? *Oh my gosh.*

"I don't need to go to the store right now," I snapped, correcting my posture and glaring right back at him. "Do I?"

He shrugged as if he hadn't given it much thought, even though we both knew he had. "Well, it would be nice."

"This morning all you could talk about was Ethel Fulton's murder. Now it's more important that you have a specific type of water than that we discuss the details and start working on the case?"

He considered this for a moment. “I never thought I’d say this, but bring on the tap water.”

“Really?” Despite his giving the desired response, I fully expected him to change his mind within a matter of seconds—or to tell me that he’d obviously been joking and then call me stupid for not getting it.

“Sometimes we have to make sacrifices for the ones we love. This one’s for Ethel.” He nodded gravely despite the fact that we were discussing one of the most mundane topics imaginable.

“Oh, how long-suffering you are.”

His eyes widened in what I presumed was shock. “Hopefully not *long* suffering. Once I tell you what I know, it should be an open and shut case.”

“Perfect,” I said, making my way to the kitchen and running the faucet for a few seconds to make sure it was the perfect temperature for my spoiled new acquaintance. “Tell me what you know.”

Octo-Cat waited until I had returned and set the bowl of water on the coffee table before him. He hopped over and sniffed hesitantly.

“This isn’t made of Lenox or crystal. Not even stainless steel.” He craned his neck to the side, turning his body into an odd, snobby twist of fur and limbs. “What is it? And is it safe to drink from?”

“It’s a normal bowl from the dollar store and is perfectly fine. I eat out of it all the time.” I pushed the bowl toward him emphatically, and Octo-Cat jumped back in fright.

“That’s hardly a ringing endorsement.” He eyed me from head to toe and shrugged his little kitty shoulders before turning and leaping back to my armchair. "Suddenly, I'm not so thirsty," he declared with a yawn.

Instead of responding to his snobbery, I popped open my soda and took a nice, long drink. The bubbles did little to calm my frazzled nerves.

"Are we going to talk about this?" Octo-Cat flicked his tail impatiently. Despite the many delays he'd caused, my single drink was now to blame for us falling behind in the two of us beginning our job as amateur sleuths.

As much as I hated to be a pushover, it was simply easier to go along with his outrageousness than to keep arguing over every little thing. The sooner we identified the murderer and brought him to justice, the sooner I could be back to my normal, cat-free life.

I took a deep, centering breath and asked, "What makes you think Ethel Fulton was murdered?"

"I don't *think* she was murdered. I *know* it. I saw everything with my own two eyes." He widened his amber gaze demonstratively. Maybe this wouldn't be so difficult after all.

"Oh, great. Well, who did it then?" I leaned forward, ready for the big reveal.

"I don't know."

Deep breaths. "But you said you saw everything?"

"I did."

"Then how can you not know who did it?"

"It was definitely a human," he said, an expression of surety spread between his whiskers.

"Really? Is that all you've got?" The couch groaned in protest as I threw myself back against it and threw my hands in the air so as not to wring Octo-Cat's neck with them. "Was it a man or a woman? Someone old or young? A stranger or someone she knew?"

He yawned. "Do you really expect me to remember that?"

"Are you serious?" And now I was yelling at a cat.

"What? It's not my fault all humans look the same."

Deep, calming yoga breaths. "So, you saw a human kill her, but you don't know who."

"Yes. That's what I said. Aren't you paying attention?"

I spoke slowly even though he was the one who assumed me to be an idiot. "Do you know how the human killed her? From what I understand, she died of natural causes."

"No, she wasn't ready to die yet. Someone definitely intervened."

I waited for him to say more, but he started grooming himself instead.

"Hello? We're kind of in the middle of an important conversation here. Can you stop licking yourself for five minutes so we can figure this out?"

Octo-Cat let out a little huff but complied with my request. "The sacrifices I make. I hope Ethel is watching from above so that my good deeds don't go unnoticed."

"I'm sure she's in Heaven, looking down at us and thinking, 'Wow, what a great cat I had.' Now, can you tell me the whole story from start to finish? *About the murder,*" I quickly specified, not wanting to hear about his mother's six nipples again.

He nodded and brought himself up onto his haunches. What

followed was a dramatic retelling that would have been worthy of an Oscar if anyone could understand him besides me.

"Let me paint the scene for you." He lifted his paw and swept it in an arc before him. "It was just two nights ago. The weather was balmy. The light had begun to fade from the sky. Ethel had invited several other humans over to eat food at the table. She cooked the whole thing herself. I remember because she made salmon and also gave me a little plate to enjoy. I'm happy to report the fish was perfectly cooked, tender but not dry, and the portion was absolutely perfect, too. Ethel always knew exactly what I needed."

"Focus, please," I said through gritted teeth. "Back to the murder, if you don't mind."

He sneered but didn't offer any verbal argument. "Everyone ate more than their fill, then they all went home. When Ethel was getting ready for bed, she clutched her chest and told me she wasn't feeling well, then tucked herself in and went to sleep. She didn't wake up again."

"It sounds like maybe she had a heart attack. What makes you think she was murdered?" I reached out to offer him a conciliatory pat on the head, but he batted my hand away.

"Ethel had a very strong heart," he insisted. "She was always telling me about it after she came back from the doctors." He made his voice high and scratchy, hunching forward in what seemed to be an impression of his late owner. "'Doc says I have a strong heart and just might live forever.' In fact, she went to the doctor just that week, and he again told her what good shape her heart was in."

I didn't know how to put this delicately, so I just blurted it out. "Yes, but she was old. Sometimes their bodies just give out on them."

He shook his head adamantly, and when he glanced up at me again, his eyes had crossed before his nose. "Maybe, but that's not what happened to Ethel. She smelled funny after dinner."

I worried my lip while thinking this over. I knew Octo-Cat loved his owner, but the more he talked, the more it sounded as if she'd died of natural causes and not some secret murder scheme. I just didn't know how to tell him this.

After a moment's hesitation, I told him, "I've heard cats can sometimes know when people are about to die. You two were very close, so maybe you just sensed it."

Again with the manic head shaking. "No, she was definitely murdered. That same weird smell was in the dinner and the tea."

"Are you trying to tell me she was poisoned? I'm not sure that pans out. Remember, you told me in great detail how you ate the fish and you are perfectly fine."

"She fed me before the guests arrived. I think someone tampered with the food after I'd left the kitchen to go take a catnap."

I raised an eyebrow and asked, "Then why didn't the other guests die?"

"Someone specifically wanted to kill Ethel, I guess." He moved his eyes to the chair before him in his first show of true sorrow. "I don't understand. She was the nicest human ever. Who would want to kill her?"

"I was hoping you'd know the answer to that one." I had to remind myself that he didn't want to be petted—at least not by me. I wrapped both hands around my drink and took another sip before suggesting, “She did have a lot of money. Do you think someone was trying to get their inheritance early?”

His head whipped back up and his eyes focused in on mine. “So, you think someone in the family killed her?”

I shrugged. “I’m still not entirely convinced she was even murdered.”

“Then I guess I’m going to have to show you.” He popped to his feet and jumped off the chair in what amounted to the blink of an eye.

“Show me? How?” I asked, following dumbly.

“Let’s go to my house and take a look around. I guarantee you’ll find the proof you need,” he said, then flicked his tail before adding, “Seeing as my word apparently isn’t enough.”

6

I considered it a small miracle that Octo-Cat actually knew his home address. He and Ethel had lived together on the exact opposite side of town close to the bay—the same as all the other wealthy folks around Glendale.

A private drive twisted about half a mile through the woods before it opened up to a gorgeous, sprawling Colonial with huge bay windows looking out the sea.

My jaw dropped in response to the unexpected grandeur. "You live here?"

"Safety first, then talk," Octo-Cat whisper-yelled, digging his claws deeper into my thighs as I navigated the last stretch of driveway and pulled to a stop before the structure that reminded me more of a palace than an actual home.

Rather than parking out front, I pulled around to the far side of the house to at least partially conceal my visit. As soon as I opened the car door, Octo-Cat hopped out onto the ground and walked in a crooked line toward the porch.

"Wait!" I called after him, taking another opportunity to survey the estate. "Are we really just going to walk right in?"

"Of course, we are. This is my home."

"Yeah, but isn't it locked?" Despite all my various degrees and random knowledge, I'd never taken the time to learn locksmithing. Perhaps I could add it to my list for later, although that wouldn't help us much now.

"*Pssh.* Only for humans. Watch." Octo-Cat ran up the porch steps and stood before a little doggie door that was almost perfectly hidden within the stone face of the house. As he waited, the slab slid open, admitting him inside and leaving no doubt that Octo-Cat's front door cost more than my entire month's—maybe even year's—rent.

I jogged up to join him, then lowered myself to my hands and knees to peer inside. The stone doorway shut right in my face but re-opened a few seconds later.

Octo-Cat trotted back outside with a smile curling across his short snout. "It's good to be home."

"Well, don't get used to it. We're only here to look for clues."

"What are you waiting for, then? Come inside." He slipped back in through his private entrance, and this time I was close enough to see a little light flash on his collar before the door slid open. Fancy.

Octo-Cat turned around to glare at me. "Aren't you coming?"

"Just one small problem." I reached my hand in after him. "I don't fit."

He shook his head slowly and raised a paw to his face in exasperation. "Then grab the key that's under the shiny rock. Hurry up already!"

I groaned as I lifted myself back to my feet and searched the porch and nearby flowerbeds for the shiny rock he'd mentioned. Even having only met Octo-Cat earlier that day, I already knew better than to ask for help or further clarification. Honestly, you haven't lived until you've been condescended to by a cat—although I don't recommend the experience if you can avoid it.

As for me, I had no choice in the matter. At least not until I either solved the murder or proved no foul play had occurred, either of which I considered an equally likely outcome.

Octo-Cat jogged back out and tapped my calf with his paw. He made no effort to conceal his claws when doing so. "You're looking in the wrong place," he informed me with a bored expression.

I glared down at him and checked my leg for any fresh pricks of blood.

My kitty companion spun in a circle then hopped off the porch and began pawing at the corner where the house met the steps. There sat the first in a series of foot path lights, none of which had been illuminated despite the descending dusk.

I trotted back down the steps after him and pulled that first light right out of the ground. Sure enough, a small silver key lay buried in the earth beneath. "Good hiding spot," I said as I bent down to pluck the key from its grave.

"Ethel was just as smart as she was kind," Octo-Cat said with a reverence he didn't normally possess. "She really was the best human. Too bad you never got the chance to meet her."

I was just about to tell him how sweet I found that sentiment, when he added, "You really could have learned so much."

"All right," I said with a grunt, turning to face the stairs once again. "Let's get on with this investigation already."

The key slid into the lock perfectly, and a moment later I stood inside the regal entryway with no clue where to begin. Letting out a low whistle, I whispered, "This place is huge."

Octo-Cat sighed. "Yeah, it's perfect. Isn't it?"

We stood in respectful silence as I took in all the expensive furnishings and decor. Even the light fixtures looked like they had been lifted from a seventeenth century castle. If I hadn't already felt guilty about breaking into a dead woman's home, then I definitely felt bad about snooping around amidst all these priceless possessions.

The tabby took off decisively toward the right, and I followed. A short while later we wound up in the kitchen.

I eyed the beautiful white oak cabinetry appreciatively. Everything about this place proved larger than life. The giant island in the middle of the space was about the same size as a king bed, and the stainless-steel fridge appeared to be at least twice the size of my tiny rental's.

"Oh, good thinking," I murmured, unable to tear my eyes away from what had just become my own personal kitchen goals. "Since the food was prepared here, we should look for any proof of poisoning we can find."

At last I shifted my attention back to Octo-Cat. At least he didn't mind me moving slowly if it was to admire his former home.

In fact, he looked quite pleased with himself now. "Mmm-hmm. The Evian's in here."

I followed his gaze to the pantry where, sure enough, dozens of bottles of his preferred drinking water were stacked on the lowest shelf. "Do we really need to do this first?"

"Yes, now hurry. I'm parched." He lowered himself to the ground and waited.

I rolled my eyes but followed Octo-Cat's orders all the same. After I poured him the specified amount in the specified dish, I went back to the pantry and grabbed several bottles of water and a couple dozen cans of Fancy Feast to help get us through our time together. At least now I wouldn't have to spend a small fortune on Octo-Cat's shopping needs.

He lapped appreciatively from the dish and then licked the outside of his mouth for good measure. "That hit the spot. Thanks."

I resisted the urge to tap my foot impatiently, which seemed the human equivalent of all his tail flicking. "Now that you're refreshed and rehydrated, perhaps you can show me around and help me see what you saw the night of the murder."

"Yes, okay." He crossed the kitchen at a slow, loping run, then jumped onto the counter.

I followed as he guided me toward the sink, which had been filled to the brim with dirty dishes.

"This is gross, but I'll do it for Ethel," he informed me before closing his eyes and sticking his nose into the middle of the mess.

He rooted around for a bit, then murmured, "It's this one."

I craned my neck but couldn't see what he meant. "Which one?"

"I'm pointing at it with my nose," came his muffled reply. "Please hurry, it's not the most pleasant smell."

One after the other, I pulled dirty plates from the sink. Each had a varying degree of salmon skin, rice grains, or butter glommed onto the surface, but I'd dealt with far worse than a couple day old dishes. The activity didn't bother me nearly as much as it did Octo-Cat.

"There. That's the one," he cried, slowly backing out of the sink and immediately licking his paw. "Smell it."

I did as he said but could only discern the faint smell of spoiled fish.

Octo-Cat rubbed his paw on top of his head, then brought it back down for more licks. "Now sniff another, and you'll see what I mean," he instructed.

I did as he said, making sure to take a good long whiff of each, but as far as I could tell they were no different. "What am I supposed to be smelling other than the fish?"

"Remember I told you about the funny smell?" He waited for me to nod, then revealed, "Only Ethel's plate had it."

"And this was her plate?" I asked, holding up the first for him to sniff again.

His face contorted in disgust. "Definitely."

"I don't know what I can do here. I can't smell the difference, and I wouldn't even know how to begin getting a forensics team on this."

"Tell them what I told you."

"Oh, sure. Tell them 'the cat told me.' That will go over real well."

"I see your point." He stopped grooming and glanced around the kitchen. "Nothing looks out of order other than the mess from dinner. But open up the trash can and see if there's any poison in there."

I did as he said, stepping on the little foot pedal to raise the lid so we could both peer inside.

"Nothing," I told him with a shake of my head. "It's starting to look like she wasn't murdered, after all."

"Or that the culprit was smart enough to take the evidence with him. Besides, we have proof from the sink. It's not my fault your weak human nose refuses to smell what's right there in front of it."

I hated to admit it, but he was right. "Fine. Where else can we look for clues?"

He shook his head haughtily and flicked his tail to match. "First tell me you believe me about the murder."

"What? Why is that important?" I fixed him with my most domineering stare. I didn't think cats had alphas the way dogs do, but I needed some way to gain leverage here.

He growled, breaking my concentration. "If we're going to be working together, I need to know you believe in what we're doing. I need to know you'll do what it takes to get justice for Ethel."

I rolled my eyes and muttered, "Fine, I believe you."

"Next time, try a little harder to sound convincing." He sneered at me then jumped off the counter, shaking his little kitty booty as he strode away. "Seeing as you're the best option I've got, I'm just going to have to put up with you. C'mon, let me show you our bedroom."

While following him back to the entryway and up the grand staircase, I asked myself whether I did believe that Ethel had been murdered. I hadn't been able to see or smell any proof for myself just yet, but I also knew Octo-Cat well enough to know he wouldn't waste his time on false claims.

Whether or not it made much sense, he was convinced Ethel had met an unnatural end—and even though it made me more than a little crazy, I believed him.

7

It felt strange standing in a room where someone had died less than forty-eight hours earlier. Even the air in Ethel Fulton's bedroom felt less oxygenated somehow, as if she'd tried to suck in every last breath she could before taking her last. At that lovely thought, I shuddered and wrapped my arms around myself.

Octo-Cat hopped up on the bed and pawed at the comforter. "This is where she died. I slept on this pillow here, and she slept on the side closest to the bathroom. Usually she got up a couple times per night to pollute her water bowl. You humans are a disgusting bunch, by the way, but I loved Ethel and was able to overlook her flaws."

"Your point?" I asked with a sigh.

He raised a lip at me but kept his hiss to himself. "That night she didn't wake up at all. It was the first sign I knew something was definitely wrong."

I hovered awkwardly near the bed, unwilling to sit down or even to touch it. "I thought the funny smelling food was the first sign something was wrong."

My companion sniffed around the bed as if in search of something specific. "That's when I first suspected, but when she didn't get up at night, I knew for sure."

I gave Octo-Cat a few uninterrupted moments to finish his investigation of the bed. When he settled back on his pillow, I said, "Okay, so even though this is where she died, I don't think it has anything to do with the murder. Downstairs there were six dinner plates. Assuming one was for Ethel, can you remember who any of the other five guests were?"

"I might be able to identify them if I saw them again, and more likely by smell than sight."

I contemplated this. Octo-Cat's heightened sense of smell was of no use to me. The only other person I'd ever be able to identify by scent would be Bethany from work—and that was only because of her essential oils obsession. At that, an encouraging thought struck me. "Were any of them at the will reading this morning?"

He yawned and stretched his paws in front of himself in some kind of sleek yoga pose. "Yes, all of them were there," he revealed.

Suddenly, solving this thing seemed not only possible, but likely. Trying not to startle Octo-Cat with my sudden burst of eagerness, I said, "But you don't know which one killed Ethel?"

"No, none of them had the funny smell from the dinner party when I saw them this morning," he confided with a frown.

"And you don't remember their names?"

Octo-Cat shook his head.

Forgetting my earlier disgust, I sighed and sunk down onto the mattress beside him, feeling all the wind leave my newly raised sails. "Seeing as there were at least twenty people at the reading, we have quite a few suspects."

He sighed, too. "Yes, it would seem we do."

I shivered upon realizing that I was sitting in the exact same spot where old lady Fulton had died not even two full days earlier. "Maybe if we try to—"

"Hush!" Octo-Cat yelled, leaping to attention. His ears twitched like tiny satellite dishes trying to find the best reception. "Someone just came in the house."

My stomach dropped past my feet and straight through the floor boards. *"What?"*

He listened a little bit longer. "Yes, someone is definitely inside."

Knowing my luck, it would be the killer, coming to scrub the scene clean of any lingering evidence—evidence I'd been too stupid to actually locate. Now it would be gone forever, and poor Ethel Fulton would have to go into the afterlife unavenged. Not to mention if the killer found us, he just might strike again—and, of course, we stood right in his path.

"We need to get out of here," I mouthed, hoping Octo-Cat could read lips.

He jumped onto the floor and trotted out through the bedroom door which I'd foolishly left wide open.

I listened for what felt like an eternity, waiting for someone to cross paths with my hapless sidekick. Would Octo-Cat recognize the danger? And, if so, would he find a way to alert me to it?

Several minutes passed without any sign of Octo-Cat or anyone else. Taking a deep breath, I tiptoed out into the hallway and toward the grand staircase. I just had to make it down these steps and out the door, then I never had to set sight on this place again.

Although I did a great job of descending quietly, I did it at the expense of a speedy getaway.

About halfway down, a shadowy figure appeared in the foyer and paused upon noticing me.

Of all the things I could have done then, I chose the worst possible one. I froze in place.

"Who's there?" the figure asked. The voice clearly belonged to a woman, which eased my fears a bit. I'd have a hard time defending myself against a full-grown man, but at five foot eight and a size twelve, I could probably fight off most other women... unless she had a weapon.

"I... I'm..." How could I possibly explain my trespassing? The truth about the talking cat and our murder investigation would be worse than pretty much any lie, but I was far too frightened to think up a good lie on the spot.

Luckily, Octo-Cat chose that exact moment to come in through his electronic cat door and race up the stairs to join me. "Tell her you're looking for my food and bed and other supplies," he commanded.

Oh, that was a great idea. It was also at least partially true.

"I'm watching the cat for a few days and came over to pick up his things. Wh-who are you?" I asked boldly, standing tall as if I had every right to be here.

She stepped back and flicked a switch that illuminated the overhead chandelier, casting light over us both. "Obviously you're not close with the family or you wouldn't have to ask that. So why don't you start by telling me who *you* are?"

"She's bluffing," Octo-Cat whispered at my side. "She's just as scared as you are. She's throwing out human stress hormones like crazy."

"I work for Mr. Fulton." I descended a few steps, keeping my eyes trained on the other woman. "Should I tell him you stopped by?"

"Nice one," Octo-Cat cheered behind me.

The woman cursed under her breath. The deep bags beneath her eyes implied she hadn't slept well in nights, and the way she twisted her mouth into a frown told me I had her outwitted.

"No, he wouldn't like that," she mumbled, glancing behind her then back up toward me. "Look, I'm not taking anything. Just looking over Aunt Ethel's things to make sure I don't get taken when divvying up the inheritance. I'm on my way out, though, so no harm done." She lifted her hands in surrender and waited for me to join her on the main floor.

"I suppose I don't need to tell Mr. Fulton about this, but we had both better leave and lock up," I said with far more courage than I felt.

"Yes, okay." She backed away slowly, keeping her eyes on me the whole time, then bumbled for the doorknob and swung the front door open so forcefully it slammed against the wall. If I wasn't suspicious before, then I definitely questioned her motives now.

"See you around, then," the woman said, peering through the door one last time before scurrying down the steps.

I watched as she got into an old car and sat mumbling to herself behind the wheel. Even though she was on her way now, it didn't mean that she—or others—wouldn't be back soon. I had to get out of there, but first I needed to grab Octo-Cat's things from the kitchen.

He followed me at a quick clip. "You did great," he said. "I'm starting to think that maybe you're up to this task after all."

"Gee, thanks," I told him as I packed my arms with the Evian and cat food cans as best I could. "Mind watching my back in case she tries to sneak up and stab me while I'm not looking?"

Octo-Cat jumped on the counter and widened his eyes. "Oh, she's not the killer."

"What makes you so sure?" I mumbled, struggling with my off balanced load. "Was she not there that night?"

"Oh, she was there, but she's not smart enough to commit a murder, let alone conceal it. Believe me, that's Ethel's niece. She's, hands down, the stupidest human I've ever met. She couldn't have concocted this."

"It almost sounds like you admire the killer," I whispered while leaving the kitchen. I didn't know whether the other visitor had left yet or whether she would return before I had a chance to make my getaway.

My companion hissed. "No, believe me, I'm mad as a human without its cell phone. I just know she doesn't have it in her. That still leaves four other guests that could have done it, though."

The front door still hung wide open, but the other woman's car had disappeared from the drive. Thank goodness, because I wasn't up for more small talk even if I could rest assured that it wouldn't end with my own murder.

"But you don't know who any of the other guests were? Earlier you said you didn't know anyone, but you seemed to recognize Ethel's niece right away."

He sighed as if he were the one suffering a fool here. "It's scent memory. Some details don't click into place without it."

"I've never heard of such a ridiculous thing." I watched my feet as we picked our way across the uneven ground to the side of the house where I'd concealed my car near a copse of tall trees.

"Well, how many cats did you have deep conversations with before you met me?"

I had to admit, he had me there. "Point taken. But this little field trip accomplished nothing, so what are we supposed to do next?"

We reached my car and I set my load of cans and bottles on the ground so I could open the trunk and stash everything inside.

"It definitely was *not* nothing." Octo-Cat jumped onto the hood of my car and looked down on me as if I were a peasant and he was king. "We got my food and Evian, didn't we?"

I shook my head and chuckled as I slammed the trunk closed again. We'd come face to face with danger but were still nowhere near solving our murder mystery. At least we had Evian, though!

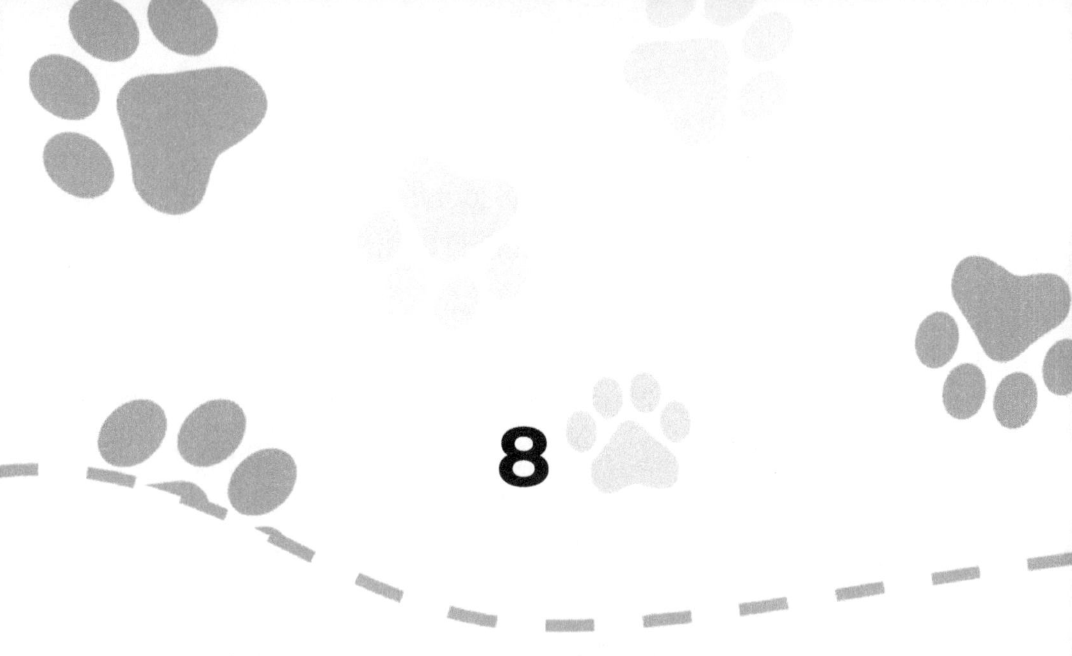

8

The next morning, I woke up to an ear-piercing cry in the wee hours. The room was still shrouded in darkness, so I groped for my phone to serve as a makeshift flashlight.

"Ack, right in my eye!" Octo-Cat shouted as he jumped from the bed to the floor to escape the path of the light.

I struggled to sit, my limbs still heavy with sleep. "What's going on? What's wrong?"

He turned to face me. His glinting eyes widened as they adjusted to my flashlight. "It's time for breakfast," he informed me.

A quick glance at my phone confirmed that it was only five o'clock, more than two full hours before I generally awoke on a work day.

"No way, not going to happen," I moaned and pulled the covers over my head. "Go away."

That same horrible banshee cry sounded again, sending shivers up my spine and digging straight into my brain.

"Is that you?" I hissed.

Octo-Cat hissed back but otherwise kept his voice slow and at its normal volume. "It's breakfast time," he repeated. "If I could open the can myself, I would, but I can't. So, get up and use those opposable thumbs the way God intended, darling."

"Fine, but I hate you," I whined as I threw my legs over the side of the bed. He had me up, but that didn't mean I needed to hurry.

He ran ahead and turned several circles while waiting for me to catch up. "The feeling is mutual. At least until I've had my breakfast."

"And me, my coffee," I said, shuddering as I remembered yesterday's run-in with the office coffeemaker. Perhaps I would switch to tea going forward.

In the kitchen I plunked his favorite congealed salmon pâté onto a plate and set it on the ground for my spoiled roommate. *"Bon Appetit,"* I mumbled, shuffling back toward my bedroom.

I didn't even have a chance to lie back down before Octo-Cat took a swipe at my feet and growled. "No, you can't go back to bed. It's morning and I need to have my breakfast."

"I just fed you. Go eat already and leave me alone." I dropped into bed and turned on my side so that I wouldn't have to look at his demanding kitty face.

"Why is this so hard to understand?" he said with a sigh, his whiskers twitching furiously. "I can't eat unless you stand nearby and watch me. Maybe tell me what a good cat I am, too."

"But you're not a good cat," I grumbled. Right now he was pretty much the worst cat in the world. After all, none of the others were rousing me from sleep at this unholy hour.

"Ethel always petted me and talked to me while I ate. Please, don't you think...?" His words broke away and despite my better judgment I turned to look straight into his huge, pleading eyes.

"Fine!" I sputtered. "But tomorrow we wake up on my schedule."

Octo-Cat didn't say anything as he led the way back to my kitchen, his tail held high and hips swaying in a way that definitely looked put on for my benefit.

"Oh, great and mighty Octo-Cat, you are such a good kitty," I said, rolling my eyes as he took his first tentative bite of that awful-smelling breakfast.

"Hey, what did I tell you about calling me 'kitty?'" He grumbled between bites. "But I've gotta say, the other thing is growing on me."

"What? *Octo-Cat?*" I regarded him suspiciously. This was a surprise given how he'd stubbornly insisted on his ridiculously long moniker until now.

"That's the one," he confirmed with a smack of his lips as he continued to gobble up Fancy Feast.

"It suits you."

"And it makes me seem hip and modern, too."

"Oh, yes, you're one cool cat." Maybe it was time to teach the poor guy some new slang. After all, he'd taken all his current lingo from a woman in her eighties.

When he finished his meal, I poured some Evian into a mug and set it before Octo-Cat. He lapped it up appreciatively and then began the first of his many daily grooming ministrations.

"Since I'm up, I guess I'll go get ready," I informed him, thanking my lucky stars when he didn't follow me into the bathroom. I was able to take a shower without any added drama.

The hot water pounded my skin, slowly bringing me back to life. By the time I finished my own grooming rituals, I found myself in a much better mood.

"Good to see you've finally woken up," Octo-Cat said with an approving nod. "What time do we head into the office?"

"We? No, no, no. There's no way I can justify taking you into the firm."

"But I was there yesterday," he argued with a child-like pout.

"For the will reading."

"Well, just have another will reading then. Besides, if I'm there, I can help suss out the killer."

I crossed my arms over my chest and stared him down without blinking. "You're *not* coming."

He ran toward the door, calling to me in a sing-song voice. "Too bad you can't stop me."

Oh, what a brat. Leave it to Octo-Cat to always want to be at the center of all the action. He was really quite outgoing as far as cats were concerned. If I had any chance of leaving him at home, then I needed to come up with something important for him to do here—or at least something I could trick him into thinking was important.

What was that saying about curiosity and cats again? I was banking on it being true.

"I'm only going to work because I haven't got a choice in the matter," I informed him. "You, however, do. And it would be much better if you stayed here and did some research into our case."

He flicked his tail, but otherwise looked intrigued. Score one for clichéd old sayings. "Oh? Well, what did you have in mind?"

If I took too long to think, Octo-Cat would figure me out so I went with the first thing that popped into my mind. "Research. On the Internet."

"I can't type," he said with a scowl. "Or read, for that matter."

"Can't read?" I don't know why I was surprised. Most cats didn't talk. Maybe I'd just assumed that Octo-Cat could do all things like my very own super kitty sidekick.

He abandoned the door and joined me in the living room. "Until I met you, I had no idea humans had such a complex system of communication," he explained. "Your different sounds mean different things! I always thought it was just about emotion, but you actually seem to assign noises to various objects and concepts. It's fascinating."

"Right back at you, cat." It still hadn't ceased to amaze me that Octo-Cat thought of humans as just another animal. In his mind, cats were the most intellectually superior species on the planet, which seemed laughable to me. Were humans otherwise deluded about their place in the animal kingdom? It sure made me wonder.

I'd been wondering something else, too, and decided to ask Octo-Cat about it. "So, you're not speaking English?"

He twitched his whiskers in confusion. "What's English? Is that your word for human? Because no, I'm not speaking human. You're speaking cat."

"I'm not speaking cat, though." At least I was pretty sure I wasn't speaking in a series of meows, purrs, and growls.

"And yet somehow we understand each other." Octo-Cat looked bored, even though I found the intricacies of our communication amazingly interesting. Maybe at the end of the day curiosity killed the human, too.

We sat in companionable silence as we both puzzled over this, one of us more than the other.

At last I said, "I suppose that's another mystery we'll have to figure out. You know, once we solve the more pressing murder mystery."

"There's no mystery about it," he informed me, his eyes flashing with untold knowledge. "It's magic."

"Magic?" I laughed at this notion. "You believe in magic?"

"You don't?" He looked authentically surprised at this.

How much did we humans not know about the rest of the world? I was beginning to think it was substantial. I'd look into this all later. Right now, I needed to focus on distracting him so that I could slip away to the office, unaccompanied.

"Okay, so that's what you can do for me," I told him, reaching forward to grab the remote from the coffee table. "I'll leave the TV on for you and you can learn to read human."

"Eww, why?"

"So you can help me with the research, of course."

"Are you going to learn cat?" he shot back.

"Sure, you can give me some lessons once I'm home from work." I agreed primarily to avoid an argument but had to admit, the idea of learning such an uncharted new language did excite me.

The TV flickered to life at the press of the button and immediately our eyes darted to the screen. After a bit of channel surfing, I settled on one of the kids' channels where a caramel-skinned little girl and her monkey talked directly to the viewer. I pressed a series of buttons, at last reaching the option to enable subtitles.

Octo-Cat meowed right back at the screen, immediately enamored of the program. I watched with him for a few minutes, then managed to slip out undetected just as I'd hoped.

I'd be painfully early to the office that day, but maybe that would be to my benefit. Little by little, a plan began to form in my mind.

Yes, today would be a productive day when it came to solving Ethel Fulton's murder. If all went according to plan, I might even be able to discover the culprit before returning home in the evening.

9

On my way to the office, I stopped by the local coffee shop to order lattes for the partners and all the associates. Even though I couldn't really afford it, I needed an excuse to talk to everyone and see what I could learn about the will reading and Ethel Fulton's purported cause of death.

Thankfully, no matter how much Nan wanted me to be a fully functional adult, she would still step in whenever I couldn't make rent. Generally, my pocket money went toward books or community college courses or online webinars, but I figured Octo-Cat's and my mystery would keep me too busy to spend much time on recreational learning for the next few days.

I'd read enough police procedural novels by this point to know it took a fair bit of work to identify a killer. Surely in the real world, many cases proved to be open and shut, but I doubted Ethel's would turn out that way.

For starters, all of my evidence was based on hearsay... *from a cat.*

And even though I believed him, I couldn't exactly use his word to justify myself to others. Octo-Cat had also given me just enough to legitimize his claims of murder, but not enough to guide my questioning when talking to anyone else.

All of this meant I'd need to keep myself casual and conversational while trying to glean information from my boss and coworkers. The surprise coffee delivery would be my way in, but I'd need to rely on my wits to learn anything of actual value.

Oh boy, I definitely had my work cut out for me.

Thanks to my rude awakening that morning, I reached work a full hour before my normal start time. Only two other cars stood in the parking lot— Mr. Fulton's and Bethany's. So much for all the extra lattes. I just hoped I'd be able to secretly warm them in the microwave later without anyone noticing.

Trying not to show my disappointment, I floated into the office with my oversized tray of coffees and a bright smile on my face.

"Good morning," I sang, passing by the front desk where I normally sat to greet any visitors who happened to drop by the firm.

Only silence greeted me.

"Hello?" I called, knowing for a fact I'd seen their cars. As I moved down the hall toward Mr. Fulton's office, I flicked on the overhead lights.

"Mr. Fulton?"

The door opened abruptly, causing me to jump back. Thank goodness the hot coffees didn't spill down my front or I'd have found myself in the hospital with a wicked work injury a second day in a row.

Once I regained my balance, I glanced up at my boss. The poor man was almost unrecognizable. Mr. Fulton appeared almost comically disheveled. His normally well-pressed shirt was wrinkled, and his tie hung askew. His eyes focused on the ground, meaning it took him an extra moment to realize I was standing right in front of him.

"Good morning, sir," I said carefully. "Is... Is everything okay?"

He glanced up at me and plastered on a polite smile, which I saw right through. "Oh, yes. Yes, I'm fine. Is this coffee for me?"

After I handed him a latte, he retreated back into his office and slammed the door behind him without so much as a *thank you*, a *good morning*, or an *I'm glad you didn't die at the hands of that coffeemaker yesterday.*

Strange. Definitely strange.

Shrugging it off, I headed toward Bethany's office next. The room sat dark and quiet even though I could have sworn I'd seen her car in the lot, too. Maybe I really had lost my mind, or maybe it was everyone else who had gone crazy.

Either way, I had the strange feeling of being watched. Did the killer know I was on to him, or was some other dark danger looming?

Danger, *phfff.* I was just being silly.

It was still my plain, old boring office, only a little bit earlier in the day. Mr. Fulton had just lost a relative and had a complicated estate to manage as well, so of course, he was out of sorts.

As for Bethany, she often liked to escape outside to grab some fresh air, which also made sense seeing as a chemical fog hung in her office from more than a year of overzealous essential oil use. In fact, she was probably hanging around in the yard now, which would give me the perfect opportunity to talk with her in private before the others arrived.

Having talked myself down from that near fright, I set the tray of coffees on my desk, grabbed one for me and one for Bethany, then headed outside. I took a lap around the entire building, but only found a shifty looking squirrel staring at me suspiciously.

Where could Bethany have gone?

Returning to the parking lot, I glanced into her car, but it also stood empty. When I turned around, I caught a flash of gray disappearing behind the building.

"Bethany?" I called, jogging after.

But again, nothing was there.

Giving up at last, I went back inside and found Bethany waiting for me beside my desk. "How did you…?"

"What?" she asked, pawing at one of the coffees before at last picking it up and holding it between her two hands awkwardly. "I was here the whole time," she offered with a shrug when I didn't say anything more. If that was true, then it meant she was more than likely in Mr. Fulton's office with him. Her office had definitely been empty, and none of the others had been opened yet for the day.

But why the secrecy?

Had I stumbled upon a new mystery altogether?

No, Mr. Fulton would never have an affair. Not in a million years. And especially not with harsh and brassy Bethany, who was so much his wife's opposite. Thanks to Octo-Cat, my imagination had run away with me, plain and simple.

Now it was time to stop speculating about my coworkers and start gathering intel about Ethel's murder. Seeing as Bethany was already a tad harried, maybe she would slip and tell me more than she would have otherwise intended.

I had to give it a shot.

"So..." I said, setting one of the coffees down and taking a small sip of the other. "Yesterday was crazy, huh?"

Her face jerked toward me as if she'd only just remembered I was there, and then a serpentine smile slithered across her face. "Seriously crazy," she agreed.

"Did you miss much because of taking me to the hospital?"

"Oh, no. I don't think so. When I got back, they'd only just made it to the part about the cat." She tucked her light blonde hair behind her ears and offered me a placating smile.

"I heard Ethel left a lot of her estate to Oct... I mean, her cat. That really had everyone up in arms, I bet."

She settled into our conversation, becoming less stiff as we gossiped. "How would you feel if you'd been denied your inheritance because of a common house cat?"

"I hear he's part Maine Coon," I said, wondering why I felt the need to defend a cat I'd known less than twenty-four hours and didn't really even like all that much, anyway. Bethany was right. I still didn't know how much Octo-Cat had inherited, but judging from the house we visited yesterday, it had to be a pretty penny, indeed.

"Well, whatever the case," she said with a frown. "I don't think that woman is going to be remembered favorably after this. At least not by her family."

"Did they like her before?" I wondered aloud, trying not to show my rapt interest in her answer as we finally got to the meat of this juicy tidbit.

Bethany shrugged. "Who knows?"

When she turned to walk away, I blurted out the first thing that popped into my head. "Do you know how she died?" I practically shouted. "Is it possible someone in the family, you know, helped her along to get a shot at their inheritance early?"

Bethany froze in place. A few awkward seconds passed before she burst out laughing. "Really, Angie? It seems you've been watching a bit too much TV. People die every day. Very few of them are murdered."

I forced a chuckle, too. "Oh, you're right. I stayed up late reading last night and then woke up early because of the cat. I'm afraid my brain is a bit fried."

She seemed interested in this. "The cat. Yes, you took him in, didn't you?"

"Yup, I wanted to help the family during this difficult time, and this seemed like the easiest way."

Bethany stalked back toward me with slow, deliberate steps. Dropping her voice to a husky rasp, she whispered, "You better be glad those murder mysteries are only in your head, because whoever gets the cat gets the money. If he stays with you too much longer, you could be next on the killer's list."

A chill crept from my fingertips all the way to my heart, and the little hairs on the back of my neck also stood tall and on alert. I was just about to ask what she was insinuating when Bethany exploded in laughter once again.

"You should have seen your face," she crowed, turning on heel and strolling back to her office. Her laughter bobbed along after her, leaving me alone with my mostly full tray of coffees.

If I hadn't known better, I'd swear Bethany was trying to get a rise out of me—or extend a warning. Did she know something I didn't? Could she be at least partially to blame?

Suddenly I didn't feel so safe anymore.

10

About half an hour later, the other attorneys began to trickle in to the office. By then I'd already decided I would never show up early ever again. Mr. Thompson sent me out for coffee when he arrived, but at least this time he gave me the cash to cover my purchase.

When I returned with a fresh tray of hot beverages in hand, I found Diane Fulton sitting in the small waiting area with a magazine folded over her crossed legs.

"Oh, there you are, Angie," she said, turning to me with an exacerbated smile. "Good morning."

"Good morning," I responded hesitantly, shifting my weight from one foot to the other. Normally I loved Diane's visits, but today her presence had me nervous considering her husband's oddball behavior that morning and my suspicions of a possible affair.

I put on a huge fake smile of my own. "Is there something I can help you with?"

Her hands shook in her lap, belying the extreme emotion she was trying so hard to keep buried beneath the surface. "Well, I came in to see my husband, but he doesn't seem to be around. I figured if I waited long enough for you to return maybe you'd know where I can find him."

"I'm sorry, no. If he's not in his office, I'm not sure where he would have gone." I hesitated again before asking, "Is everything okay?"

Diane tucked her normally neat hair behind her ears and swallowed hard. It was only then I noticed how disheveled she appeared, too. Rather than her usual wardrobe of trendy designer blouses and skirts, she wore an old T-shirt that had a large, blotchy stain across the chest. She'd paired that monstrosity with track pants and flip flops, neither of which I ever would have guessed she even owned, let alone would ever be seen wearing in public.

I set the coffees on a side table and stooped down to talk to my friend, who now visibly had to work to fight back tears. "You can always talk to me," I cooed, wondering if I should offer a tissue or a hug.

"It's Richard," she confessed with a sob. "He didn't come home last night, and he's not answering any of my calls or texts. I don't know what to do."

I thought back to that morning. I'd never seen my boss so out of sorts, and I was willing to bet Diane had never seen him lose his composure like this either.

"Tell you what," I said, hoping I wouldn't regret this. "I'll shoot you a call whenever I next see him."

Her eyes widened, the unshed tears now sparkling with mirth. "Oh, would you? That would be such a huge help."

"Sure." I really didn't want to insert myself into the middle of their domestic drama but also couldn't ignore my friend in her hour of need.

"He's been acting so strange this past week," Diane continued after grabbing a tissue for herself and giving her nose a good blow. "We've been married almost thirty years, but suddenly it's like he's a stranger."

I really didn't know what to say to that, so I patted her on the shoulder and offered a placating smile. "There, there, I'm sure everything is fine. He's going through a rough time with the death of his aunt. Right?"

Diane nodded. "Ethel was always my favorite in the family. I just wished we would have spent more time with her in the final days. I think we all half expected her to live forever. It's been such a shock."

I would have loved to ask her about the dinner party, but there was no way I could justify having that knowledge. Instead I said, "I really am so sorry for your loss."

She sniffed and tucked the used tissue into her purse. "Oh, look at me. I'm keeping you from your work." She tossed the magazine back on the coffee table and stood, attempting and failing to brush the wrinkles from her outfit. She laughed sarcastically. "I'm such a mess. Maybe a salon day is in order."

"That sounds like the perfect idea to me."

"You promise you'll call me if you see him?"

"I promise." That at least I could do. Solving the murder, though? I was seriously beginning to worry about what other unsavory secrets I might uncover if I kept digging.

Diane nodded, glanced around the office, and then surprised me with a tight hug. "Thank you, Angie. You have no idea how much you've helped."

Less than a minute later, she was gone and I was just as confused as ever.

Our youngest associate, Derek, emerged from the office he shared with another of our blue blood frat-type attorneys in training, Brad, and made a beeline straight for the coffee. "Thanks for this," he said, grabbing two and spinning on his heel to dive back into their office.

I followed sitting at the corner of Derek's desk, so neither man could ignore me. "You guys were at the will reading yesterday, right?"

Derek took a slow slurp of coffee. "I wasn't invited, but Brad was." He didn't seem too happy about this fact, but I didn't have time to unpack Derek's feelings when there was still so much more to learn about the Fultons.

I fixed my gaze on Brad and tried to show my interest in the topic without encouraging any flirtations on his part. "I've heard the craziest things. What happened?"

He spun in his chair with a self-satisfied smirk. "Well, there was this hot secretary who got electrocuted and had to be rushed to the hospital."

Non-detective me would have either slapped him knowing full well I could lose my job for doing so, or she would have stormed out without so much as a second glance. Brad had asked me out once or twice or a few dozen times, and each time I'd said no. I would forever say no, that was one certainty I'd happily stake my life on.

Add to all this the fact he referred to me as the firm's secretary on a regular basis, and I was more than a little irked. I was a paralegal. Just because I happened to bring everyone coffee most days didn't change that. Besides, I was pretty sure Brad had only scraped by in law school because of his father's connections. Everything I had career-wise—which admittedly wasn't much—came from my own merits.

I forced a smile. "After that, I mean?" As skeezy as I found Brad to be, at least I could count on him wanting to impress me. That meant he might be a little looser with his tongue than some of the more tight-lipped attorneys. And that's exactly what I was banking on now.

He cleared his throat and adjusted his tie, sitting straighter in his seat as he revealed, "The old lady left almost everything to her cat. And one lady lost her cool completely when she heard."

Oh, now we're getting somewhere!

"What lady?" I asked, quirking an eyebrow in curiosity.

His face contorted in a grimace. "She was short, had gray hair, pretty frumpy. I think maybe it was the niece?"

Hmm, that sure sounded a lot like the person Octo-Cat and I found lurking around Ethel's estate the night before. "What did she do when she found out?"

"She started yelling all these profanities, said how much she had looked after Ethel over the years while all the cat ever did was catch some mice and poop in a box. She said *she* deserved the money."

I laughed and silently tucked away the second-hand insult to deliver to Octo-Cat later. “And what did everyone else say?”

“Basically, to stay in her lane. She sat down and shut up pretty quickly after that, then rushed out of there as fast as her feet could carry her when it was over.”

I chuckled and tried my best to picture the fiasco. “Sounds like I missed quite the show.”

Brad popped to his feet and popped his collar in a move I’m sure he thought was sexy, but I found ridiculously clownish. “I’d be happy to give you a recap over dinner.”

I yawned and shook my head. “Thanks, but I’ll have to pass.”

He shrugged off the bruise to his ego. I was beginning to believe he had freaky healing powers like the Wolverine or the cheerleader girl from *Heroes.* Nothing ever seemed to faze him more than as a glancing blow.

“See you guys later,” I said with a polite nod to Derek, whom I’d always liked far more than Brad. Then again, I liked everyone in the office better than Brad. Except maybe Bethany. Those two were probably tied for last place on my list of favorite coworkers.

Maybe if she wasn’t having an affair with Mr. Fulton, she’d consider Brad a possible suitor instead. That would be great for getting him off my case, but I wasn’t sure if it would be worth the nightmare possibility of those two teaming up.

When I passed back through the main area, I noticed all the to-go cups of coffee had been claimed while I chatted with Brad and Derek about yesterday’s will reading. That meant either someone was being greedy or that Mr. Fulton was indeed nearby and had consciously hidden from his wife during her visit.

I took a deep breath before going to check his office. Nobody responded to my knock, but the door hadn't been latched all the way, so I gently pushed my way inside. I knew it was wrong to snoop, but it was also wrong to murder—and I needed to at least try to bring the culprit to justice.

After my strange run-in first with Mr. Fulton and then with his wife, I was beginning to suspect my kindly boss could have blood on his hands, which made breaking into his office even riskier.

I moved slowly through the space, ready to bolt at the first sign of danger—or of Mr. Fulton's return. At first everything appeared normal, but then a swath of bright purple lying in a heap under his desk caught my eye. Wheeling the chair back, I bent down for a closer look.

And came face-to-cup with a frilly silk bra. It was way fancier than anything I would ever wear, and too sexy for Diane. Could that mean…?

I didn't want to believe the worst about my boss, but I was already beginning to suspect him of murder, so maybe adultery wasn't too far a stretch by comparison.

As easy as it would be to peg this whole thing on the most obvious and immediate suspect, I still had a hard time picturing my favorite boss as the killer of a kindly old cat lady.

It just didn't make any sense. He'd always seemed like such a nice guy even, and perhaps especially, for a lawyer. Had it all been a ruse to lull us all into overlooking his culpability?

But why now?

Why would he kill his aunt? Was it cold and calculated or more of a passion thing? It sure seemed that slipping poison into someone's dinner was something you planned in advance. If he'd really done this horrible thing—had slowly and surely carried it out—then why did he seem so frazzled now?

I just couldn't figure it out, but one thing was for sure: I needed to get out of there before I was caught purple-handed with this newfound evidence. Sure, what exactly it was evidence for remained to be seen, but soon the truth about everything would come out.

Yes, even if I had to force it.

11

I didn't see Mr. Fulton for the rest of the day, which only raised my suspicions that much more. Diane called just before the end of my shift to check in, and I absolutely hated disappointing her with my lack of news.

On the drive home, I rolled down my windows and let the cool ocean breeze sweep through my car. It was really quite nice to be able to drive without claws stuck into my thighs for a change. And, speaking of claws, I really hoped Octo-Cat hadn't made a disaster of my house while I was away.

A few short minutes later I pulled into the gravel lot of my rental, sucked in as much fresh air as I could, and entered expecting the worst.

Octo-Cat greeted me at the door by rubbing against my pant leg and shaking his tail. "You were gone forever!"

I thought about bending down to pet him but didn't want to spoil his mood so soon after returning. "Just a little longer than my normal nine to five. Not forever," I explained.

"Nine to five? Sounds like a prison sentence to me." He had a point; I could give him that.

"Yeah, well, you're not exactly wrong," I admitted with a weary sigh.

"Then why do you go?" He sat down and studied me without hissing, flicking his tail, or otherwise expressing displeasure. Had he been body-snatched while I was away? This was definitely not the crabby tabby I'd come to know and loathe.

I rubbed my index finger and thumb together. "It's all about the Benjamins, babe. And what's this? You actually missed me?" I didn't want to risk turning him back into a striped version of Grumpy Cat, but I had to know.

He shrugged. "I like knowing you're nearby. You know, in case I need some fresh Evian or help with a particularly tricky hairball."

That made me laugh. "Thank goodness you survived."

He grinned like... well, like the Cheshire cat, then informed me, "Speaking of which, it's time for my supper."

I saluted him and headed for the kitchen. After I plopped a fresh chunk of pâté down for him and filled a cup with Evian, I proceeded to tell him what a good cat he was, just as I'd been instructed earlier that day.

When he finished his evening meal, he jumped up onto the counter and said, "Well done. You may pet me now."

"Um, okay." It felt strangely intimate to run my fingers through his brown and black fur and rub him all the way from the top of his head down to the base of his tail. It felt even stranger to hear him purr.

"You're welcome," he said after a few more strokes. "I know you've been wanting to do that for a while, and—*hey*—you've earned it. But please stop now or I will have to bite you."

I yanked my hand away faster than you could say, "Oh, brother." Then I said it aloud anyway for good measure.

Octo-Cat hopped back onto the floor and guided me into the living room where my TV still sat tuned in to the kid's channel I'd selected for him earlier that day. "Did you learn a lot today?" I asked with a smirk.

He yawned and nodded. "In between napping, yes."

"Aren't you going to ask me about my day?" I was eager to hear his thoughts about Mr. Fulton's strange behavior coupled with the fact that he seemed to have gone missing.

"The thought hadn't occurred to me," he admitted with another yawn. "Besides, I still have so much more to tell you about mine."

"Oh, I'm sorry. Please go ahead." I took a seat on the couch and motioned for him to regale me with all the many, varied events that had filled his day. It was the least I could do after he'd managed not to wreck everything I owned in some kind of irrational hissy fit as I had expected.

He jumped onto the coffee table and paced back and forth, speaking rapidly as he recounted his day. "First I woke up hungry as I often do. It took me a while to get you out of bed, and even longer to teach you how to properly serve me my morning repast. All in all, I'd give you a C for effort. Average, but not special."

"Okay, great. Can we skip ahead please?" I asked in irritation. I'd never met someone who could turn on a dime as quickly as this cat. One moment he lovingly greets me at the door and the next he's back to insulting me. This inconsistency seemed to be a staple of his character. At least I could trust him to always tell me exactly what was on his mind. That had to count for something, especially when it came to solving a murder mystery.

Octo-Cat continued to pace back and forth, speaking in rhythm with his quick steps. "After you left, I watched the cartoon girl solve mysteries using the items in her backpack. We should really get a backpack to help with our case, too. Oh, and a map."

I chuckled, which apparently was the wrong response.

"I'm dead serious here," he said, his amber eyes boring into my blues. "I also learned about pineapples under the sea and other oddities of the human world. I'm understanding your language a bit better, but you as a species a lot less. Why broadcast shows about a sea sponge and his pet snail? Why not focus on your own species, or at least a superior species like the *Felis catus?*"

"Um, I don't really have an answer to that one. People do weird things all the time, like commit murder or have affairs. You'll never believe what I discovered today at work."

"Oh, I'm sure I will believe it. You humans are also quite predictable," he informed me, plopping his rear down on the coffee table and wagging his tail ominously. "But first I must tell you about the rest of my day."

There was *more?* How much more could there possibly be?

I really wasn't looking forward to a blow by blow of all the cartoons he'd watched that day, especially not when we had far more important matters to discuss. Still, it seemed important to him that I give him my undivided attention, so I leaned back into the couch cushions and motioned for him to continue.

"At first I tried napping on the back of the couch, but I found it too lumpy for my liking. After scouring the premises, I found the perfect spot where a patch of light landed on the carpet and warmed it nicely. I napped there for roughly an hour before the sun moved, rendering the spot unsatisfactory."

He waited for me to say something, so I settled for, "Of course."

Pleased, he continued, "Then I went to your bedroom and found a nice twist in the comforter where I made something of a burrow. Unfortunately, I was unable to jump down in time when I woke up with a hairball clogging my windpipe. So, you may want to do a load of laundry before turning in for the night."

He puked on my comforter? *Gross.* At least he'd told me rather than letting me discover it for myself. Thank goodness for small miracles.

"When you came home, you fed me, and this time you made a much better showing of it. I'll give it an *A minus,* I think. Now we are here. How the rest of the day unfolds remains to be seen."

"Sounds like you had a busy day," I summarized sarcastically.

He winked at me, not catching the humor. "Yes, it was a good day, considering."

I considered asking him what he meant by that, but decided I'd rather not get in another long conversation about the intricacies of daily cat life when we still needed to discuss what I'd stumbled across at work. "May I tell you about mine?"

"It will be hard to top my day, but you may try."

I thought this meant he was happy with me, and for some reason that made my heart swell with pride. Maybe like Brad, I craved affection from someone who didn't easily offer it. Octo-Cat's kindness felt like a reward that I had earned for good behavior, and I was lapping it right up.

Without going into too much detail—because I knew how easy it was to lose his interest—I recapped the events of my day, ending with the purple bra I'd discovered in Mr. Fulton's office.

Octo-Cat shook his head. "And humans think we're the ones who need to be neutered. At least the only thing we do is make kittens, not trouble."

I had to agree with him there. "Does it surprise you that Mr. Fulton could be having an affair?"

"Not really, but I don't know him well and I don't understand your human marriages, anyway. Those tiny collars you wear on your fingers... It's like being micro-chipped, right? You can try to run away, but they'll always find you again and bring you home. Frustrating."

"Something like that," I said, trying to hide my smile. "Do you think Mr. Fulton could have been the one to poison Ethel?"

Octo-Cat thought about this for a good long time. "He's the one with gray hair and extra padding, right?"

Mr. Fulton was fit and slim, and most of his hair was still brown. Something wasn't adding up. "Are you talking about the woman we saw at your house yesterday?"

"Yes! That's Mr. Fulton, right?"

"Um, no. That was Ethel's niece. Can you really not tell men and women apart?"

"I told you, all humans look the same. Can you tell whether a cat is a man or a woman just by glancing at them?"

Okay, he was right about that, so I decided to cut him a bit of slack.

He flicked his tail as he thought, then said, "I don't suppose you could describe what this Mr. Fulton smells like? It would be so much easier for me if you would."

"Um, no. Sorry." I shook my head to erase the mental image of me attempting to surreptitiously sniff my boss.

He shrugged and began grooming himself.

I slumped back against the couch again and sighed, something I sure was doing a lot of lately. "Then I guess nothing I tell you is of value because you don't even know who I'm talking about. How are we supposed to solve this thing if we can't even fully communicate with each other?"

It seemed like a cruel joke that I'd somehow gained the ability to talk to animals but couldn't use that power to actually accomplish anything. Someone upstairs must be getting a good laugh out of the two of us right about now.

"You could take me to work with you," Octo-Cat chanced with a sly grin.

"No way. I already told you why that won't work." I still had no idea why he wanted to go to the office so badly, but this was one point on which I refused to waiver.

He looked bored as he suggested, "Okay, then how about the viewing tomorrow?"

I leapt up straight in my seat at this. "A viewing? Like the pre-funeral thing?"

"That was what I gathered. The humans were discussing it yesterday between the time you left and the time you came back." He meant when I'd gone to the hospital. It seemed no one was overly concerned about my near brush with death, not even my new friend, the talking cat. I tried not to let it hurt my feelings, but jeez. You'd think at least someone would be worried after a display like that.

"I don't know how," I told him, forcing myself to focus on the matter at hand once again. "But yes. I'm going to find a way to take you with me. Since the killer was someone Ethel knew well enough to have over for dinner, then he'll definitely be making an appearance. We need to be there, too."

"I was hoping you'd say that," he said with a wink. "Now, if you'll please excuse me, I need to pay a visit to the little kitty box."

12

I snuck out of work early the next day so that Octo-Cat and I could get ready for the viewing happening early that evening. Mr. Fulton didn't come into the office at all that day, which made it quite difficult for me to do any further investigation into his means or motive. The longer he stayed away, however, the more and more suspicious I became.

One way or another, I'd need to find a way to learn more. Maybe I could invite myself over to his house to visit with Diane. Or maybe the viewing would reveal everything I needed to know. I sure hoped it would be the latter.

Knowing that there was a killer on the loose—and that it was more than likely someone I personally knew—had started cutting into my sleep lately. Add Octo-Cat's early morning wakeup calls to the mix, and I was practically a dead woman walking. *Yikes.*

Until we had enough proof to take our case to the police, I'd just need to drink lots and lots of extra coffee, a pretty cruel irony considering how I'd first acquired my ability to talk to animals in the first place. I tried not to dwell on my near-death experience too much, considering that there was nothing *near* about Ethel Fulton's death.

On the way home I stopped off at the local charity shop to find a suitable mourning outfit. I also found an over-sized shoulder bag that I quickly claimed for that evening's use. Even though its tan and black wicker design appeared a tad on the beachy side, it would conceal Octo-Cat's furry bulk perfectly, thus allowing me to sneak him in and out of the funeral home undetected.

"It smells," he told me with a flick of his tail when I presented my idea to him a short while later.

Even though I knew the second-hand bag wouldn't be an easy sell for my spoiled cat friend, I still frowned with disappointment. "Unless you have a better idea, I'm afraid we're stuck."

"I was invited to the will reading. Why am I not invited to this?" His upper lip quivered, and he let out a pitiful, weak mewling sound. It actually made me feel bad for him even though his ego could stand to be taken down a few pegs.

"Look, I didn't make the rules," I explained. "It's a public showing, which means pretty much anyone who wants to come is welcome, but I still worry they'll turn us both away if I show up with you out in the open. Sorry, it's just how most people would react to a cat showing up in a public place. Especially if you're still all freaked out from the car ride."

And now I'd made him angry. Well, angry was better than sad, I guess.

"You said I was getting better," he reminded me with a growl.

Okay, yes, I did tell him that on the way home from Ethel's estate a couple nights back, but it had only been a polite, little lie to make him feel better.

"Yes, that's right," I said now, unwilling to take the time to explain the intricacies of human etiquette to him when the clock was already ticking.

I left my feline friend to pout while I quickly changed into my new get-up. Sarcastic or not, Bethany had been absolutely right about Goodwill being a great place to find clothes within my budget. This new black dress fell just below my knees and could just as easily be repurposed for a cocktail party as it could a funeral.

"Let's go," I said, sweeping back through the living room and pointing to the wicker vehicle I'd purchased expressly for this mission.

Octo-Cat's eyes widened in horror. "Surely I don't need to get in there now. Can't it at least wait until we reach the funeral parlor?"

"Nope, I'm not taking any chances." I put one hand on my hip and used the other to hold the bag open wide. "Now in!"

He hissed and growled, but ultimately complied.

"Good kitty," I said.

Another hiss rose out of the bag. "I warned you about that."

"Yeah," I murmured as I twisted the lock on the front door after closing it behind me. "But you already puked on my bed once, so I figured I'd earned that one."

"You figured wrong," he said, popping his head out of the bag to scowl at me.

I laughed as I set his makeshift carrier on the floor of the passenger side, then off we went. Once or twice he tried to flee the bag for the safe harbor of my lap, but each time I managed to talk him off the ledge and back into his hiding place.

"I hate you so much," Octo-Cat snarled when at last we arrived.

"Shh," I warned him. "Nobody can know you're here."

Luckily the bag's weave gave him some visibility without revealing his hidden form. Just as much as I wanted to catch the killer, I also believed Octo-Cat deserved the chance to pay Ethel his respects. After all, she'd been an all-encompassing companion for him his entire life and I knew he missed her like crazy.

"Remember the plan," I murmured without moving my lips. Maybe all these years my hidden talent had actually been in ventriloquism. I'd definitely have to explore it in more detail later.

"If you see—or, *umm*, smell—someone who was at the dinner party," I continued, "reach through the bag with your claws and tap my arm. Please note this is the only time I am giving you permission to claw me."

"Understood. Now please let's get this over with. This thing really stinks." He wasn't the only one who'd rather be at home, but it seemed I had to be strong now for the both of us.

I hoisted the bag further up my shoulder and strode forward with the confidence of someone who didn't have a talking cat secretly stashed in her bag. No sooner had we entered than I found a familiar, wrinkled visage staring right at me. Honestly, it gave me the heebie jeebies, especially after what Brad had revealed to me about her tantrum at the will reading.

"I recognize you," I said, striding straight up to her. "What's your name again?"

She glanced around then murmured, "Anne Fulton."

Octo-Cat chose that exact moment to sink his claws into the soft flesh beneath my arm.

"Ow," I cried, then caught myself, chuckled nervously, and said, "'Ow did you know Ethel?"

"She was my aunt," Anne said, giving the answer I already knew.

"I'm sorry for your loss," I said, ducking my head and charging away. The last thing I needed was to be trapped with this strange, temperamental, breaking-and-entering woman all evening. Yet, then again, I was kind of all those things, too. Maybe Anne and I had more in common than I wanted to admit.

The bag weighed heavily on my shoulder, making me think that maybe Octo-Cat would benefit from a diet and me from some more weight lifting. We passed gracelessly between the guests, making our way toward the casket.

There Ethel Fulton lay upon a bed of light pink silk, her short hairstyle curled in a perfect halo, her makeup heavy but elegant. I hadn't known her in life, but seeing her dead body laid on display like this sent a shiver of sorrow straight through me.

Octo-Cat clawed me a second time, and it stung. "Yes," I hissed quietly. "Ethel was at her own dinner party. I know that."

He let out a low growl then mumbled, "Incoming from behind."

I spun on my heel, resisting the urge to check my arm for little pin pricks of blood, and came face to face with Diane wearing a simple, black shift dress with an understated pillbox hat.

"Oh, Angie," she cried, falling into my arms so fast the bag almost slipped off my shoulder. "I'm so glad to see a friendly face."

She held tight to me for a long time, sobbing and sharing stories of all the good times she'd had with Ethel. "When I was a young bride, Ethel took me under her wing and taught me everything I needed to know to keep a good home and to keep my husband happy." Diane burst into another hysterical sob. "Oh, you don't have time for this."

"There, there," I said, patting her back and praying she would let me go.

She tensed in my arms and yanked away as if she'd been burned… or perhaps electrocuted.

I turned to see what she was staring at and saw Mr. Fulton standing in the entryway to the funeral home, with Bethany close at his side.

"I have to go," Diane sobbed, fleeing the scene before I had a chance to stop her.

Visions of the purple bra in Mr. Fulton's office danced before me menacingly. Now that I thought about it some more, that thing had looked like it was about Bethany's size. I watched in disgust as our boss placed his hand at the small of Bethany's back and guided her toward the casket, openly flaunting their intimacy for all to see.

Oh, poor Diane!

She had come to say goodbye to a beloved relative and instead her husband chose to humiliate her in front of the entire community.

I waited at the casket, wondering if they would even try to excuse their behavior. Octo-Cat slipped his claws through the bag's weave and dug those tiny pin missiles into me once more, alerting me to the fact that Mr. Fulton had, indeed, been present the night of the murder, too.

Well, now we knew the identity of three of the five guests from that night. Octo-Cat had already ruled out Anne for us, and I knew better than to suspect Diane. That narrowed our suspects to exactly three people. Either Mr. Fulton or one of the remaining mystery guests had done the deed—and more and more it looked like Fulton was our man.

"Angie," he said with a sad smile, dropping his hand from Bethany's back as he approached. "Thank you for coming to pay your respects."

Bethany nodded curtly but didn't say anything.

"It was the least I could do," I said, not knowing what I meant by that.

Apparently, however, my words were well received.

"She was such a special lady," Fulton said with a sigh. "Almost like a second mother. I've been having such a hard time admitting she's gone."

His voice cracked, and Bethany patted his arm consolingly. It only made me angrier and angrier.

They both turned to look into the casket, and I excused myself before I could say something we all regretted. Octo-Cat tapped me again as I charged through the other guests toward the door, but I didn't even notice who he wanted me to see.

At this point, I had all the proof I needed to know Mr. Fulton was guilty of at least two unforgivable crimes.

13

A hand on my shoulder stopped me before I could tear my way across the parking lot. I whipped around to see…

Bethany, of all people.

"What do you want?" I growled, not even bothering to disguise my disgust now.

Her wispy blonde hair rippled in the wind, and her lips pinched together in a tiny bow. I'd never seen her look this vulnerable—or this feminine—before. "I want to make sure you're okay. You looked like you were going to be sick back there. Have you never seen a dead body before?"

"I've seen bodies," I spat. "What I haven't seen is my boss flaunting his affair right in everyone's faces and at the very worst possible time, too."

Bethany gasped and took a step back. "Affair? You couldn't possibly think…"

"What else am I supposed to think?" I demanded, actually wishing she'd offer up another answer. I'd been quite happy working for Fulton, Thompson, and Associates until this recent turn of events. I'd never be able to look at Fulton or Bethany the same ever again, not without picturing that awful purple bra, his hand at her back and —*oh, yeah*—the murder of a sweet, old lady who definitely didn't deserve it.

Bethany frowned and shook her head. "I thought you knew me better than that by now, Angie." It almost looked like she might cry. Who was this frail woman before me, and why was she suddenly so different than the office shark who would sink her teeth into anyone to get ahead?

"I hardly know you at all. And I guess I don't know Mr. Fulton very well, either." I laughed bitterly. "You know, you guys did a great job hiding it. I actually had no idea until I came in early and found you two alone in the office. Then there was that bra—"

"A bra?" Bethany asked aloud, then mumbled something to herself that I couldn't quite make out. Maybe now that she knew she'd been caught, she'd finally start telling me the truth here.

I crossed my arms, narrowing my gaze at her. "Yeah, *your* bra."

"Wow." She stared at me, unblinking. "Just wow."

"You honestly thought no one would ever find out? Just because I'm a paralegal doesn't make me any less intelligent than all you know-it-all lawyers." All my grievances were coming out now, all the things I'd kept to myself over the months in the name of creating a positive workplace environment. The way Bethany just stared at me with something that resembled hurt in her eyes was quite unsettling, though. I'd almost rather be dealing with Brad and his obnoxious come-ons right now.

Bethany kicked at the pavement in frustration. When her eyes snapped back up to mine, they were cold and unyielding. "Yes, and just because you're a woman doesn't mean you're not being terribly sexist right now, either. It's one thing for me to get this from the guys, but from you? I expected more of you, Angie."

"Oh, don't give me that whole 'I'm not angry, I'm disappointed' spiel. I heard it from my nan a million times growing up. And don't go placing the blame on me when you're the one sneaking around with a married man—who just so happens to also be our boss."

She widened her stance as if bracing for impact, then enunciated each word as she insisted, "I am not having an affair with Mr. Fulton."

"I don't know," I said with a shrug. "You two looked mighty cozy in there."

She glanced over her shoulder demurely. "That's different."

"Yeah, right." I smirked and gave her a sarcastic thumbs up. I wasn't normally such a confrontational person, but for some reason, Bethany just got under my skin, especially today at the viewing when emotions already ran high.

"It is," she insisted through gritted teeth. "You don't understand."

"Oh, I understand perfectly," I yelled. There was nothing I hated more than being condescended to—well, except maybe murder and adultery.

"No, you don't," she shouted back, then dropped her voice several notches. "And you're starting to make a scene."

What Bethany didn't understand is that I'd never been bothered about making a scene. I was raised by a retired stage actress, for crying out loud! As far as we were concerned, making a scene was a good thing just so long as it didn't get us into trouble.

I could tell Bethany was getting ready to put an end to our exchange, so I finally decided to ask the million-dollar question. "Hey, you're the one who stopped me from leaving. But, okay, tell me this: if you're not having an affair, then what are the two of you doing?"

She wrapped both arms around her own waist and looked toward the ground as she murmured, "I can't tell you that. At least not yet."

"How convenient," I muttered while shaking my head.

When Bethany didn't say anything else, I charged the rest of the way across the lot and tossed my bag onto the passenger seat of my car, forgetting momentarily that Octo-Cat was stowed away inside. *Oops.*

"Do you mind?" he shouted after making the same terrible sound he most often uses to wake me up in the mornings. "Some of us are trying to avoid losing lives unnecessarily here."

Despite his irritation, he seemed to be okay.

But me? I was so angry that my hands shook and turned bright red. I needed a moment to re-center myself, but Octo-Cat did not like being ignored.

"Uh, hello, I'm talking here!" he shouted, taking a swipe at my arm with claws extended, which made me angrier still.

"Don't you ever shut up?" I yelled back at him.

"Wow, who pooped in your party?"

"That's not the expression," I said, still seething from the confrontation with Bethany. I just wanted to get home, but I didn't trust myself to drive safely yet.

My tabby nuisance put his two front paws on my leg and began to knead the muscle as he spoke. "It fits, though. Now you're the one who dragged me into this, you can at least include me. What was that back there?"

"Me? Dragging *you?* Yeah, that's not how I remember it."

"Semantics." He waved a paw dismissively and sat back down on his seat. "Who started this isn't what's important. What I want to know is why you got so hung up on a human that wasn't even there that night. Don't you care about finding Ethel's murderer?"

Suddenly, all the fight drained out of me as if Octo-Cat had twisted a spigot. No matter how scandalized I felt about the affair, Octo-Cat, no doubt, felt far worse. He'd lost someone important to him, and here I was making a circus out of her viewing.

"I'm sorry," I murmured, feeling like the worst friend in the world.

"Hey, it's okay. Humans get emotional sometimes." He licked at his paw idly, then added, "Okay, a lot of times. But we can work through this."

His words were oddly comforting and just what I needed.

"Okay," I said, letting out a slow, shaky breath. "Okay."

Octo-Cat nodded. "We need to go back in," he informed me. "We still haven't found everyone who was there that night."

"I think I already know who killed Ethel," I confessed. "All signs point to Mr. Fulton."

“The man. My boss,” I clarified when I noticed he still looked confused.

As it turned out, what my kitty companion said next shocked me with its wisdom and depth.

“Look,” he said. “He could very well be the one, but we can’t know for sure until we rule the others out. It’s like how sometimes you might think that the chicken pâté is your favorite flavor of Fancy Feast, but then the next day you have the salmon and shrimp blend and it tastes even better than the chicken. When you think about it some more, you may have just been extra hungry before which made the inferior flavor of the chicken seem extra delicious, or you mistakenly thought chicken was best only because you hadn’t tried all the other wonderful flavors yet. Do you get what I’m saying?”

Strangely, I did. “That Mr. Fulton could be our salmon and shrimp blend, or he could simply be chicken pâté, but we won’t know until we’ve finished our meal?”

“Exactly.” He seemed to glow with pride, but maybe that was just his eyes glinting in the waning sunlight. “This meal’s only just getting started, so make sure you save some space in that belly of yours.”

“Thanks, Octo-Cat. I needed that.”

“And I may need you to swing by the store after this and grab some chicken pâté. I know, I know. I usually don’t eat the poultry flavors, but suddenly I find myself with a craving.”

I scratched him between the ears. “You’re a good cat.”

“And you’re a very good human. Yes, you are,” he told me in a goochie-goo voice that made us both smile. “Now let’s get back inside and see who else we can find.”

14

Even though Octo-Cat convinced me to go back into the funeral home for the viewing, we were too late to do any meaningful sleuthing. The close family and friends had already departed for a private function, leaving only distant acquaintances and curious casket-gawkers to mingle in the parlor.

Unsurprisingly, Bethany had left, too, only further supporting my suspicions.

Octo-Cat and I were among the last to remain behind, which gave him a chance to surreptitiously poke his head out of the bag and speak his goodbyes to Ethel.

"Oh, Ethel," he cried without a trace of his normal over-the-top theatrics. "You were my whole world, and you didn't even know it. I know we had our disagreements on occasion, but you were truly the best thing that ever happened to me. The world won't be quite as bright without you in it. I'll always think of you when drinking Evian or stretching out in a sun spot. I love you and am so happy you were my human."

I teared up a bit as I listened to his heartfelt goodbye. "That was beautiful," I told him, searching around for one of the boxes of tissues I'd spotted earlier, but coming up short.

"Yeah," he said with a sniff and a twitch of his whiskers.

"By the way," I said, settling him back into the bag with the utmost care. "She knew how important she was to you."

His voice came out muffled. "How can you be sure?"

"I just am."

After that, we drove home, and I briefly stopped off at the supermarket to purchase fresh shrimp for our dinner. Octo-Cat had kept it together when I couldn't. As far as I was concerned, he'd more than earned this special treat. Seeing as it would be impossible for me to prepare such a nice meal without also indulging, I bought enough to feed me, too.

Octo-Cat didn't eat as much as he normally did, which worried me. "Is your dinner okay?" I asked regarding the morsel on my fork suspiciously. Could he sense something I didn't? My mind briefly flitted back to smelling dishes in Ethel's kitchen in an ill-fated attempt to detect poison.

He sighed. "I just miss Ethel."

"Of course, you do. I'm so sorry you had to see her like that."

"It's just..." He sniffed as he padded his paws on the table anxiously. "It's just, I thought we'd be together forever. Then suddenly she was gone."

"Life works like that sometimes," I admitted, never having felt this acute sense of loss myself but hoping I could still offer some measure of comfort.

"If you want, maybe..." I hesitated, something new and most definitely unexpected overtaking me.

"Yeah?" he asked sadly, when I didn't continue.

"Maybe after this is all said and done, I don't know..."

Just say it!

"Well, maybe I could be your human."

His eyes widened with surprise, and then a rumbling purr filled the silence between us. "I'd like that," he said.

"I mean, it's better than having to break in another new human." He dropped his head and nibbled on the largest and most succulent shrimp I had placed before him.

Now that he was otherwise occupied, he was unable to see the tears welling in the corners of my eyes.

What could I say?

That ornery tabby had really grown on me the past few days. Maybe I was a cat person after all.

The next morning, I woke up before Octo-Cat could rouse me—and unbelievably I felt refreshed and ready to go. Excited for the day ahead, even. It was such a drastic change from how I'd felt upon going to bed that it couldn't have been anything other than a gift from above.

Rather than questioning it, I decided to pay it forward.

"I have a present for you," I told Octo-Cat after he'd finished his breakfast.

"Not another foul-smelling bag, I hope," he complained, but I could tell he was excited. Something about the twitch of his tail and the perkiness with which he trailed me back toward the bedroom suggested he was in just as good a mood as me that day. Perhaps how we'd bonded over our shrimp dinner last night had something to do with it.

"Hop up," I told him as I took a seat on the bed and rooted around in my night stand.

He joined me, padding across my lap to sniff at the drawer.

When I pulled out what I was looking for, he leapt back with a start. "What's that thing?" he said between quick, panicked breaths.

"This is my iPad," I explained, pushing the power button to wake the screen then setting it on the bed between us. "Well, actually now it's yours."

"It's shiny," he commented, sniffing it hesitantly.

I nodded enthusiastically. "Yes, and I think you'll really like what it can do."

"Oh?" Now I had his interest.

"I'm guessing Ethel didn't have one of these," I said, presenting it once again with a flourish.

He shook his head in confirmation.

"Well, we can install apps for you to play with when you're bored, like a virtual fish tank or a keyboard or even the radio, and we will... But the main reason I'm giving this to you is for FaceTime."

"FaceTime?" He laughed after trying the name aloud for himself. "That's an odd mash up of unrelated words."

"Yeah, but they already had iPhone, so they had to come up with something else to name this app. Look." I pulled my phone out of my pocket and called the tablet using FaceTime.

Oct-Cat swished his tail as he watched me reach over to answer the call. "Whoa," he murmured in awe when my face popped up on the screen, followed by his own when I pointed the phone on my camera toward him.

"Cool, right?" I gushed. I loved teaching others new things just as much as I loved learning them for myself.

"What else can it do?" he asked, spinning in an excited circle before settling back down before the iPad.

"I know you miss me while I'm at work, so I figured we could use this system to talk to each other," I explained with an ingratiating smile, just in case he planned to argue this point. I was pleasantly surprised when he didn't.

My iPad was part of Nan's family network, while my phone was funded by Fulton, Thompson, and Associates, which thankfully meant I had two separate numbers. Earlier, I'd found that to be a pain, but it worked out quite well now that my talking cat needed his own line.

I sat with him for about half an hour, teaching him how to unlock the device, click on the FaceTime app, and press my photo to call me. We also practiced having me call him, so he could answer by stepping on the screen with his paw.

And he did it all splendidly.

Who said cats couldn't be trained?

By the time I had to leave for work, Octo-Cat was pleasantly pre-occupied with a koi fish app he'd selected all on his own. He didn't play the game quite right, but he sure had fun swiping at the fish on screen.

So, I left him to it and headed to the firm to see what more I could learn that day.

As it turned out, it wasn't much. Mr. Thompson had taken Derek to court with him. Bethany refused to speak so much as a word to me, and I generally preferred to avoid Brad as a rule. That left a few of our less talkative associates, Mr. Fulton, and me.

For his part, my boss seemed far more composed today than he had earlier in the week. I wondered if he'd made up with Diane. I also wondered if Bethany had told him about our heated exchange last night in the parking lot, but if she had, he showed no signs of knowing I suspected him of anything unsavory, affair or otherwise.

He approached my desk and cleared his throat. "Angie," he said, his mouth set in a firm line. "I need you to work on a special project for me today."

I looked up from my keyboard and nodded. "Sure. What can I do for you?"

He rapped his fingers on the edge of my desk, and we both watched his hand as he spoke.

"I need you to search for some precedents about wills being thrown out due to the guarantors being of unsound mind at the time of signing. What were their arguments? What happened to the estate after the original will was discarded? How long did the cases take to settle?"

He paused, slipped both hands in his pockets, and glanced over his shoulder before continuing.

"But before that, could you, um, do a quick review of a petition for me and then send it through the courier? I'd really like it to go out today, please."

"Yes, absolutely," I answered without hesitation.

He broke out into a huge smile. "Great. That'll be a huge help. I'll email the petition shortly." He turned and walked back to his office with a somewhat lighter gait than he'd used to approach.

It hardly took a minute for the document to pop up in my inbox. Curious, I clicked to download the attachment.

It was a petition for divorce.

His divorce from Diane.

15

After a quick scan of the divorce petition, I snuck into the bathroom at work to call Octo-Cat. It took two tries before he answered, and when he did, I couldn't see anything on the screen.

"Hello?" I asked, unsure about the stability of our connection.

"Hello," he answered, his voice coming over loud and clear and full of pride. "I did it!"

I stared at the screen, still unable to make out his picture. "Why can't I see you?"

"I don't know," came his befuddled response. "I mean, I'm sitting right on the thing!"

Well, that explained a lot. I'd have to gently remind him how the camera works later that night. For now, I was far too excited about the new information I had to share and preferred not to spoil it by getting in to a lengthy argument over proper iPad usage for cats.

I dropped my voice to a whisper to make sure no one else in the building could hear me. "Mr. Fulton is filing for a divorce. He also has me researching a bunch of old cases related to overturning wills. I think he might be our shrimp and salmon blend after all."

"What does that mean?" Octo-Cat asked without the slightest hint of irony in his voice. Could he have really forgotten his own metaphor?

"Yesterday, you... *Never mind."* I couldn't get into this with him, not when we had far more important matters to discuss. Not when I already had a massive headache forming at the edges of my brain.

"Just tell me this," I said, determined to make something of this call. "What do you think it all means?"

Octo-Cat let out a loud and long yawn. "You're right that it makes him seem guilty. Mr. Fulton, *hmm...* Which one is he again?"

I sighed and clutched my forehead in my hands. We were quickly heading to migraine status. "I'll point him out at the funeral, okay?" I offered with a whimper.

"Sure." He yawned again. "When is that again?"

I was seriously beginning to worry here. It's like my cat's entire mind had been wiped clean overnight. "Hey, *um,* are you okay?"

"I just woke up from a nap, so I'm a little out of sorts," he admitted with another high-pitched yawn. "And the longer we talk, the warmer this thing is getting. It's making me so sleepy."

That's what happens when you sit on your iPad, I thought. "Okay, well, I'll let you go then. Enjoy your nap."

"Oh, I shall," he said right before I ended the call.

Well, that had accomplished nothing, other than telling me that

FaceTime could possibly work as a method of communication for us with a bit more practice on Octo-Cat's end.

I washed my hands and then stepped out of the bathroom, back into the main office.

Mr. Fulton was waiting just outside the door. "Did you finish that petition for me yet?" he asked anxiously.

"Just about," I promised.

"Good." He nodded, but continued to frown. "I need that research ASAP, too."

"You've got it." He looked like he wanted to say something more, so I stood awkwardly by and waited for him to gather his thoughts.

Mr. Fulton frowned as he regarded me, which I tried not to take personally. Even though I was trying to prove him guilty of murder, I was still great at my job as a paralegal.

"I'll be headed out of the office soon and plan on taking tomorrow and Monday for personal affairs," he informed me with a dismissive nod.

Affairs. I practically choked at his choices of words but managed to hold it together well enough to say, "Okay, I'll put everything else on hold until I get that done for you."

Finally, he switched his expression to something less aggrieved and a bit more neutral. It still wasn't quite a smile, but I'd take it. "Good. Thank you, Angie. See you next week."

I watched him return to his office, then shut and lock the door. What could he possibly be hiding in there? And where was he headed for the long weekend?

I briefly debated calling Octo-Cat again, but the poor furball clearly needed his rest. Still, I needed someone to talk to, so I took a big gamble and headed to Bethany's office, hoping enough time had passed that she'd at least be willing to talk with me.

I knocked softly at her door, wishing I had some kind of peace offering. For now, my apology would have to do.

"Go away, please," she called without opening the door.

"I'm sorry about yesterday," I pleaded into the cherry-stained wood. "I was hoping we could talk about it."

The door flung open to reveal my still very clearly enraged coworker. "What's there to talk about?" she demanded with a hand on her hip and a scowl on her face.

"I'm just worried about you and wanted to see if you needed to talk." This much was true. If she was carousing with a murderer, she definitely needed to know that. As much as Bethany got on my nerves sometimes, I'd much rather have her on my team than playing against me.

"No thanks," she answered, trying to close the door again.

I stuck my foot into the door's path just in time. "Please, just give me two minutes," I begged.

"Fine." She retreated back to the safety of her desk and stared daggers at me.

I closed the door behind me and slowly approached.

"Time's a ticking," she reminded me, pointing at her wrist even though she'd never worn a watch as long as I'd known her.

"Look, I don't know what's going on with you and Mr. Fulton, but I'm worried about you," I started.

She let out a sigh so big, it ruffled some of the papers on her desk. "Not this again."

"Bethany, listen to me. I have reason to believe he's dangerous."

She shook her head. "That's ridiculous. Mr. Fulton is one of the most legitimately kind people I know."

"He's leaving the office for several days," I blurted out. It was definitely unusual behavior. Normally, he worked straight through the weekends, and I wanted to know what had changed about this week. "Do you know why?"

"I don't know... Maybe mourning? Why can't you just leave the poor man alone? And leave me alone, too, for that matter. Time's up, by the way."

"What? But we hardly even said anything at all," I protested.

"This is my office," she said as she rose from her seat and marched toward the door. "I decide who is and isn't welcome. And right now, you most definitely aren't."

Defeated, I trailed after her. "Just be careful, okay?" I said once I'd made it into the hall.

"Sure, whatever," she said with a grimace, hesitating with her hand on the door knob. She hadn't closed me out, not yet.

Bethany bit her lip and studied me for a moment before suggesting, "I think you should talk to Brad about that bra you mentioned yesterday. I overheard him bragging to Derek about some after-hours conquest, and well... I'm sure he'll be more than happy to tell you the rest."

She shut the door in my face—a bit gentler this time, so at least we were making progress. Opting to take her advice, I headed to Brad's office next.

I hated that we didn't have Derek as a buffer today. He was usually the only one who could keep Brad even close to in control. Still, I needed answers, and I needed them much sooner than later.

"What's up, doll face?" he asked when I clicked his door shut behind me.

"Doll face? Really?" I shuddered. First of all, that pet term was from at least eight decades ago, and second, it wasn't at all appropriate for work.

"What? You prefer sweet cheeks?" He glanced pointedly toward my rear and widened his eyes in what I assumed was appreciation. *Gross.*

"What I want is for you to call me my name and only my name," I ground out, taking great care not to slap him across the face—at least not before getting the info I'd come for. "It's Angie, by the way," I reminded him.

"Okay, Angie," he said pointedly, smirking up at me. "What can I do you for?"

I decided to just spit it out so that I could spend as little time alone with this walking lawsuit as possible. "What do you know about the purple silk bra I found in Mr. Fulton's office yesterday?"

His smile widened to a sickening degree. "Heard about that, did you?"

"I *saw* it," I said, shuddering again.

He chuckled. "Aww, don't be jealous. There's plenty of Brad to go around."

"So, it *was* yours," I spat.

"Not mine, but..." He shot me a creepy smile as he thought of how to put it. "A friend's," he finally settled on.

"If it was your friend's, then what was it doing in Mr. Fulton's office?" I demanded.

He shrugged casually. "My friend may have thought I was the junior partner here."

"And why would she think that?"

He sighed and shook his head. "C'mon, Angie. Do I really need to spell it out for you?"

Ick, ick, ick. "Does Mr. Fulton know?"

He cleared his throat. "Of course not. You think I want to be put on suspension?"

"No, but you deserve it. Worse, even," I hissed, giving him one last withering look before charging out of his office.

Finally, the firm had enough reason to send Brad packing. I didn't care how influential and well respected his father was. Brad was, hands down, the biggest creep I'd ever met. He should have been fired months ago for sexual harassment, but then again, it was possible that neither Thompson nor Fulton knew since Bethany and I tended to let his disgusting behavior carry on unchecked.

Well, no more.

I barged straight to Fulton's office, forgetting to knock.

I found him on the phone, speaking in a raspy whisper. "I don't care what it takes," he growled. "Keep it buried. At least until the divorce is final."

Our eyes locked, and his face contorted in momentary rage before he wiped his expression clean once again. I should have turned on my heel and run away but was too startled to move a muscle. Stupid deer in headlights effect.

"I'll talk to you later," he whispered into the phone, then turned his full attention to me and plastered on the most inauthentic smile I'd ever seen in all my life. "Angie, do you have my petition ready?"

"Yeah, let me just go get it," I lied, then I booked it out of there as fast as my legs could carry me.

Brad's dismissal would have to wait for another day. Right now, I had to make sure that I wasn't next on the chopping block. I'd happily give up my job, however, if it meant keeping my head.

16

Luckily, Mr. Fulton left shortly after I summoned the courier, which meant I was safe for the time being. I'd definitely be looking over my shoulder extra until he was behind bars, though.

When I told Octo-Cat about the call I'd overhead, even he had to agree that no one but Mr. Fulton could be to blame for Ethel's murder.

"And if he's killed before, it'll be easier for him to do it again," he added.

I shivered in fear. "You're right, and I'm pretty sure he knows that *I* know."

"Based on what you've told me, you're probably right." Octo-Cat rubbed his head against my arm affectionately, but it wasn't enough to put my mind at ease. Suddenly, every lingering shadow, every unexpected sound transformed into a warning that my boss was coming to kill me for what basically amounted to being too good at my job. Then again, I was supposed to be researching legal precedents, not clues in a murder mystery.

"We need to get out of here," I said, panic rising in my chest.

Octo-Cat looked up at me with large, amber eyes and an understanding nod. "Where to? Ethel's house?"

"Heck no!" I practically shouted. "We're going to Nan's."

I packed up his Fancy Feast, Evian, and freshly cleaned litter box in a hurry, feeling far too exposed in my own home.

"Don't forget my iPad," he reminded me as he pawed at the bedroom door. He seemed far less frightened than I did. Was this because he had nine lives to draw on? Whatever the case, he hadn't seen the livid expression on Mr. Fulton's face when he caught me eavesdropping on his call. If looks could kill...

No, if I focused too much on my fear, I wouldn't be able to act to keep myself safe. Right now, I just needed to focus on getting us out of there. Once we were out of there, we could brainstorm the best way to present our case to local law enforcement. Maybe Nan would have some good ideas about how to repackage our evidence in such a way that excluded the fact our primary informant was a talking cat.

Less than fifteen minutes later, Octo-Cat and I turned up at Nan's door with our overnight bags. Thank goodness for small towns and short drives.

"Angie?" my grandmother asked, blinking first at me and then at the tabby who stood at my side.

"What a nice surprise," she exclaimed, motioning us in and saddling me with a huge hug. She didn't even ask about the cat I'd randomly acquired since our last meeting. It all made me feel very guilty and like I should probably visit my nan more often.

She led us to the couch, and Octo-Cat immediately hopped up on her lap and began to purr.

"I like her," he announced. "She reminds me of Ethel."

"He likes you," I told her.

"I like him, too," she cooed. "Is he yours?" Today she wore an emerald green blouse with gemstones hand-sewn around the neck, and it suited her perfectly. I glanced down at the jeans and T-shirt I'd changed into after work, suddenly feeling underdressed for our visit. Then again, I was always coming up short compared to my elegant and talented Nan.

I shook my head and frowned. "*No.* Well, maybe. It's kind of a long story."

"I have time. Tell me what's going on." She continued to pet Octo-Cat while she listened to my tale of unexpected workplace terror.

Once I started talking, I just couldn't stop. It felt so nice to be able to unload it all on someone I knew was actually paying attention for a change. I caught her up on all the evidence against Mr. Fulton and what were more than likely false accusations toward Bethany. Now that I thought about it, I definitely owed her an apology. A sincere and heartfelt one.

"It sounds like something straight out of an off-Broadway script," Nan said, summing things up pretty accurately. "One thing I don't quite understand, though, is how you suspected murder in the first place."

I glanced toward Octo-Cat for guidance.

"You might as well tell her," he said, leaving Nan to take up residence on my lap. "You can pet me, if it helps," he offered selflessly.

"Thank you," I mumbled.

"Thank you for what, dear?" Nan asked with an unassuming smile.

Why was I holding back? If I couldn't trust Nan—the very woman who had raised me—then I had no hope left for this life, anyway. Besides, it would be nice to finally share my secret with someone outside of Octo-Cat.

I took a deep breath, pushing my fingers through his fur as I prepared for my big reveal. "Remember how you picked me up from the hospital earlier this week?" Man, could it really only be Thursday with all that had happened these past few days? My entire world had changed in the blink of a cat's eye.

Nan nodded. "You said it was a mild electric shock. Was it something more than that?" she pressed, reaching for her bifocals so she could study my face more closely as we talked.

"It was an electrical shock, that part's totally true. What I didn't tell you, though..." I bit my lip. What would I do if Nan didn't believe me?

"Go on," Octo-Cat encouraged me. "She can handle it."

"Go on," Nan also said. Her wrinkled brow knitted with worry while she waited. As much as my forthcoming confession unnerved me, I couldn't leave her hanging like that.

"I can talk to cats," I blurted out, finally putting it out there for the wider universe's consideration.

She glanced from me to Octo-Cat and back again. "Does he talk?" she asked considering my big reveal for a few seconds.

"Yes, he does," I nodded enthusiastically. Did this mean she actually believed me? "He's the one who told me about Ethel's murder. She was his owner, and he saw the whole thing," I further explained.

"I'm so sorry your owner was murdered like that," she told Octo-Cat, patting her lap and inviting him to return to her. "Is there anything I can do to help?"

And this right here was one of the many reasons I loved my nan so dearly. She didn't question my crazy claim. She just automatically believed what I told her. We all need someone like Nan in our corner.

Relief washed over me as I realized I'd done the right thing by trusting her with my secret. "Did you understand her?" I asked Octo-Cat.

"Yes, I did," he informed me, then looked up at Nan and said, "Thank you for your condolences."

"Oh," Nan cried. "He's talking to me! What did that adorable, little meow mean?"

Octo-Cat beamed with pure and unadulterated joy. Apparently, it was okay for Nan to dote on him in a way that I wasn't quite allowed yet.

"He thanked you for your condolences," I passed on.

"What a well-mannered fella you are," she said, stroking him up and down his back. Octo-Cat now seemed to live on cloud nine, and I didn't want to ruin the moment for either of them by reminding everyone of just how rude my cat companion was on the regular.

"I'm worried, Nan," I confessed. "I'm almost positive Mr. Fulton poisoned his aunt, but the police probably won't believe the whole talking cat informant angle as readily as you did."

"Good point," she said with a defeated frown.

"So where does that leave us?" I begged for an answer. "I can't exactly live the rest of my life on edge until he's caught, but I also can't go to the police with this. Even if I were to quit my job and move back in with you, that still wouldn't guarantee anyone's safety. And it wouldn't avenge Ethel, either. Besides, what if Mr. Fulton is planning to strike again?"

Nan and I both thought on this in relative silence as Octo-Cat purred his content at receiving Nan's idle attentions. I meditated on my last question. Even if Mr. Fulton did kill again, would I really be the most likely candidate? It made far more sense that…

"Oh my gosh, Diane!" I shouted with this sudden realization. "She doesn't know!"

Of course! Add the fact that Mr. Fulton had said he wanted to keep his dirty secret until after the divorce was finalized to the other simple fact he was filing for divorce in the first place, and it clearly painted Diane Fulton as the one who was most in danger should he decide to strike again.

The divorce itself already showed he had no love left for the soon-to-be-former Mrs. Fulton. What if she pushed him too hard during the divorce proceedings? What if she was next? She didn't have any idea she could be in danger…

I popped to my feet, suddenly desperate to get to my friend and make sure she was okay.

"Now just you hold on, missy," Nan said, pulling herself to her feet and placing a hand on my shoulder. "You came here because you were afraid for your safety. I'm not letting you rush off straight into the lion's den. Regardless of the source, you have a pretty solid case against Mr. Fulton—and it sounds like he might know it, too. The last thing you want to do now is to turn up at his house with these accusations of yours."

Our eyes met, hers pleading while mine stared ahead unblinking. This was my nan, the one person who loved me more than anything in the whole wide world. Of course, she only wanted what was best for me. But at the end of the day, I couldn't stand by if it meant possibly signing my friend's death warrant.

I ripped my arm away from Nan. "I'm sorry, but I don't have any choice," I shouted, already on my way out the door.

17

I was surprised when Nan didn't try to stop me. Far less surprising, though, was the fact that Octo-Cat seemed to think he was coming with me. A brown blur shot past me as I ran toward my car.

"Let's do this," the tabby said with a look of determination I would have found comical if not for the seriousness of the situation.

"You're not coming," I shouted. I didn't have time for this. What if I was too late to warn Diane? "Now get out of my way."

He kept his focus glued firmly on my car door, waiting for me to open it. "Oh, I see. I'm only allowed to come when *you* think you need me."

"That's right," I grumped. "And I don't need you for this. Go stay with Nan and wait for me to come back."

His tail flicked wildly back and forth as he regarded me with hurt reflecting in his eyes. "You're really mean sometimes. You know that?"

"And you're really annoying all the time," I yelled back while silently begging for him to give up the fight. The last thing I needed was for him to be in danger, too. Despite my better judgment, I'd really come to love the little nuisance.

"Whatever," he said with a growl, staring me down. When at last I opened the car door, he hopped right in despite my consistent objections.

So, I did the worst possible thing I could think of. I picked him up by the scruff of his neck and marched him straight back to the house.

"Let go of me," Octo-Cat cried as he twisted violently in a futile attempt to escape my grip. "This is not okay!"

Without saying anything more, I tossed him into the house and slammed the door shut before he could regain his bearings. As much as I'd miss my sassy sidekick, it was better this way. Besides, if I brought him with me, Diane might suggest I leave him with her. I couldn't stand the thought of losing my new friend—but I also knew I wouldn't be strong enough to refuse if she asked.

I still didn't know how to convince the extended, non-murdering side of the Fulton family to let me keep him, but I'd have time to figure that out later. Right now, I had to save Diane from meeting a fate similar to Ethel's.

Although we probably wouldn't see each other much anymore, considering the divorce and the likelihood of her ex eventually ending up in jail, I still cared about her and wanted her to be all right. At the end of the day, I wouldn't wish death on anyone, not even Brad and especially not poor Diane who had been through so much already.

I owed her at least this much in honor of the brief, reality-TV based friendship we'd shared these past few months.

I'd only been to the Fultons' home once before to attend a company potluck over the holidays, but I still remembered the exact location of their fancy McMansion. After all, Blueberry Bay wasn't that big of a region, and our town of Glendale was even tinier.

I pulled up outside the white vinyl facade, which was offset by a massive front lawn, and cut my engine. Perhaps a call to announce my arrival would have been in order, but I didn't want to risk Mr. Fulton finding out I was headed here before I at least had a chance to warn Diane about the dangers that lurked right in her very own broken home.

Marching right up to the front door with far more confidence than I felt, I tried the handle without first ringing the doorbell to announce myself. Of course, since this was small-town Maine, the door stood unlocked. I let myself in, hoping that I wasn't too late to make a difference.

Inside, the house was dark as dusk settled over the land.

"Hello? Diane?" I called, groping about for a light switch but coming up short.

I padded toward the living room but turned abruptly when I heard the sound of a floorboard creak from a few paces behind me. There, within the pale light of the large bay window, a tall shadowy figure stood with its arms stretched high overhead.

"Diane?" I asked, squinting at the figure and praying it was my friend rather than her husband. I didn't have long to puzzle it out, though, because...

CRACK!

A tremendous pain radiated from my forehead, and before I had the chance to figure out what was going on, I crumpled to the floor, having once again lost consciousness.

* * *

When I came to, every inch of my body screamed with pain. I looked to my left and saw a massive fire roaring in the fireplace less than a foot away. It was too close. My skin had already begun to turn red from the excessive warmth. Struggling to move out of its range, I realized then that both my hands and my feet had been bound together in front of me.

"You think you can just break into somebody's home?" my captor rasped, moving into the light. I fully expected to see Mr. Fulton standing before me, but no. It wasn't him at all.

It was Diane, my friend. *My attacker? What?*

"Diane," I wheezed. "It's me, Angie. We need to get out of here."

"I know who you are. What I don't know is why you couldn't leave well enough alone." The contempt that filled her eyes as they combed over me was so blatant that I could hardly recognize the kindly woman I'd come to consider a friend.

My head pulsed with pain, making it hard to think straight. Why was she acting like this? Had Mr. Fulton lied to her about everything? Did she somehow think I was to blame for all of this?

None of this was adding up.

"Ethel was murdered!" I screamed at her. My throat ached just like the rest of me, but I didn't care. "We have to tell someone."

Diane groaned and paced the room in search of something. "Keep quiet," she warned. Maybe this was all an act. Maybe she was scared, too, and trying to convince Mr. Fulton she was on his side so that he wouldn't harm her.

"Let me go," I pleaded. "It's not too late. We can go to the police, and—"

She rushed back toward me and stooped down so we were at eye level. "Nobody's going to the police," she said in an eerie whisper before slapping me right across my face.

As this new pain stung my cheek, I finally saw the truth that stood right before me. Mr. Fulton had never been guilty—not of murder, not of this.

"It was you the whole time," I spat.

She smiled a wicked grin and rolled her eyes. *"Obviously.* Don't act like you didn't know. I couldn't believe my dumb luck when you woke up at the will reading talking about a murder. I've heard about psychics before, but I had no idea you were one of them."

"You think I'm a psychic?" I hissed. Everything hurt, but most of all my heart. I'd been so naïve, blindly trusting Diane because we liked the same TV shows. Now this oversight could very well cost me my life.

"How else would you explain your inexplicable knowledge of Ethel's murder? At first, I thought maybe you were playing some kind of joke and had just accidentally blurted out something true without even knowing it, but then you kept turning up everywhere."

I shook my head and struggled against my bonds to no avail. It made sense that Diane thought I had psychic powers. In a way I did, just not in the way she'd assumed.

"The viewing, Ethel's house..." Diane continued, kicking me back when she saw that I was trying to untie my feet.

"Oh, don't look so shocked. Of course Anne told me about that. The one thing I couldn't piece together is why you hadn't gone to the police to turn me in. But then when you tried to break into my house, I realized you actually planned to take me out yourself. Well, great job, you did." She laughed an evil villain laugh that seemed so at odds with the sweater-set-wearing, pearl clutching housewife I knew.

"But *why?* Why would you kill Ethel?" I choked out. As much as I wanted to hear the answer, I needed to keep her talking until I could figure out a way to escape. For all I knew, she planned to kill me after our little talk here. Clearly this madwoman was capable of anything.

Diane snarled like a wild animal, baring her teeth and sending another chill straight to my gut. "Didn't you figure that part out when you helped my philandering oaf of a husband serve me with a petition for divorce today?"

I gasped, a response she clearly appreciated.

"So, he *was* sleeping with Bethany!" I said, playing it up to keep her talking as long as possible. I'd been wrong about our killer, but right about the affair. Whether or not the bra belonged to Bethany, she was still guilty.

“Sleeping with her?” Diane curled her nose in disgust and pushed off the floor back to a standing position.

My phone vibrated in my hip pocket, which gave me an idea. If I could just find a way to FaceTime Octo-Cat, he could get Nan and she could get the police. I needed to distract Diane enough that she wouldn’t see me reaching into my pocket. It would be hard to be sly with my hands bound together, but I at least had to try.

“So he wasn’t?” I asked curiously.

“I should hope not, seeing as she’s his daughter. Then again, Richard’s illegitimate child is the least of my problems right now.” She moved fast, muttering to herself on occasion before speaking more to me.

How had she hidden so much of her true self? How had I never seen through the pleasant housewife act? Did Mr. Fulton know? Is that why he was leaving her? I wanted to know so much more, but first, I needed to get away from the crazy murderess who now paced the floor in front of me.

“And you wanted all of Ethel’s money for yourself,” I said, hoping it was enough of a prompt to get her to fly into another monologue about her motives.

“Who wouldn’t want the money? It’s not like the old lady was long for this world anyway. I gave her an easy death which, if you ask me, was far better than she deserved.”

As she talked, I inched my hands closer to my pocket. Luckily, my phone was on the opposite side of the fire, which gave me some shadows to help disguise my movements.

"You're already rich," I murmured, happy she wasn't looking at me anymore.

Diane had now returned to her frantic search of the room. I prayed it wasn't a gun she was hoping to find. I may be able to think fast, but I didn't think I'd be able to act fast enough to dodge a speeding bullet aimed straight at me, especially considering my recent head injury.

She laughed bitterly. "Already rich as Mrs. Fulton. What do you think will happen to me after the divorce, though?" Luckily, this was a rhetorical question as she kept talking without waiting to see what I had to say. "I thought I had more time. Richard was supposed to inherit everything from his aunt, then I'd get half if I could just keep him happy long enough for the will to go through. I got sick of waiting for the old lady to kick the bucket, so I helped her along. I couldn't believe my rotten luck when we found out she'd recently changed her will to leave almost everything to that stupid cat!"

I kept my eyes glued to Diane as I slipped the tips of my fingers into my pocket and began to slip the phone out from inside. She continued on her diatribe about her poor, unfair life, but I only heard enough to offer the smallest of replies. Instead, my focus had shifted toward my phone.

I pressed to unlock it—thankful I'd disabled the passcode—clicked the FaceTime app icon, and placed a call to Octo-Cat on my iPad.

Fingers crossed he wasn't too mad to help save my life.

18

The call went through, and Octo-Cat answered after just a couple rings. I swear I'd never been happier to hear anyone's voice in all my life.

"Let me guess," he said, sounding almost bored. "You're in danger and need the cat to come save the day."

Yes! I wanted to scream, but I couldn't alert Diane to the call without causing serious trouble for myself. Instead, I needed to find a way to keep her talking until my cat could come up with a way to rescue me. Seriously, of all the things my life could hinge on, it all came down to a talking cat with a bad attitude—one whom I'd recently made very, very angry with me.

I needed to find a way to keep the conversation going, but Diane wasn't paying any attention to me as she ripped through drawers and containers in search of whatever it was she needed. A couple minutes later she found what she'd been searching for all this time and strode back across the room to show me. Oh, how I prayed Octo-Cat was still with me!

I pushed the phone behind my back by making a big show of struggling against my bonds, managing to get it out of sight just in time.

"I'd stop that if I were you," Diane warned, holding up the newly acquired object so that I could see it clearly. An old revolver caught and reflected the light of the fire in its smooth metal body, and no matter how much it terrified me, I just couldn't tear my eyes away.

"That's right," my captor said with a smirk. "You're going to die."

My mind reeled, turning back to Octo-Cat once more. I couldn't hear his voice anymore. For all I knew, we'd lost the connection or he'd gotten bored and given up waiting. Still, I had to press on with my plan, hoping he was there and listening with Nan.

"I can keep quiet," I pleaded with Diane. "I don't have to tell anyone you murdered Ethel. You can take the money and leave. Or I can leave. Please. Just let me go."

"Oh, Angie," she said with false pity. "You're forgetting that I know you. You can't even keep the results of a TV singing competition secret. What makes you think I'd trust you with something like this?"

"Are you going to shoot me?" I asked, my voice tremoring with fear. I'd like to say that it was put on for effect, but that would be a lie. I had no idea whether my lone escape plan was working or whether I'd survive this horrible experience to live another day. If I did, I'd sure take a lot less for granted going forward.

Like people's guilt or innocence, for one thing.

Diane kicked my leg and lowered the gun from my head to my chest. "That's plan B," she revealed coldly.

"What's plan A?" I whispered as my heart galloped wildly in my chest.

"You like swimming. Don't you, Angie?" she asked, kicking me again. "I figured we could go for a nice night swim at Deadman's Wharf. What do you say?"

"Deadman's Wharf?" I repeated loudly. "But the undertow there... I wouldn't be able to... I'd..." I cried openly now.

"Oh, I know." Diane's face flashed with sick delight as she loosened the bonds on my ankles. "Now get up."

"I don't want to go to Deadman's Wharf," I wailed. *Please, Octo-Cat. Please be listening. Please understand what I'm trying to tell you.*

"Now it's about what *I* want." She kicked me a third time. "Get up."

Somehow I had to find a way to get up without her seeing my phone on the floor behind me. I made a big show of struggling to my feet then stumbled forward, knocking Diane over in the process.

"Oh, you're going to live to regret that," she growled before breaking out in a creepy laugh. "Luckily it won't be very long."

She pulled us both to our feet, stuck the gun into my ribs, and led me outside. It looked like we were on our way to Deadman's Wharf.

I just hoped we weren't the only ones.

* * *

Despite driving in Diane's large luxury SUV, the ride over was bumpy and painful. Well, I wouldn't be volunteering to lay tied up on the floor again any time soon—that is, if I even managed to reach tomorrow with my life intact.

She'd tied my ankles tight again after forcing me onto the floor of her vehicle, then kept her eyes on me through the rear-view mirror the entire drive over. Even if I'd had the strength to mount an escape, carrying it out would have been impossible under her watchful eye.

By the time we arrived at Deadman's Wharf, I had already lost feeling in my feet. Well, except for the mess of tingles that had taken up residence and made it so that I no longer trusted myself to stand without the very real risk of toppling over.

Diane parked near one of the darkened buildings dotting the wharf and did a quick search of the premises before finally forcing me out of the car.

Wind whipped violently at the waves as Diane dug her nails into my wrist and yanked me toward the nearest pier. But my ankles were still bound too tightly for me to shuffle along. I had to hop along instead, which was especially difficult given the fact my feet had fallen asleep and my brain had gone crazy with fear.

"I did like you before," Diane muttered when we reached the midpoint of the pier. "It's going to be much harder killing you than it was to kill Ethel."

Gee, thanks. She was still going to kill me, but at least she'd feel a little bit bad about it.

"You don't have to do this," I said with great difficulty before falling face forward on the old, weathered planks below when one of my hops failed to land properly.

"Stop being dramatic," Diane hissed in my ear as she put an arm beneath each of mine and pulled me back to a standing position with a series of insulting grunts and groans. "I'd tell you to maybe try a diet, but..." She made a flippant gesture and actually laughed.

"Fat shaming me, really?" I ground out. My legs burned beneath me. The new wounds on my face stung from where my cheek had hit the pier. "I'm sure you'll feel way less guilty about killing me now."

Diane said nothing but quickened our pace toward the end of the pier.

I tried to glance back over my shoulder to see if Octo-Cat and Nan had gotten my message to come out and help. Maybe some lone lobsterman would be out checking his traps. Maybe a car would just randomly happen to pass by...

Or maybe no one was coming.

Maybe I was really going to die.

We were less than ten feet from the end of the pier now. The tide was high and the waves crashed so violently that they lapped at the edge, sending ripples over the wood. I was a good swimmer, having been raised near the ocean, but not nearly good enough to escape waves like this when both my hands and feet were tied tightly.

I had one last chance to make it out of this alive, and it was time for me to take it. Drawing in a deep, labored breath before my next hop, I angled myself so that I landed partially on Diane's foot, knocking us both sideways across the pier.

"Oh, you're going to pay for that!" she whisper-screamed while clutching her jaw from where it had hit on the firm wood planks. I was banking on her to scream and curse at the top of her lungs, but that didn't happen. We didn't both pitch off the side, either.

I glanced around frantically, searching for someone who could save me. *Octo-Cat,* I begged in my mind. *Please, please help me!*

Then I realized I was probably dying one way or the other, so I began to scream at the top of my lungs, praying with all my might that someone was near, that someone would reach me in time. "Help! She's going to kill me!"

All this did was make Diane even angrier and even more determined to kill me quickly. She hobbled back to her feet. "Thanks for making this so easy, Angie," she growled with animal-like anger in her eyes.

We hadn't reached the end of the pier, but apparently we were close enough. She kicked me in the ribs again and again, forcing me to the edge.

"No, please stop!" I screamed as loud as I could into the empty night.

Much to my surprise, Diane did pause for a moment, regarding me from above with not the slightest flash of pity in her eyes. "You had the chance to stop this, but you just kept digging into things that were none of your business. This isn't my fault. It's yours."

And with that, she swooped down and pushed me with both hands. It was enough to send me rolling straight off the pier and into the unforgiving ocean below.

I sucked in a deep breath just before I hit the water, just before the darkness of the churning waves pushed me under.

Well, that settled that question. Now I knew...

I was definitely going to die.

19

Two near-death experiences within one week has got to be some kind of a record. Then again, time was ticking, and I wasn't sure how much longer I could hold on. No, I probably *wouldn't* survive being pulled down into the undertow of Deadman's Wharf. They called it Deadman's Wharf for a reason, after all.

And if they ever did manage to find my body, it would be far from the first they'd recovered from this perilous stretch of sea.

Diane would be long gone by then.

I thrashed my arms and legs, but only sunk deeper below the waves. The salt of the ocean water stung all my fresh wounds, blinding me with a fresh onslaught of pain. I held my breath past the point of comfort, even as panic overtook me completely. I knew that the first inhalation of sea water would be the thing that ultimately killed me.

But I also knew I didn't want to die.

No matter how much the odds were stacked against me, I had to keep fighting to survive. So, I continued to thrash and hope against hope as the dark depths drew me deeper and deeper into their embrace.

As my brain began to starve from the lack of oxygen, the pain also started to fall away. My body felt lighter, warmer, almost as if it was rising back toward the surface. More likely, though, was that I had died without noticing the exact moment of my demise, and now God was lifting me to Heaven. I even saw a light shining right in my eyes.

And it hurt.

Which meant…

Was I safe now?

I finally gasped for air, unable to hold my breath for even a second longer. The overwhelming pain surged again. It was truly amazing the human capacity for pain. Somehow, I was still finding new ways to hurt, even in the final moments before my death.

I coughed and sputtered, expelling the mistakenly inhaled water in big bursts. A cold chill overtook my entire body when just seconds ago I'd felt warm and peaceful. Even though it felt as if they were weighted down by heavy blocks, I managed to open my eyes just long enough to notice I wasn't underwater anymore.

Somebody pulled me up and onto the pier, and somebody else climbed up after. Had he been the one to pull me to the surface?

I didn't have time to figure out their identities, because everything went dark again as I lost consciousness.

Yes, *again.*

Yes, that makes three times so far this week.

This was by far the worst, though.

* * *

My throat was on fire as I vomited lava onto the ground beside me. At least that's what it felt like.

Nan's voice was the first I discerned from the jumble surrounding me. "That's right, dear. Cough it all out."

I took her advice and coughed and coughed until it didn't hurt quite so bad. When I opened my eyes to see who had saved me, I came face to face with a set of amber eyes glinting in the darkness as they regarded me with pity.

No, not pity. *Fear.*

Octo-Cat's entire body shook, and I didn't think it was from the dampness of his fur or the chilliness of the night. "I thought I'd lost you now, too," he said between panicked kitty breaths.

"I'm okay," I said, reaching out to pet him. My hand came away soaked, making me wonder if he'd jumped in after me despite his hatred of any water that didn't come from an Evian bottle.

I continued to stroke him until his labored breathing became gentler and was ultimately drowned out by the beautiful, contented sound of his rumbling purr.

"Diane Fulton," I ground out, sputtering even still. "Did she get away?"

A familiar pair of strong arms lifted me to a sitting position and wrapped a shiny insulated blanket over my shoulders. "We got her," the police officer said with a reassuring smile. Seeing as he was just as drenched as I was, I assumed this was the brave man who had jumped in to save me before Deadman's Wharf could claim me forever.

Nan appeared at my side, sitting right down on the pier and crossing her legs like we were at a slumber party and not a rescue mission. "That was good thinking, calling your iPad," she told me, careful to leave out any direct references to Octo-Cat I noticed. "We were able to record our end of the line and gave it to the police as evidence. And her intention to kill you," Nan revealed, rubbing my shoulder over the insulated blanket. "It was just awful to listen to, especially when the call went silent."

My heart clenched, reimagining tonight's events from poor Nan's perspective. Luckily, she was a tough, old kook, and I seemed to be okay now.

"Of course, you're going to need to buy me a new iPad now," Octo-Cat added, pushing his way under the blanket with me. "And seeing all you put me through tonight, you might have to make that two iPads."

"You did the right thing," the officer told Nan. "Your quick thinking saved your daughter's life."

"Oh, granddaughter, actually." Nan giggled and coquettishly twirled a ringlet as she looked the officer up and down. The officer, who was way, way too young for her to be flirting with. "What's your name again?"

Some things never changed, and thank goodness for that.

"Officer Damon Bouchard, ma'am." He smiled kindly at her, but I felt Nan stiffen beside me at the polite nickname. Her crush had ended just as soon as it had begun. That was good considering we had enough to deal with already.

"Are you ready to get in the ambulance?" the other officer asked —a woman—approaching us from the pier.

"Can my cat come, too?"

Officer Bouchard shrugged and glanced toward his partner. "I guess he can ride over with us, but unfortunately he's not going to be able to come into the hospital with us."

"But…" I hesitated. After all we'd just been through, I didn't want to leave him again especially so soon.

"It's okay, dear," Nan said, turning her full focus to me once again. "I'll take care of him until you're well enough to come home."

"Could you just give me a moment alone with him?" I asked, knowing the request made me sound crazy.

"Um, sure," Officer Bouchard said.

"We'll just be over there," the other officer said, pointing somewhere to the right, but I didn't care enough to notice.

"You can stay, Nan," I said as she began to struggle to her feet.

She settled back down and wrapped both arms around me, then we waited together until we knew we had the privacy we needed.

"Thank you for saving my life," I whispered toward my chest, where Octo-Cat still sat nuzzled against me. "I'm sorry I scruffed you, and I'm sorry for all the times I was rude or didn't understand. During this past week you've become my best friend… well, other than Nan, I mean… and I'm so glad you're in my life. Can you forgive me?"

A few tense moments of silence passed before Octo-Cat finally extracted himself from the warmth of the blanket and came to stand before me on the wharf. "You're my best friend, too," he said, rubbing his head against my hand and purring in earnest. "But if you ever scruff me again, I'll kill you and eat the evidence."

I erupted with laughter, and Nan joined me even though she didn't quite know why.

"Thank you for avenging Ethel," he said when our peals of laughter faded out. "She would have liked you, you know."

My eyes teared at the compliment. *Ugh,* more salt water was not what I needed just then. Still, judging from how awesome her cat was, I bet I would have liked her, too.

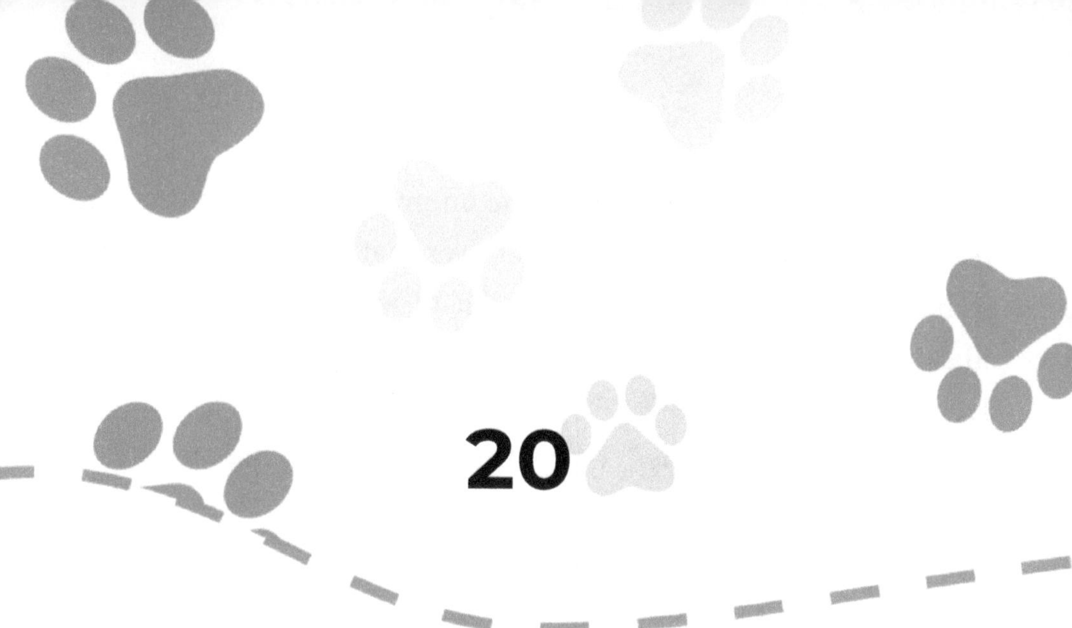

20

I felt fine—all things considering—but the hospital insisted on keeping me for at least twenty-four hours since I was still in danger of succumbing to my near-drowning even now.

I groaned audibly when a familiar face popped into my room.

"So…" Dr. Artie Lewis, the same ER doctor who had treated me earlier that week, said with an obnoxiously large smile. "You decided to up the ante this time, eh? You know, real life isn't an action movie. You can't keep putting your life at risk and expecting to survive."

Yes, this was the same guy who had made me feel like an idiot when I came to him for care after getting zapped unconscious by the office coffeemaker. It was upsetting to see that his bedside manner hadn't improved since I'd seen him last.

The doctor bobbed his head, ignoring the fact that I hadn't responded to his greeting—or his advice. "Drowning is definitely a more impressive way to lose consciousness. Good job."

Did he really just compliment me on my method of getting hurt? Yeah, because I had a lot of control over that. I briefly wondered if perhaps the not-so-good doc was a bit of a thrill seeker in his life outside of the hospital. He seemed almost excited as he discussed the details of my near drowning.

"Just leave me alone," I pleaded, finally breaking my silence. Hadn't I already been through enough that day?

I'd nearly died, for crying out loud!

He shot me a withering glance before chuckling to himself and saying, "No can do. This time you need a lot more than some regular strength Tylenol. You know, a smile wouldn't hurt you much, either."

If I had any strength left, I'd have shot out of bed to punch him in the face. I'd had enough violence for one day, however—even though it sure seemed like this doctor guy was cut from the same sleazy cloth as my least favorite colleague, Brad.

Maybe it was time to start exploring some alternative medicine therapies… or to stop getting knocked unconscious every other day. Either worked.

"I'll be back later," Dr. Lewis announced after a brief glance over my vitals. "By the way, you have some guests waiting in the lobby. Should I send them in?"

"Yes, please." I nodded excitedly, wondering if Nan had somehow found a way to sneak Octo-Cat into my room. I definitely wouldn't put it past her.

It wasn't Nan who came to see me, though.

A few minutes later, Mr. Fulton and Bethany shuffled into my room. Mr. Fulton carried a giant pink teddy bear that said *It's a Girl* which made me giggle.

Ouch. Laughing hurt deep in my chest.

"How are you doing?" Bethany asked, trailing her fingers along the foot of my bed. I'd never seen her out of office clothes before and was surprised to find her personal style was actually pretty fun. She wore red polka dotted pants with a white button down shirt, an outfit that would have fit perfectly with either Nan's or my own wardrobe.

"Pretty good, considering." I smiled to show her I was all right and that there were no hard feelings between us.

"I'm sorry my wife almost killed you," Mr. Fulton interjected, catching me off guard. I mean, I'd only been in the hospital a few hours. It seemed strange that he and Bethany already knew what had happened.

"How did you find out?" I asked, wondering just how much he knew about what had transpired between me and Diane, if he knew that she was also to blame for killing his beloved aunt.

He rushed to explain. "I came home from my trip early and saw your car in front of my house and the door wide open. A short while later, officers showed up and brought me in for questioning. Let's just say they caught me up on my wife's shocking extracurricular activities."

"And you?" I asked Bethany. I remembered now that, in the middle of her maniacal raving, Diane had mentioned something about Bethany being Mr. Fulton's daughter. I still had so many questions about that but was hoping they might fill me in without being prompted. After all, it technically wasn't any of my business.

Bethany glanced toward Mr. Fulton nervously. “He called me on the way over.”

“It’s okay,” I coaxed, apparently unable to play it cool. “Diane told me the truth. At least, I think she did.”

I turned to Mr. Fulton. “Is she really your daughter?”

“Yes,” they answered in unison, both regarding me with similar expressions.

“How come you didn’t just tell me that?” I asked Bethany, recalling the hard time I’d given her at the funeral. Of course, I felt terrible now.

“I didn’t want it getting out,” Mr. Fulton explained. “Diane was already so upset.”

I glanced back toward Bethany. “Did you know all this time?”

“Not all this time. I suspected he might be my mysterious missing father when I took my position at the firm, but we only just had it verified by DNA testing. In fact, that’s why I decided to apply in the first place.”

Mr. Fulton looked like he was going to be sick as he explained, “I cheated on Diane while we were dating. Just once, but—”

“It led to my mom getting pregnant,” Bethany supplied. “I’ve had some strange… health issues these past few years, and I’ve been trying to learn more about my best options. So, finally my mom caved and told me more about my father.”

“Oh,” I said simply. It sucked for Diane that her husband had cheated on her. Sure, they hadn’t been married at that time, but they’d still been committed to each other. You always assume that your partner will be faithful—but then again, you also assume they won't try to murder anyone you care about, too.

"We figured since you were already part of the family drama, thanks to Diane, you at least deserved to know the full story," she said with a sniff.

"I'm so sorry, Bethany. I treated you horribly." It all came rushing to me then. She'd grown up without a dad. She'd suffered health issues she didn't feel comfortable disclosing, and she'd recently lost an aunt she never even got the chance to know.

"Yes, you did," Bethany said with a frown that quickly transformed into a smile. "But I've treated you horribly on so many other occasions that perhaps we're just even now. Let's stop trying to tear each other down and start lifting each other up instead now, okay?"

"We girls have to stick together," I said in agreement. "By the way, I really like your outfit."

She smiled and sashayed playfully at the compliment.

"Again, I'm so sorry that my wife tried to kill you," Mr. Fulton said with a pained expression. "What I don't understand is why. Do you know?"

Both he and Bethany studied me with curious eyes.

I took a deep breath to steady myself before revealing, "She thought I was psychic and that I had figured everything out. As part of that, she confessed to killing Ethel in a scheme to get more money out of your divorce."

Mr. Fulton sighed and shook his head.

"Are you?" Bethany asked, her breathing hitched slightly as she awaited my response.

I scrunched up my face in confusion. "Am I what?"

"Psychic," she supplied.

"What?" I chuckled nervously. No one besides Nan could ever know the truth about me and Octo-Cat. "No, of course not. Don't be silly."

Bethany laughed, too. "Just seeing if you still have your wits about you after that massive loss of oxygen to your brain."

Mr. Fulton placed a hand on his daughter's shoulder. "Bethany, could you give us a moment?"

"Sure. I'll be waiting for you outside," she answered, smiling at me one more time before leaving the room and clicking the door shut behind her.

Fulton grabbed a nearby chair and pulled it up beside my bed. "I think it goes without saying I'll be resigning from the firm."

I nodded, unsure of what he wanted from me now.

"I'll actually be using it as an opportunity to retire, get to know my daughter, and enjoy life outside of work for a change."

"That's great," I said, happy for him but finding it hard to maintain my enthusiasm. My brain felt heavy with the weight of all the new knowledge I'd acquired that day, and I needed my rest.

"I had no idea what Diane was up to all this time, but I'm so sorry you got hurt because of it." He reached into his suit jacket and pulled out a check book. "I know I can never make it fully right, but let me help you somehow. Do you think one hundred thousand is enough to...? Well, to forgive me?"

I edged my hand toward his, but couldn't quite reach. "You don't need to pay me off. I forgive you."

"Please let me do something. This money and more was going to go to Diane in the divorce, but now that she'll probably be spending the rest of her life in prison, I suddenly have far more than I need." He seemed so sad, so desperate to give me a small fortune in recompense. But he had never done anything wrong. Well, not for the past thirtyish years, at least.

"I don't need anything," I said, realizing as soon as I said the words that they weren't entirely true.

Mr. Fulton must have caught onto my ambivalence, because he said, "I can see you do. How about one hundred and fifty? Two hundred? Please, just tell me what you need."

For the briefest of moments, I allowed myself to envision what life would be like with that kind of money. I could stop working, put a sizable down payment on a house all my own, or even take a couple years off to travel the world.

I could do anything my little heart desired.

But, honestly, I liked my life, no matter how lackluster it may appear to an outsider. Sure, I wanted to be rich one day—*who doesn't?* —but I also wanted to make my own fortune, my own way.

There was one thing, however, I now desperately wanted that only Mr. Fulton could provide.

"I do have a request, if you don't mind," I said after licking my cracked and dried lips.

He perked right up and poised his pen over the checkbook. "Anything. Name your price."

"Would you mind if I keep the cat?" I asked, almost afraid to breathe until he gave me his answer.

He closed his checkbook and stared at me blankly. “The cat?” he asked to clarify.

“Yeah, Octavius Maxwell...” I broke off in a laugh. “You know, Ethel’s cat, the one I’ve been looking after this week.”

“The cat!” Recognition at last lighted in his eyes. “I forgot about him with everything else that’s been going on these past few days.”

I smiled and waited for his answer.

It came with a wink that I didn’t quite understand. “Of course, you can have the cat. I’ll send over his things in a couple days when you’re settled back at home.”

My heart filled with joy over being able to keep an animal I had until very recently considered the bane of my existence, but now wouldn’t trade for the world—or for two-hundred thousand dollars.

“Thank you so much,” I called after Mr. Fulton’s departing figure, absolutely beside myself with delight.

I couldn’t wait to get home and tell Octo-Cat the good news.

I was given the next two weeks off work to recover from my ordeal and spent most of it curled up on the couch with Octo-Cat, catching up on all our favorite human TV shows. We even found a show about a cat trainer, which we both found hilarious. Every time the “expert” interpreted what the cat was feeling, Octo-Cat corrected him and we both broke out laughing.

A few days into my forced vacation time—yeah, they really had to twist my arm on this one—a parcel arrived by courier.

"What's this?" I asked, after signing my name on the dotted line.

He shrugged and trotted away, leaving me alone with the mysterious letter. It was a very thick letter, at least twenty pages long.

"Whatcha got there?" Octo-Cat asked, coming to sit beside me at the table as I continued to puzzle over the manila envelope lying before me.

"I honestly have no idea," I answered while fiddling with the clasp.

"Well, open up! I'm dying of curiosity here."

I decided to let that one go, since I was also quite curious myself.

After pulling out the bundle of pages, I quickly scanned the first, then flipped through, glazing over the headlines for each subsequent section of the legal document before me.

"Say, Octo-Cat," I murmured, unable to tear my eyes away. "What's your full name again?"

"Octavius Maxwell Ricardo Edmund Frederick Fulton Russo," he said, each syllable rolling off his sandpaper tongue seamlessly.

"Aww," I cooed. "You added my last name."

"Well, of course I did. You're my human," he said with an endearing twitch of his whiskers.

"Um, for legal purposes, you'll have to drop the Russo, though."

"Why?"

I pushed the papers toward him, even though he couldn't read very well yet.

"What's that say?" His tail flicked in agitation.

"This is the paperwork for the trust fund Ethel set up for you.

Now that you live with me, I'm your official guardian and thus guarantor of your estate."

He yawned. "And that means?"

"Two things," I told him with a huge smile on my face. "One, you're legally mine now. And two, we will receive a stipend of five thousand dollars per month to contribute to your care and provide the lifestyle to which you are accustomed."

Octo-Cat's eyes grew wide.

"Finally!" he cried. "I knew Ethel would come through for me. Now let's have a little talk about these living quarters..."

TERRIER TRANSGRESSIONS

I'm finally coming to terms with the fact I can speak to animals, even though the only one who ever talks back is the crabby tabby I've taken to calling Octo-Cat. What I haven't quite worked out is how to hide my secret...

Now one of the associates at my law firm has discovered this strange new talent of mine and insists I use it to help defend his client against a double murder charge. To make things worse, Octo-Cat has no intention of helping either of us.

Our only hope rests on a spastic Yorkie named Yo-Yo, who hasn't quite figured out his owner is dead. Can we find a way to get Yo-Yo to help solve the murder without breaking his poor doggie heart?

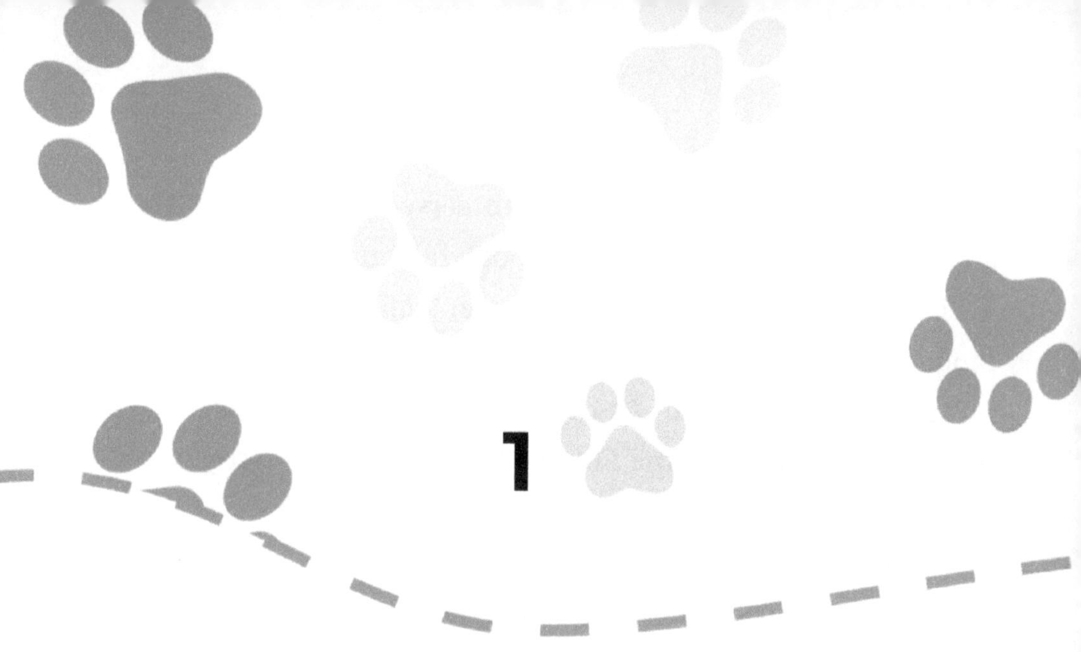

1

Hi, I'm Angie Russo, and I have a talking cat for a pet. Well, he only talks to me, but still. A few months have passed since he came to live with me following the murder of his owner—a sweet old lady who was poisoned by a member of her own family in a greedy inheritance grab.

Since then, Octo-Cat and I have been settling into our new life as roommates, and he's nice to me more often than not just so long as I feed him his breakfast on time and never, ever call him "kitty." He's even learned how to use his iPad to call me on FaceTime so we can check in with each other while I'm at work.

Yes, *his* iPad.

Have I mentioned just how spoiled he is?

Not only does he have his own tablet—and a trust fund, too—but he insists on drinking Evian fresh from the bottle and will only eat certain flavors of Fancy Feast when served on specific dishes and according to his rigorously kept, though fully unnecessary, schedule.

I have to admit he's grown on me, something I honestly never thought would happen. I even kind of like my job as a paralegal at Fulton, Thompson and Associates these days. Things have been pretty interesting since the Fultons left town rather abruptly and our firm lost its senior most partner.

A cutthroat competition as to who will take his place has ensued. Until Mr. Thompson decides whom he'd like to promote, though, we're simply Thompson and Associates. Lots of candidates—both from within our firm and from outside—have been passing through our office in hopes of securing the coveted position at Blueberry Bay's most respected law firm, but Thompson is having a hard time making up his mind.

Can't say I blame him. I definitely wouldn't want to be in his shoes.

Our firm is now a bit infamous following the surprising murder involving one of its partners and his family. Everyone wants the scoop, but Mr. Thompson has made it very clear: we aren't supposed to discuss what happened with anyone.

In the meantime, he has hired a new associate to help keep up with the newly increased workload. Charles Longfellow, III, came to us highly recommended with a great resume and even better looks.

It's been a while since I've had a crush but—boy—do I have it bad for Charlie. He's got this thick, wavy hair that falls in a perfect dark swoop on his forehead. He's tall, like *maybe-played-basketball-in-high-school-but-probably-not-in-college* tall, and you could easily get lost in his deep green eyes. I know, because I already have a few times.

Yes, as much as I usually prefer books to boys, I often find myself a bit twitterpated whenever Charles is near. That's probably how I made such a colossal mistake in the first place...

Now I'm being blackmailed about my biggest secret, the fact that I can talk to animals.

The worst part? I kind of like it.

I should probably start at the beginning, huh?

Well, here goes nothing...

* * *

Octo-Cat called me via FaceTime just before noon. I was at the office, of course, but since he knew not to call unless it was an emergency, I decided to put my research on hold to answer him. Besides, almost everyone had left the firm for an early lunch meeting, leaving me more or less alone in the building.

"What do you need?" I asked after scanning the premises just in case I wasn't as alone as I'd thought. Normally I took my calls with Octo-Cat in the bathroom, but one of the junior associates had been holed up in there for at least half an hour before he left—and I definitely wanted to avoid whatever disaster scenario he'd left behind.

"There's a fly in my Evian," my cat complained with a keening mewl. His face looked utterly scandalized as he leaned in close to the camera.

"Oh, you poor thing," I cooed while rolling my eyes just out of his view. Octo-Cat was definitely too spoiled for his own good sometimes, but then again, I received a five-thousand-dollar monthly allowance for his care, so I really couldn't complain too much.

"My thoughts exactly," he answered with a grimace and a sigh. "I need you to come home immediately to rectify this situation."

"I can't. I'm at work," I reminded him with a beleaguered sigh of my own while clicking through my overfull email inbox idly.

Octo-Cat growled when he noticed he didn't have my full attention. "I thought you were supposed to only be going part-time now?"

Why was I constantly explaining my life choices to a cat? He rarely remembered what I told him, anyway. We'd had this exact same conversation about my work at least three times already. Rehashing it now felt like the ultimate exercise in futility.

Still, it was easier to explain yet again than to deal with one of his hissy fits.

"Yes, technically I am part-time," I explained patiently. "But I need to help out extra until Thompson finally hires a new partner. It's been really busy around here, and unfortunately I just don't have time to stop home and pour you a new cup of water right now. I'm sorry."

His eyes narrowed, ready to go to war over such a simple thing. "But don't you receive a generous monthly stipend to ensure I'm cared for in the manner to which I am accustomed? Because I most definitely am *not* accustomed to having a wiggly-legged fly swimming in my Evian."

Once again, it was easier to cave than it was to argue for hours or days on end. "*Aargh,* fine. I'll send Nan by to pour you some more water. Happy?"

He yawned, which only annoyed me more. "Not exactly. It will take me days to recover from this horrible event. Could you make sure Nan knows she needs to throw out the contaminated cup?"

"You are a cat," I said between clenched teeth. "You are supposed to be a fearsome hunter, not a spoiled baby. You know, other cats even—"

"Angie?" a deep, dreamy voice broke into the middle of our conversation.

Oh, no, no, no. Everyone was supposed to be gone!

I spun around in my chair to find none other than Charles Longfellow, III standing behind me and gawking over my shoulder at the image of Octo-Cat on my phone screen.

"Um, hi, Charles." I tittered nervously as I pushed the button to end our call, but it was too late. He'd already heard and seen more than enough to figure out my secret. The best I could hope for now is that he would think one or both of us had gone crazy.

I took it as a good sign that he stood looking at me as if I'd sprouted a second head. Perhaps that would have been less strange than what he'd really walked in on.

"Is everything all right?" he asked, raising one thick eyebrow in my direction. The air suddenly felt impossibly thin like the office had been transported to the top of the nearest mountain.

I nodded, desperate for Charles to go away and stop questioning me. "Perfectly all right. Thanks," I lied, wishing I'd inherited Nan's legendary acting skills. As it was, I could tell my colleague wasn't fooled by my feeble attempts to downplay the situation.

Sure enough, his voice dripped with sarcasm as he said, "Really? Because it seemed like your cat needed some help with his..." A delicious smile crept across his face, stretching from one high cheek bone to the next. "Evian? Is that right?"

My mouth fell open from shock, but no additional words came out to explain away the freak show my crush had just witnessed.

"Well?" he prompted, widening his eyes at me. "Were you or were you not just having a conversation with your cat?"

I tucked my hair behind my ears and swallowed hard before stumbling over my answer. "Um, I call him sometimes when I'm away. He has separation anxiety so..." I gave him my most ingratiating smile, but it didn't seem to work. I was seriously outmatched here.

"But it sounded like maybe he was talking back to you," Charles insisted. "Like you were having an actual conversation with each other."

I blinked hard as I stammered, "What? No, don't be silly. Of course I can't talk to animals. I mean, who can?"

"You, apparently," Charles said, narrowing his gaze at me. Clearly he wasn't going to let me off the hook until I revealed the one thing I most wanted to hide.

I swallowed the giant lump that had become lodged in my throat, then broke out in hysterical laughter. "*Gotcha!* I can't believe you fell for my little office prank."

Charles shoved both hands in his pockets and rocked back and forth on his heels, but didn't say anything.

Oh my gosh. Why wasn't he saying anything?

My heart galloped like a wild stallion as my nervous laughter fell away.

Charles studied me for a long time, and stupidly I couldn't bring myself to look away. "You're coming with me," he said.

"What?" I crossed my arms over my chest in defiance. "No. I have too much work to catch up on here."

He placed his palms on my desk and leaned down so our faces were only a few inches apart. Given pretty much any other circumstance, I'd have enjoyed having his gorgeous face so near to mine.

As it was now, though? I was absolutely terrified.

"You're coming with me," he repeated with a devilish grin. "Unless you want me to tell everyone what I saw."

I gulped. "Everyone?"

"Everyone," he confirmed before returning to his full height and straightening his tie.

Completely bewildered and unable to see any practical alternative, I rose to join Charles.

"Excellent," he said, leading me to the door and motioning for me to go through it.

I turned back to study him. "Where are we going?"

"My place," he answered coolly as we strode through the parking lot toward his car. Charles had never invited me anywhere before, especially not his apartment. Unfortunately, something told me I wouldn't like what was waiting for me there one bit.

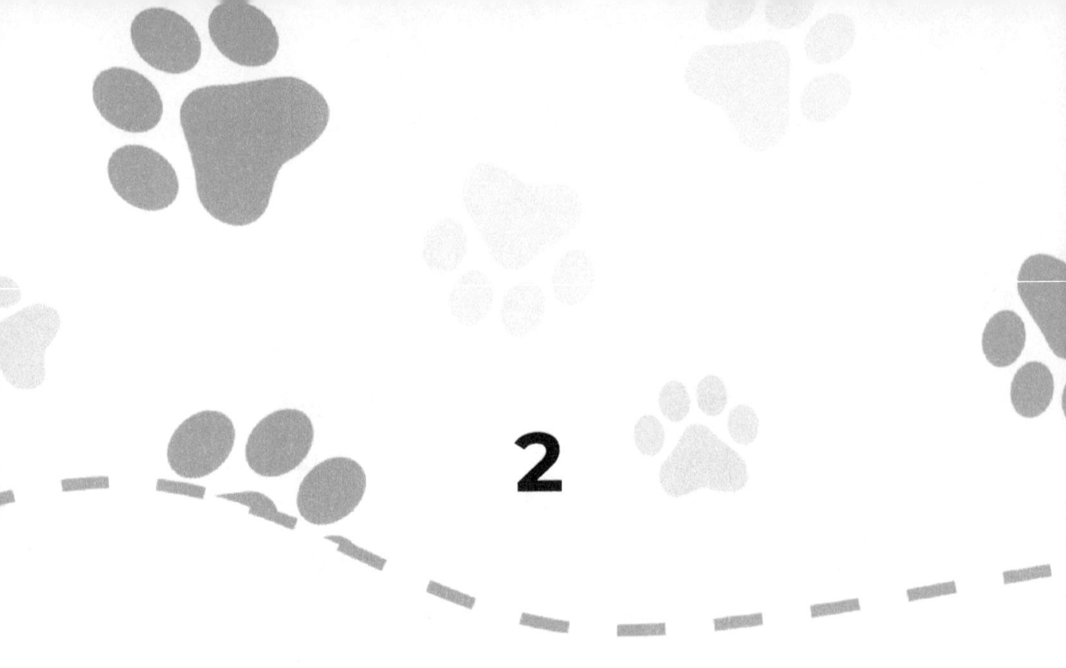

2

About five minutes after leaving the office, Charles and I pulled up to the Cliffside apartment complex. I was surprised to find that he lived in the budget apartments rather than the nicer condos on the other side of town. Normally, Cliffside was for newly graduated students or those who were otherwise just passing through.

As an attorney, Charles could easily afford somewhere nicer—and safer, too. Crime rarely occurred in Glendale, but when it did, nine times out of ten it happened here. As a criminal defense attorney, perhaps he wanted to be closer to his client base. Still, most of the crimes our firm dealt with fell under the category of white-collar crime. With its stained carpeting and peeling paint, Cliffside was anything but white collar.

Did Charles living here mean he wasn't planning on making Blueberry Bay his long-term home? Was he just passing through like so many of the others who lived in this run-down cluster of buildings?

Even though he was kind of blackmailing me, I hoped he'd stick around a bit more permanently. Despite everything, I still liked him and preferred his company to the others at the firm. Lately, Bethany and I had formed a tentative friendship, but we often found it hard to relate to one another. We just came from two very different worlds.

Despite his fancy name, perhaps Charles and I weren't so different, after all. No, I hadn't grown up poor, but Nan had raised me to be humble even as others were showering me with praise. Her mantra had always been that the stage was for stars, and real life was for real people.

Maybe Charles had grown up under similar guidance, although Cliffside was a little more "real life" than even I preferred.

He'd remained tight-lipped on the drive over and stayed quiet still as he led me up the stairs to the third floor.

"This is me," he said, turning his key in the door.

I shrugged and followed him in.

Immediately we were greeted by a hyper, barking dog, who was so excited to see us he piddled right on the floor at our feet.

"Sorry about that!" Charles cried, grabbing a roll of paper towels from the nearby counter. "He just gets a little excited sometimes."

"I'll say." I politely patted the little dog on the head but resisted the urge to pick him up, seeing I was in no mood to be peed on today.

Something struck me as odd, though. Charles had already been in town for at least a month, but a quick glance around his apartment showed more unopened boxes than actual furniture or home decor.

So, how did he already have a dog? And what did it do all day while he put in the long hours Thompson required of all his associates?

Charles finished cleaning up the mess, washed his hands, and motioned for me to make myself comfortable on the lone futon that sat against the living room wall.

"Where's all your stuff?" I asked conversationally, feeling more than a little unnerved when he sat down beside me on the much too short futon.

The terrier also hopped up when he patted the seat beside him.

He just shrugged, not seeming the least bit embarrassed by my question. "I sold everything before moving east and haven't had the time to pick up much since arriving."

That made sense. He'd come to Maine by way of California, and as far as I knew, he didn't have any family nearby. Why anyone would want to leave guaranteed sunny weather to hole up in small-town Maine, I'd never understand, but still, I was happy to have him here in Blueberry Bay.

The little dog spun in happy circles, racing from Charles's lap to mine and back again and again. The poor thing was obviously deprived of the regular attention he needed.

"If you're so busy, then why do you have a dog? That isn't really fair to him." I didn't mean to sound accusing, but I knew very well from Octo-Cat that animals hated being left alone all day while their owners pursued lives outside the home. No wonder the little guy peed on the floor the moment he came through the door.

"No, I've only had him for a little while," he said with a frown. "And before you can say anything more, I know I don't have time for a dog but... well, it's kind of a long story, and it's why I asked you here."

My curiosity was definitely piqued now, but first, I had to clarify one thing. "You didn't ask me here," I said with a knowing look. "You forced me."

His handsome face pulled down in a frown. "I'm sorry. Really, I am. It's just.. I didn't know how else to get you to come, and I'm kind of desperate here." At least he had the decency to appear apologetic now.

I nodded even though I didn't really understand what he was talking about yet. Obviously, *he* didn't understand that I would have been more than willing to follow him anywhere if only he'd asked nicely.

Charles stroked the tan and gray, silky-coated dog and launched into his story. "This is Yo-Yo. He's not mine. I found him, actually."

I immediately went into fix-it mode. "How long ago? Did you call the shelter? I'm sure someone's really missing him and hoping he'll come home."

Charles shook his head and cleared his throat, glancing from me to Yo-Yo before he said, "No. His owners are dead."

I scooted a little farther from him on the futon. "What? How could you possibly know that if he's just some dog you found?"

"The address listed here." He thumbed the tag on the Yorkie's collar. "And I know his owners are dead because I'm defending the person accused of their murder."

Well, I'd heard more than enough now. Jumping to my feet, I cried, "Whoa, whoa, whoa. I may not be the one who's taken an oath of ethics, but this seems really, really wrong. What are you hoping to accomplish by keeping this poor dog hostage?"

Charles stood, too, holding Yo-Yo against his chest with one arm and reaching the other toward me. I yanked myself away before he could make contact, though. The last thing I needed was my batty hormones intervening here.

"My client didn't kill Yo-Yo's owners," he said, his eyes begging me to understand. "He's innocent."

"Yeah, everyone says they're not guilty, but you know what? Usually, they are." I briefly considered grabbing Yo-Yo and making a run for it. That poor, little dog. First his owners had been murdered, then he'd somehow inexplicably wound up with the man defending their killer.

"No, it's not like that," Charles insisted. "*I know* he didn't do it, but the evidence against him, it's bad. Like I said, I'm desperate here. So when I saw you talking to your cat, I thought maybe, just maybe, you could be the answer to my prayers. You could save an innocent man from jail and help get justice for Yo-Yo's owners, too."

I considered denying my ability, insisting that there was no way I could do what he was asking for, but Charles just looked so needy—and Yo-Yo also chose that exact moment to whimper and stare at me with sparkling, little doggie eyes...

"*Ugh,* fine!" I shouted, sinking back down onto the futon. "I'll see what I can do."

Relief washed over Charles's face as he lowered himself beside me. "Thank you. You're a lifesaver!"

"Yeah, well, I haven't actually done anything yet," I grumbled. There was absolutely nothing about this situation I liked.

"The fact that you're willing to try means everything," Charles said, and for the briefest of moments something passed between us.

Love?

Longing?

That special bond between a blackmailer and his blackmailee?

Really, I had no idea.

He stood again, then set Yo-Yo on the futon beside me. The dog jumped on my lap where he immediately began licking my face, his tail wagging wildly with each lap.

"Hey, Yo-Yo," I said, completely unsure of myself. The only animal I'd ever actually carried on a conversation with was Octo-Cat, and he'd talked to me first. This thing right now with Yo-Yo felt crazy, unnatural, and uncomfortable by comparison. Still, I had to try for the sake of Charles and his client. And for Yo-Yo, too.

"I understand you lost your owners," I said slowly with an even voice. "Can you tell me what happened?"

The Yorkie continued licking my face without any signs of slowing down, so I picked him up and put him on the floor to see if it could help him focus.

"What happened to your owners?" I asked again. "Did someone murder them?"

Yo-Yo yipped merrily and hopped back up on the futon beside me. Now he decided it was a good time to douse my hand in a slobber bath.

"What did he say?" Charles asked eagerly. His eagerness made this whole thing that much more frustrating. I'd always hated letting people down. Yes, even when they were blackmailing me, I guess.

"He barked," I said simply.

"Yes, but what did it mean?"

"I don't know," I admitted honestly.

His face fell. "But I thought you could talk to animals?"

"I talk to my cat, but that's it."

"So why can't you talk to Yo-Yo?" This was the hundred-thousand-dollar question. I'd stopped questioning my sanity when it came to my ability to talk to Octo-Cat but still had no idea why I could speak to him or what the extent of my powers might be.

I raised my palms and shrugged. "I don't know, but I'm trying."

"Well, try harder," he urged. "It's really, really important."

"I *am* trying," I muttered to Charles through gritted teeth, then turned back to Yo-Yo with my most pleasant expression. "Hey, there, little guy. If you could talk to me, it would be a huge help. Maybe start by telling me what you really think of this guy you're living with now?"

I hooked a thumb toward Charles and made a goofy face, which resulted in Yo-Yo grabbing hold of my sweater and giving it a firm tug.

"Hey, stop!" I cried, but this only made him tug harder. When I finally managed to wrestle my shirt away from him, it had been stretched beyond repair. I leaped to my feet so he couldn't destroy any other parts of me before we were through here.

"What did he say?" Charles asked, hope reflecting in his dark eyes.

"He said you've got the wrong girl," I answered. "And that he liked my sweater but still thought it deserved to die a horrible, untimely death."

Charles deadpanned. "Just like his owners, huh?"

Okay, now I felt bad, but it didn't change anything about my inability to speak with Yo-Yo. I'd tried. It hadn't worked. It was time to move on.

"I don't know what he said or even if he said anything," I explained, hoping Charles would finally take me at my word. "I guess I can't talk to dogs."

"But you can talk to cats?"

I shrugged noncommittally, but he seemed to interpret this as my agreement.

"Great," he said, shuffling through the items in a junk drawer before extracting a long, black leash. "C'mon, Yo-Yo. We're going for a walk," he cried in a slightly higher pitched voice that made me forget my irritation for a moment—but only a moment. "Want to go for a walk?"

"And I'm going back to work," I said, traipsing toward the door. "Drop me off on your way to wherever it is the two of you are going."

"Sorry, can't," Charles answered while the Yorkie ran furious, barking circles around the apartment to convey his enthusiasm. "We need you to come with us."

I crossed my arms and eyed them both suspiciously. "Why?"

"Because we're going to your house to talk to your cat," Charles explained, grabbing Yo-Yo into his arms and clipping on the leash.

To my house?

Crud. Octo-Cat was definitely not going to like this.

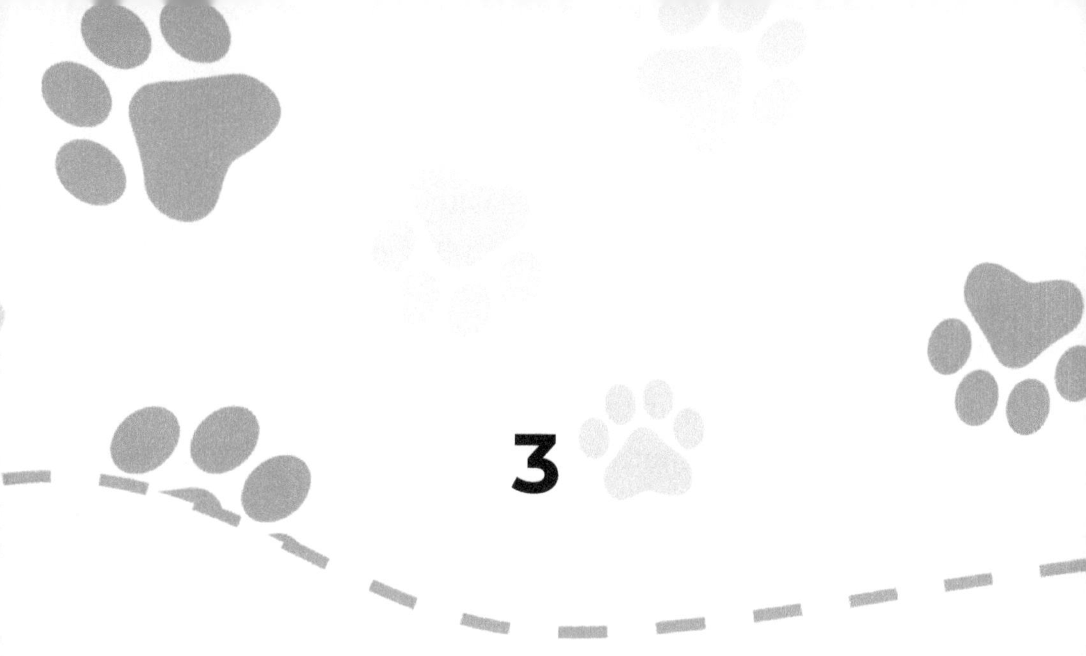

3

Less than two miles stretched between Charles's apartment complex and my rental home, which meant we were in one place almost as soon as we'd left the other.

I opened the door to find Octo-Cat waiting for me with a rapturous look upon his face.

"Finally!" he cried. "I've been so thirsty." His expression quickly changed to outrage, though, when Yo-Yo nosed his way into the house and gave Octo-Cat a big, wet kiss right on the nose.

Charles pulled back on the leash, then lifted the visiting dog into his arms.

Octo-Cat shook with fury as a bead of drool dripped down his face and onto the carpet below. "Why would you do this to me? Haven't I already been through enough today? First the fly and now a-a-a *dog?*" he spat out that last word as if it were the foulest curse word he could imagine.

"What's he saying?" Charles asked with rapt interest.

"He's mad at me," I admitted. "And he's not happy about Yo-Yo being here, either."

Octo-Cat arched his back and hissed. "You can say that again," he muttered before jumping onto the kitchen table.

"Just give me a minute here," I whispered to Charles before joining my irate tabby in the kitchen.

Octo-Cat took a giant leap from the table to the counter, then sat with his tail flicking back and forth wildly. "Unbelievable," he growled without so much as looking at me.

I knew I was in the wrong here, but I also had no other choice but to comply with Charles's wishes. If anyone else found out about my special ability to talk to cats, I'd lose my job, be made a laughing stock, and possibly have to move away from the only home I've ever known to start life over with a clean reputation.

Hopefully Octo-Cat would understand that my hands were tied once I had the chance to explain a bit more. First, though, I needed to find a way to give Charles what he wanted. Once I did, the threat hanging over my head would be eradicated, and Octo-Cat could go back to being mad at me for the usual reasons.

I grabbed a fresh bottle of Evian and a clean china tea cup from the cupboard. The cup came from the set we'd inherited from his late owner Ethel and was used for the sole purpose of offering Octo-Cat his daily libations. After presenting the fresh water to him, I made quick work disposing of the dead fly.

He took one quick lap from the dish, then trotted off to my bedroom without so much as a thank you.

"You're welcome!" I called after him with a scowl. Jeez, it felt like no one appreciated me today.

"So what now?" Charles asked, bending down to unleash Yo-Yo.

"No, wait," I cried, but unfortunately it was too late.

The Yorkie immediately darted into my bedroom, barking manically the whole way. A dreadful hiss-growl-meow hybrid reverberated through the house, and a second later Octo-Cat appeared with his tail poofed out so large that it resembled that of a raccoon.

"I hate you!" he screamed, tearing through the house as the dog gave chase.

"Grab him!" I yelled to Charles, who made a leap for the rambunctious animal and missed.

"Hey, Yo-Yo!" I called, racing back toward the kitchen. "Want a treat?"

The Yorkie immediately turned in his tracks and trotted after me, releasing a joyous series of high-pitched barks. I reached into the fridge and grabbed a slice of lunch meat to offer him as a treat just as Charles managed to re-clip the leash to his collar.

"Well, that was an experience," he said with a weary chuckle.

"I wouldn't laugh if I were you," I told him. "It's going to take forever for my cat to forgive me now."

Charles stared at me in confusion.

"If he won't forgive me, then he also won't help. Don't you know anything about cats?" I grumbled, despite the fact that I hadn't really known anything about them myself until a few months prior.

He looked properly chastised as he hung his head and let out a giant sigh. "Sorry. What should we do?"

"We aren't going to do anything just yet. *You* are going to take Yo-Yo outside, and I guess I'll go offer up my firstborn in a last-ditch attempt to get Octo-Cat to talk to me."

Charles began to smile but quickly retracted it immediately upon seeing the stone-cold serious expression on my face.

"Uh, okay. C'mon, Yo-Yo," he said, yanking the little dog toward the door.

"Don't come in until I tell you it's okay," I shouted after them.

"It's never going to be okay," Octo-Cat hissed, emerging from wherever it was he'd been hiding. "Why would you do that to me?"

"I'm sorry. I didn't want to," I rushed to explain. "He made me."

Octo-Cat wagged his tail, which had mostly returned to its normal size. "So you sold me out for a pretty face," he cried. "I thought we were friends! I thought we were family!"

My heart clenched. Normally I didn't let his dramatics get to me, but this particular reprimand cut deep. This is what I got for confiding my workplace crush to my cat. He was thankfully getting better at telling humans apart and could accurately guess gender about four times out of five now. Of course, when I needed him to identify a murderer, he was hopeless, but when it came to figuring out my crush? Sure, *that* was no problem.

"I didn't want to," I repeated yet again. "He walked in on us Face-Timing earlier and forced me to help him."

Octo-Cat scoffed. "So he walked in on you. *Lie!* Seriously, Angela, how hard is that?"

He rarely used my name, and even more rarely my birth name. Oh, yeah, I was in serious trouble now. Someone would most definitely be waking up to vomit in her shoes tomorrow—and, sadly, that somebody was me.

"Look," I said, trying to reason with him. "Regardless of whether you would have handled things differently, we're here now. Charles wants us to talk to that dog to learn about how his owners died so that he can better defend his client who is being wrongfully accused of their murder."

Octo-Cat nodded but maintained his cold, narrow gaze. He'd been watching a lot of *Law & Order* reruns lately in an effort to better understand my job, and I was glad to see he'd learned enough to keep up with the legalese required to understand the situation.

"Okay, fine," he said after a thoughtful pause. "But why didn't you just talk to the dog yourself? Why did you need to drag me into this circus?"

"Because," I whined, wishing that he could just take me at my word for once in our lives. "I couldn't understand Yo-Yo, and I don't think he could understand me, either."

"Again, why couldn't you have lied? For goodness' sake, Angie, make something up so we can all move on with our lives."

Well, it was nice to know my cat had no problems with lying to get out of a scrape. My morals were less questionable, however. Also, I'd already tried lying to Charles and it hadn't worked.

At this point I had seriously begun to worry about the ramifications of my midday work break. How much time had passed? Had Thompson and the other associates returned to the office and realized I was missing yet?

"I am not going to lie to him," I said, choosing to take the high road. "Especially not about a case. What if his client really is innocent? What if he has to spend the rest of his life in jail because my lie messed up the case? Yeah, no thank you."

Octo-Cat groaned and rolled his eyes, a new human gesture he'd picked up from me. "So what? You need me to translate because you can't speak dog?"

"Yes, please." I clasped my hands in front of me. I wasn't above begging, and Octo-Cat just so happened to love it when I groveled.

He took on a self-important air, glancing down his nose at me. It made his eyes cross, and I had to fight to suppress a laugh. "You know dogs have a much simpler language than cats. It matches their simple minds. If you understand me, then you should definitely be able to talk to Dum-Dum out there."

"So you'll help?" I asked, praying he could see how desperately I needed him.

"Fine, I'll help" he said with a growl. "But you owe me. *Big time.*"

I raced to the door to let Charles and Yo-Yo in before my cat could change his mind. "Keep him on the leash this time," I instructed as they passed back through the threshold into my home. "Better yet, keep him on your lap."

Charles took a seat on my living room couch with the dog perched on his lap. "What now?" he asked as I took up residence in my arm chair.

"First, promise me that you won't tell anyone about any of this."

He bobbed his head in rapid, enthusiastic agreement. "Yes, I promise."

I nodded, too. "Good. Now remember I don't even know if this is going to work, but give me a few minutes and we'll be able to find out."

Charles fell silent, his eyes fixed squarely on me. It seemed that maybe Octo-Cat frightened him a bit, and that was just fine by me.

I turned to my tabby companion and said, "Would you please ask Yo-Yo what happened to his owners?"

Octo-Cat hopped up onto the coffee table and faced the dog on Charles's lap before repeating the question.

Yo-Yo gave a happy, little yap and began to pant, which my cat translated as, "He says his owners are the nicest people in the whole world and that the guy he is staying with right now is nice, but he misses his family and wants to go home."

"He said all that?" It took Octo-Cat at least ten times longer to translate that than it took Yo-Yo to speak it.

"I told you," Octo-Cat said, taking a quick break to lick at his paw. "Dog language is incredibly simple. What he actually said translates to 'best, miss,' but when dealing with dogs you have to add a ridiculous degree of enthusiasm to get a proper sense of what they want to tell you. It's exhausting, really."

"What are they saying?" Charles asked.

"Shhh," Octo-Cat and I both hissed.

Charles slumped back on the couch and watched us with a mix of intrigue and fear.

Turning back to my cat, I requested, "Would you please ask him if he was present when his owners were murdered?"

When Octo-Cat relayed my question, Yo-Yo let out a long, shrill series of screams and clawed at Charles's lap in a panicked attempt to get away.

"Oh my gosh, what happened?" I cried at the same time Charles asked, "What the heck was that about?"

I looked to Octo-Cat for an explanation.

The cat's eyes widened as he revealed, "He says his owners aren't dead, and that pretending they are is a mean and terrible joke to make."

So much for using Yo-Yo to plan a defense for Charles's client. It sounded as if the little dog were being murdered himself simply by being asked about their deaths. How could we get any useful information from him if he didn't even realize they had died?

One thing was for certain: I wasn't going to be the one to break this poor, sweet doggie's heart.

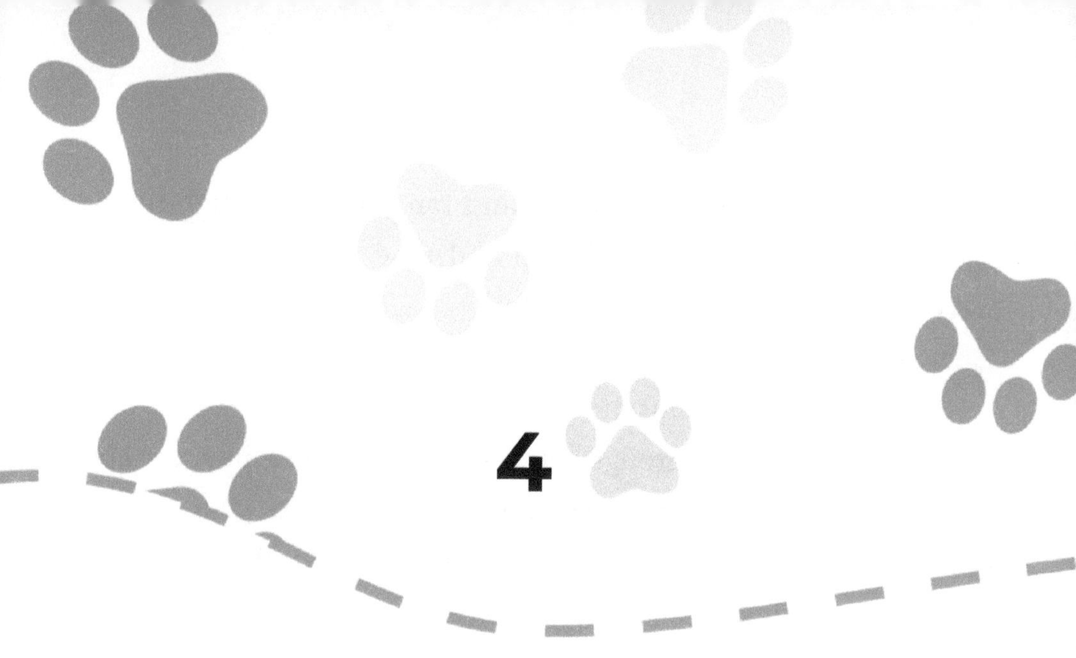

4

I watched helplessly as Charles raked both hands through his hair in distress.

"I just don't know what to do anymore," he admitted with a deep, guttural groan. "I thought for sure when I saw what you could do that it was fate, that you were meant to help me defend this case."

I leaned forward in my chair and placed a consoling hand on his knee. It was the only part of him I could reach, but still, the minor contact sent a little thrill racing from my fingertips straight to my chest. "Maybe I can find another way to help. There's still one thing that really doesn't make much sense to me, though."

He raised his head to look at me. A series of wrinkles lined his brow as he waited for what I had to say.

I cleared my throat before asking, "If you're so sure your client didn't do it, then how come you don't have a defense for him outside of talking to the victims' dog?"

He slumped back on his chair and ran a hand through his hair again, releasing the scents of soap and pine into the air. "Because everyone's already decided he's guilty."

"Except you," I said flatly.

Charles sighed. "Seems that way."

"Okay, so walk me through this, then. Can you tell me more about what happened and why everyone's so convinced your client is guilty? Also, I'd love to know how you ended up with this dog."

Octo-Cat settled in on the chair beside me. "Actually, I'd love to know that, too."

We both waited while Charles composed himself enough to tell us the story.

"If he starts this thing with 'it was a dark and stormy night,' I'm going to puke," Octo-Cat remarked with an exaggerated yawn.

"Hush up, you," I said to the impatient tabby at my side before offering Charles an apologetic glance. "Sorry. Go on."

He cocked his head and studied the pair of us for a moment. "What did he say?"

"You don't want to know," I muttered, stroking Octo-Cat with more force than he generally liked as my way of sending him a silent warning.

Charles let his gaze linger on Octo-Cat as he launched into his description of the murder. "It happened in the morning. The victims—their names were Bill and Ruth Hayes—had just put their house on the market. Apparently they'd already had an offer accepted on a new place and needed their old place to move fast, so a big open house was planned for that day. I guess property in their subdivision rarely goes up for sale, so there was a lot of interest. At least a dozen couples arrived to check the place out, and one of them discovered the victims' bodies shoved into the master bedroom closet upstairs."

I took this all in before asking, "Okay, so lots of people means lots of potential suspects. Why did the blame get pegged on your client?"

"The crime scene guys said they'd been dead for close to ten hours before they were discovered the next morning, and it was my client's hammer that was used as the murder weapon. Besides his sister, he was one of the only people who had access to their home and knew the code to disarm the security system." Charles's face was grim as he recounted the details. The more he told me, the more familiar the events started to feel. I hadn't been brought in to research this case for the firm, but I had heard all these details before from another source...

"Wait, is this the Brock Calhoun case? I've seen that all over the news." I wasn't sure whether Charles knew that my mom was the anchor for our local station or that she was part of the reason everyone assumed his client's guilt. I decided not to mention that part. Otherwise, he'd never let me help him, and clearly he needed as much help as he could get right now.

Charles nodded. "He and his sister Breanne were the ones responsible for selling the place. Someone used Brock's hammer to bludgeon the two homeowners to death."

"Ouch. Yeah. It doesn't look good for your client." I sucked air in through my teeth and glanced toward Yo-Yo, who was now snoozing on the floor by Charles's feet. Thank goodness he couldn't understand what we were saying now. No one wants to picture their loved ones meeting such a violent end, and this particular Yorkie seemed less equipped than most to deal with such a harrowing mental picture.

Charles also looked down at Yo-Yo before meeting my eyes again. "Like I said, everyone's already decided he's guilty, and now the community's pressing for a quick conviction and harsh sentencing."

I tried to keep my expression neutral as I asked, "What makes you believe he's innocent?"

"Part of it is the fact that the evidence is largely circumstantial. Another reason is that people seem to have decided he was guilty based on the fact that he wasn't the nicest person during his high school years, and also..." He seemed to debate whether he actually wanted to tell me this next part.

"You can tell me," I said with what I hoped amounted to a reassuring smile.

He shrugged. "Well, it's just a feeling I get when I talk to him. I know he's telling me the truth when he says he didn't do it."

I nudged his knee again and made a funny face. "Is intuition one-oh-one something they're teaching in law school these days?"

My joke didn't even get him to crack a smile.

Octo-Cat, however, sighed and said, "Was that supposed to be funny? We really need to get you a joke book or something."

Charles hung his head and continued to frown. "I know I'm new to town, but it just seems ridiculous that stupid teenage behavior from nearly ten years ago could cost this guy everything. So what if he bullied some classmates? I mean, it's not great, but it's also not murder."

I nodded. Brock had been a year ahead of me in school and—yeah—he'd been a jerk, but just like Charles, I also had a hard time picturing him as a killer.

"You said the Hayeses were bludgeoned to death with a hammer, right? That seems an awful lot like a crime of passion to me. What possible reason could Brock have had to kill them, especially so brutally and at close range?"

Charles perked up at this. "That's the crux of my defense so far—that he had zero motive even if he had the means and opportunity."

"And the police aren't helping?" I thought back to my encounter with Officer Bouchard and his partner a few months ago. They'd saved my life without even a moment's hesitation. Could the same force really be turning their back on Brock in his hour of need?

Charles laughed bitterly. "If only. Once they made their arrest, they just kind of clocked out. That's really the worst part of all of this. How can the justice system do its job properly if the police don't do theirs?"

"Yeah, yeah, yeah," Octo-Cat complained with an emphatic flick of his tail. "He's still leaving out the most important part. How did he wind up with that doggie menace in the first place?"

"Where does Yo-Yo fit into all of this?" I translated for Charles as I placed a stilling hand on the tabby beside me.

"That's the weirdest part. He was missing on the morning of the open house. Everyone assumed he'd just run away, but when I was driving through the Hayes's neighborhood last week, desperate for any clue or lead I could uncover, I found him waiting on the porch asking to be let in."

Okay, that was weird, but it still didn't explain why Charles had kept him all this time. "And you decided the best thing to do would be to steal him?"

He rushed to defend himself, but I wasn't buying it. "No, no, of course not."

"Then why do you still have him?"

"It was already pretty late that night, so I was going to take him to Animal Control the next morning. Only Thompson called me in early to go over the case, and I really needed his input. So then I decided I would take Yo-Yo in after work."

I couldn't argue with this. After all, Thompson was my boss, too, and I knew how demanding he could be. "Let me guess, it was too late again?"

Charles nodded emphatically. "Exactly, and the longer I hung on to him, the more the little guy began to grow on me. Also, the harder it became to just dump him off at Animal Control, or to confess that I was the one who had him all this time."

"Well, not all this time," I pointed out. Charles had hung on to Yo-Yo for less than a week, so where was he all that time before? How did he just disappear and then show up again as if no time had passed at all?

"A terrible reason to keep a dog," Octo-Cat said with a sneer. "I guess your hots for this guy have to be extinguished now. You can't end up with a dog person, Angela. That just won't do."

Heat pooled in my cheeks from morbid embarrassment, but then I remembered that Charles couldn't understand Octo-Cat—and seriously, thank goodness for that!

"Everything okay?" Charles asked, glancing from me to my cat and back again.

This was the exact moment Yo-Yo chose to wake up from his nap. Upon spotting the cat sitting just a few feet away, he resumed his hyper chain of barks almost as if he'd never stopped in the first place.

"Well, isn't this pleasant?" Octo-Cat growled as he hopped to the top of my chair and took cover, using me as a human shield. "I don't like this dog, and I don't like your boyfriend."

"He's not my boyfriend," I corrected without thinking.

Now Charles was the one blushing. Oh, great.

"Will you please just stop embarrassing me in front of Charles?" I whisper-yelled at the cat.

Octo-Cat laughed but refused to back down or even apologize.

"Anyway," Charles said as he scooped up the noisy terrier. "Do you think you could help with—?" He continued talking, but it was impossible to hear him over Octo-Cat, who decided now was the perfect time to start in on one of his annoying diatribes.

"Charles is far too classy a name for this oaf," he mused. "It sounds more like the name of a cat person, and a cat person would never have tormented me with Dum-Dum the way this guy did."

"Keep your commentary to yourself, please," I begged, trying to focus my attention back on Charles.

"I'm going to give him a new name, one that fits him better."

"Great, tell me about it later," I mumbled to the cat. "Charles, I'm sorry. Would you mind starting over?"

"Sure, I was hoping you could help me with—"

"What might some good nicknames for Charles be? Charlie,

Chuck... *Huh.* More like Upchuck, because being around him and his dog make me want to barf up my breakfast."

I had almost managed to drown out Octo-Cat's voice when he shouted at the top of his lungs. "Yes, Upchuck! It's the perfect name for him. Upchuck, Upchuck, Upchuck," he sang in absolute merriment and at the fullest possible volume his tiny kitty lungs could produce.

And he didn't stop after saying it a few times. He'd already repeated this cruel new moniker at least fifty times when Charles asked, "What do all these meows mean? I've never heard a cat talk so much in all my life."

"*Um,* he's just wondering if you have a nickname we could call you by," I hedged. What? My explanation was mostly true. While I wasn't big on bending the truth, I was even less a fan of hurting others' feelings when it was in no way warranted.

Charles broke into a smile at last. "Sure," he said, his eyes lingering on mine. "My grandfather was Charles. My dad was Charlie... And since I'm the third, they call me Chuck. You can, too, when we're not in the office. I mean, if you like that better."

Of course his nickname would be Chuck. Of course it would.

Octo-Cat just about died laughing.

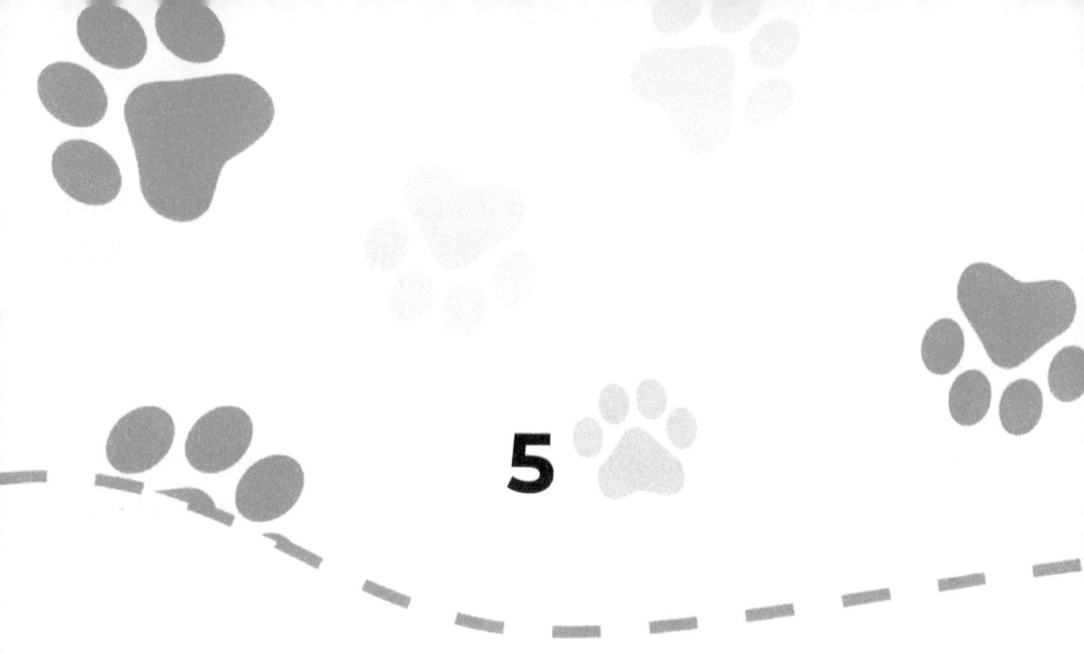

5

Even with our multiple pit stops, Charles—I'm sorry, I just can't bring myself to call him "Chuck"—and I still made it back to the office before the others returned from their long working lunch.

Charles locked himself into his office for the rest of the day, while I did some research on prior cases that could help defend Brock Calhoun from the double murder charge hanging over his head. Charles had probably already pulled every possible case, seeing as he was so desperate he'd now turned to my newly discovered pet whispering abilities to help suss out leads. Still, it felt good to know I was doing something to assist on the case.

Toward the end of the day, the mailman came and handed me a thick stack of bills, flyers, and correspondence for the office. After discarding the ads and circulars into the recycle bin, I made a round to deliver the letters by hand.

Charles groaned when I brought his to the office he shared with Derek. Previously, another associate named Brad had sat at his desk, but he was fired a few months back for workplace misconduct—which was a gentle way of saying the guy was the biggest, most sexist jerk you could possibly imagine.

"More hate mail, I take it," Charles said as he studied the postmark and sighed. "Great. It's coming all the way from Misty Harbor now."

"Hate mail? You have got to be kidding." I sat down on Derek's empty desk. He must have gone home early after the big lunch meeting. Whatever the case, I was thankful to have some alone time with Charles now. Yes, I'd already forgiven him for the blackmailing that had taken place that morning. Maybe I needed to re-evaluate my life choices, or maybe it was just impossible to stay mad at a guy who already seemed so defeated.

"I wish," he said as he tore his thumb through the top of the envelope and extracted the folded paper inside. His eyes roamed down the page quickly, and then he handed the letter to me. "This is pretty much the usual these days."

The short letter was typed in a large serif font and wasn't signed by its sender. *You should be ashamed of yourself* was the general gist, but it also included threats of picketing the trial and appealing to the bar to get Charles's ability to practice law revoked.

"Is this for real?" I asked, shaking my head as I handed the letter back to him. "People are ridiculous."

"If they're sending me this much mail, I can only imagine how much Brock must be getting." Charles balled up the note and tossed it in the trash.

No wonder he was so desperate to defend his client. I hadn't seen the people in my hometown—and even the neighboring towns, too!—this worked up since a popular football player got suspended for dealing drugs to underclassmen. He lost his college offers, scholarships, and even had his Homecoming King title retroactively pulled.

And back then it was just drugs.

Now we were facing murder, and things definitely didn't look good for Brock. Small towns never forget, which meant that even if he was found innocent, his reputation would be forever tainted and he'd probably have to move somewhere new to start over.

Poor guy.

"It gets even worse," Charles said, his mouth arranged in a firm line. "I just found out the local news station is devoting their entire broadcast tonight to a special they're calling *Brock Calhoun: A Murderer Amongst Us.*"

Ugh, leave it to my mom to go full-on sensational over this.

"I might be able to help with that," I said with a cringe and an apologetic smile.

He turned to me with excitement shining in his eyes. "Of course! Why hadn't I put two and two together before? The sports guy, Roman Russo, you're related, aren't you?"

"Yes," I admitted through clenched teeth. "He's my dad. Also Laura Lee is my mom."

His expression soured instantly. Generally my mom was well-liked all across Glendale and the greater Blueberry Bay region.

Usually, though, people didn't find themselves on the receiving end of her passion for investigative journalism.

Most people also didn't realize that our locally famous news anchor was actually my mom, seeing as she decided to keep her maiden name just in case Nan's lingering showbiz connections could help her own career get a leg up.

That strategy had worked well, and Mom had boasted a very successful career pretty much ever since I was in diapers. Lately, though, she seemed to be growing tired of all the puff pieces and human-interest stories that dominated Glendale's news. I hadn't talked to her in a couple weeks, but I could almost guarantee that she saw the Brock Calhoun case as a way of getting national attention—and possibly a better job offer for both her and my dad.

"Let me talk to her," I said with a sigh. "Maybe I can get her to ease up a little."

"More like ease up a lot," Charles said with a groan.

I nodded. "Yes, okay. I'm not sure I can catch her before tonight's story runs, but I promise you I'll do my best."

"Thanks." Charles frowned and shuffled some papers around on his desk, which I took as my dismissal.

Halfway to the door, though, he stopped me. "Angie?"

"Hmmm?" I whipped around, pleasantly surprised by the smile he offered me.

"Thank you," he said in earnest. "I know I kind of pulled you into this case against your will, but it means a lot that you're willing to help me."

"No problem," I said with a giant grin of my own. Yes, I'd definitely forgiven him for the whole blackmail thing now.

Charles returned to the papers on his desk, and I left his office to return to my own work spot near the firm's front door. As soon as I reached my desk, I shot a quick text to my mom:

SOS. We need to talk ASAP. XOXO.

I usually preferred to text in complete sentences and with proper punctuation, but it was a well-known fact that the more acronyms I used, the more likely my mom would be to respond quickly. Sure enough, I received a message back almost as soon as I'd hit *send* on mine.

What's wrong? She included an exploding head emoji and also one that looked like an alien, which I didn't quite understand, given the context. It kind of rankled that my middle-aged mother was more up on the current lingo than I'd ever be.

I drew in a deep breath before composing my next text. I had her attention now, but getting her to agree wouldn't be easy. *Need you to cancel the Brock Calhoun special you're planning for tonight.*

My phone buzzed with an incoming call not even a full minute later.

Mom's voice sounded panicked, which made me feel a bit defensive. "Why do you need me to cancel my report? It's one of the best pieces I've ever put together."

I pinched the bridge of my nose while speaking, hoping it would help to stave off the migraine pressure I felt building in my head. "I'm sure it is, Mom, but he hasn't been put on trial yet. It isn't fair to turn the whole area against him before he even gets a chance to defend himself."

Please understand. Please understand. Please understand.

It was hard to predict how my mom would react. Growing up, we hadn't shared the close relationship that many mothers and daughters do. She worked hard and never deprived me of anything, but it was Nan who had put in the emotional work raising me. Nan had always been the one I came to with my secrets, my dreams, my fears. Mom supported me in everything I did, but she was also so busy living her big life that being a mother sometimes felt too small by comparison.

I think this was a big part of the reason I hadn't settled down myself yet—not just the whole starting a family thing, but also really committing to a single career path. I liked having my options wide open and only being accountable to myself—well, and my cat, too. I couldn't imagine the pressure my mom felt whenever her home and work lives collided, and especially when they crashed into one another as was the case with my request today.

"We all know he did it," my mom said in little more than a whisper. "Besides, I heard my piece might get picked up all across the state and maybe even farther out on the Eastern seaboard, too."

I inhaled sharply before revealing, "Mom, my firm is defending him, and now I'm helping with the case, too."

It took a moment for her to respond. When she did, she didn't seem at all sure of the words she spoke. "Perhaps you could recuse yourself. We all know paralegaling isn't your real passion, but sharing important stories with the public is mine. Please, Angie. I don't want to hurt you, but can't you see that this is my big shot at finally breaking out of local news?"

"I know, and I wouldn't ask unless it was really important."

"We've already been advertising it, too," she said, her voice getting weaker with each syllable.

"So I heard." I racked my brain for a solution that would satisfy both of us, finally landing on something that I thought might work. "Tell you what. Do you think you can hold the story until Friday? That will give us some time to work on the case without the added cloud of bias."

Mom's words came out a little surer. "Okay, but what happens Friday?"

I presented the first option with as much as enthusiasm as I could muster. After all, it would be the better option for both of us, and I thought maybe that saying it aloud would give it more of a chance of actually coming true. "Either we prove beyond a shadow of a doubt that Brock Calhoun is not guilty, and we give you the exclusive right to break our story."

"Or?" Something rustled on the other end of the line, and I pictured my mom twisting nervously in her seat as she waited for me to make my full offer.

"You run it as-is and I won't try to stop you."

The line went silent for a frighteningly long time.

At last, my mother returned, her voice sweet and placating. "Honey, are you sure? You seem really upset about all of this."

I gulped down my anxiety. The clock had been set, and already it was ticking. "I'm sure. Thank you, Mom. If anyone at the station gets mad at you, send them over to me."

She laughed, and I felt all the stress we'd each been holding bubble up and float away into the sky. "I just might have to do that," she said with a sigh. "I love you, Angie. Good luck on the case," she added before ending the call.

Yes, luck—Charles and I would definitely need it. We'd also need a certain pair of talking animals to get over their hang-ups to help us figure out some new leads. Otherwise, we might as well sign Brock's sentence now, because we seemed to be out of any other reasonable avenues for his defense.

Perhaps I'd stop by the grocery store and pick up some fresh shrimp as a way to bribe Octo-Cat into spending more time with Yo-Yo. Here's hoping my feline friend loved shrimp more than he hated dogs.

6

TUESDAY

I awoke the next morning with a growing sense of dread lodged right between my lungs. The weight of knowing that Brock's freedom seemed to now rest squarely on my shoulders made it difficult to catch my breath.

I couldn't let him—or Charles—down. I also wanted to find the real culprit and secure justice for poor Yo-Yo, who still had no idea his owners were even dead.

Despite my vow to never come to the office before nine in the morning, I sucked it up and headed to the firm almost as soon as I could string a coherent thought together.

As expected, only Bethany had arrived before me. I'd never understand why she insisted on showing up so early every single day, but at least she looked happy to see me when I knocked on her office door to say hello.

The cloying and heavy scent of citrus combined with freshly

brewed coffee to create a nauseating aroma as I breezed into her office. Bethany may have become a softer, kinder person lately, but the one thing that would never change was her obsession with essential oils. Hey, everyone had their weird little things. I definitely wasn't in any place to judge.

Besides, Bethany was my own personal hero these days.

After I got electrocuted by the old office coffee maker, she brought in a Keurig machine, which she kept in her private space rather than the common area. Honestly, I was still terrified of that horrible appliance in all its forms but—much to my surprise and relief—Bethany had kindly taken to brewing me a cup each morning. I never needed to ask or to work up the courage to press the *brew* button on my own.

Thus her having become one of my favorite people lately.

"Good morning," she said with an alert smile on her fair face. My guess was she'd already imbibed two to three cups before I even arrived. "You're here early."

"Yeah," I said with a tiny wave hello. "Seeing if I can help Charles with the Brock Calhoun case."

Bethany rose to approach the coffee maker, and I was so happy I almost hugged her right then and there. Bethany and I were slowly becoming friends, but making physical contact would probably be more of a detriment than a boon to our relationship. She usually avoided hugs, handshakes, and the like whenever she could. Maybe it was something about being the only female associate at our firm, or maybe it was just her personality. Whatever the case, I knew better than to judge the woman responsible for caffeinating me five days out of seven.

"You know," she said as she popped a morning blend cup into the machine. "I was really surprised Thompson assigned such a prominent case to our newest associate. Honestly, it's one he should have handled himself."

I shrugged. "Maybe everyone else was too busy to add to their workloads right now. We have been getting a lot of business ever since... you know."

She took a couple steps closer to me and lowered her voice. "I know but—and please just keep this between you and me—I had time to help, and I'm pretty sure Derek and some of the others could have made time, too."

"What are you trying to say?"

Bethany dropped her voice even lower. "I'm saying that I think Thompson gave this case to Charles on purpose, knowing he'll probably lose it."

"And?" I may have been awake enough to drag myself to the office, but my real thinking ability wouldn't kick in until after I'd drained my first cup of joe.

"Well, think about it. Charles is brand new to the firm. When he loses what amounts to a more or less impossible case, it'll be easy for Thompson to fire him and move that stigma away from the firm."

"Like a sacrificial lamb?" Even as I questioned her, I knew Bethany was right. Our senior partner definitely wasn't above such underhanded tactics.

Her eyes glowed an unnatural hue as she nodded. "Exactly. That way Thompson gets to keep enjoying our new-found wave of success without having to worry about one notorious trial dragging him down."

That all made perfect sense, but how could Thompson be so sure Charles would lose? He was giving his everything and then some to this case. He could still win it in the end. I raised an eyebrow and asked, "But what if Charles wins?"

"Even better," Bethany answered, grabbing my coffee cup from the machine and placing it directly into my outstretched hands. "Then he'll get to brag about how his firm won the unwinnable, how he discovered Charles almost straight out of law school and recognized his talent instantly. We'll become even more popular, and Thompson will be able to pad his retirement account nicely."

"Well, that's super fun," I muttered before taking an appreciative sip from my mug.

"Isn't it though?" Bethany nodded as she paced across the office to return to her desk. "I think it's nice you're helping Charles. He's going to need every last bit he can get."

Bethany and I chatted about other things for a few minutes, but my mind stayed on what I had just learned about Charles. Did he know his job was on the line, too? Is that why he so badly wanted to win, or did it still come down to his belief in Brock's innocence?

Whatever the case, it wasn't fair for Thompson to move him clear across the country only to set him up to fall on the sword at the first available opportunity. I needed to help him win this case, and not just because the office would feel sad and empty without him...

But also because it was the right thing to do.

* * *

By nine o' clock, the rest of our colleagues had joined us at the office. I snuck into Mr. Thompson's office after giving him a few minutes to settle in.

"Good morning, sir," I said, clasping my hands in front of me and offering my most ingratiating smile. "I have a request if you're not too busy."

Our lone partner glanced up from his computer monitor and looked at me briefly before returning his attention to whatever was displayed on the screen before him. "Go ahead," he said in a way that suggested he would rather not deal with me just then. Still, I had to get his okay before going forward with my plan, whether or not he was in a good mood that day.

"I'd like to devote my week to helping Longfellow with the Calhoun case," I informed him bravely. While our previous partner, Mr. Fulton, had called everyone by their first names, Mr. Thompson only used last names. It was cold and impersonal and part of what made him so scary.

He dropped his hands from the keyboard and raised his eyes to mine, at last giving me his full attention. "Why?"

Luckily, I'd spent the last half hour or so preparing for this conversation and was ready with my response. "Longfellow is doing a great job, but his job is being made more difficult by the media. More specifically, by my mother. Adding me to this case will get her to ease up some while we work out a defense. It could be the difference between a win and a loss for Thompson and Associates on this case."

My boss studied me for a moment before offering a quick nod of agreement. "Good thinking, Russo."

"Thank you, sir," I said, ready to book it out of there and head straight to Charles's office to share the good news.

"Next week you return to business as usual, though," Thompson called after me. And, yes, that was fine, seeing as we really only had until Friday to figure out our defense, anyway.

I ran into Charles just as he was leaving the office he shared with Derek.

"Leaving so soon?" I asked, unable to hide my enthusiasm at officially being assigned to the case.

"Yup. I'm meeting with a client at ten," he informed me as we walked together toward the door.

"If it's Brock Calhoun, then I'm coming, too."

He paused to study me, and those same worried wrinkles from the other day stretched across his forehead.

"Thompson assigned me to the case for the week," I explained with a flippant wave. "Now let's go."

Charles shrugged but didn't argue when I followed him out to his car and climbed into the passenger seat.

"Since I guess you're on the case now," he told me while navigating us toward the state prison where Brock was being held on remand. "I'll share the discovery with you when we get back to the office." He bit his lip and hesitated. It looked as if he'd missed a shave or two, and I hoped my help wasn't too late to keep him from coming undone.

"What?" I asked, eager to know what had him so upset now.

Charles risked a quick glance at me before returning his gaze to the road ahead. "It's pretty gruesome. The crime scene photos, I mean. Are you going to be okay looking at them?"

"I'll be fine," I said, even though I wasn't so sure. I hadn't struggled much with blood and gore before. Heck, I'd even completed a phlebotomy certification in my early days of college. But something about being tied up as a hostage and almost offed by a crazed killer a few months back had made me more squeamish than I'd once been.

I needed to suck it up for Charles, for Brock, and for Yo-Yo, though. They were all counting on me.

"A fresh set of eyes could help," I offered, secretly picturing the worst in my mind's eye.

Okay, time to change the subject before I had a mini freak out.

"What are we meeting Brock about today?" I asked, feigning calm.

"Normal attorney-client stuff," Charles answered rather unhelpfully. "I can introduce the two of you and let him know how you helped to get the news story delayed, but I really don't have anything else to tell him at this point."

"Then why go? Why not call with a quick update?"

Charles sighed and tightened his grip on the steering wheel. "I'm hoping he might have something new to tell me, something to help with the defense."

I sighed, too. While I was happy for the chance to meet Brock and decide for myself whether I believed he did it, I doubted he'd suddenly remember the one detail that could save him after weeks of sitting in prison. Charles didn't need to hear me express my doubts, though. I was sure he had his own.

It also seemed I'd recently become the unofficial case optimist. If I started acting defeated now, we wouldn't stand a chance of securing an innocent ruling.

When we arrived outside the state prison, I was surprised by how small and unassuming it appeared from the outside. Maybe I was expecting a giant, sprawling facility containing watchtower turrets with snipers and barbed wire fencing that stretched two stories high, but that definitely wasn't what I got. The concrete-faced building looked like something you might spot in a strip mall—not like a secure detention center for nearly a thousand inmates accused of everything from drug possession to murder.

"You going to be okay?" Charles asked, pulling the car into the visitors' parking lot.

"I'm fine." I unbuckled my seat belt with shaky hands while keeping my eyes focused straight ahead. "Let's get this over with."

The inside of the prison felt much closer to what I'd expected—the guards, the metal detectors, the holding cells. Frankly, the whole scene gave me the creeps. I followed Charles wordlessly as we were guided into one of the private attorney-client rooms. Once there, we had to wait several minutes before Brock was brought out to join us.

There, our client stood with shackles securing his hands and feet and an unbecoming beige uniform that washed out his light complexion. His dark hair appeared overgrown and poorly washed. His gray eyes were deep-set, with heavy circles painted beneath them.

When he saw us waiting for him, he smiled and ducked his head politely. Even though he was easily six foot four and had sizeable muscles to round out his physique, he seemed so small standing there before us. And then I felt it, that same gut feeling I'd teased Charles about just one day earlier. It was as if a thunder bolt of understanding struck me in my very core.

Boom!

Just like that, I knew for sure that Brock Calhoun didn't belong in this awful place and that he couldn't possibly have murdered those people.

Brock turned toward me askance, waiting for an introduction perhaps. He smiled hesitantly, politely, un-killer-ly.

"Hi, Brock," I said after clearing my throat. "My name's Angie, and I'm going to help win your case."

7

Just as I feared, Brock had nothing new to share with us during our visit. That meant it was up to me, Charles, and the pets to find a new angle for his defense—and finding a new angle meant finding the real murderer.

Was I scared? Oh, yeah.

Last time I'd gone head-to-head with a killer I almost ended up dead myself. For now, I'd try my best not to think about that. When all this was over, though, I'd definitely be booking some therapy sessions.

Back at the office, Charles handed me a thick folder filled past bursting with the prosecution's discovery, all the facts and files they believed would prove Brock guilty of the Hayes's murders.

"Wow," I said, letting out a low whistle as I flipped through the many, many pages it contained. "They sure have a lot."

Charles groaned and slumped into the chair beside me. “Yeah, they really do.”

I only looked at the crime scene photos for a few seconds before pushing them aside. The gruesome pictures showed that poor Bill and Ruth had not died a gentle death. The deep crimson puddles of blood that pooled around their heads made my stomach churn.

Who would do such a horrible thing? And, perhaps even more importantly, *why?*

Charles returned to his desk for a moment. When he came back to our shared workspace, he placed a much thinner folder on the table before me. “Our discovery,” he said.

“Oh.” He had a few prior cases and character witnesses for Brock, but not much else to go by. It definitely didn’t look good. “Who gave these statements?” I asked, holding up the character testimonies.

Charles grabbed the thin bunch of papers and described each one as he placed them back before me. “His sister, a few previous clients of his handyman business, an old girlfriend.”

“Have you talked to anyone who knew the victims?”

He shook his head. “Just Brock and his sister.”

“What about the witnesses for the prosecution?” I asked, returning to the thick discovery folder and pulling out several pages of testimony from inside.

Charles didn’t even bother reaching for these papers. Instead he shrugged and explained, “They prefer not to talk to our side pre-trial.”

“Well, that’s convenient,” I grumbled, blowing out a big puff of air that ruffled my bangs.

No one seemed to be playing fair here—nobody except for Charles, that was. And this fact put us at a huge disadvantage.

Charles could take the high road all he wanted. I knew perfectly well that sometimes back roads were the only way to reach your destination, and I was definitely not opposed to taking them. "Okay, so hear me out on this... What if they don't know they're talking to us?" I suggested with a sly grin.

He crossed his arms and shook his head. "Everyone knows I'm the attorney on Brock's case. Even if I wanted to be sneaky, I couldn't. And, no, I don't want to be sneaky. I want to win this case and clear Brock's name fair and square."

"Oh, sure. I understand," I acquiesced quickly. "Forget I said anything."

Charles and I spent the next several hours reviewing both sets of discovery and planning our cross-examination of the witnesses. He didn't need to know that I'd secretly made a list of people to visit outside of office hours. No one would recognize me as being part of the case.

After all, few people ever paid any real attention to paralegals.

I could use that to my advantage to learn more about the victims and figure out who might have wanted them dead. Nothing needed to come out in court unless I found our smoking gun—or, in this particular case, our bloody hammer.

* * *

"Are you ready, Nan?" I asked when I showed up to collect her for our after-hours private investigation. Because I'd arrived at work early that day, I was also able to sneak out a bit early. This gave us just enough time to stop by Bill Hayes's former place of employment and see what new information we could learn about him and any potential murder suspects that might be lurking around his office.

"Oh, yeah," Nan drawled with a vaguely Southern accent. "Let's do this."

Have I mentioned that my grandmother used to be a huge star on Broadway? She acted in the occasional community theater production now, but still jumped at any opportunity to dust off her underutilized talents. That's why I'd invited her to tag along with me tonight.

The late Mr. Hayes had worked at a place called Bayside Printing Company. Most of their jobs involved printing promotional materials for the many businesses scattered across Blueberry Bay, but a quick search on their website informed us that they also helped independent authors and micro-presses publish their books. This gave us the perfect excuse to stop in for a chat.

You see, for years, Nan had been telling anyone who would listen that she had a book in her—and more specifically, an autobiography. She'd even decided upon a title despite the fact she had yet to write a single page.

"It's called *From Broadway to Blueberry Bay: The Life and Times of Dorothy Loretta Lee*, and I guarantee it's the most fabulous piece of printing that will ever come across your desk," she told the printing manager with a big jazz hands finish.

I studied the unassuming middle-aged man sitting across from us. His name was Mr. Weber, and with his thinning hairline and well-ironed shirt tucked neatly into his pants, he definitely didn't look like a murderer. He smiled at Nan with genuine interest as she regaled him with all the stories of her fake youth growing up in the South.

"It truly sounds fascinating," he said, mirroring her accent.

I had to fight hard not to crack up laughing at them both as they spoke chummily in their matching set of fake accents.

"Let me run some numbers so we can get settled on a quote," he said as he made a big show of pulling his keyboard toward him on the desk.

"Lovely," Nan said, folding her hands in her lap.

Mr. Weber's smile didn't leave his face as he clicked a series of boxes on his computer screen, pausing occasionally to ask Nan questions like how many pages her book would contain, what trim size she needed, if she wanted cream or white paper, paperback or hardcover.

Nan didn't hesitate one bit as she flawlessly trotted out each response to Mr. Weber's apparent satisfaction. It made me wonder if perhaps she was really serious about this autobiography despite the fact she hadn't yet begun to write it.

Well, I would just have to make the time to figure out how I could be more supportive of her dream later. Right now, the investigation needed my full attention.

"*So...*" I said, drawing out the syllable until Mr. Weber turned his attention to me. "Isn't this the place where that poor Bill Hayes worked before he was so tragically murdered?"

Mr. Weber turned red and sweat began to bead on his forehead at the mere mention of the victim's name. "Yes," he said with poorly concealed rage. "No one deserves to be killed like that, but especially not Bill."

"Such a terrible thing that happened," Nan said, patting his hand and offering a sympathetic nod.

A calm washed over Mr. Weber following Nan's touch. "Bill was the best employee I had and was even poised to take over for me when I retire next year," he explained with a frown. "I guess that won't be happening now."

"That's too bad," Nan said while I silently thanked my lucky stars that I'd decided to bring her with me. "I can tell you work very hard. You deserve a break after so many years of devoting yourself to the company."

He shook his head sadly. "Bill was the very same. Everyone in the office loved him. All the customers, too. There were so many times a client would come to us with a crazy rush deadline, and Bill wouldn't even think twice before offering to stay late and put in extra hours to make sure they got their order on time."

"It sounds like he was a wonderful asset to Bayside Printing Company," I added with a reassuring nod, not wanting to be completely outdone by Nan.

Mr. Weber kept his eyes glued to Nan, though, as he sighed and said, "I still can't wrap my head around it. What did that handyman have against Bill? And to kill his wife, too? I hope they put him away for a long, long time."

I shifted in my seat uncomfortably as Mr. Weber forced a smile back on his face and turned his computer monitor toward us.

"Anyway," he said after clearing his throat twice. "As you can see, you're looking at a cost of $2,500 to $6,700, depending on how many copies you'd like to print for your first run."

Nan nodded. "What would you rec—?" Suddenly, she broke into a terrible coughing fit, unable to speak another word as she clutched at her chest dramatically.

"Excuse me," she croaked out once the coughs had subsided. "Mr. Weber, would it be possible for me to have a cup of water?"

He popped to his feet quicker than I might have expected a man of his girth and stature to be able. "Sure, that's no problem at all. Excuse me. I'll be right back."

As soon as he'd rushed out of the office, Nan began rummaging through the papers on his desk and snapping bursts of pictures with her cell phone camera.

"What are you doing?" I whispered.

Nan didn't pause as she ground out her answer. "Seeing if we can find anything he's not telling us. When he comes back with my water, excuse yourself to use the bathroom and see if you can find anything in the main office."

Wow, my nan made an excellent private investigator. Perhaps I'd have to include her on my cases more often. Then again, this was only my second case to date and already she'd proved indispensable to both. Hey, I'd take help wherever and from whomever I could get it, just so long as nothing I did ever put my dear nan in any danger.

When heavy footsteps clopped their way back down the hall, Nan slipped her phone back into her purse just in time to greet Mr. Weber with a gracious smile. "My hero," she cooed as he handed her the cup of water.

"If you'll excuse me," I said, rising to my feet. "I just need to use the bathroom real quick."

"Turn left, then it's the second door on the right," Mr. Weber muttered without looking up to see me off. He'd fallen under Nan's spell as so many did, and I couldn't fault him for that—especially since it would make my investigation that much easier.

"Thanks," I muttered before clicking the door shut behind me. Even though Nan was obviously an old pro, I myself was still new to this whole snooping business and didn't really know where I should be looking. Somehow, I doubted Bayside Printing Company would just leave their financials or security tapes in plain view. Come to think of it, a place like Bayside probably didn't even have security tapes, although if they did that would make this whole thing so much easier.

Man, I wished Octo-Cat was here with me. Where I was gangly and untalented, my cat was an expert at sticking his nose in others' business. Heck, *snooping* might as well have been one of his middle names. With such a long list of them, it might actually be hidden in there without me knowing. He even put Nan to shame with his immense spying skills and the zero remorse he showed over exercising them. Maybe I could channel some of that now...

Now, if I were Octo-Cat, where would I look first?

I didn't get a chance to find out, because a moment later I found that I wasn't alone in the main office. The tall, slim woman who sat silently in the waiting area perked up upon noticing me.

"Can I help you?" I asked hesitantly. It seemed rude to just ignore her, even though I hadn't a clue how I could actually help her with anything of consequence.

"Is Mr. Weber in?" she asked, tucking a fluffy red curl behind her ear and offering me a friendly smile. "I was hoping to grab my order before he closed up shop for the night."

"Um, sure. I'll just go tell him you're here," I said, turning back toward the office in defeat.

I sure hoped Nan was having better luck with Mr. Weber than I'd had out here. Or that she had captured something valuable on her camera during her sleuthing micro-burst.

Otherwise, it looked like Bayside Printing Company might be a big, fat dead end. All we'd managed to do was waste valuable time.

Wednesday was almost upon us, and we weren't any closer to finding the Hayes's real killer. Might tomorrow turn out to be our lucky day?

Oh, I sure hoped so.

8

WEDNESDAY

The next morning I told Charles about the reconnaissance Nan and I had attempted at the Bayside Printing Company the night before.

"I knew you were up to something," he said before widening his eyes and asking, "Did you find anything that can help?"

I caught him up on the little things we'd learned, like that Bill was well-liked at his job and slated for a promotion the following year. In the end, we really hadn't gained anything more than that. Most of Nan's pictures had turned out blurry, and the few we could see clearly showed nothing useful.

I tapped my pen on the desk and chewed my lower lip. "Are you sure that none of the prosecution's witnesses would be willing to talk to us before the trial?"

"I'm sure," Charles answered with a weary sigh. "They all said *no.* Well, except for one, but I haven't been able to get a hold of her despite trying to call multiple times." He shrugged and took a sip from his coffee cup before adding, "I'm not sure she'll be taking the stand, anyway."

"Oh? Who might that be?" I leaned in closer, eager to hear more. Had Charles been sitting on this lead the whole time? I wished he would have said something earlier.

He didn't seem to think it was a big deal as he casually informed me, "Michelle Hayes, the daughter."

My heart quickened at this revelation. Could Michelle be the missing key to unlock the perfect defense?

"Don't get so excited," Charles warned me. "I'm telling you, she's all but impossible to get a hold of."

"Just like this case is impossible to defend?" I quipped, shooting him a wry grin. Suddenly, a dark thought occurred to me. "You don't think she's not returning your calls because *she* did it, do you?"

"Absolutely no way. She loved her parents. They were paying *beaucoup* bucks to put her through private college, and she still came home almost every weekend to visit even though her school is a good three-hour drive from here."

"I thought you couldn't get a hold of her?" I asked suspiciously. He seemed awfully quick to jump to Michelle's defense. Was it possible he wasn't sharing everything he knew with me? And, if so, why?

Charles seemed unperturbed by my question, and he held his coffee firmly between both hands as he said, "That was in the statement she gave the police."

"What's her number?" I asked, crossing the office to grab his landline. This week, Derek had graciously agreed to switch workspaces with me so that Charles and I could have unfettered access to each other while I assisted on Brock's case. It definitely made things easier.

Until Charles yanked the phone right out of my hand.

"It's way too early in the morning to be calling a nineteen-year-old student. You think she's going to want to talk to us if we wake her from a dead sleep?"

I cringed at his choice of words, but ultimately agreed. "Later then."

"Do you think we could try the animals again today?" Charles asked with a similar puppy dog expression to the one I'd seen on Yo-Yo's face when we'd first met.

"Sure. Why not?" I answered. We had to do something. Maybe I could put in a call to Michelle when he wasn't paying attention.

"Okay," Charles said before letting a relieved whoosh of air escape from his lungs. "Let's go."

"Not so fast," I called after him.

He'd already grabbed his things and made it halfway out the door. Talk about eager. Charles turned back to me, properly chastised. "What's wrong?"

"We need a plan first." I returned to my seat and flipped to a new page on my bright yellow legal pad.

Charles sat back down, too, but began to bounce both legs nervously.

When I was sure I had his attention, I continued, "We need to treat the animals just like we would any other witness, and we need to approach Yo-Yo as a vulnerable witness. You saw the trauma he went through at the mere suggestion his owners might be hurt. We can't upset him like that again or he may close off to us completely. Also, if we push too hard, I worry it could negatively impact his long-term mental health."

Charles thought about this for a moment. By the time he spoke again, his nervous bouncing had ceased. "Do you think Yo-Yo saw the murder?"

"He definitely could have seen it," I said with a nod.

Understanding sparked within his pine-colored eyes. "He saw it, and then he suppressed the memory to protect himself."

"That's what I'm thinking." I brought the pen to my mouth but stopped short before I began to gnaw at the cap. It was a nervous habit of mine—a disgusting habit—I definitely didn't want to trot out in front of Charles.

Luckily, he didn't seem to notice. "So how do we get him to acknowledge these hidden memories in time to save Brock?"

"We don't," I said, recapping the pen and placing it back onto the desk. "I think Yo-Yo can still help even without remembering what happened or knowing that his owners were killed. I mean, who knows a person better than their dog? He saw their daily routines for years. He would definitely know if anything had changed shortly before their deaths."

"Smart," Charles said with a nod while my heart secretly swelled at the compliment. "Do you want to take the lead on the questioning?"

"Yes, I think I do." I could talk to animals for a reason. At first I thought helping Octo-Cat solve Ethel's murder had just been a fluke, but more and more it seemed like this was my calling: to uncover justice one fluffy critter at a time.

* * *

A couple hours later, we'd prepared an exhaustive list of questions and prompts, and even role-played how a conversation with Yo-Yo might go. That only left one variable for which we hadn't properly accounted—Octo-Cat.

His mood changed so regularly, it would take far too long to draw out the various scenarios we might be faced with while trying to secure his compliance. Also, I was too embarrassed to admit to Charles how much I let my cat walk all over me on a daily basis. Instead, we planned to just show up at my house and tell Octo-Cat what we expected of him, plain and simple.

Oh, he'd definitely find a way to punish me for it, but I could handle a little cat puke or a fresh claw wound if it meant saving an innocent man from a life in prison and protecting a sweet terrier's innocence.

We stopped off at Cliffside Apartments to grab Yo-Yo, then made a quick detour to the pet store where we purchased a leash and harness for Octo-Cat. Unfortunately, the only get-up they had in his size was bright neon green with a series of fluorescent bones patterned along the leash.

This would make it that much harder to convince him to wear it, but we didn't have time to stop off at multiple stores just to assuage my cat's vanity.

Sure enough, Octo-Cat baulked when presented with his shiny new walking gear. "So let me get this straight. You not only want me to spend more time talking to Dum-Dum while you make heart eyes at Upchuck, but you also expect me to wear this monstrosity? *Ma'am, I am a cat,* not some common, mouth-breathing dog."

I crossed my legs and sat down on the floor in front of him, arranging my face in the best approximation of puppy-dog eyes any human could hope to muster. *"Please.* It's just for a little while, and I wouldn't ask unless it was really important."

He flicked his tail a few times before responding with, "So you're asking then? That means I have a choice. I choose *no.*"

I gave Charles the signal we had discussed, knowing in advance that it would most likely prove necessary. I watched as he slowly slipped his hands into a pair of oven mitts and tiptoed toward Octo-Cat from behind.

"I want you to know..." I told my soon-to-be furious furr-enemy. "I was hoping it wouldn't come to this."

Octo-Cat's eyes widened with the knowledge of my betrayal at the same time I shouted, *"Now!"*

A furious cry ripped through the house as Charles scooped my cat into his arms, clutching him tightly and very much against his will.

"Unhand me, Upchuck!" he screamed as he swiped his claws in any and every direction. "I will not be disrespected like this!"

"Shh," I said in a futile attempt to coax him into a belated agreement as I worked his arms through the harness. "You do this for me, help us find who killed Yo-Yo's owners, and I will owe you a favor. It can be any favor you want. I swear. Please just help us. We need you.

And, if you'll recall, it wasn't so long ago I risked my life to help you get justice for Ethel."

At these words, all the fight drained from his furry little body, and Octo-Cat sighed heavily. "Fine," he growled as I clipped the harness under his belly.

Charles set him back on the ground, and Octo-Cat took a few tipsy steps. His fur stuck out in various directions from the struggle, and he twitched spasmodically while keeping his posture low and defensive.

"You owe me a big favor," he shouted in my direction. "The biggest favor you've ever given anyone in all your nine lives!"

I nodded, eager to put this confrontation to an end. I'd braced myself for a much bigger fight than he'd given me, and things could still go south if I wasn't careful. "You've got it," I promised. "Anything."

Octo-Cat let out a maniacal chuckle that made the small hairs on the back of my neck stand on end, too.

"What?" I asked, my voice suddenly shaky and unsure.

"Oh, you'll see. You'll all see!" He swept a paw toward Charles, which only increased my worry—but my crazy cat's demands could be dealt with later. Thinking of which, I should also probably put parent controls on the TV later to discourage this kind of crazed villainous behavior. Right now, though, we had to move on to the next phase of our plan, just in case he suddenly changed his mind and retracted his offer to help.

"Let's get out of here while we still can," I told Charles while bending down to clip the leash to Octo-Cat's new harness.

"Fully unnecessary," the tabby grumbled. "What makes you assume I'd run away? Remember, I chose you despite your many, *many* shortcomings."

"It's more for your safety than your compliance," I explained.

Even if Octo-Cat fully intended to stick with us on this trip, he had a tendency to become a different cat from the moment he stepped paw outside. Inside the house, he was a cool intellectual who freely offered an unsolicited running commentary on my life. Once he got out into the wide open, though, he became flighty, unpredictable, and highly excitable. For all I knew, he could spot a butterfly and run three miles straight before realizing we weren't right there chasing it with him.

Yes, as annoying as he could sometimes be, I loved my cat and wanted to keep him with me for many years to come.

Unfortunately for him, that meant he needed to wear the harness.

I only hoped the favor he requested of me would be something I could legally and physically obtain for him. You just never knew with this guy. That's part of what made living with him so exciting most days.

Then there were days like today...

I knew the worst of his agitation was yet to come.

Grabbing a thick, long-sleeved jacket from the closet, I took a deep breath and led our motley party toward Charles's waiting car.

It was time for phase two.

9

We arrived in the Hayes's old neighborhood less than ten minutes later, and Yo-Yo immediately perked up upon taking in the familiar sights and smells. He barked, howled, whimpered, and whined, all before we even managed to find a place to park the car.

"What's he saying?" I asked Octo-Cat, who sat velcroed to my lap in the passenger seat. Since I wasn't driving this time, I'd had the blessedly bright idea to bring a cushion to place between his claws and me. Never before had I enjoyed such a nice car ride with my agoraphobic cat.

Octo-Cat, of course, was still less than thrilled to be in the moving vehicle. It took a few moments before he answered. "He's calling out to his mom and dad and letting them know he's come home," he explained between nervous pants.

"Oh, that's really sad," I responded after offering a quick translation for Charles. Despite the obvious seriousness of the situation, speaking to each other like this reminded me of the old schoolyard game of telephone. How warped did Yo-Yo's words become by the time they finally reached Charles?

"Definitely a vulnerable witness," Charles agreed with my earlier assessment while pulling up to the curb and putting the car in park. "Poor guy."

"You still haven't told me the plan," Octo-Cat said as I helped him untangle his claws from the cushion and placed him gently on the pavement outside.

Charles grabbed Yo-Yo's leash and came around the car to stand beside us. The excited terrier strained so hard against his leash, he began to wheeze.

"Yup. Dum-Dum is definitely a much better name for this dog," Octo-Cat said with a contented grin, clearly feeling like himself again now that he was back on solid ground. "Upchuck suits the human, too."

"Yes, yes, you're a great nicknamer," I said to placate him, resisting the urge to roll my eyes now that he knew what the gesture meant. Instead, I chose to answer his earlier question. "The plan is to walk around the neighborhood and see what Yo-Yo can tell us about his life before. Something he says could give us a clue as to who besides Brock might have committed the murder."

"Wouldn't it be easier if you just told Dum-Dum the truth about what happened and asked him to help?" Octo-Cat almost seemed as if he was trying to help, but I suspected the real goal was to end his involvement with our case as soon as felinely possible.

"No!" I shouted at the same time Yo-Yo screeched and began to twist at the end of the leash. Any passerby would have thought we were torturing the poor Yorkie. Thankfully, we had the street to ourselves for the moment.

"Dum-Dum says he wants to know the truth," Octo-Cat explained with a bored expression and a yawn.

"Ugh, stop making things harder than they have to be," I scolded him. "And stop being such an elitist. His name is Yo-Yo, and you know it."

"Yes, I'm the one making things harder here," my cat said, widening his eyes in the direction of the neon-colored leash that tied me and him together. He let out an exasperated huff and looked away.

I'd had more than enough of his complaints, especially since Yo-Yo was still panicking—and doing so loudly. Dropping to my haunches, I stared the obstinate tabby down and said, "If you want your return favor, you'll do things the way I want them done. You hear?"

He cringed. "Say it. Don't spray it. And you don't have to shout, either."

Okay, that was it. I would definitely be restricting his TV access. It was bad enough when he was watching educational cartoons all hours of the day, but now he'd turned into a snarky teenager—and that was just too much when combined with his already snarky feline temperament. Besides, he needed to learn that his actions had consequences.

Ugh. Here I was still in my twenties and yet somehow also a single mother to a whiny teenager. I owed Nan and my parents a huge apology for all the irritating know-it-all things I'd done as a teenage brat myself.

"Are we agreed?" I asked pointedly as I stood up and Charles bent down to pick up Yo-Yo so that he would stop hurting himself.

"Fine," Octo-Cat spat out. "What do you want me to tell him?"

I put on a huge smile to show Octo-Cat how pleased I was about his cooperation. I knew better than to call him a good boy in front of mixed company, even though he loved hearing those words when it was just the two of us at home. "Tell him his mom and dad are away on a trip right now, but we're going to take a walk around his neighborhood together because we'd love to hear about all his favorite memories with them."

"You do realize this is going to be torture for me, right?"

"You'll live," I shot back.

Octo-Cat conveyed my message to Yo-Yo, who briefly stopped panting and slipped his tongue back inside his mouth. A few seconds later, his enthusiasm returned, and he struggled to break free of Charles's grasp once more.

"Ready?" Charles asked.

When I nodded, he placed the terrier on the ground, and the four of us began our walk around the neighborhood with Yo-Yo proudly leading the way.

"Do I have to translate everything he says?" Octo-Cat whined less than a minute into our jaunt.

"Yes, everything," I answered.

Charles stayed oddly silent as the animals and I conversed. On the rare occasion we ran into another walker, he spoke, too, so that I would appear at least somewhat less insane. I was still walking a very angry-looking cat on a leash, after all.

"Careful, he bites," Charles warned a pair of blue-haired ladies in track suits when it looked like they were going to try to pet Octo-Cat.

Octo-Cat hissed and arched his back for good measure, then laughed when they quickened their pace and power-walked right on by us. "That was kind of fun," he said as he shook it out.

"Awesome, so glad you're enjoying yourself. Now, what is Yo-Yo saying?" I demanded. I was glad Octo-Cat had found a way to make the experience more palatable, but we needed him to stay focused on the entire reason for this trip in the first place.

The tabby sighed and twitched his whiskers and moved his ears back and forth. "Let me just turn on my Dum-Dum receptors... *There.*"

"Haha, you're hilarious. Now stop with the stand-up comedy and start with the translation already."

"Fiiiiiiine," he drew that single word out for at least seven syllables before finally doing as he was told. He sighed and said, "Well, that rock we just passed a few paces back, that's one of his favorite places to pee. Once he saw a squirrel crossing the road here, and it ran so fast he couldn't catch up. Birds like to sit in that tree over there. He also enjoys peeing there. There's usually a nest every spring. The kids who live in that house up ahead like to run through the sprinklers in summer, and sometimes they invite him to play..."

I was starting to get his hesitation about translating *everything* Yo-Yo said. It all came out so fast there was no way I could relay it to

Charles. I offered him an apologetic glance before asking Octo-Cat, "Do you think you could ask him some questions for me?"

He just kept walking without so much as looking at me.

I took his silence as agreement. "Ask him if he likes all the people who live in this neighborhood."

"He says, 'yes, very much,' then he told me about the time he saw two red cars in a row right on this block."

I needed to keep both of them talking, but I also needed to keep them on topic. "Were Bill and Ruth particularly close to anyone in the area?"

"Apparently they liked everybody, and everybody liked them," Octo-Cat relayed. I was beginning to wonder if our terrier friend might not be the most reliable of witnesses. It seemed he saw the best in everybody—and every situation, too.

"Anything yet?" Charles asked.

I shook my head and kicked at a pebble in our path. "No. Unless you count knowing all the best places to mark your territory along this block."

Charles laughed, but I could tell he was at least a little—and probably *a lot*—disappointed. I was just about to suggest we head back when Yo-Yo barked defensively. He stopped walking and grew stiff, pointing his nose to the next yard over.

"What is it?" I asked my cat as excitement surged through my veins.

"He says that's the bad lady. He wants her to go away."

I followed Yo-Yo's gaze to the "For Sale" sign down the block. There, a blue and white notice announced that the property was being sold through Calhoun Realty, and a picture of Brock smiling beside his twin sister, Breanne, graced its countenance.

"Lady, right?" I asked carefully. "Not man?"

"Definitely lady," Octo-Cat concurred. "He said that she always shoved him into a closet whenever people came to visit and that made him sad and scared."

"*Hmm,* I wonder if that could be the same closet that Bill and Ruth's bodies were found inside."

Octo-Cat took a deep breath and turned toward Yo-Yo.

"*Don't translate that!*" I shouted.

"What are they saying?" Charles nudged my arm while wearing an expression of utter glee. "Do we have a lead?"

I glanced from the sign to Yo-Yo and then to Charles. "Well, the dog that likes everyone has a very negative impression of Breanne Calhoun. It seems we might need to pay her a little visit."

* * *

As we walked back toward the car, Charles placed a call to Breanne —or at least he tried to get through to her.

"Straight to voicemail," he said with a frustrated groan.

"Text her?" I suggested.

Charles did, and we heard back from her almost right away. He handed me the phone, so I could read the message for myself:

Showing houses to a client. Everything okay?

I gave the phone back to Charles, who deftly composed his reply while speaking each word aloud to keep me in the loop. "Can we meet about the case?"

A quick series of pings followed, and Charles relayed, "She can't tonight, but says we can stop in tomorrow any time after lunch."

"Great," I moaned. Tomorrow would be Thursday, and my mom's story was set to run Friday. That sure didn't leave us much time, especially if Breanne turned out to be yet another false lead.

"So what now?" I asked.

"I'm kind of hungry," Charles answered. "Do you know of any place we can get a good lobster roll? I've been craving one ever since I moved here."

I stopped dead in my tracks. "Are you serious right now, Charles Longfellow, the Third?"

"What? What did I do?"

"You've been in Maine how long and haven't had one of our famous lobster rolls?"

He laughed. "Have I mentioned I'm kind of a workaholic?"

"This won't fly, Chuck," I said, finally feeling comfortable using his nickname. "Since you've waited this long, not just any lobster roll will do. You need the best."

"I'm definitely okay with that. Which place has the best?"

"C'mon, we're headed to Misty Harbor and a little place called the Little Dog Diner. I just know you're going to love it."

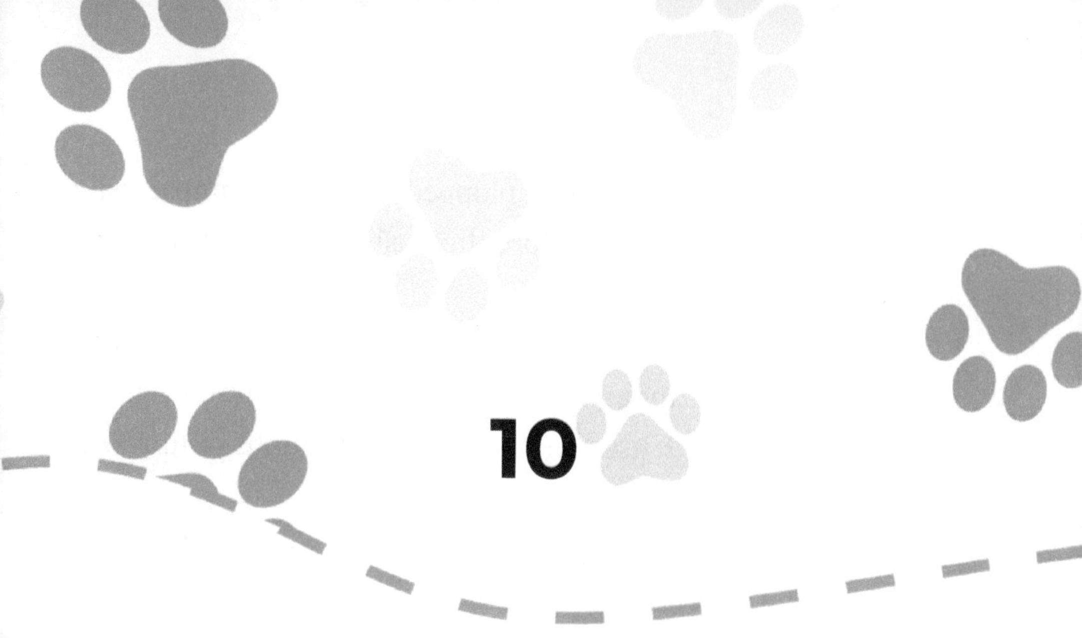

10

Our dinner detour in the nearby town of Misty Harbor proved to be just the thing both Charles and I needed to ease our frazzled nerves. Of course, we'd stopped by my house to drop off Octo-Cat along the way—a fact for which he was exceedingly grateful—but we brought Yo-Yo with us and dined at one of their outdoor tables that looked right onto the bay. We even got the pup a fish dinner of his own, which he devoured with aplomb. I saved a small portion in a to-go box for Octo-Cat as a thank you for his help that day, and also with the hope he'd go easy on me whenever he revealed the favor I'd need to grant him in return.

Charles and I sat and chatted over lobster rolls until the sky began to darken and another restaurant-goer needed our table. I thought I recognized the woman with red, fluffy hair, who approached us with a smile and a request to take over our spot, but I couldn't quite place her. Anyway, it looked like she was busy, because the moment we gathered our things to leave, she plopped down and unpacked a laptop from her bag. That was before the busboy had even managed to clear away our plates.

I felt bad for her, having no one to dine with her on this beautiful Wednesday night, even though I'd be home in my jammies fighting with Octo-Cat by now if it weren't for this impromptu outing with Charles.

"See," he said, bumping my shoulder with his own. "At least I know not to mix work and lobster rolls."

Work, ugh. Yes, our momentary break from the case had come to an end. There wasn't much time left now.

"Can we try calling Michelle now?" I suggested as we made our way back to the parking lot.

"Sure, use my phone," he said. "I have her number saved just in case."

I tried my luck but got sent straight to voicemail where a robotic voice informed me the mailbox was full and thus unable to take any new messages. "So much for that," I said with a defeated sigh.

"Hey. At least tomorrow's a new day," Charles told me with a wistful glance in my direction.

Yes, a new day—and the last full one we had when it came to proving Brock's innocence and stopping my mom's big exposé. Even with the animals' help, this was not turning out as easy as I'd hoped.

Could we possibly hope that a new day would make that any different?

* * *

THURSDAY

Charles and I put in a full morning at the firm before heading over to Calhoun Realty around noon. He'd practically insisted we bring the animals with us, but fortunately I was able to convince him that we should meet with Breanne on our own before getting Octo-Cat and Yo-Yo involved—especially since we had no idea how the little dog would react to seeing Breanne in person. If she was our killer, all heck could break lose once Yo-Yo's memories came rushing back. And, judging by his reaction to seeing her printed image yesterday, that was a very real possibility.

We had to wait more than half an hour before Breanne ushered us back into her office. Even though I was sure she was a very busy person, this immediately soured her to me. One of my biggest pet peeves was people who didn't respect others' time. Didn't she know her brother's freedom was on the line here?

"Sorry about that," the realtor said when at last she waved us back into her private office. Of course, she didn't seem the least bit apologetic despite her words to the contrary.

Charles and I sat in the matching pair of chairs in front of her desk and waited for Breanne to settle herself. She seemed rather put out by our arrival even though she'd known we were coming.

"How is everything?" Charles asked, putting on the same drawn expression I'd seen him use when speaking with Brock at the prison.

"Not so hot," she admitted, tossing her auburn hair into a messy bun at the nape of her neck. With her hair pulled back, I noticed how strongly she resembled her brother. I guess that made sense, them being twins and all, but still I found the similarity quite striking and a bit shocking. The only differences seemed to be the feminine curve to Breanne's face and the alternate hair color.

She pinched her features in dismay before jumping into a lengthy explanation. "Half the people I take out on showings don't even want a house. They just want to gossip about my brother. Or, worse, sometimes they want to chew me out on his behalf. Still, I'm taking as many extra hours as I can, because your firm doesn't come cheap. And, if Brock is convicted, I can pretty much kiss this realty goodbye." Breanne laughed sarcastically and let out a long sigh. "So, yeah, not so hot."

"I'm sorry to be intruding on your busy schedule," Charles said. He didn't seem too apologetic, either. "But we need to explore every possible lead that comes before us, and your brother has asked that I keep you informed of all new developments for his case."

I shifted uncomfortably in my chair as I tried my best not to stare at her with open hostility. If there was one thing the past few months had taught me, it was that I could trust what animals said far more than I could trust humans. For all we knew, Breanne might just be playing the part of the aggrieved sister, all the while framing her poor brother for a crime she committed.

The most convincing evidence I had to support my theory, of course, was the fact that the happy-go-lucky Yorkie who loved everyone became insecure and defensive when confronted with a mere picture of her.

What else could something like that mean?

I did wish Charles would've been open to the idea of having Nan accompany us. She could have engaged in some of her grade-A sleuthing while Charles and I spoke directly to Breanne. I'd only met this realtor minutes ago and already knew better than to trust a single word that came out of her glossy red mouth.

"Has there been a new development?" Breanne asked, crossing her legs above the knee and staring Charles down. "Go on, tell me about it, then."

Charles glanced toward me and took a deep breath. Oh, gosh, I hope he wasn't planning on telling her about the talking animals or that we now suspected her because of them.

"This is Angie Russo," he said as he gestured toward me.

I smiled and waggled my fingers at her awkwardly.

"She's Blueberry Bay's best paralegal and has recently signed on to help me defend your brother's case."

"That's all well and good," Breanne said with a disappointed shake of her head. "But I hired a lawyer, not a paralegal. With as much as we're paying, Mr. Thompson should really be defending this case himself. Please tell me you didn't request this meeting just to tell me you have a new assistant. That is not news I should have to pay $275 an hour to hear!"

"Don't worry. This visit is off the clock," Charles said with an ingratiating smile. Somehow it actually seemed to work, too.

"Oh?" the pretty realtor said, sitting a little higher in her chair. "Then how can I help you today?"

"In reviewing the discovery with Angie here, we came up with a few new questions regarding the crime scene. Would it be possible for us to have another look around this afternoon?"

"You want to see the house again," she said flatly. "I guess that's fine."

"Great, thank you so much." Charles rose to his feet and extended a hand across the desk. "If you could just give us the key then, we'll be on our way."

"Not so fast," Breanne said as she stood up with him. "The State Licensing Board is already watching me like a hawk. Even if Brock gets off the hook, the fact still remains that the killer could have gained access to the Hayes's home through my lockbox. Someone even suggested that maybe I didn't close it up properly and that's why my clients were murdered. Can you believe that?"

"Tough break," I muttered. Apparently, this was the wrong thing to say.

Breanne's eyes narrowed in on me and she pinched her lips together in quiet contemplation before shifting her gaze back to Charles. "What did you say her name was again?"

"Angie Russo," I answered on my own behalf, purposefully not offering to shake hands on our re-introduction. "Now can we please go see the house?"

Her eyes zipped back to mine, and this time she sneered openly. The two of us stared at each other for a few moments before Breanne finally caved and showed us out of her office.

"We'll meet you at the house in about fifteen minutes," Charles said. "We have a quick pit stop to make first."

"Fine, but please don't be longer than that. I have a lot of paperwork to get through tonight and would prefer not to be up all night."

I didn't say anything until Charles and I were buckled safely back inside his car. "Well, isn't she a peach?" I scoffed.

Charles appeared thoughtful as he watched Breanne pull away in her large cherry red SUV. "She's under a lot of pressure these days. Maybe even worse than her brother," he explained. His expression became almost tender, which made me feel queasy.

"But that doesn't mean she needs to be rude," I argued. "What's your plan for checking out the house, anyway? I thought the whole point of this visit was to find out if Breanne framed her brother for the murders."

"We can't exactly come right out and ask a client if she's guilty, especially since she's not the one we've been hired to defend. I figured we could grab the animals, grab the discovery, and check the place out. After all, you haven't seen the crime scene yet. You might notice something I haven't. Yo-Yo might remember something once we get him back inside."

"Yesterday, Yo-Yo seemed pretty convinced that Breanne was to blame. He even called her 'the bad lady,'" I reminded him.

Charles kept his eyes straight ahead as if gathering his private thoughts, ones he wasn't quite ready to share with me. "Yeah, well, I know Breanne better than you, and I still don't think she did it."

"And I do," I shot back, crossing my arms over my chest like an angry toddler. If I didn't feel threatened by Breanne before, I definitely did now that Charles was going out of his way to defend her despite our evidence against her. It seemed maybe my crush had a little crush of his own.

Maybe Octo-Cat was right. Maybe I needed to find a nice cat person to settle down with and leave pining for Chuck in my past.

But then he smiled a full-on toothy grin, grabbed my hand, and gave it a good squeeze. "Only one way to find out. Let's go."

My breathing hitched in my chest. Oh, yes, I was ready to follow him anywhere. Not just because he was handsome, but also because he was smart, kind, and committed to justice.

And all of that was a good thing, too, since we were heading to the place where two people had recently been murdered...

11

Charles and I pulled up to the Hayes's home some twenty minutes later and found Breanne waiting in her SUV idling in the driveway. When we each exited with an animal sidekick, she scrambled out and slammed the door with more strength than I thought she had in her.

Yo-Yo growled and bared his tiny incisors, but made no effort to escape Charles's arms despite either his anxiety over spending more time with a person he loathed or his unbridled joy at having finally returned home.

"What are you doing with these animals?" Breanne demanded, marching right up to us and blocking our path to the house.

Octo-Cat and I cut across the grass and let ourselves inside, leaving Charles to charm the angry realtor since neither of us would be much help there.

The moment we entered, the sharp tang of chemicals hit my nose.

Octo-Cat smelled it, too, and immediately began rubbing his paw over his face. "*Ew, ew, ew,*" he complained with each step we took further into the house. "You humans sure have a knack for fouling up your environment. I'm not sure how long I'll be able to take this."

"Me either," I said, lifting the collar of my shirt over my face to form an impromptu breathing filter. "I guess they had to give the place an extra deep cleaning after..."

Octo-Cat picked up where my words had trailed off. "The brutal murders? Yeah." His words came out muffled from beneath his paw.

I looked to him, wondering where we should go next, but the cat ignored me. Instead, he lifted his head and bravely sniffed the air, then broke into a trot and headed straight up the stairs without another second's hesitation.

"Wait," I called after him, struggling and failing to keep pace. "Where are you going?"

He didn't answer, but after climbing the stairs myself, I found him sitting in a bedroom at the end of the hallway. The large area was completely devoid of furniture, unlike the other rooms I'd passed through on my way here. It also appeared to be the source for the strong chemical smell, but otherwise the walls and carpeting appeared pristine and untouched.

I felt a little guilty stomping through the room, but that feeling left me when I managed to pry open the windows and let some fresh, non-toxic air into the space.

Octo-Cat hopped up onto the window sill appreciatively. "Now I can breathe again," he said with a contented sigh. "For a while there I thought *I* was going to die in this house, too."

I placed a hand on each hip and stared him down. "Too soon, Octo. Too soon."

He flicked his tail in agitation. "Is my punishment to lose yet another part of my name? What happened to the *Cat* in *Octo-Cat?* Hmmm?"

"I don't know," I answered truthfully, a devious smile creeping across my face. "You're giving everyone new nicknames lately, so I guess I thought I'd try it out, too. Besides, unlike you, I'm trying to lighten the mood a little bit, considering I'm pretty sure this is the room where Bill and Ruth died."

"This is the room where they were *murdered,* you mean," Octo-Cat corrected, taking deliberate care to enunciate the terrible term. "And don't forget the *Cat* next time. It is the most important part of my name."

"Fine, but let's try to focus now. Okay? This is the place two people were killed." I dropped my voice to a whisper just in case Breanne could hear us from outside. I couldn't hear her and had no idea where she, Charles, and Yo-Yo were at the moment, so perhaps we were in good shape for now. Still, it always paid to be extra careful when letting my freak flag fly. "We need to see what we can find out while we're here and have the chance to look around."

"Yes, boss," my tabby said wryly and with another energetic flick of his tail.

A bird chirped in the tree outside the window and immediately drew his attention away. Octo-Cat slowly rose to his feet while keeping his head perfectly still, then wiggled his butt and let out a laughable impression of a bird call.

Rather than tease him, I just rolled my eyes and walked the perimeter of the room. One of us needed to get to work before this golden investigation opportunity completely passed us by. And it seemed that would have to be me.

Tucked into a little nook, I found the door to an impressive walk-in closet. This was the place the bodies had been found, although nothing—other than the chemical smell—hinted at its uncomfortably recent and gruesome history now. It was simply a plain, empty space.

"This is where they were found," Charles said, coming up behind me and causing me to jump in my skin.

"You don't just sneak up on someone in the middle of a crime scene," I hissed, turning toward him so that he could read the displeasure on my face.

His eyebrows pinched together, and his mouth drooped in a frown. Well, at least he looked properly chastised. "Sorry about that. I didn't mean to scare you, but I also worry we don't have much time. Breanne is not happy right now and even threatened to call Thompson and issue a complaint."

I shook my head and took a step back when I realized Charles and I were still standing too near each other for comfort. I had the hots for the guy, sure, but this hardly felt like the time or place. "All because we brought a couple animals with us? Does she even recognize Yo-Yo?"

Upon hearing his name, the Yorkie zipped into the room, running huge looping circles so fast, he was mostly a gray and brown blur.

"Well, someone has the zoomies," Octo-Cat declared, hopping

down from the window sill and joining me and Charles by the closet. "Also he scared my bird away. I almost had it, too."

I decided not to mention that Octo-Cat also got the zoomies from time to time or that there was absolutely no way he was catching that bird—not just because his bird call was extremely unconvincing but also because of the screen window that hung between them. Add to that his whole inability to fly and we had the very definition of an impossible situation.

We watched the Yorkie run joyous circles until he collapsed in an exhausting, panting heap right in the middle of the room.

"What's going on with Breanne?" I asked Charles while Octo-Cat dutifully approached the dog and began a conversation with him.

"She says we're overstepping, and she questions our sanity." His face remained unreadable as he delivered this unwelcome news, but I could guess how he probably felt in that moment.

My heart began to gallop. It was bad enough that Charles knew my secret, but now he was telling others, too? "You didn't tell her about—"

"No," he cut me off. "But I had to tell her something, so I said they were emotional support animals."

Well, no wonder she thought we were crazy. Charles had basically confirmed that for her.

"How long do we have?" I asked, unable to resist the urge to gnaw on one of my many hangnails. I really needed to treat myself to a manicure when this whole thing was over.

"Half an hour, tops," he revealed with another deep frown.

"Then we better get to it." I approached the animals slowly and sat down beside them cross-legged. Hopefully, the chemical smell from the carpet wouldn't rub off on my clothes, but even if it did, it would be a small price to pay for information that would save Brock.

"What did he say?" I asked Octo-Cat while nodding toward our doggie eye witness.

"Lots of things. Too many things," Octo-Cat said, rolling onto his back so that his belly was facing the ceiling. He looked utterly exhausted even though he couldn't have been talking to Yo-Yo for more than two minutes before I interrupted.

"Care to tell me any of them?" I asked, resisting the urge to pet his fluffy tummy. Something told me he was already looking for a reason to bite me as an outlet for his anxiety, and neither of us needed the extra hostility right now.

He yawned, and the smell of the tuna blend breakfast on his breath mixed with the chemicals in the carpet made my stomach churn with bile. "Something about his owners and missing home. He was in the closet. They were in the closet. Yada yada yada."

"What? No *yada yada yada.* What did he say? His exact words, please." I nudged him until he rolled onto his side then forced him to look up and focus on me.

Octo-Cat growled, picked himself up, and moved a couple feet so that he was out of my reach. "I told you everything I could remember. He talks fast. And incessantly, I might add. It just all kind of runs together after a while."

Hmm, kind of like Octo-Cat himself.

I groaned, and Yo-Yo crawled onto my lap to frantically lick my face. "I cannot believe you," I told my naughty kitty. "We came here specifically to investigate the murder and you can't be bothered to pay attention for two minutes?"

"I don't need to lay here and listen to this," Octo-Cat said, pulling himself to his feet with great agitation and trotting out of the room.

Yo-Yo perked up in my lap, then hopped off to give chase.

"Well, I'm guessing we have even less time now," I told Charles, returning to my feet as well. "Where is Breanne hanging out, by the way?"

He stood in the closet studying the walls as if they were the most interesting thing in the whole world. "In her SUV," he mumbled without looking away. "She said she had some calls to make."

I swallowed the giant lump in my throat. We both knew that one of those calls might be to our boss. As much as we needed to make the most of our time here, I also needed to tread lightly as far as my boss was concerned. Mr. Fulton had always been kind and complimentary of my work, but Mr. Thompson—the only partner left at this point—made his dislike of me clear at every possible opportunity.

If Bethany was right about him planning to throw Charles under the bus when it came to this unwinnable case, I had no doubt he'd all too happily discard of me as well.

Sigh. Why were things never easy?

"Should we go after them?" I asked, pointing my chin toward the door through which the animals had just noisily departed.

Charles glanced from me to the door and back again, then shook his head. "In a little bit. First, there's something about the crime scene that's always struck me as a bit odd. Maybe you can help me figure it out." He reached into his messenger bag and pulled out the giant discovery folder from the prosecution.

Just as I feared, he flipped straight to the photos of Bill and Ruth's bloody, lifeless bodies. I hadn't wanted to see these pictures the first time, and I certainly didn't want to see them now.

But I also didn't want to see an innocent man spend the rest of his life in prison, so I grabbed some antacids from my purse, placed one on my tongue, and willed myself to examine the photos that Charles extended out to me now.

I looked closely this time. Carefully. Just as Charles had asked of me.

And wouldn't you know it? We finally found something that might actually help our case.

12

I may not have much experience with murder or crime scenes, but something about those photos jumped out at me.

"Can we lay these out in the closet?" I asked, shoving them back toward Charles.

He nodded, got down on his hands and knees, then matched the photos up to their corresponding spots in the actual physical space. Together, we spent a few minutes making sure the angles were represented perfectly.

"Okay, walk me through this," I said, rubbing my chin with the side of my index finger. "What exactly do we know from the pictures?"

Charles pointed to one on the left-hand side of our spread. "From the angle of the blood splatter, we know that the killer approached his victims from the right."

We both studied the wall, which had once been painted red with blood. Now it was a pristine and perfect white.

"Okay, what else?" I asked, chewing on a fingernail now that the antacid had fully dissolved. I needed something to ground myself in the now so my fears wouldn't get the best of me.

Charles swept his vision across the arc of photographs before turning back toward me. "Well, we believe Bill was killed first and that Ruth was killed a few minutes after when she came to investigate."

I hadn't heard this bit before, but I also hadn't asked for many details about the crime scene, either. One thing was for sure: I definitely needed to work on thickening my skin or at least strengthening my stomach when it came to these things—especially since it seemed investigating murders was becoming something of a habit for me as of late.

I nodded. "Okay. What makes you say that?"

"Bill's blood was more saturated in the carpet and spread further than Ruth's, but really it was a matter of minutes between the murders, so it's hard to say," Charles explained, keeping his voice steady. I wondered if thinking about the brutal killings upset him as much as it upset me. If it did, he certainly didn't make his feelings obvious.

"Hmm," I said, considering my investigative partner just as much as the information he'd presented. After a moment of tense silence, I grabbed a pencil from my purse and did my best to trace the area of blood splatter on the wall. Art was one of my many failed talents, but I did okay considering.

Charles panicked and tried to wrest the pencil away from me. "What are you doing?" he demanded with a look of horror on his handsome face. Although, I had to admit, he seemed less handsome today than he had at the beginning of the week. Maybe I was unconsciously beginning to associate the Hayes's double murder with him, and that definitely wasn't swoon-inducing or crush-worthy.

"Trying to match the evidence to the conclusion." I had to admit, I felt very Sherlock Holmes in that moment. Well, if Holmes had secretly harbored an on-again-off-again crush on Watson. Yeah, I still hadn't found anything groundbreaking, but something told me if we kept following this line of thought, we'd find exactly what we needed to save Brock.

My Watson unfortunately wasn't the most agreeable when it came to my current tactics. He argued, "But Breanne—"

"She's already mad," I said through gritted teeth. "It's not like this will make things any worse."

Charles sighed but moved aside and let me finish my work.

Ignoring the small droplets, I reproduced the outline for the main burst of the blood splatter carefully. A few minutes later, I stepped back, satisfied with the effort.

"Now," I said, brushing my hands off on my pants even though they hadn't gotten the slightest bit dirty. "We need to finish setting the scene. You be Bill, and I'll be the killer. Do you have anything that can work as the hammer?"

"Um..." Charles shifted his weight uncomfortably. He didn't seem to have the slightest idea what I was on about, but I didn't want to waste time explaining, especially when Breanne could barge in and disrupt us any minute.

"Never mind, we can use this." I grabbed Octo-Cat's neon leash and folded it over several times to approximate the length of a standard hammer, then tied it in place with a hair tie on each end. "Got any sticky notes in there?"

Charles fumbled around in his bag, then pulled out a mini pad of brightly colored notes, which he promptly handed to me. "Never know when these might come in handy," he said with a shrug. "In fact, I still don't know how they're going to help right now, but I'm ready to find out."

"Good," I said, eyeing him carefully for a moment. He smiled instead of grimacing, which I took as a win. "Now go lay down the way Bill was found and in the same spot, too."

He did, lowering himself gently down onto his stomach and reaching his arms overhead at odd angles. It was eerie, seeing him there sprawled out like the victim from our photos—especially since my mind automatically filled in the missing details like the blood and the giant, blossoming bruises.

I shook my head to clear my mental Etch-a-Sketch of that gruesome picture, then picked up the photo of Bill's prone body and put a series of sticky notes on Charles's back and head in the same spots where the hammer had wounded Bill. There were three in total—one near the base of his neck, one on the side of his face, and the last on his upper back near his shoulder.

"Okay. Now stand up," I instructed, taking a big step back to give him space.

Charles did without saying anything. I could tell he was intrigued and also wanted to see where this was going.

"How tall was Bill?" I asked as I motioned for my colleague to turn around so that I could study his back from behind.

"About five foot ten," he answered after a brief moment's thought.

"And how tall are you?"

"Six feet even."

"Now how tall is Brock?"

"Six-four."

I kept all these numbers in my head, adding my height of five foot seven to the mix as I brought my makeshift murder weapon up and down on each of the sticky notes. I caught each shot with the camera on my phone.

"Okay. You can turn around now." I made a quick trip to the app store to download a measuring app while I explained the next steps to Charles. "Brock is six inches taller than Bill. So now we're going to make me six inches taller than you. Can you crouch to about *yea*-high?"

I drew the phone from the floor to about my shoulder height and held it there while Charles got into position. He was a bit shaky as I redid my measurements and snapped pictures of each.

"Now check these out with me," I said, helping him back to his feet so we could both examine the six new photos on my phone. "These first three photos are from when we were both at our normal height, and the next three are from us recreating the height difference between Bill and Brock. What do you notice?"

Charles grabbed the phone from me excitedly and flipped back and forth reviewing each photo several times, then we placed my phone onto the floor next to the crime scene photos of Bill. He looked from the walls where I'd traced the path of the blood splatter and back to the pictures.

"Given the angle of the blood splatter and placement of the wounds, the first pictures look much more accurate."

I nodded. "If Brock had landed these blows on Bill, he would have needed to angle his wrists awkwardly like this and taken a wide, golf-like swing. It would have been much more natural—and more effective—to hit him from above."

"So you think someone shorter committed the crime?"

"I do, but let's recreate Ruth's death before deciding for sure."

We went through all the same motions again, with me playing the victim this time. Ruth had only needed one blow to go down and it was directly to the top of her skull.

"See," I told Charles as we were going through the resulting photos. "Why would the murderer hit Ruth over the top of the head and not Bill?"

"Because he couldn't reach on Bill," Charles answered excitedly.

I nodded, happy to see that my companion both understood and supported my theory. "Actually, I'm pretty sure the culprit is a she. Or a very short man. In any case, it's not Brock."

"So we're looking for someone about..." His eyes found and held mine.

"My height, yup," I confirmed.

Charles grabbed the discovery folder and flipped through it quickly, mumbling the names of each witness and person of interest as he went. "It couldn't be Brock. Also couldn't be Bill's boss. Both are too tall."

I already knew exactly who this new evidence implicated, but I needed Charles to arrive there on his own.

"Almost everyone is either too tall or too short to be considered," he murmured while stashing the folder back in his bag.

"We know at least one person related to this case who's exactly my height," I pointed out.

"Breanne," Charles said with a sigh. "I was afraid of that."

A series of footsteps stomped up the staircase, causing us to share a horrified expression. We knew exactly who had come to find us now.

"Okay, time's up!" Breanne called, charging angrily into the room and growing even more livid when she found Charles and me sitting on the closet floor with the crime scene photos and a matching pair of guilty expressions on our faces.

"What are you doing?" she demanded, placing a hand on each hip. "And where are your animals?"

Uh-oh. This was not good. Not good at all.

13

I bolted out of that room so fast, Breanne couldn't have stopped me if she'd tried. Maybe I was being a bit overdramatic, but I didn't feel like being trapped in the same small, enclosed space with a possible killer. Her arrival also reminded me that I hadn't heard from the animals in quite some time, and I had no idea whether they'd somehow managed to escape outside.

Luckily, I found Octo-Cat almost right away. He stood on top of the fridge with his fur puffed up and his expression angry. Yo-Yo whined and stood on his hind legs scratching the surface of the refrigerator in his desperation to reach the cat.

"Why did you abandon me?" Octo-Cat raged.

I put my hands up in surrender. "Hey, you're the one who left in the middle of our investigation. You could have come back at any time."

"Not with Dum-Dum cornering me here," he ground out.

I knew he was irritated, but so was I. He was supposed to be finding a way to connect with our doggie witness, and that clearly had not happened.

"So, I'm guessing you did nothing useful this whole time?" I asked with a frustrated sigh.

His angry, unblinking eyes fixed right on me. "I defended my life and my dignity, and that is the most important thing of all."

I shook my head and bent down to collect Yo-Yo. "We have to go," I whispered to Octo-Cat. "And when the other humans come downstairs, I have to stop talking to you."

"What's that?" Breanne asked, appearing suddenly at the foot of the stairs. Seriously, what was it with people sneaking up on me in this house? It gave me the heebie jeebies big time.

"Just telling them it's time to go," I answered truthfully.

Charles joined us a few moments later. "I was just gathering our things," he said, handing me Octo-Cat's bundled up leash. "And telling Breanne that I would be happy to apply a new coat of paint myself."

Right, to cover the huge damage I'd made with my light pencil marks.

"I hired you to make things easier for me. Not harder," Breanne said with a scowl.

"Sorry," I apologized for all of us. "It was one-hundred percent my fault."

Breanne regarded me coldly. "Oh, I know. That's why I want you off my brother's case."

A pit of fear formed deep in my stomach. This wasn't supposed to be happening. Charles and I were supposed to take our new theory about the killer's height and use it to clear Brock and save the day just in time. That would be much, much harder if Breanne stood in our way.

How could I explain this all without making her angrier? I didn't know, but I at least had to try. "But..."

"But nothing. All you're doing is making a mess of my sale property and distracting my lawyer from the job he's supposed to be doing."

"Brock's lawyer," I corrected without thinking.

Breanne fumed, stomping a heeled foot on the kitchen tile for added emphasis. "Yep. I definitely never want to see you again or your therapy animals. I'll also be having a talk with Mr. Thompson about my grave disappointment with his firm's performance to date."

I gulped and forced myself to keep quiet even though my instinct was to either defend myself or accuse her. Yo-Yo tensed in my arms and growled at Breanne.

"What is it with small scrappy dogs and their hatred for me?" Breanne asked flippantly as she shoved our entire party toward the door. "The homeowners had one just like this. It was the most irritating thing. Definitely reminded me why I'm a cat person."

"Did she say cat person?" Octo-Cat asked, quickening his pace so he could rub against the realtor's ankles. The whole thing was uncomfortably flirtatious, and I seriously had no idea what my tabby expected to gain from such an exchange. "I think I like this one," he purred.

Breanne bent down to pet his striped head, softening a bit as she stroked his silky fur.

"Oh, yeah! I like her very much!" Octo-Cat said, flipping onto his side and presenting his belly. What a traitor.

She sighed. "I guess I can hold off on the call to Thompson, if only for this little cutie. But I still don't want you working on my case anymore."

"Noted," I answered coolly.

"What was that about?" I demanded once Charles, the animals, and I were tucked securely back in his car.

"What?" Octo-Cat shrugged, still calm and collected since the car hadn't begun to move yet. "Sometimes a guy just needs a little bit of attention from a pretty lady. Besides, I really saved your butt back there, so I wouldn't be complaining if I were you."

I groaned and shook my head. If I wasn't careful, I'd soon have a killer migraine.

"What did he say?" Charles asked, gesturing toward Octo-Cat with his chin.

"Never mind," I murmured.

Charles didn't push me any further on that, but he did ask, "Where to now? I think we need some time to catch up with the animals, and I doubt they'd be welcomed back at the firm."

"No," I agreed thoughtfully. "But I know somewhere even better we can go. Take a left out of here."

* * *

Nan answered the door in a rose-printed kimono so long it pooled at her feet. Her all-white hair clung to her jawline in a stylish bob that included a thick shelf of bangs that fell just above her brow.

"Looking good," I said, pushing straight into her house. This had been my home until about six months ago, when Nan had forced me to get a place of my own as part of the whole growing up thing. Even still, I visited her at least a couple times per week. She wasn't just the woman who'd raised me, but she was also my best friend and the person I trusted most in this entire world.

That's why I'd brought everyone here now.

Both animals followed me inside as I hooked a thumb back at Charles. "This is Charles. He's the head attorney on the case you helped me with the other day."

Wow, had it really only been two days since our dead-end trip to the printing company? *Unreal.*

"He's cute," Nan said, batting her eyelashes.

Charles cleared his throat and glanced toward the ground, which gave me the giggles. Nan had always been a shameless flirt, but she did it for fun, not to land a date. It had been more than ten years since Gramps passed on to a better place, and she hadn't taken on a boyfriend since. I doubted she'd make an exception for Charles, no matter how handsome we both found him. Besides, she'd no doubt soon associate him with the Hayes's double murder the way I did now.

Turning back toward me, Nan asked, "Here to work on the case?"

"Yup, you up for helping us out?" I led our party into the dining room as it had the best work area to seat all of us.

"Oh, dear, you know me," she answered, making eyes at Charles again. "I'm always up for anything."

He blushed, not quite knowing what to do with the geriatric flirt. "Actually, I'm not sure..."

"You can trust Nan," I insisted.

"I'll sign a Non-Disclosure Agreement," she added.

Charles looked trapped, but ultimately agreed with a shrug. "Fine," he said. "Do you have a printer I can use to print that NDA for you?"

Nan led him to the little office she kept upstairs, then returned to join me and the animals in the formal dining room. "Does he know about...?" She widened her eyes at Octo-Cat. "Well, you know."

"I'm afraid he does," I said with a groan. That was probably another reason why Charles and I could never become an item.

Nan sucked air through her teeth and shook her head in disappointment. "You shouldn't just go around blabbing your secret, dear. It's really not wise."

"Trust me, I didn't." I took a quick moment to catch her up on the whole blackmail scenario.

When Charles returned with his printed form, Nan hit him on the chest.

"Ouch," he mumbled. "What was that for?"

"You're lucky my granddaughter is such a forgiving person. If you ever blackmail her again, though, you'll have to answer to someone much less forgiving. Me." She pulled herself onto tiptoe and stared at him menacingly despite her small stature.

"Yes, ma'am," he answered at once as he clutched the NDA to his chest defensively. He almost looked afraid to offer it to Nan now.

I rolled my eyes at them both. "Enough posturing. We've got a lot of work to do and not much time to do it."

Charles unpacked his messenger bag and began to lay out papers on the table, while Nan excused herself to make a pot of coffee. I took the opportunity to head to Nan's little office so that I could print out the photos I had taken while at the Hayes's house.

When I returned, Octo-Cat sat in the middle of the table, shedding all over everything as he flopped his tail back and forth.

"He wouldn't move," Charles told me with a frown.

"Keeping myself front and center is the best way to ensure you protect me from Dum-Dum," Octo-Cat explained. "I don't want you getting so caught up in your work that you forget all about the handsome cat who made this all possible."

Ugh, he was so vain. And even more stubborn.

"What did I tell you about calling him Dum-Dum?" I asked in irritation.

Octo-Cat yawned unapologetically. "Hey, I calls 'em like I sees 'em."

"Well, if you're not going to cooperate with us, then we're not going to cooperate with you. Oh, Yo-Yo!" I called, grabbing the cat and placing him on the floor so that the dog could slobber him with kisses.

Octo-Cat screeched, got puffy-tailed, and fled in the direction of the kitchen, shouting kitty curses the whole way.

Nan appeared a couple minutes later, holding the tabby in her arms and stroking him kindly. “What did you do to this poor guy?” she demanded.

“Don’t believe a word he says,” I shot back. “He is not the victim he makes himself out to be.”

“Oh, hush. He’s just an innocent little kitty,” Nan argued, peppering the smug feline with kisses. Even though she couldn’t talk to animals the way I can, sometimes it felt like it. This was one of those times.

Charles couldn’t help but chuckle. “How does it feel when the tables are turned on you, *hmmm?*”

Octo-Cat laughed, too, but not kindly. “Your nan likes me better than you,” he teased, then actually had the audacity to stick his tongue out at me to add an extra layer of awfulness.

Nan put him down on the table, then returned to the kitchen to fetch the coffee.

“See?” Octo-Cat said. “If you won’t appreciate me, I can always find someone else who does.”

I picked him up again and was ready to give him back to Yo-Yo when Nan returned and scolded me. “You leave that handsome boy alone. He’s such a good cat. Isn’t he?”

Octo-Cat laughed again and immediately moved to Nan’s side of the table where he snuggled up against her chest and purred at a ridiculous volume.

“By the way, here’s your form,” she said, pushing the Non-Disclosure Agreement in Charles’s direction. “Now catch me up on the case.”

I took a deep breath and explained everything.

"*Huh,*" Nan said, sitting back in her chair pensively. "You sure have a doozy on your hands, but I think I have an idea."

I couldn't wait to hear what she had to say.

14

All eyes zoomed to Nan, even Yo-Yo's despite the fact he still didn't know what we were investigating, and I was pretty sure he couldn't understand any of us humans, either.

"Well, here's what I think..." my eccentric grandmother said, placing the Yorkie in her lap, much to Octo-Cat's annoyance.

He skittered across the table and back to my side. "Yuck. Dog germs," he said with an exaggerated twitch.

"I think," Nan continued in a baby voice directed at Yo-Yo. "That nobody's tried buttering this little guy up. You keep putting him in all these excitable situations and expecting him to be able to perform. Why not spend a little time getting to know him, making him feel comfortable, and then broaching the...?"

She hesitated before deciding on the word she needed to finish her sentence. "Um, conversation," Nan concluded with an awkward smile.

Charles and I looked to each other and shrugged.

"I guess it's worth a try," I said with a quick nod. I'd hoped she would stay with me and Charles to study the photos and files some more, but once Nan had an idea, it was hard to get her to focus on anything else. Actually, she was kind of like Yo-Yo in that way.

"Great." Nan stood, still clutching the terrier to her chest delicately. "You two get back to your work with those grisly photos, and I'll work on plying the key witness."

"We don't actually know that he saw anything. It's possible that —" Charles corrected, but stopped short when I placed a hand on his wrist and shook my head.

"Just let her do her thing, and we'll do ours," I said. "Now help me pull out the testimonies of all the women involved in the case—officers, witnesses, friends, neighbors, coworkers, anyone we have."

We shuffled through the papers, having all but memorized the order of the statements and evidence. It didn't even take five minutes to pull out the documents we needed.

"Now," I said, appraising our work. "Are there any men that we know for sure are my height or shorter?"

Charles thought for a few moments before handing me a couple of additional files. "This one is a colleague of Bill's from Bayside Printing Company, and that's one of the potential buyers from the open house."

I fanned everything out before us, attempting to group similar people together. We had one group for colleagues, one for people from the open house, one for friends and family, and one for miscellaneous folks who had somehow been called into the case, such as police officers or crime scene cleaners. Most documents weren't official testimonies at all, but rather bio sheets Charles had made himself before I joined the case.

"Let's go through them all one at a time," Charles suggested, reaching for the colleagues stack. We spent the next hour talking through each person and taking notes about who had either means, motive, or opportunity. For those that had more than one of those, we added a star to their sheet and placed them in a new pile.

After all that work, we were left staring at our two most probable suspects: the daughter and the realtor, Michelle Hayes and Breanne Calhoun.

I sighed and leaned back against my chair. "I keep hoping the facts will line up differently, but it really looks like one of these two is to blame."

Charles crossed his arms and shook his head, staring me directly in the eye as he defended our—or at least my—prime suspect. "No way. I know Breanne can be a bit brusque, but she didn't do it."

"Maybe so," I said, even though I still hadn't even come close to clearing the rude realtor in my mind. I like to think I learned my lesson from investigating Ethel Fulton's death. I'd been so convinced of who the killer was that I wouldn't even consider anyone else—and ended up putting myself in a very dangerous position besides.

Still, from everything I'd seen and heard so far, Breanne made sense. Maybe if I eased Charles into this realization a little more slowly, he'd put his hesitation aside and finally see things my way.

"Okay, so then let's discuss the daughter. How do you explain the fact that Michelle has more or less disappeared into thin air?"

"She hasn't disappeared," Charles argued this point, too. If we kept disagreeing over every single possibility, we might as well hand over Brock's conviction now.

"She's just not answering our calls," he said, tapping his pen on the table and frazzling my nerves.

"Okay, then where is she?" I demanded, grabbing the pen and moving it out of his reach.

Charles sighed and folded his hands in front of him. "At her college up state."

"Well, given that we have no other leads to pursue, I think I know where we're headed next."

"It will be a waste of time," he insisted with another heady sigh.

"Charles," I said gently. "Please. We have nothing else at this point. We at least have to try. For Brock."

"Fine. For Brock," he answered in defeat.

"Good," I said, even though his lack of enthusiasm made it an empty victory. "Let me go check with Nan and Yo-Yo. C'mon, Octo-Cat." I roused my tabby from his nap and motioned for him to follow me.

"Are we finally getting somewhere with all of this?" my cat asked after letting out a massive yawn.

"Soon, I hope," I said diplomatically.

Charles groaned and laid his forehead on the table as we walked away.

"Oh, hi, dears!" Nan cried as Octo-Cat and I joined her in the living room. "Yo-Yo and I are having a great time getting to know each other out here. Aren't we, boy?"

The terrier barked, and Nan praised him profusely.

"Well, she's lost at least ten points in my book," Octo-Cat said drolly. "It's always a shame when a good human falls to the dog side. I must say, I never expected this kind of betrayal from Nan. You, maybe, but definitely not her."

"She's not changing allegiances," I said as he jumped to the back of the couch and settled in. "She's just doing what she can to help out."

"Says you," he complained, shaking his head in disgust.

"Is everything okay?" Nan asked with a quick glance toward the perturbed kitty.

"It's fine, or at least it will be. Hey, Octo-Cat," I called to get his attention again.

"What?" he whined, mid-paw lick.

"You can take a bath later," I scolded. "The whole point of us coming out here was to see if Yo-Yo has anything new to say. Could you please ask him if he remembers anything new?"

"No, not like that," Nan interjected, continuing to pet the Yorkie enthusiastically. "Tell him his new friend Nan would like to know if anyone has hurt his family that he can remember and if he can tell us about it."

"Barf," Octo-Cat responded before shouting, "Hey, Dum-Dum!"

The terrier's head immediately snapped toward him. It definitely didn't help that Yo-Yo had started responding to the cat's cruel nick-name for him.

Octo-Cat asked his question exactly as Nan had worded it, which caused the other animal to whimper and bury his face in

Nan's lap. The fact that he wasn't yipping in terror was definitely progress.

My bored-looking cat nodded as he listened to the little dog, who had now lifted his head to look directly at Octo-Cat as he made sad puppy noises.

When Yo-Yo grew quiet again, Octo-Cat said, "Wow. I'm actually really surprised that worked."

I sat up straighter in my excitement. "What did he say?"

"He said it was really dark that night and he couldn't see well, but the person who hurt his mom and dad had red hair. He also wants to know when he can go back to his family."

The poor dog still didn't know he wouldn't be seeing his parents again, but he had finally given us enough to finish clicking all the pieces together. Red hair could only mean…

"So it was Breanne!" I shouted triumphantly. "I knew it!"

"Good kitty," I called back to Octo-Cat as I marched back to Charles in the dining room.

"Do not call me kitty," Octo-Cat growled after me, but from the note of happiness in his voice, I could tell the correction was just to remain consistent in his attempts to train me out of certain behaviors he didn't much appreciate.

"Did you hear?" I said, placing a palm on each side of the table and leaning toward Charles, who still looked utterly defeated.

"You think it was Breanne," he answered. When he lifted his head, one of our case documents was stuck to his cheek. "Why?"

"Yo-Yo doesn't know they're dead, but he remembers them

getting hurt. He said it was late at night, which matches up with what we know about the crime."

Charles finally looked as excited as I felt. "And?"

"He said it was dark so he couldn't see well, but that the person who hurt them had red hair. That could only be Breanne."

"Think again," Charles said, pulling out his phone and browsing through his email. When he handed it back to me, there was a young woman with bright red locks who looked vaguely familiar even though I wasn't sure I'd ever seen her before.

"Who's that?" I demanded.

"That's Michelle Hayes."

Uh oh.

We stared at each other for a moment before I finally came up with an argument. "But wouldn't Yo-Yo recognize his own sister?" I sputtered.

Charles frowned. "Not necessarily. Especially if it was too dark to make things out clearly."

"So what now?" I asked, gnawing on one of my few untouched fingernails as nerves overtook me.

"Road trip!" Nan cried from the other room.

Charles nodded. "It's our last shot at solving this in time to stop your mother's story."

Shoot, he was right. Even though just minutes earlier I'd been the one insisting we pay Michelle a visit, I felt much more anxious knowing that she may actually be the killer.

15

FRIDAY

The next morning, I woke up before Octo-Cat for what was probably one of the first times ever in our strange relationship. The alarm on my phone sounded at five thirty and I had to nudge him awake so that we could both get ready for the long day ahead.

In hindsight, I really wished we had gone to bed earlier the night before, but when Mom joined us at Nan's, we all wanted to hear her opinion on the progress we'd made so far.

"I have to admit," she told us, shaking her head. "It really seems like you're right about Brock not having done it."

Mom offered to hold the story longer, but I insisted that she wouldn't have to. We would solve this thing before the six o'clock news was set to air, and we'd give her the exclusive true story, too.

Charles didn't share my optimism, but he did agree to wake up before dawn so we could make the long drive to Michelle's college where we'd grill her live and in person so we could finally uncover the important answers we'd been missing all this time.

Predictably, Yo-Yo was excited for our big road trip, even though we hadn't told him we were going to see his human sister.

I'd offered Octo-Cat the opportunity to stay at home, but he refused to get left out of the action. This worried me, because he had made zero progress in dealing with his car phobia and we had a very long drive ahead of us that day. Because I knew it would be impossible to change his mind, I decided to help him out. With his permission, I slipped some crushed-up medicine into his morning meal. It was just the kitty Benadryl his vet had previously prescribed in case of emergency, but it did cause him to snooze for a large part of our journey—and for that, everyone was very thankful indeed.

He really did look like an angel when he wasn't insulting me, or clawing me, or questioning my life choices in general. And I suspected he was also starting to enjoy our crime-solving gig, even though for the time being it included a dog.

Nan joined us for the road trip, too. Yes, now that she'd been brought up to speed, she insisted on coming along for the ride. "In case Yo-Yo needs a friend," she'd said, making me wonder why I was the one who'd gained the ability to talk to animals when it seemed she was the one who understood them so much better.

Despite trying hard not to, I snoozed for part of the trip right along with Octo-Cat. After all, I didn't have Bethany to make coffee for me, and I'd already thrown out my home coffee maker for fear of sustaining another near-death experience, or worse—gaining weird, new superpowers. Luckily, Nan was more than happy to keep Charles company while Octo-Cat and I caught up on our beauty sleep.

"Rise and shine!" Nan shouted from behind me, forcing me to wake up again. Yes, indeed, the previously absent sun was now shining bright and high in the sky.

"We're here," Charles announced, maneuvering his car into the guest parking lot that serviced our suspect's small liberal arts college.

"So what's the game plan?" Nan asked eagerly, leaning forward with a hand on the edge of each of our seats.

"Didn't you figure out the plan on the way over?" I asked in irritation. If I'd have known they were just going to shoot the breeze, I never would have allowed myself to nod off when there was still work to be done.

"Route One is lovely this time of year," Nan answered in a cheery tone. "We were too busy admiring the scenery to worry about what we'd do when we got here. Besides, you seem to be the designated worrier of the bunch. So, why don't you make the plan?"

I slapped a palm against my forehead. "I guess that's what I get for sleeping on the job."

Octo-Cat woke up and yawned in my face, sending a giant whiff of tuna breath straight up my nostrils. Let me tell you, it worked better than a double shot of espresso to snap me wide awake.

"It's a small college, so I guess let's just ask around," I said with a sigh, hating that this was now our plan. Then I realized we had one very distinct advantage we hadn't considered yet. "Maybe it's time to let Yo-Yo in on who we're here to see. He may even be able to sniff her out for us."

Before Charles had a chance to either agree or disagree, Octo-Cat relayed the message to the Yorkie, who responded immediately and with great enthusiasm to the idea.

"He's ready," Octo-Cat said as he stretched his legs and spine to finish waking up himself. Miraculously, he only hissed at me once while I worked the harness onto him.

Nan had a much harder time readying Yo-Yo, who continuously threw himself against the car door in his eagerness to reunite with Michelle.

Once both animals were safely leashed, we were on our way. As we walked around the seaside campus, it struck me that we were probably one of the strangest groups of five who'd ever wandered these paths. It was still only about nine in the morning, which meant the campus was mostly empty, but that didn't stop the people we did come across from sending pointed stares our way.

I smiled at each as they passed, but by the time the third or fourth person grimaced our way without so much as a proper "good morning," I'd had enough.

"So what if I'm walking my cat on a leash?" I called, holding my chin high. They couldn't possibly judge me any harsher than I already judged myself. "He likes to get some fresh air, too. And why should dogs have all the fun?"

"Yes!" Octo-Cat cheered, skipping a little as he ran beside me. "Now you get it. You finally get it!"

Yo-Yo stopped abruptly and went rigid, making the same pointing gesture he'd taken on when first seeing the sign for Calhoun Realty. This time his gaze was fixed on a three-story stone building that lay across a neat and tidy lawn.

He woofed once, twice, then stopped.

"He says his sister is in that building," Octo-Cat translated.

"Is that a dorm?" I asked my human companions.

Charles jogged around the front and read the sign. "Yes, it is," he said when he returned, not even the least bit winded from the tiny burst of exercise.

"He wants to see his sister," Octo-Cat said as the Yorkie began to whimper and pad his paws on the ground impatiently.

"I'm going in," Nan said, forging confidently ahead.

"Wait. Why you?" Charles demanded.

"None of us are relatives, but I'd wager whatever security they have in this place is far less likely to question a kindly old lady." Nan paused for a moment. When neither of us argued with her, she straightened her posture and asked, "The mark's name is Michelle Hayes, right?"

The mark? What? Had Nan been watching those con man adventure movies again? She was really getting way too into this.

Now that I was awake enough to notice things a bit better, I realized that she had actually put together an elderly granny costume, complete with a knitted shawl and a high-waisted skirt. The ensemble was so very not her that it could only be intentional. She'd had this plan all along but hadn't told me because she'd known I'd argue about her forging ahead alone.

Well, she was right about that much.

“I’m coming with you,” I said, handing Octo-Cat’s leash to Charles before trailing after her.

Charles grabbed me by my shoulder, forcing me to stop short. “She’s right. We’ll wait here until you come back or text us.”

Nan nodded.

Charles nodded.

I groaned and motioned for Nan to carry on her way. “Are they even going to let Yo-Yo into the dorms?” I called after her.

“Only one way to find out,” Charles answered as we both watched Nan turn the corner to the front of the building.

“I don’t like this,” I pouted. “And I don’t think Michelle did it.”

“Yes, we’ve established what you think,” my companion said with a groan.

“It’s not just that I think Breanne’s hiding something,” I explained. “I mean, why would Michelle kill her own parents? And wouldn’t Yo-Yo have recognized his own sister?”

“I don’t know,” Charles answered coolly. “But you’re the one who insisted we come out here. Remember?”

“Only so we can eliminate Michelle and see if she has any direct proof that points to Breanne,” I reminded him. Yes, I’d vowed not to jump to conclusions after my wrong assumptions nearly got me killed on the last case, but this was different. Yo-Yo had more or less identified Breanne already, and she was still the only person in the whole world he seemed to dislike. That had to be more than a simple coincidence.

Charles seemed far less convinced. “Well, I guess we’ll see,” he said with a shrug.

“Yeah, I guess we will.”

Neither of us said anything more as we waited for Nan to return, although I sent out a quiet prayer that she’d have a ready and willing partner to help us finish our investigation once and for all.

Time was ticking away fast.

16

Nan reappeared about fifteen minutes later. At her side stood a fiery-haired, freckle-faced girl wearing pajama pants that had been liberally patterned with smiling cartoon tacos.

"Hello, darlings," Nan sang out proudly. "This is Mitch Hayes."

"Yeah. Nobody's called me Michelle since grade school," the college student explained before plopping a kiss right on Yo-Yo's fuzzy head. The little dog looked as if he were floating on a cloud as Mitch hugged and doted on him.

"Thanks for coming out to talk to us," Charles said. He rose and offered his hand to Mitch, and she struggled to adjust the terrier in her arms to accept his greeting, leading to a rather awkward introduction.

"Why weren't you answering any calls?" I demanded. Maybe I

was being a tad rude, but none of us had time to waste if we wanted to meet my mother's deadline for clearing Brock.

The girl shrugged. "I dropped my phone in a toilet a couple weeks ago and haven't felt the need to replace it since I'm pretty much always on my computer or tablet, anyway."

"But why not return any of the many, many calls from people trying to get in touch with you?" Charles asked, crooking his eyebrow.

"I was sick of people calling to make themselves feel better about offering condolences while only making me feel worse with the constant reminders that my parents are dead." She buried her face in the Yorkie's fur and mumbled, "Maybe I don't want to talk about the fact my parents were murdered in cold blood."

Nan placed an arm around Mitch and pulled her in close. "You two can stop with the third degree now. Mitch doesn't have to help us, but she's kindly agreed to anyhow."

"Thank you, Mitch," I said, offering a smile I hoped would get through to her. "We do really appreciate it."

She kicked at the ground and kept her eyes focused there. "So you really think this Brock guy is innocent?"

I placed a gentle hand on her shoulder and waited for her to look up at me. "We know he is."

She shivered beneath my hand and her face took on a new pallor. "That means the person who killed my parents is still out there."

I let go of her shoulder and grabbed my shoulder instead. "Yeah."

"Tell me what you need me to do." Mitch set her mouth in a determined line, her brows furrowed in anger.

"Over here." Charles cleared his throat and motioned for everyone to sit on a nearby retaining wall. "We need you to tell us anything that could help us identify the real killer."

Poor Mitch looked a bit lost. "But you have my statement, right? I already told the cops everything I could think of."

"We do, but do you mind if we ask you a few more questions in light of recent things we've learned?" Charles asked, reaching into his bag. I seriously hoped he didn't plan to pull out the crime scene photos right now. Mitch shouldn't have to see that.

Even before Charles could find what he was searching for, a sudden burst of tears fell from the girl's bright blue eyes.

"Oh for goodness's sake, you two. Slow down a bit. Can't you see this is hard on her?" Nan grumbled, pressing the girl's head into her shoulder. "You just go ahead and cry all the tears you need to cry. That's right. Nan is here for you now."

Yo-Yo whined and licked his sister's face, offering a hesitant tail wag.

As I watched them and tried to come up with a new way to approach questioning Mitch, Octo-Cat pawed at my shoulder.

"Excuse me," he said, shocking me with his sudden politeness. "Dum-Du—I mean, *the dog* says he remembers who hurt his owners now. Also, he says he thinks his humans might even be dead."

"He remembers?" I asked, not even caring when Mitch lifted her head to study us curiously. "I thought he said it was too dark to see."

"Yes, but he smelled everything just fine, and apparently remembers who it was now," Octo-Cat explained slowly.

Yo-Yo fixed his eyes on me and gave an urgent bark.

"So, yeah." Octo-Cat dropped his voice to a hissy whisper and leaned in close. "Can I finally just tell him already?"

"Tell him what? Oh..." That his owners are dead. Yo-Yo still didn't know for sure. I nodded my agreement. "Yeah, I think it's time."

Octo-Cat spoke to Yo-Yo calmly and much kinder than he ever had before. When he'd said all he needed to say, I waited for the inevitable high-pitched screeching and crazy escape attempts from Yo-Yo, but he just let out a soft whimper and snuggled in closer to Mitch.

"Why isn't he freaking out?" I asked my cat.

Octo-Cat had something akin to respect written across his face. I couldn't be one-hundred percent sure, since I'd never seen him make that expression before and it didn't seem likely I'd ever see it again, either.

"He wants to be strong for his human," he told me.

I brought a hand to my chest and said, "Awww, that's so sweet."

Octo-Cat shrugged his little kitty shoulders. "Yeah, dogs might not be the smartest, but they are loyal. I guess that's their one redeeming quality."

Yo-Yo licked Mitch a few more times, then untangled himself from her arms and came to sit right next to me. He let out a string of four or five barks, keeping his eyes trained on me the whole time he spoke.

"He didn't see much, but he remembers her smell now," Octo-Cat said. He lifted a paw to his mouth, but then thought better of beginning a new grooming session at this key investigative moment and dropped his paw back to the ground.

"Her, right." So far everything was lining up with what Charles and I already knew—or at least theorized—and things weren't looking very good for our realtor friend. "Who was it?"

Sure enough, Octo-Cat confirmed my suspicions with what he said next. "He says it was the lady selling the house."

"Breanne, I knew it!" I shouted before turning to Charles. "Give me that picture of Breanne from her flyer, please."

He stared at me wordlessly for a moment before finally reaching into his messenger bag and retrieving the requested photo.

"Is this her?" I asked, holding the paper up to Yo-Yo.

He let out a bark that quickly turned into a growl.

"See!" I said, shoving the paper back at Charles. "You let your crush on Breanne blind you to the truth. It was her this whole time."

Octo-Cat pawed me again. This time with a bit of claw.

"Ouch!" I cried. "What now?"

"That's not what he said," he told me with a smug smirk.

Not Breanne? How could that possibly be? We already knew it wasn't Mitch. Glendale wasn't very big. How many five foot seven redheaded killers could we possibly have in our small town?

I widened my eyes at him, waiting.

"He said it wasn't the lady on the paper," Octo-Cat explained, visibly losing patience with each word. "It was the other one."

"What?" I asked as my heart crashed to my feet. "All this just to find out it really was Brock all along?"

Octo-Cat turned to the terrier, and the two spoke quietly back and forth for a couple minutes before he looked back to me.

"Not the man," he said. "The other lady."

"Charles," I said, reaching out my hand. "Give me a photo of Brock to show Yo-Yo."

Mitch, who'd kept quiet during this whole exchange until now, piped up. Her eyes were wide and unblinking as she asked, "Are you actually talking with that cat?"

"It gets less weird the more you're around it," Nan explained with a kind chuckle.

"Looks like the cat's out of the bag," Charles added with a laugh that was way too generous for his bad joke.

I didn't have the time to worry about some college student learning my secret. I was so close to figuring this out, and just in the nick of time, too. We only had about ten hours before my mom's story would run. Maybe—just maybe—it would actually be enough.

Charles held up the picture of Brock, and Yo-Yo made a high-pitched yipping noise.

"Not him," Octo-Cat translated.

"Then who does he mean when he says it's the other one?" I complained. Something just wasn't clicking. Maybe Yo-Yo wasn't the key to solving the case, after all.

"Brock *is* the other one," I insisted, speaking to Octo-Cat but keeping my gaze on Yo-Yo as I did so. "Who else is there?"

"I'm calling Breanne," Charles announced already mid-dial.

"Give me that," I said, yanking his cell phone right out of his hand.

"Hello?" Breanne answered full of an energy and friendliness I certainly hadn't heard from her before.

I caught the eye of each of my companions and raised a finger to my lips to let them know they needed to be quiet. "Hello, Breanne. It's me, Angie Russo, the paralegal on your brother's case."

"I thought I told you I didn't want you working on it anymore," she growled, every ounce of kindness having evaporated within a split second.

"I'm off the case after today," I explained quickly. "But Charles asked me to drive up to Michelle Hayes's school and see if I could find her. She only had a few minutes before her class started, but she told me the realtor did it."

Yeah, like I was about to confess my strange abilities to someone who already hated me.

"Impossible," Breanne spat back. "I didn't do it, and neither did my brother. It's awfully funny that she's blaming me now when she swore she didn't have a clue in her statement to the police."

I made a tight fist and then let it go, bracing myself for what came next. "If you didn't, then who did? I mean, who else could she possibly mean?"

Breanne made a series of infuriated noises that started with a huff and ended with a yell. "That's it! I'm definitely calling Mr. Thompson to file an official complaint."

"Please just answer the question," I insisted, praying she wouldn't hang up on me before offering anything good.

"The realtor," Breanne yelled. "That could mean absolutely anybody. Do you know there are more than three-thousand realtors licensed just in the state of Maine? It could have been any of the ones who showed up at the open house or had a showing before that, or even the one who was helping them to buy their new house. Anyone could have had access to the lockbox. Anyone could have killed them."

"Wait," I said. My breathing hitched, and I shook from the sudden excitement of my realization. "Go back."

"Anyone could have access. The fact you insist on blaming me when I'm the one paying—"

As much as I knew she liked yelling at me, I had to cut Breanne off in order to keep her focused. "Not that. Before," I begged.

"Despite your fondness for blaming me, Michelle could have literally been talking about any other realtor. If she had some insider information, then why hasn't she shared before now?"

"Forget about that for now," I said. "You mentioned another realtor. You're not the one helping buy their new house?"

Breanne drew in a sharp breath. Maybe she was finally beginning to understand now. "No. I mean, I wanted to, but they already had someone picked out before they came to me to list their house."

"Do you know who that other realtor was?" I asked, then held my breath as I waited.

Her answer would determine everything.

17

All eyes watched me as I waited for Breanne's answer to come through the line. Even my heart seemed to beat more quietly for fear of missing a single word.

"I don't understand why this is important," the realtor grumbled, disappointing us all.

Charles grabbed the phone from my hands and practically shouted into the speaker. "Breanne, it's Charles. We think the other realtor is the key to clearing your brother. Can you tell us who it is?"

I followed after Charles as he paced a small path, making sure I remained close enough to hear both sides of the conversation.

Surprisingly, Breanne seemed just as irritated with Charles as she had been with me. "Really?" she shot back sarcastically. "Because a couple seconds ago your assistant accused me of killing the Hayeses."

Charles shot daggers in my direction but kept his voice even for

Breanne's benefit. "I promise that's not what she was doing. She just... has a hard time expressing herself clearly sometimes."

"I want her off my case," Breanne reminded him with a heavy sigh. "And you should really consider getting yourself a new assistant, anyway."

Charles's voice became small. "Could you please just—"

"Oh for Pete's sake!" Nan shouted, yanking the phone away from Charles and delivering it to Mitch, who stared down at it in confusion.

"Go ahead, honey," Nan coaxed. "Tell her who you are and what you want."

"Hi, this is Michelle Hayes," the girl sputtered into the phone.

Everyone grew silent again as we watched to find out what would happen next.

"Would you please tell me the name of the realtor helping my parents buy their new house?" Mitch asked, her voice shaky. I couldn't tell whether the fresh tears in her voice were authentic or for added dramatic effect, but I hoped they would work on the coarse woman on the other end of the line.

Of course, the phone had gotten too far away for me to clearly hear Breanne's response, but Mitch nodded along as the realtor said whatever she needed to say.

"Please," the girl said next, her voice cracking on that solitary word. "I just want to find out who killed my parents and make sure they're punished for it. Can you help?"

She listened some more, nodded a bunch, then turned to the rest of us and flashed a thumbs up sign before saying, "Great. Thank you so much for your help... Yes, we'll definitely do that... Bye."

"Well?" Nan practically shouted, ready to explode with excitement.

Mitch looked quite pleased with herself as she handed Charles's phone back to him. "She says she doesn't know off hand, but the info will be in the realtor database. She's looking it up now and will text the info to Charles. She said, um, that she prefers not to deal with the assistant anymore."

Of course. I was beginning to think Breanne's problem with me was much bigger than just me drawing on some walls, but honestly, it didn't really matter. Not when we still had a double murder to solve.

Charles shot me a sympathetic look. At that same moment, a new text notification flashed across the screen. "Sandra Lynn of Lighthouse Realty & Brokerage. Anyone recognize that name?" he asked, glancing toward each of us in turn.

We all shook our heads and waited as Charles returned his attention to the phone.

"Hold on," he said, squinting down at the phone. The clouds had just cleared, sending a direct beam of brightness down onto the campus. It was almost as if God Himself wanted to spotlight the importance of this moment.

"Breanne just sent a link," Charles explained as his fingers swept across the phone.

I slid close to him and stared at his slowly loading web browser. When the site finally did load, I recognized the woman splashed across its front page almost immediately. There she stood in front of a spiraled black and white lighthouse with her wavy red hair blowing softly in the breeze as she smiled and held up a giant, hulking *SOLD* sign.

"Is that the woman we ran into at the Little Dog Diner?" Charles asked. "The one who wanted our table?"

I blinked hard and looked again. Yes, that was her, too. The diner wasn't the place I first remembered seeing her, though. "She was at the Printing Company when Nan and I went to investigate. She said she was hoping to pick up an order before they closed for the evening. She was the reason I couldn't do any snooping around the storefront."

Understanding lit in Charles's eyes. "So that means she would have known at least Bill already, if not Ruth, too," he surmised.

I'd only ever rented, but something about that didn't make sense to me. "But if they were close enough to have her buy their new house, why wouldn't they have hired her to sell their existing one, too?"

Charles shrugged. "People don't always use the same realtor for both transactions, but I do find it weird she wasn't brought into the investigation before."

"It says here she's based out of Misty Harbor, which would explain why we saw her at the diner," I pointed out. "That's in Misty Harbor, too."

Charles worried his lip, then asked, "Should we call her?"

"And let her know we're coming? Heck no!" Nan broke in, then once again stole the phone from Charles. "Give me that," she said with a huff, then marched right up to Yo-Yo and held the device in front of his face.

The dog immediately growled and snapped at the air.

Nan had to jump back to avoid getting bitten.

Octo-Cat trotted over to my side. "He says—"

"Yeah, I don't think we need that one translated," I said with a giant smile. We'd done it. We'd really done it. And just in time, too.

"Let's go get our perp," Nan said, already marching back toward the parking lot. She paused a moment to call over her shoulder, "You coming, Mitch?"

The girl hopped off the half wall. "Let's do this!"

And just like that, we were all running back to the car—Charles, me, Nan, Mitch, Octo-Cat, and Yo-Yo—which we reached in record time for such a motley crew.

"It all lines up," I said between heavy breaths while my fingers fumbled with the seatbelt's clasp. "Sandra looks enough like Breanne that it confused Yo-Yo. They're also both realtors who were working with the Hayeses, which would have only added to his confusion."

"Plus, all humans look the same," Octo-Cat pointed out.

"And that," I said with a freeing laugh. Oh my gosh, we had done it. "Now we just have to prove it in a way that will hold up in court, and Brock will be a free man."

"You leave that to me," Nan said, cracking her knuckles on each hand as if readying for war.

"No way!" Charles answered for me. "You've already done more than enough."

"Hold on," I said calmly, doing my best to be the voice of reason.

"We have a long drive ahead of us. Maybe we can reconsider all the facts we already know about the case in light of this new information and try to figure out what possible motive Sandra Lynn could have had for..." I stopped, remembering Mitch with was us now. "Well, you know."

"Sure," Charles answered, sending a sly grin in my direction. "Just so long as everyone stays awake this time."

"Hardy har har," I shot back. "This isn't a time for making jokes. It's a time for finding answers."

"Let's get you caught up, Mitch," Nan mumbled from the backseat, then placed a hand on the side of Charles's seat and mine. "Where's that briefcase of yours?"

"I have it here," I said, reaching down to grab it from my footwell. "Give me a minute to do some... um, tidying up, and then it's all yours." I grabbed each of the photos and the written reports describing the crime scene and stashed them in the glove box, then handed Charles's bag back to Nan.

Nan began to explain what we already knew to her rapt audience of one.

"So are we done now?" Octo-Cat asked from the cushion on my lap. "Case closed?"

"We're almost there," I assured him with a gentle pat on his head.

"How do we go from almost to all the way?" he asked with a growl. I tried not to take it personally since I knew how much he hated car rides, and I hadn't thought to bring him any Benadryl for our return trip home.

"I need to go home and sleep for the next six or seven days at least," he informed me with a weary sigh.

"Based on what Yo-Yo's told us, we have a very strong case against Sandra Lynn," I explained. "The only problem is that won't be enough for the other humans."

"Because he's a dog?" Octo-Cat asked.

I rolled my eyes. "I think you know why. Don't be such a smart aleck."

"So what now?" he insisted.

"Now we need to find evidence they'll accept without questioning our sanity in the process. So we already have the answer. Now we need to work backward to find the clues that support that answer. Make sense?"

"Yeah, but it sure seems like a lot of work." Octo-Cat's posture grew more rigid as Charles took a sharp turn. "You know you have another option. Right?"

"Oh, really, and what's that?" I challenged, placing a hand on his back to help steady him.

He flicked his tail with one giant movement before revealing, "Get a confession. *Duh.*"

Finally, all the TV he'd been watching lately seemed to have paid off. I was very glad he'd graduated from *Dora the Explorer* to *Law & Order*, which was no doubt what inspired this little nugget of wisdom.

Charles turned to study me briefly before training his eyes back on the road. "What did he say?"

Well, this created quite the conundrum. While I didn't want to lie to Charles, I also knew he wouldn't be a big fan of the forced confession plan.

On my last case, I'd headed into trouble all my own and just barely managed to escape with my life. Well, this time I definitely wouldn't be making the same mistake.

Nope.

This time, I'd be sure to bring the cat with me when I marched straight into Sandra Lynn's office and demanded an explanation.

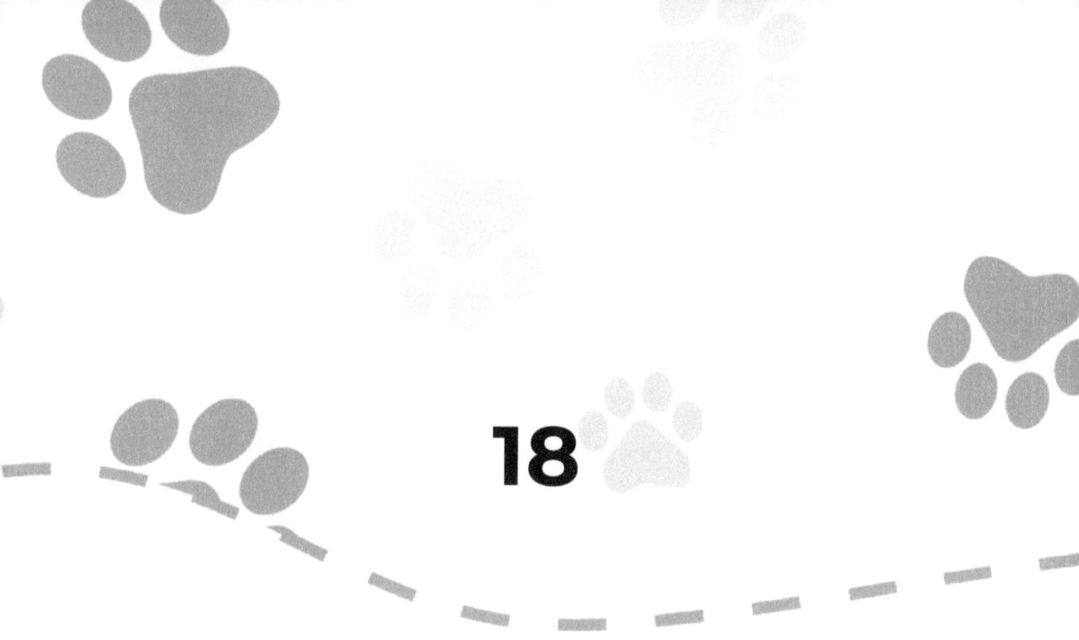

18

By the time we got back to Glendale, the noon sun already hung high in the sky. Nan invited everyone over to her house for lunch while they once again reviewed the evidence, this time trying to prove what Yo-Yo had revealed to us that morning.

I excused myself from the shindig by providing the very valid excuse of needing to take Octo-Cat home to use his litter box. They didn't need to know what I had planned after that quick pit stop.

"Okay, so what now?" Octo-Cat asked after visiting his little kitty box and wiping his paws off on the new mat I'd purchased expressly for his use.

"What do you mean?" I asked, searching the fridge for some food I could quickly inhale to calm my growling stomach.

He regarded me with a piteous look. "What do you mean 'what do I mean?' *I mean* we're going to get that confession, right? I assumed we didn't talk about it in the car because you didn't want Upchuck to know the plan—not because you'd given up on it already."

While he made his harangue, I found an old but not yet expired package of string cheese shoved into the back of my vegetable drawer and grabbed a couple of pieces to tide me over. After tearing into the first with great aplomb, I peeled off a thick piece and shoved it in my mouth.

Then I attempted to answer my cat's concerns by saying, "Of course we're going to get the confession. I figured we could start with me pretending to be an interested client, and you hiding in your wicker bag."

Octo-Cat wrinkled his nose. "I hate that bag."

"Got any other ideas?" I challenged, putting another thick string of cheese into my mouth.

He paced back and forth on the table in frustration as he talked. "I do have ideas, but none that don't put at least one of my lives at risk. I'd be willing to make that sacrifice for the team, but something tells me you wouldn't."

"I only have one life, remember?" I probably should have been insulted that he kept forgetting—or at least completely disregarding—this very important fact, but right then I was too keyed up to care.

"Ahh, yes." Octo-Cat plopped his rear down and shook his head. "So fragile."

I inhaled the final stringy thing from my first cheese and opened the second package, rolling my eyes as I did. "Fine, I'm fragile, but I still think putting you in the bag for half an hour is preferable to the possibility of me dying. Don't you?"

Octo-Cat responded by lifting a rear leg over his head and licking his kitty bits.

"Um, excuse me? I'm talking to you!" Suddenly I had less of an appetite.

"What? I'm still thinking. Give me a minute here," he mumbled while he continued to groom himself. It was so nice to see that protecting my life held comparable importance to avoiding a perfectly normal smelling wicker bag. That whole superior sense of smell was a total excuse, and I knew it. The snobby cat claimed it stunk mostly because he hated that I'd picked it up at a charity thrift store.

"Fine," he said at last, dropping his leg back to the floor. "I'll get in the bag, but you owe me."

"I already owe you from the harness," I pointed out, regretting my big mouth instantly. I shoved another bite of string cheese in with the hope it would keep me from saying something else I'd come to regret.

What could only be described as an evil smile crept across his furry face. "Yes," he answered with a malicious laugh. "And the size of that favor just grew. Keep going, sweetheart. Daddy needs a new... well, everything."

Uck. I didn't know whether to be more afraid of the threat or disgusted by the manner in which he'd made it. I gulped down my anxiety and with it the too-large piece of unchewed cheese. It only took a millisecond to realize I was choking on the stupid thing.

Octo-Cat sat by and watched as I gestured wildly to my throat. He didn't so much as move a paw as I coughed and pounded on my chest, finally dislodging the misplaced morsel.

"What would you have done if I died?" I demanded, my voice hoarse. "I was choking, and you didn't even try to help!"

He yawned. "Oh, is that what that display was all about? I thought you were just stalling for time. You know, if we don't hurry, Upchuck and the gang will come looking for us. Is that what you want?"

Ugh. I hated that he was right even more than I hated the complete lack of sympathy.

"Fine, let's go," I said after filling up my water bottle at the sink.

Octo-Cat followed me hesitantly. "No harness this time?"

"Nope," I said, grabbing my prize from the coat closet and holding it up for him to see. I looked forward to knowing he would suffer just a little bit. Such was the nature of our relationship. "Bag instead."

He raised his paw in a gesture I hadn't seen from him before. He must have learned that from one of his many kids' TV shows. "Um, I have a question."

I raised my eyebrows and motioned for him to go ahead.

"What is my role in all of this?"

"If anything bad happens, use your iPad to call for help. And if anything really bad happens, use your claws and attack. Can you do that for me?"

He nodded. "As long as you remember to bring my iPad."

I groaned and tracked back to the bedroom to retrieve his favorite toy. "Good?" I asked, tucking it into the rear pocket of the bag. This was such an odd way to prepare for what could be a risky situation, but it was a fair representation of what my life looked like now.

"One more thing," I told him as we made our way to the car. "I'm calling my mom."

"Why? Aren't I enough for you?"

"Trust me," I said with a laugh. "You're more than enough most days, but I did promise my mom a scoop. And I'm going to make sure we get it."

He still appeared confused. "Won't she try to stop you? Isn't that why you didn't let Charles or Nan know?"

"Yes, that's why I didn't tell them, but Mom doesn't worry the same way they do. She understands the need to do whatever it takes to get the story."

Octo-Cat climbed onto my lap and dug his claws into my thigh as I started the engine. "It's your life," he said.

What a great attitude for a wingman. If the time really did come to save my life, I hoped he would take the necessary actions. I felt less sure, though, after the brief choking incident.

I couldn't focus on that right now. I needed to save an innocent man from spending the rest of his life in prison. Last time I'd gotten caught because I hadn't realized I was walking into a dangerous situation. This time I knew and was prepared, too.

After buckling my seatbelt, I connected Octo-Cat's iPad to the car's Bluetooth and placed a voice-only FaceTime call to my mom.

She answered so fast, I didn't even hear it ring. "Hey, Angie. Any luck today?"

"As a matter of fact," I announced, speaking loudly to make sure she could hear me over the sound of the car's engine. "I'm on my way to Misty Harbor now. Think you can join me with a film crew?"

"It may take a little bit to get everyone together. We're not used to breaking news in Glendale. But I will be there as fast as I can. Any particular place?"

"Lighthouse Realty & Brokerage," I told her, rattling off the address.

"I'm impressed. How'd you find out who really did it?" she asked.

My daughterly heart swelled with pride, but still, I hesitated. She didn't know the truth about my abilities yet, and this didn't seem like the right time or the right method by which to tell her.

"It's a long story. Let's get it on camera," I said, knowing full well I would never, ever reveal my quirky powers on the local news. It would be hard enough just to tell Mom, but I knew that I'd be doing just that before the day was through.

"There's my smart daughter. That associate degree in communications really paid off. I still think you should go back for journalism. We'd make a great team, you and me."

"I'll think about it, Mom," I said, knowing full well the newsroom held zero appeal to me. I'd hate to be in direct competition with my ambitious mom, and I'd hate even more to have to work at her side every day. We definitely loved each other, but mostly in small doses.

She chuckled good-naturedly. "I know what that means, but you're right. Let's just focus on the story in front of us for now."

There was still one more thing I needed to say, and it was the hardest part. "Mom?"

"Yeah?"

"If you get a call from me within the next hour, even if—especially if—I'm not talking on the other end of the line, call the cops. Okay?"

She sucked in air through her teeth then asked, "Are you doing something dangerous?"

I sure hoped not.

"No. It's just a precaution," I lied. Of course, I knew that Sandra had killed before—*twice!*—and that there was no guarantee she wouldn't turn on me once she found out I'd uncovered and planned to expose her crimes.

"I guess it's always good to have a backup plan," Mom said resignedly. "I'll be up there soon."

"Okay," I responded. "Call me when you get there. My phone may be off, but I'll call back as soon as I can. And Mom?"

"Yeah?"

"I love you."

"Love you, too."

I took a deep breath and turned to Octo-Cat. "There," I said. "Now my mom's cell is the last number in your call history. Call her if there's any trouble, okay?"

His face looked grim. Whether he was finally beginning to see just how dangerous this situation could be for me or simply upset about the car ride, I couldn't say for sure.

The only thing I could say for sure was that we were going to catch a killer today. *No matter what.*

19

"It's go time," I muttered from the front seat of my car, which now sat parked in the small lot outside Lighthouse Realty & Brokerage. My hands shook as I grabbed my striped wicker bag from the passenger seat floor well and held it open for Octo-Cat to climb inside.

He growled but otherwise complied without too much complaint.

"Remember, your iPad is tucked into the back pocket," I informed him. "I'll keep your bag on my lap. If there's an emergency, jump out and knock the bag off my lap. That should make the iPad fall out onto the floor so you can use it."

"Understood," he said. "But what if it ends up upside down?"

"Let's pray it doesn't," I said, wishing I would have seen this flaw in my plan earlier. But we were here now, and I had to take action.

"Just put it in the bag next to me," he said, popping his head out of the bag to study me.

"But you don't like things touching you," I pointed out.

"It's an inconvenience, yes. But it would be much more inconvenient if you died and I had to train another human on my likes and dislikes."

"Aww, so you do love me, after all!" I cooed, slipping the iPad out of the back pocket and into the main compartment of the bag.

"Enough with the mushy stuff. Get in there and catch the bad guy," he said, lowering himself back into position.

Right. I took another deep breath and clambered out of the car, adjusting the bag carefully over my shoulder as I approached the front door. Hopefully Sandra would be in. I hadn't called ahead, preferring to play things by ear. Yes, I didn't have much of a plan, but hoped the acting genes in my family would come in handy.

When I pushed through the glass door, a little bell chimed to announce my arrival. The office smelled pleasant like warm vanilla, and the waiting area was flanked with two overstuffed couches and an inviting array of magazines. It even had a mini cooler filled with bottled water, several kinds of soda, and coffee shots.

Seeing that no one was waiting at the front desk, I took the opportunity to snag one of the cold coffee shots. Maybe I could buy these for myself at home. I popped the can open and took an appreciative swig, downing the entire thing in three big gulps.

Liquid courage?

I sure hoped so.

"Hello, and welcome to Lighthouse Realty & Brokerage," a woman's voice greeted me from across the room. "How can we help you?"

I glanced over and immediately recognized Sandra Lynn with her unmistakable curly red hair and that huge smile that I now knew hid dark secrets. I grabbed the straps on my bag, needing the connection to Octo-Cat to keep my wits about me and stay on task.

"Good afternoon," I said with what I hoped was a pleasant smile. "I'm here because I'd like to buy a house."

Sandra laughed, and the sound was startlingly shrill. I wonder if I would have been so put off by it without the knowledge of her after-hours criminal activity. "Well, I can certainly help with that. Why don't you come on back to my office?" She began taking sure, steady strides down the hall, and I followed after.

"You're in luck," she prattled on over her shoulder as we walked. "Usually walk-ins have to deal with one of our junior agents, but I just so happened to have a cancellation this afternoon. As the owner of this realty and the most experienced agent, I'll make sure you have the house of your dreams in no time at all."

She simpered at me as she stopped and waited for me to enter the small, dimly lit office ahead of her.

"That is lucky," I said with a polite smile of my own.

"What's your name, dear? And will this be your first time purchasing?" Sandra took a seat behind her desk and leaned forward slightly as we spoke.

"I'm Angela," I said, reaching forward to shake her hand. It wasn't quite a lie, but it wasn't quite the truth. Nobody called me Angela except Octo-Cat—and even then he only did it on occasion. "Yes, it's my first time," I finished.

"Well, let me give you a run-down of the basics," Sandra said, launching into a lengthy monologue that gave me time to search the office with my eyes. Nothing stood out as being particularly incriminating, but I hadn't exactly expected to find a bloody hammer sitting on top of her desk, either.

Sandra finished her speech and waited for me to say something, but I hadn't been paying close enough attention to figure out what.

"What are you looking for, dear?" she repeated. Her smile faltered somewhat as she waited for me to keep up my end of the exchange.

"Um..." I thought back to all the mental gymnastics Charles, Nan, Mitch, and I had done on the car ride home to Glendale. They all centered around the question: *What reason could a realtor possibly have to kill her clients?* Money seemed the safest bet. I didn't understand what all that entailed but decided to broach the subject delicately.

"I'd really like a nice three bedroom, but I'm worried I may not have enough money to make my dream house a reality."

She frowned briefly before shaking her head and bringing back the smile. "That's okay. We can work around it. What's your credit like?"

"It's pretty bad." Unfortunately, that part wasn't a lie.

She pressed her coral-colored lips together in a flat line. "Hmm."

"Is there anything you can do to help?" I asked, calling up my best impression of a desperate aspiring homeowner.

Sandra stiffened, taking a moment before answering. "There are government programs that may be able to help get you into a house. Your interest rate probably won't be that good, but that's the case for a lot of first-time buyers."

"Okay," I said helplessly.

"Why did you decide to buy now if money is so tight?" she asked.

I had to think fast to avoid suspicion, so I said the first thing that popped into my head. "Well, with my current rental, it feels like me and my cat are living on top of each other. We need some more space. Oh, and I have a dog, too. A Yorkie."

She blanched at this and swallowed before letting that shrill laugh loose again. "Sounds like you have your hands full," she said.

I'm not sure if I imagined it, but she definitely faltered upon the mention of "my" Yorkie. If I could push this topic a little further, maybe I could unsettle her enough to trick her into a confession.

"Are you a dog person?" I asked, hugging my bag tight on my lap to reassure Octo-Cat, who no doubt hated not being able to join this particular conversation. After all, one of his favorite pastimes since meeting Yo-Yo was pointing out how superior cats are to dogs.

"I watched a dog for a friend once," Sandra answered, turning away from me to organize some papers. "I'm not sure I'm cut out for a dog companion myself, but since you are, let's get you a place with a fenced-in yard." She handed me a printed-out list triumphantly.

I puzzled over her words while pretending to review the listing. Watched a dog for a friend? Was she talking about Yo-Yo? Is that why he'd disappeared for a few weeks before turning back up at the Hayes's door where Charles then found him? And, if so, why hadn't Yo-Yo told us?

I thought his traumatic memory loss had been resolved once we reunited him with Mitch, but perhaps he'd still chosen to forget some of the other details that weren't directly pertinent to remembering who'd done it.

"I'm not sure this one is for me," I said, pushing the listing back across the desk. "Thank you, though."

"Have you done any shopping around online? Those listings aren't always the most up to date, but if you have an idea of what you like, it could help me to refine our search."

She was very good at staying right on topic and pushing me closer to buying with each comment. It would take something major to knock her off her game. Luckily, I still had an ace up my sleeve.

"Actually..." I said, trying to still my shaking hands by hugging the wicker bag tighter to my chest. "There is a place I like out in Glendale. It's above my price range, but I'm hoping we might be able to get a good deal."

"I'm happy to negotiate with the homeowners to see what we can do," Sandra said with an ingratiating smile. "Is that the house you want? Are you ready to start putting together an offer?"

"Well, it is a really nice house. I guess we could try," I said, feigning hesitation.

She nodded enthusiastically. I'm sure it must be nice to make a big commission with hardly any work at all. She probably looked at me and saw a giant, sparkling dollar sign now. "Fabulous. Do you have the address?"

I pulled out my phone and pretended to search for information before rattling off the Hayes's address, which I already happened to know by heart.

Sandra didn't say anything in response—just sat there staring at me, so I added, "Like I said, I'm hoping we can get a good deal, because two people were murdered there."

"I don't think that's the house for you, dear," the realtor spat out at last.

"Why not?" I argued. "It's in a great location and has plenty of space for me and my pets. Can't we at least put in an offer and see?"

"I'd really urge you to consider a property with a less sordid history," she said, turning back to her files and pulling out another listing, seemingly at random. "This looks nice. How about this one?"

I didn't even look down at the paper. Keeping my eyes glued to hers, I licked my lips and said, "You said we could put in an offer, and that's what I want to do. Can we get started please?"

She shook her head. "I probably shouldn't be saying this, because it makes me look a little, well, like I'm not all there..." Sandra paused to laugh, but I kept my face neutral, waiting.

"But that place you mentioned?" she continued. "It's very, very haunted."

"Oh? Just a sec." I placed my bag on the floor right in front of her oversized desk so that she wouldn't be able to see what I was doing unless she chose to stand up. I grabbed the iPad and motioned for Octo-Cat to creep out as well. Once both were settled on the floor and I confirmed that the tabby was indeed placing a call to my mom, I straightened back in my chair and returned my focus to an increasingly nervous-looking Sandra.

"It's haunted, huh?" I asked, shaking my head. "Well, how about that?"

She nodded eagerly; relief flashed across her face. "I know some people don't believe in ghosts and all, but they are there and very angry. It's best not to get involved with that mess."

"Wow. Hmm," I said, pretending to think this over carefully but only to buy us a little more time. If Octo-Cat could get Mom on the line before I showed my hand, she'd be able to hear what happened next. I heard a little murmur sound from the floor. That had to be her.

"What was that?" Sandra asked, shifting her gaze around the room to find the source of the speaker.

"Wait. I have a question," I blurted out to draw her attention back to me. "You say the ghosts are angry. Is that because you murdered them?"

20

"Why, I've never been so insulted in all my life. Go! Get out of my office!" the realtor cried. All traces of her earlier smile completely wiped clean from her face, which now pinched in rage. Sandra popped to her feet so quickly, I instantly recoiled in fear.

And, in my attempt to stumble to a standing position, I stepped on Octo-Cat's tail.

He let out a terrible yowl and jumped onto the desk between us, hissing up a storm.

"What? Where did he come from?" Sandra demanded, turning redder and redder as each moment passed.

"Why don't you answer my question first," I shouted at her. "I know you killed the Hayeses, and I can prove it!"

"You can't prove anything," she spat. "Now get out of here!"

I crossed my arms over my chest and stared straight into her eyes, hoping she couldn't see how afraid I was in that moment. "I'm not going anywhere until you admit what you did."

"I didn't do anything," she said, taking care to enunciate each word, but I was not convinced.

"You killed the Hayeses in cold blood. You bashed out their brains with a hammer and framed the handyman," I said. "Hey, if I agree to work with you, will you kill me, too?"

Sandra let out an enormous huff and lunged for me, but I was too fast for her.

I ran out of her office and back into the main waiting area. "Help!"

"No one else is here," Sandra told me, approaching slowly, deliberately.

I saw my chance, so I took it. Squeezing past her down the hall, I bolted back into her office and locked the door behind me.

"You're going to regret that!" she screamed, pounding furiously on the door.

I tuned her out and began pulling open drawers and cabinets in search of evidence. "Help me find proof!" I told Octo-Cat, who sat licking his wounded tail.

Soon we were both tearing through the office.

Surely something had to be here.

"I called your mother just like you said," my tabby informed me.

"I'm calling the police!" Sandra screamed from the hallway.

"Good, that will make it easier for them to arrest you!" I shouted back, calling her bluff while shooting the cat an appreciative smile.

"Thanks for your help," I told him. "You did good."

We searched frantically for another couple moments, my desperation growing by the second.

"What's this? The words look familiar," Octo-Cat said, nudging a pile of mail from on top of the filing cabinet until it fell and scattered to the floor. He still didn't know how to read, but he was beginning to recognize familiar patterns of numbers and letters.

Sure enough, I combed through the pile and found a sealed envelope addressed to Charles at the firm.

"Oh! Think you can get away with blackmailing my colleague, do you?" I called to Sandra, waving the letter around wildly even though she couldn't see it. "But why threaten him when you know perfectly well that Brock Calhoun didn't kill Bill and Ruth Hayes?"

She didn't come back at me with an angry retort. In fact, Sandra said nothing at all as the entire office fell silent. The only sound in my ears was my own blood as it flew through my veins at a rapid tempo. My heart went crazy as I sent up a silent prayer that Sandra hadn't somehow gotten her hands on a gun or some other weapon she could use to attack me through the closed door.

A moment later, the front door burst open, sending the greeting bell into a violent jangle.

"Laura Lee, Channel 7 News. Do you care to tell our viewers what's going on here?" my mother's voice rang out, loud and clear, and I could just picture her there with her probing microphone that she swung around like a sword when she was really on the warpath. I imagined now would be one of those times.

Feeling safe enough to exit now that I had backup, I swung the door open and stepped back into the main area just in time to see Sandra Lynn make a run for it.

"Mom! Stop her!" I screamed as I began to run after the fugitive. I had absolutely no idea what I would do if I caught her, but I at least had to try.

"Wait here," my mom said, dropping her mic and wrapping her arms around me. Her cameraman gave chase, but his gait was mired by the giant apparatus on his shoulder.

I watched through the glass door as a police car squealed to a stop and two armed officers jumped onto the scene.

"I've got her!" Charles called from somewhere I couldn't see.

My mom let go, and I raced outside to extend my view. Sure enough, Charles stood with the very distraught murderess in his embrace.

"You don't have any evidence!" she screamed.

"Actually, I have this," I said, waving the envelope in the air. "It was in her outgoing mail," I explained, handing it to the nearest officer.

"Threatening letters, huh?" the officer said with a smirk after scanning the letter. "Thanks for this," he told me as he slipped it into his pocket. "But the mass collusion and double homicide should be more than enough to put this one away for a long time."

"I have rights!" Sandra shouted pathetically.

"That's right," the other officer said. "Let me read them to you now. You have the right to remain silent..."

Charles ambled over to me with a bit of a limp, which made me think Sandra put up some kind of fight when he subdued her. "Are you okay?" he asked, checking me over.

"I'm fine."

Once he realized that was true, his handsome features contorted in an angry mask. "Why did you come out here on your own?"

"I had to find a way to prove Brock's innocence, and this seemed like the most surefire way."

"Well, it was the most ridiculous way," Charles said. "The most unsafe way, too."

I shook my head, going back over what the officer had said. "Did you find another way to prove she did it?"

He ran a hand through his hair and sighed. "Yes, and if you would have come back to the house, I could've told you that in person."

"How?" I insisted. I still couldn't figure out why the realtor had turned on her clients, and that was driving me crazy.

"Mitch," Charles said simply. "She set everything in motion by texting a few key people during our drive."

"But she said her phone—"

"She used Nan's," he cut me off. "Anyway, you were on the right track with the Bayside Printing Company, but you didn't have the right access. Bill's former employer, Mr. Weber, was able to do a system restore to recover previously deleted files. Once he knew to examine Lighthouse Realty & Brokerage's past jobs and records in particular, he found exactly what he was looking for."

I was so happy we'd found the answer, but it still didn't make sense to me. "Which was?"

"The motive," Charles said with a winning smile. "It was small and easy to miss, but on her latest print job, Sandra provided one page too many."

"Meaning?" I asked, motioning for him to hurry up and answer the question that had plagued me all week long.

"Meaning she gave Bill a financial document, which showed some illegal activity involving false documentation and offshore accounts," he explained.

"And so she killed him over that?" I asked. "Because she was worried he'd turn her in?"

"He blackmailed me!" Sandra screamed. "He said since I already knew how to skirt the rules that it shouldn't be a big deal to get him a new house free of charge, the selfish jerk! I didn't just have half a million to throw around. What was I supposed to do?"

"Not steal in the first place," one of the officers said as he pushed her head down and shoved her in the back of the cruiser.

"Yeah, and you definitely shouldn't have killed him or anybody else," the other said.

"Well, there you have it," my mom announced, coming to stand between me and Charles. "Brock Calhoun is innocent, and the real murderer has now been apprehended. And you saw it all unfold live, only on Channel 7."

As my mother began to interview Charles, I quietly slipped out of the frame and went to retrieve my cat and his iPad from inside the brokerage.

I found Octo-Cat curled up on Sandra's desk chair. Somehow he'd actually managed to fall asleep despite all that excitement.

"Hey." I nudged him awake gently. "We did it."

He blinked up at me, yawned, and then said, "Great. So what now?"

"How about a lobster roll from the Little Dog Diner?"

* * *

Charles joined us for lobster rolls and he even paid for everyone, including Mitch, Nan, and Yo-Yo who all joined us shortly after Sandra's arrest. I let him recount all the gritty details while I focused on the delicious meal before me.

Toward the end of his explanation, Nan hit me on the back of the head, almost causing me to choke again.

"What?" I cried, my mouth still stuffed with food.

"If you do something that stupid again, I'm going to kill you," she said, fixing me with a scowl.

"Sorry," I muttered. "Does Brock know yet?" I asked in an effort to change the subject to happier outcomes.

Charles licked a bit of mayo from his thumb. "They're processing him for release now. He'll be a free man by nightfall."

This news made me so happy I couldn't help but smile as I devoured a second lobster roll.

Mitch finished eating first, then picked Yo-Yo up and sat him on her lap. That reminded me of something that still didn't sit well with me.

"When I was talking with Sandra," I said, waiting for a beat to make sure everyone was listening, "she mentioned dog-sitting for a friend once. Do you think it's possible she meant Yo-Yo?"

"Do you really think she stole him, kept him hostage for a few weeks, and then let him go? That seems kind of improbable," Charles said. "What reason would she have for doing that?"

"Let's ask the dog," Octo-Cat said before taking a giant hunk of shrimp into his mouth.

"Would you?" I said, adding "please" when he didn't immediately comply.

"What's—?" Charles began, but I shushed him while I waited for the animals to finish their exchange.

"Affirmative," Octo-Cat said a moment later. "She took him that night when he wouldn't stop barking, but he got away and came home. It took him a while to find his way back from Misty Harbor, but he was determined to get home, no matter what."

I quickly relayed this information to the rest of the group.

"So, why didn't she kill him, too?" Charles asked, stating the obvious.

"I guess even evil has its limits," Nan said with a pert nod.

"He says he's sorry for not remembering everything sooner," Octo-Cat informed me. "And he said thank you for helping his family."

"What's going to happen to Yo-Yo now?" I asked the others.

"Charles is helping me petition the school to keep him with me on campus as an emotional support animal," Mitch answered with a sad smile. "I just couldn't imagine losing him again. He's the only family I have left now."

"And until then, he'll stay with me," Charles said. "But we should have no problem getting our petition approved, in light of..." His voice trailed off, but Mitch picked up the thread for him.

"My parents being recently murdered."

"What a day," Nan said with a giant sigh. "Let's take a break before investigating our next big case, if that's okay with you," she said, turning to me.

"What makes you think there will be a next case?" I asked, surprised.

"Because, my darling, you might not always go about things in the safest way, but I think you've finally found your true calling."

"Which is?"

"You're the best private eye in all of Maine," she said with a proud smile.

"I'll drink to that," Charles said, raising his glass of soda.

"Me too," Mitch said.

That's when Mom came swooping into the restaurant to join us. "I'm here!" she cried. "What did I miss?"

"Nothing," Nan said, sending a wink my way. "Nothing at all."

Well, I guess I could tell Mom later. I'd had more than enough excitement that night already.

Octo-Cat nudged me with his paw. "Now that that's over with, I'm ready to collect on my favor."

Mom was busy giving her order to the waitress, so I bent down and quietly hissed, "What is it?"

"I want you to buy me a house," he said with a Cheshire grin.

"A house!" I exploded.

He nodded excitedly. "And not just any house. *My* house. I want to go home."

My jaw hung open as I searched for the appropriate response. Nothing came to me, though.

"Don't worry, you're coming, too," Octo-Cat added in a futile effort to answer my objections. He'd learned a lot about human society lately—I'd give him that—but there were certain things that still went way over his head, money being a prime example.

"You want me to just buy Ethel's house?" I hissed again. " There's no way I can afford that huge place."

"We'll figure out the details later," he assured me, returning his attention to his meal.

When I glanced back at my human dining companions, I saw Mom staring at me with a look I instantly recognized.

She knew.

HAIRLESS HARASSMENT

I never signed up to be a private investigator with a snarky, talking cat for a partner, but there's no backing down now. Especially considering a prominent politician was murdered pretty much right in my backyard.

The only witnesses were the senator's two hairless cats, Jacques and Jillianne. Normally pets want to help us solve their owner's murders, but this time it seems the two devious felines might actually be the ones who committed it...

Surprisingly enough, my own partner in crime, Octo-Cat, actually wants to help this time, but he can barely understand our two prime suspects because of their strange Sphynx accents. And I thought speaking tabby was hard!

So, there you have it, even with two successful cases behind me, I really don't know how I'm going to solve this one. Is it too late to go back and pick another career?

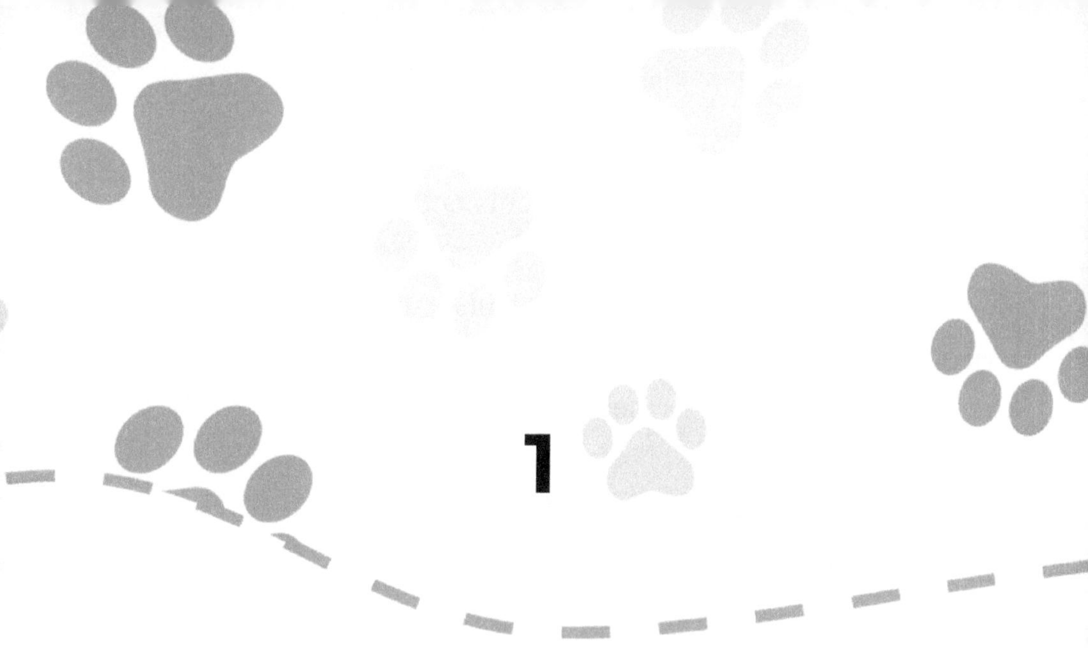

1

Hi, I'm Angie Russo, and my pet cat never ever stops talking. Not just mews and meows, but actual words that I can understand. So far, I'm the only one who seems to have this ability, and I still have absolutely no idea why.

It all started when I got zapped by a faulty coffee maker at the law firm where I work as a paralegal. Since then, Octo-Cat and I have used our special connection to solve two murder investigations together. Yeah, even I have to admit, we make a pretty great team.

Only a few weeks have passed since our super sleuthing earned the local handyman Brock Calhoun a *get-out-of-jail-free* card. And already my feline sidekick is begging for another case. Apparently, napping and complaining all day isn't an exciting enough life for him now.

All my life I've been on the search for that one amazing talent that would make me special and give me purpose. My nan starred on

Broadway in her prime, and my parents both work for the local news station and love what they do.

They were all so sure of their talents early in life, but I've really struggled to pinpoint mine. I couldn't even figure out my passion well enough to nail down a bachelor's degree, racking up seven associate degrees instead.

I definitely never expected to find my true calling as a paralegal, especially considering how much I've always hated lawyers. But now that I have Octo-Cat and my special ability, I find that working at the offices of Thompson, Longfellow & Associates provides the perfect way to use my new-found abilities for good—especially considering that the newest partner knows all about my ability to speak to animals.

Oh, yeah! Charles didn't get fired. Instead, he got promoted. I was so proud of him that I even suggested we go back to the Little Dog Diner in Misty Harbor to celebrate with the world's best lobster rolls. He told me it would have to be some other time, though, because he already had plans with his new girlfriend, Breanne Calhoun.

Yeah, I don't get that, either.

The news that he'd started dating the cold and snippy realtor we'd very recently suspected of murder was enough to extinguish my crush on Charles once and for all, though. I've also decided that the next time Octo-Cat refers to him as "Upchuck," I'm not going to correct him.

The thought of him and Breanne together makes me sick, too.

It's for the best, though, I suppose. I really need to focus on understanding my new pet-whispering abilities, and Octo-Cat and I both need to get better at investigating cases without raising the community's suspicions. That pretty much means I have no time left for love or infatuation or whatever it was I once felt for Charles.

Anyway, who needs a boyfriend when you have a talking cat?

Not me. Well, at least not for right now.

Lately I've been spending a lot more time with my mom. Ever since she helped us catch the real murderer in our latest case, she's been on this kind of career high. She got the exclusive scoop and even managed to record our showdown with the murderer live and on camera. The feature was picked up all over the nation, and she and my dad have received job offers from clear across the country.

The latest was from San Antonio, I think.

She's not saying yes to any of them, though. At least, not unless I agree to move with them, too. But I would never leave Nan, and Nan would never leave Blueberry Bay.

So we're all staying put exactly where we are.

Sure, if enough people learn my secret, I probably will have to leave eventually. Right now, a total of five people know—Nan and my parents, who I told on purpose, along with Charles Longfellow, III and a college student named Mitch, who both figured it out by accident. Hopefully I can keep that number from growing any larger, but it seems like several people are on the verge of figuring things out already.

And that definitely worries me.

Especially since my mom just invited me to help her with her newest investigative journalism assignment...

* * *

I'd finally switched to a part-time schedule at the firm, and today was one of my days off. And by off, I meant I got to stay home and pack up my tiny rental house under the supervision of one very demanding tabby.

Not only did I have to discard a number of my belongings that he found to be inadequate, but he was also the reason I had to move in the first place. Granted, I'm the one who said I'd owe him a big favor if he allowed me to put him in a harness to take him outside. I hadn't counted on that favor amounting to more than six-thousand square feet, though.

As it turned out, the favor he wanted was for me to purchase the old manor house he had lived in with Ethel Fulton before she was murdered and, through a truly unbelievable series of events, he came to live with me. Now a twelve-dollar harness was costing me the better part of my five-thousand-dollar monthly stipend, and I'd learned to be more careful about promising my kitty companion open-ended favors.

Yes, my former boss, Richard Fulton, did offer me a generous break on the price. Also, there were fewer interested parties once the greater populace found that the former homeowner had been murdered, but still—*still!*—owning Fulton Manor would require a pretty penny from me not just to keep up with the mortgage, but also to carry out the many repairs that seemed to be more or less essential for safety purposes.

At least that's what the home inspector said.

Hardly any time has passed at all, and yet somehow the sale is final and the house is ready for me and Octo-Cat to move in. It's funny how bureaucracy can either slow things way down or speed them way up depending what side you approach the red tape from. Around Blueberry Bay, the Fultons owned the spool from which the red tape was unraveled, which meant I bought myself a manor house with very little effort on my part.

Nan, who adores both me and my cat in equal measure, decided to help out, too. Even though she'd owned her little Cape Cod style home for more than thirty-five years, she decided it was time to sell and move in with me at my new Eastern seaboard mansion.

"The difference is," she explained, "this time I'll be living with you and not the other way around." That was how she justified kicking me out of her house less than a year ago, only to move in with me now.

Honestly, I'm more than a little thrilled to have an added buffer when it comes to Octo-Cat. I love him more than anything, but he also infuriates me on a regular basis, constantly finding new and exciting ways to push the poorly constructed boundaries I've tried to erect.

And so all of us are moving in this weekend, even though Nan hasn't even had an offer on her house yet. Breanne says it will be easier to sell without a current resident. Yes, I couldn't believe Nan hired Calhoun Realty to list her house, either. She and I needed to have a serious talk about family loyalty.

But first we had to survive the big move.

"Someone just pulled up outside," Octo-Cat informed me,

hopping onto the end of the bed where the better part of my wardrobe was laid out for evaluation. I took packing as a good opportunity to downsize, even though my living space would increase nearly ten times.

A moment later an urgent knock sounded on the front door and my mom's voice called out, "Angie? Angie, are you here?"

"Coming!" I yelled, letting the half-full box in my arms fall to the floor.

I flipped the deadbolt and my mom immediately pushed her way inside. "You'll never guess what happened!" she told me, reaching into my closet and grabbing one of my jackets, which she thrust at me excitedly.

"What?" I asked, still a bit sleepy and not quite ready for this level of enthusiasm.

She followed me into the kitchen where I grabbed a can of Diet Mountain Dew and flipped the tab. It was my latest attempt at a suitable coffee replacement, and so far, so good.

"Lou Harlow was murdered!" she squealed with delight.

"Um, Mom. How about a little less bliss over someone dying, please?" Lou Harlow wasn't just some random local, either. As one of the two senators appointed to represent the great state of Maine, she was one of the most famous people to reside in our little corner of Blueberry Bay.

And now she was dead. And for some reason, my mother was terribly excited about it.

"I'm sorry. I know it's sad she died and everything, but guess who's been asked to cover it?" She bit her lower lip and pointed both thumbs toward her chest while widening her eyes to a comical degree.

"Congrats," I murmured, still feeling icky about her reaction to this whole thing.

"Thank you," she said with an airy smile. "Turns out I did such a great job covering the Hayes murders, the station would like me to do another investigative piece."

"I'm really happy for you, Mom." And I was. She'd worked hard to get here, and at last everything was coming up... bodies in the morgue, I guess.

"Good, because I need you to do it with me."

"What? No, no, no, no." Yeah, I'd done the legwork to find the Hayes's real killer and clear Brock Calhoun's name, but that didn't mean I wanted to jump straight into another murder investigation, especially one as prominent as this one would no doubt prove to be.

"Angie, I don't really think you have a choice."

I groaned and shook my head. "Oh, yeah, because that's the way to win me over."

"The senator was killed in her home," she revealed. "Do you know where that home is?"

"Somewhere in Glendale?" I guessed with a sigh.

"Not just somewhere," my mom corrected with a new light dancing in her hazel eyes. "Right next door to your new house."

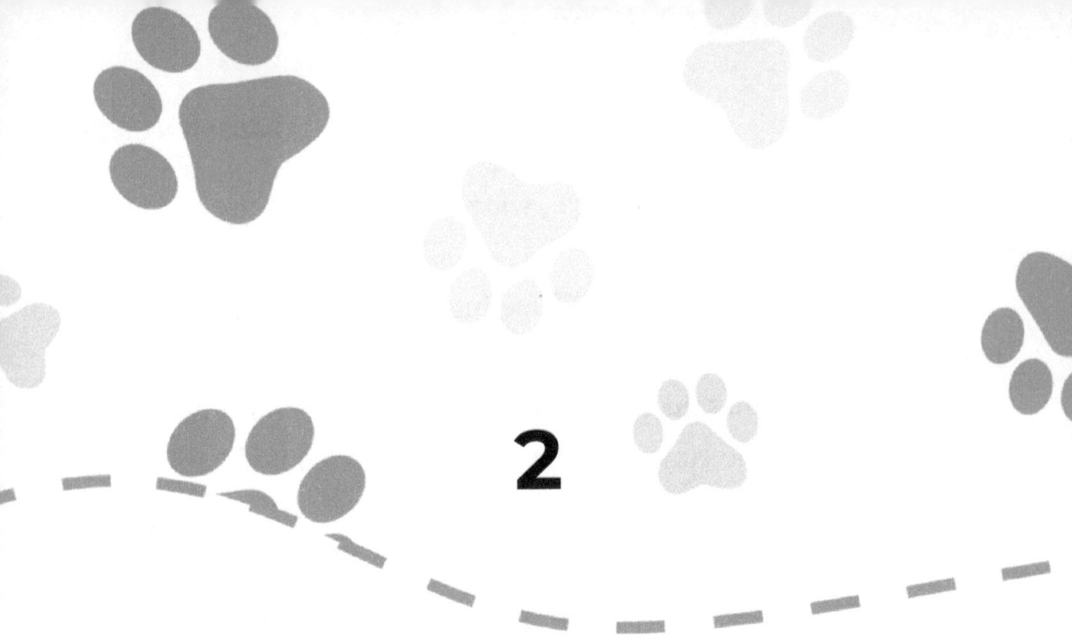

2

Well, this was exactly *not* what I needed on moving day. My new home had already been tainted by murder, and now the place next door had become an active crime scene as well.

My mom stared at me with wide, sparkling eyes. "Well?" She nudged me with her elbow as if we were doing something as harmless as discussing reality TV gossip. This wasn't reality TV, though. It was actually real life. *My life.*

"I know that look," Octo-Cat proclaimed from his seat beside me. "It's the same one you get right before you decide to do something stupid."

"Well, good luck on the investigation," I mumbled, hoping to silence them both so I could get back to packing.

It didn't work.

My mom grabbed both my wrists and attempted to drag me from

my chair. "Come with me. I need you," she whined, drawing out each word dramatically. No wonder she'd become Blueberry Bay's go-to newswoman. Even I found myself both wanting and dreading to know what would happen next.

I yanked my arms away and wrapped them around my waist defensively. "In case you forgot, it's my moving day, and I still have lots to do before the movers get here in a few hours."

Mom baulked at this excuse as she moved behind my chair and put a hand on each of my shoulders, causing me to flinch. "A few hours? Why, that's way more than enough time to take a quick glance. Besides, aren't you curious?"

I bit my lip and tried really hard not to say anything. The truth was I had, in fact, begun to enjoy the thrill of the investigation. And despite my better judgment and bigger priorities, I was definitely intrigued by the newest murder in town having happened right next door to my new place.

A fresh corpse next door. What a housewarming gift!

Seeing that she had me on the hook, Mom began to reel me in. She put her face beside mine and tipped my chair back. "Tell you what. How about you come with me now and, after we take a quick look-see, I'll come back to help you finish packing. Deal?"

I groaned and pressed my forehead to the table. The chair's front legs landed back on the floor with a jarring thud. "Deal," I murmured into the cold wood.

"Right back into the thick of it. Why am I not surprised?" Octo-Cat commented drolly before trotting off without so much as a glance my way.

"Yay!" My mom clapped her hands several times and began to yank on my arm again. Sometimes I felt like the most grown up person in my entire family, which was saying something since Mom was in her early fifties and Nan had already high-tailed it well past seventy.

"Let's go," Mom said, tugging at my arm once again. This time I got up and followed. "I'll fill you in on what I know on our drive over."

True to her word, the moment the car doors closed beside us, my mom jammed her key in the ignition and started to talk. "I know you were never interested in politics too much, but Lou Harlow was a four term senator. She won every term by a huge landslide and was probably going to be re-elected the next time, too. Everyone around here loved her, which makes her death all the more shocking."

I chewed on my thumbnail as she spoke, a bad habit that had gotten more and more out of control lately.

My mom swatted me with one of her perfectly manicured hands. "Stop that. It's gross!"

"Sorry," I muttered, running my index finger across my jagged thumbnail as I switched my focus back to the matter at hand. "So, a political rival wanted her seat and it was easier to murder her than to try to win fair and square?"

"Maybe," my mom said, bringing both hands back to the steering wheel now that she'd decided she didn't need to hit me a second time. "We'll definitely work that angle and see what we come up with."

I sensed a *but*. When Mom didn't provide it, I decided to give her the lead in. "But?"

"Why kill her at home when she spends most of her time in Washington?" she asked as if I might actually have the answer.

I shrugged. "Maybe it was more convenient."

"It's too obvious, though. Don't you think?" She frowned as she considered this.

"Well, maybe our killer isn't very smart. How did the senator die, anyway?" In my experience, killers usually were pretty smart, actually. Smart, but vain. Combine those two traits with their lack of a moral compass, and it often spelled trouble—both for their victims and for me, the fiery upstart who did my best to help bring them to justice.

Well, lately, at least.

Would I continue chasing killers around Blueberry Bay forever?

Only time would tell, but I had a sneaking suspicion that the answer just might be a resounding *Oh, heck yeah!*

Mom pulled up to a stop sign and switched on her blinker, then turned to look at me. Once again, her expression was filled with utter joy as she revealed, "Somebody pushed her down the stairs!"

Oh, for the love of...

"Then how do they know it wasn't just some stupid accident?" It looked like we might have both gotten ahead of ourselves, and here I was considering myself the sleuth of the century—at least as far as Glendale, Maine was concerned.

Mom seemed flustered. *"They?* Who's they? We are the ones investigating this, and we don't know for sure, but we definitely suspect foul play."

I bit my tongue to keep from mentioning that the police were still the true detectives here and that I was too new to the case to be a part of her royal *we*. It seemed I still had to learn this lesson for myself, too.

Shaking off my disappointment, I turned my head to watch the scenery flying past my window. Greenery stretched as far as the eye could see—trees, flowers, grass, everywhere life. Well, except at Lou Harlow's manor house.

Gulls drifted on the breeze, reminding me that gorgeous Blueberry Bay was just beyond the horizon. We lived so close to the ocean that the air always tasted slightly of salt. My new house sat so close to the shoreline, in fact, that I could walk there in ten minutes flat.

"I really wish people would stop turning up dead around here," I told my mom with a sigh. We were a small town to begin with. If the murders continued at their current clip, we'd be down half our population by the end of next year.

"Don't you think it's just a little bit exciting?" my mom said as she navigated us down the private drive that served all the most elite homes in Glendale—including now, rather inexplicably, *mine*.

I understood where my mom was coming from, though. For years, she'd wasted her journalistic talents on puff pieces and human interest stories. This new dastardly turn of events in our small town made for big news and a far more interesting job for her.

Still, people were dying, and that was definitely a problem.

I was saved from answering her question by the appearance of red and blue flashing lights on the top of the hill. My mom drove one turnoff past my new house and pulled right up to the late Lou Harlow's estate. Cops were everywhere, definitely more than technically worked for our sleepy little town. It seemed as if the whole county had arrived—whether to help investigate or merely to gawk remained to be seen.

A few officers stood by the entryway chatting over takeout coffees. Others paraded around the property talking into their radios and trying to look important. Somebody else worked on stretching that jarring yellow crime scene tape around the porch.

I hated it. I hated it so much. The good senator deserved better than this. We all did.

Mom pulled straight up behind the nearest cop car and shut off the engine. "Ready?" she asked with a quick glance my way before charging out of the car and right over to the group of officers who had gathered by the house.

"Quite the scene you've got here," she said jovially while I struggled to catch up. Even though I was taller than my mom and should have had a quicker stride, she'd always buzzed around like a hummingbird, sometimes moving so fast you could scarcely keep track.

"Yeah, and it's a private one at that," a county officer informed us both, making a little shooing gesture with her hand.

"Laura Lee, Channel 7 News," Mom answered proudly, shoving a hand forward in greeting.

The officer sneered and refused to take the proffered hand. "Oh, then we definitely don't want you here."

One of our local boys spotted us from across the yard and shouted, "It's okay. She's with us." Officer Bouchard jogged over to join us. "She's got the needed clearance," he told the others.

"Thank you," my mom said, simpering at the county officer who had tried to deny our access. "Now, be a dear and catch us up, please."

I sighed and made a mental note that *How to Win Friends & Influence People* would be the perfect gift for my mom on the next holiday that required such things.

"Officer Raines?" my mom read from the angry lady cop's badge. "I just want to help."

"Like heck you do," the other one spat back.

I tried to block their bickering out as I studied the massive stone façade before us. Just like my new house—Fulton Manor—this one was at least five-thousand square feet and probably about as old as the state of Maine itself. Gorgeous bay windows stuck out at odd intervals around the second floor in what appeared to be a recent remodeling job. I wondered if you could see the ocean from up there. Whatever the case, they seemed like nice little nooks to hang out with a good book. Maybe I could add a window seat as part of my own remodels as well.

I'd almost fully immersed myself in this bookworm fantasy of mine when a flash of something caught my eye. I squinted to try to make out what was up there, but was met only with the fluttering of drapes. Whoever or whatever was looking out upon the chaotic scene below had now disappeared.

I left mom to continue her battle with Officer Raines and inched slowly toward the entry. Her preferred method of investigation may have been talking, but I'd always preferred to jump straight in with both feet and see what I could discover.

At least if I found trouble waiting for me on the inside, I knew there were a dozen-odd officers loitering nearby. Any of them could offer up some help in a pinch.

See?

I had nothing to worry about as I tiptoed right into the middle of this fresh crime scene.

3

Despite the flurry of activity outside, the inside of the manor house sat empty—eerily so. As soon as I entered, I came face to face with the grand staircase. It had been cordoned off and the area was already scrubbed clean, though the recent disturbance was obvious.

One of the lower steps had caved in on itself, calling into question the soundness of the entire structure. A few feet from the landing, the body position had been marked in a shining white outline. *The poor senator.* She'd been a huge force in life, but the outline marking her death seemed impossibly small.

As much as my mother assumed I didn't know about the political scene or about current events in general, I'd actually voted for the senator in her two most recent elections. She'd fought hard to protect the natural beauty of our great country and the citizens within it.

Even though I liked to think of myself as non-partisan, I agreed with Senator Lou Harlow's stances more often than not.

Plus, from the few televised interviews or online news articles I'd managed to catch, I liked her. She reminded me of Nan, but in a tailored pant suit instead of a flowy silk kimono.

She'd done so much tireless work on behalf of the people, and now one of those people had killed her. I bowed my head and said a quick prayer, hoping that her death had happened quickly and without pain, and that the killer would soon be brought to justice.

I'd been around murder a lot lately, but somehow this one felt more personal. Lou Harlow wasn't a stranger. She was someone I'd seen on the TV, the Internet, and even the odd newspaper that still found its way into the firm where I worked.

"There you are," Mom shouted after me, disturbing the sanctity of the moment as she flew in through the open front door.

I kept my eyes fixed straight ahead. Was there some important clue I'd missed because emotions were clouding my judgment with this one?

"Such a shame," Mom clucked, finally showing a blessed bit of remorse.

We stood side by side, studying the scene. A glint of yellowish green at the top of the stairs drew my eye and I stepped forward to get a better look.

"What is it? What do you see?" Mom asked in an excited whisper.

I still hadn't figured out what was up there, but I pointed anyway.

We both craned our heads and shifted our angles until finally I saw a scary, mummy-looking face watching me from above. "It's some kind of animal, I think." Although it looked like none I'd ever come across before. Maybe in a zoo, but in the wilds of coastal Maine? I think not.

"The senator did have two pet cats," Mom pointed out, still struggling and twisting in an effort to discern the animal for herself.

"Whatever's up there, I'm not really sure it's a cat." I took another step forward, bending my neck straight back to achieve a fresh perspective. All that did was hurt me, though. "*Ugh.* I wish it wasn't so dark in here," I moaned.

Mom lifted her phone high and then snapped a picture of the area using her flash. The burst of light was more than enough to fully illuminate that same little animal that had first caught my eye. A second larger one of the same kind also sat farther back away from the bannister. They still looked like something that had come straight out of a horror movie, but now at least I could clearly tell they were cats.

Cats with no fur and lots of wrinkles. *Eww.*

I shuddered as I pictured Octo-Cat shorn down in a similar fashion, and that particular mental image was even scarier than the two odd Sphynxes sitting before me.

Mom showed me the picture she'd managed to get on her phone. "They're hairless cats," she said matter-of-factly.

I shivered again. "Why would anyone want a cat without hair?"

"Allergies? Attention?" Mom guessed and offered me a casual shrug. "Could have been either with the Senator."

A growl sounded above, and I swear the little hairs on the back of my neck shot straight up. I was a newly branded cat person, so why did these two freak me out so much? Was it that they were hairless or that they were staked out at a murder scene? Both?

After another emphatic growl, the larger of the two cats appeared at the top of the stairs, peering down at us like a dissatisfied overlord. Or a prison guard. Or a killer.

"Hi," I said, even though I knew he couldn't understand me without Octo-Cat here to translate.

He opened his mouth wide, then let out a terrible hiss before turning tail and stalking off with the smaller cat in pursuit.

"I am officially terrified of those things," I said.

Mom shoved her phone back into her bag and turned to me with that same excited expression she'd worn most of the morning. "Know what I'm thinking?"

"I'm not sure I want to know," I admitted. I should have been at home packing the last of my boxes for the big move, not shaking in my flip flops at the sight of these two bizarre felines. There was absolutely no reason this little investigation of ours couldn't have waited.

Mom grabbed my hand and gave it a squeeze. Obviously, we were not thinking the same thing here. "I'm thinking," she revealed with a happy squeal, "that this looks like a job for Pet Whisperer, P.I."

"Pet Whisperer? P.I.?" I shook my head and tried very hard not to roll my eyes. Of course, she'd given me a special headline-worthy moniker. She'd probably already written and rewritten my featured story in her head several times over.

"That's your new name," she said, squeezing my hand again. "Do you like it?"

"Um, I'm fine just being Angie." *Must not encourage this.* I wanted my special ability to remain a secret, not become front page news.

"Not for you," Mom said with a sigh. "For your business."

"I don't have a business," I pointed out. I still didn't like where she was headed with all of this.

"Wrong again," she crooned. "You're already doing the work. You might as well hang out your sign and get paid for it."

"Interesting idea, but I don't want people to know I can talk to animals," I reminded her. Besides, I still had my part-time salary from the law firm and my full-time stipend for being Octo-Cat's official guardian and the overseer of his trust fund.

"Everyone will think it's a gimmick," Mom countered with a wink. "But only we'll know the truth. Besides, it will give you an excuse to bring your cat with you while investigating, which is what you need anyway, right? I mean, if he'd been here this morning, we could have cracked the whole case wide open by now. Those cats definitely know what happened. I just know it."

"Why do you have to be so excited about this?" I asked, resigned to the fact that I was apparently opening a business now—and, worse still, that my cat would be my new business partner.

"That's branding, baby," Mom answered with a glamorous flip of her hair.

Oh, brother. Or rather—*oh, mother.*

I took a couple big steps back, careful not to upset the crime scene as I walked away from the crazy lady who just so happened to be my mother. Turning to the door now, I said, "Okay, great. So, I'm just going to go make sure the police know the cats are up there. With the stairs cordoned off, it might not be easy to get them down."

Mom followed after me as I returned to the bright world outside. I squinted from the sudden onslaught of sunniness and swept my eyes over the premises in search of the one officer I knew well enough to approach. Once my eyes adjusted to the light again, I spotted Officer Bouchard at the edge of the property examining a small copse of evergreens at the edge of a much larger deciduous forest that divided Harlow's property from mine.

I jogged over to him, knowing my mom would have no trouble keeping up if she wanted to.

"Did you know there are cats inside?" I asked him, embarrassed by the fact my breaths came out labored from that short burst of exercise.

"That would be Jacques and Jillianne," he said with a chuckle. "Ugly little things, aren't they?"

"They're... cute. Um, in a different way," I insisted. In a *very* different way. Still, even though I'd just had the same thought myself, I suddenly felt defensive on their behalf.

My mom joined us then, having chosen to stroll elegantly across the field rather than run like I did. I guess it was now part of her persona or something. *The news waits for no man,* she'd often told me, *but for a woman, it just might.*

Officer Bouchard smiled kindly at Mom. "Yeah. The senator picked them up from a breeder in France, thus the fancy names. They're slippery little buggers, too. I've been trying to catch them all morning, but so far, no luck. Figure with the next of kin on the way, the cats can be his problem when he gets here."

"Next of kin?" Mom inserted herself between me and him. She'd already pulled out her phone and started the recording app, which she now held up to him like a microphone. "And who might that be?"

Officer Bouchard stared at the phone, then cleared his throat and answered in a crisp, clear voice, "Her son, Matthew Harlow. Lives in Chicago. Should be here by nightfall."

"And who do you think killed Lou Harlow?" Mom asked, pressing the phone even closer to his face.

He sighed and pushed her hand aside. "I think it's too soon to say. We haven't even ruled out the possibility of it being an accident yet."

Until today, I'd only seen one crime scene before—Bill and Ruth Hayes, who were murdered in their own home. I saw it long after the fact, but I'd had the same feeling today as I'd had then.

Call it my gut.

Call it intuition.

Or maybe even just a lucky guess.

Whatever the case, I knew it had been no accident that killed Lou Harlow. Someone had wanted her dead and decided to take matters into his or her own hands.

Now we just had to figure out who.

The Pet Whisperer P.I. was officially on the case.

4

As promised, Mom stuck around to help me finish my packing and, as much as it pained me to admit, I almost wished she wouldn't have. For starters, she had an opinion on *everything.*

I'm not exaggerating either. *Everything.*

As she picked up each of my possessions one by one, she frowned and turned them over in her hands. Apparently she believed that if she studied my things from all angles, they might suddenly transform into something that would match her expectations.

Growing up, I had often wondered if she felt the same way about me, but now I knew better. Mom was a nice lady and I know she loved me as best she could, but she had most definitely not been cut from the divine maternal cloth.

"Do you really need to take this with you?" she asked me now. "I can get you a newer one. A better one."

After about an hour of this same conversation over and over again, she'd basically promised to buy me a new life as part of my housewarming gift. I know our tastes didn't match up—Mom was far more sophisticated than I'd ever be—but still, it would have been nice for her to give it a rest.

The other problem I had just then was that I desperately wanted to discuss the crime scene and those weird Sphynx cats with Octo-Cat. Yes, even though Mom knew I could talk to him, it still felt weird to carry on a conversation right there in front of her.

Our tastes weren't the only thing that differed. Mom was all cold, hard facts and evidence. She'd ask a million and one questions, including many I wouldn't know how to answer. Namely, *how come you two can talk to each other?*

I still had no idea why Octo-Cat and I had formed this connection or even really how it worked. One day I'd love to figure all that out, but I was too busy with my move at present to sit around and speculate all the many possibilities with my mom.

"You know," Mom said as she studied the plates and bowls stacked in one of my kitchen cupboards. "You're going to be living in a manor house now. A lot of your things don't really match that aesthetic. It may be jarring for visitors."

"It's fine, Mom," I said, nudging her out of the way with my hip and packing away the offensive dishes myself. "I don't really plan on having a lot of visitors, and I'm not really the hoity toity type. You know that about me."

She stepped to the side and opened another cabinet. "Maybe there's a middle ground here," she insisted. "Nan has a nice set of dinnerware. You could throw yours out and stick with hers instead. Oh! Or you could donate yours. You love those charity shops, right?"

"Maybe," I said to acknowledge the topic so that we could both move on. I did like the thrift shops, but I much preferred buying from them over donating my own things.

Mom frowned, and I hugged one of my cheery red plates to my chest. I liked my plates, and I liked my life, too. Why couldn't Mom just accept that she and I were never going to see eye to eye on certain issues? So what if most of the things in my kitchen came from the dollar store? They all worked just as well as the things Mom bought for a hundred times the price at her fancy chain boutiques.

"Oh, I like these," she said, staring into the next cupboard over as she grabbed a floral-patterned Lenox teacup and studied it with wide eyes.

"I don't want her messing with my stuff," Octo-Cat informed me, hopping up onto the counter and giving Mom such a startle, she dropped the much admired teacup right onto the ground.

The three of us watched what followed in slow motion, but it was already, regrettably too late. The delicate cup burst into smithereens and Octo-Cat let out an ear-piercing cry. "My Evian vessel!"

Mom took a step back. "I'm so sorry," she told me, and I could tell she genuinely meant it. Maybe she picked at me not to be mean, but just because she sometimes had a hard time thinking of other things to discuss. Maybe that was why she got so excited over sharing the Lou Harlow murder investigation with me.

"I'll get you a new set, I promise," she said, blinking back tears. Suddenly, I felt like the absolute worst daughter in the world. Why did I have such difficulty spending more than a few minutes at a time in my mom's company? I'd need to try harder.

Of course, I didn't have the heart to tell her that this particular set was irreplaceable. They'd belonged to Octo-Cat's previous owner, the late Ethel Fulton, and they were one of the few things he still had left of her. Granted, we'd soon be moving into her mostly furnished manor home, but still. This tea set had been special to Octo-Cat. It was the only way he'd take his food or water, and now that he was down a cup, I'd have to increase my dish-washing schedule to boot.

"Look," I said, trying to be as gentle as possible. "I think I can handle things from here. Why don't you go see what else you can find out about the Harlow murder?"

She twisted her hands anxiously. "Are you sure?" Despite her hesitation, I could tell she was just as eager to go as I was to have her leave.

Did I feel guilty? *Sure.* I'd probably never stop feeling guilty when it came to my strained relationship with her and Dad.

Still, Mom and I had always gotten along best in brief bursts. I loved that we were becoming closer these last few weeks, but we needed more time to navigate our new relationship—and this really wasn't the best day for us to put in the work, as calloused as that sounded even to my own ear.

It just couldn't be a priority with all the other things I needed to do.

I side-stepped the broken teacup and gave my mom a tight hug. "I'm sure. I can tell you're dying to get back on the case. I'll be fine here."

Mom sighed happily. *"Mmm,* you know me so well," she said before quickly gathering her things and racing toward the door. "I'll text with any updates. Bye!"

And just like that, she was gone again.

Octo-Cat resumed his agonized mewling. Even though we could understand each other, sometimes he still reverted to the classic cat sounds—usually in periods of intense emotion—like now.

"I'm sorry," I told him, carefully stroking his head. I hoped it would offer comfort and also that the kindly gesture would not result in me getting bitten, but you kind of never knew with Octo-Cat.

"It's like Ethel just died all over again," he told me. His ears twitched then fell flat against his head. His tail swished back and forth like a metronome. His eyes grew so wide and dark that I was sure he would have cried, were such a trait in his biology.

"I'm really sorry," I told him again, unsure of what else I could do.

He stared at the tiny fragments of Lenox that lay scattered across the kitchen floor. Whites, pinks, gold-trimmed, all nothing more than broken pieces of the life he'd once known. Great. Now I was tearing up, too.

"I'll just go get the broom," I mumbled, not wanting him to see how moved I now was on his behalf.

But before I could turn away, Octo-Cat shot out in front of me and screamed, "No!"

My heart beat ratcheted up a few notches, thumping wildly as I wondered what crazy thing my cat might do next. "Whoa, what happened?"

"I'm just not ready yet," he informed me. "I need some time with it first."

"With the broken teacup?" I asked gently. He'd gotten better at detecting sarcasm and punished me whenever he heard it in my voice or saw it on my face. He was allowed to talk to me however he pleased, of course, but I had to maintain the utmost respect at all times.

Even times like this.

Octo-Cat sniffed and lifted his nose high as he did whenever he wanted to appear superior. "Yes," he answered simply.

"Unfortunately, we don't really have time." I kept my face placid, understanding. "The movers will be here in an hour or so. And we can't keep stepping around the mess. It's dangerous. One of us could cut a foot on those sharp shards."

He let out a mournful meow, then turned away. "Do as you must."

I resumed my journey to get the broom and dustpan, feeling like the worst cat owner in the world. That made me the worst daughter and the worst cat owner all within the span of about ten minutes. My stock would not be rising anytime soon.

When I returned, Octo-Cat still stood frozen in that dramatic pose of his. Normally, his antics bugged me, but at that moment, I truly felt sorry for him and his loss.

"Would it help if we said a few words?" I suggested.

The morose tabby turned his head slightly and peered at me from the corners of his eyes. "Like a funeral?"

"Yeah," I said with a shrug. "Like a funeral."

He shifted the rest of the way out of his pose and faced me

straight on. Already he looked better, like his heart had started to piece itself back together. "Where will we bury it?" he wanted to know.

"Oh. *Umm.*" I did not have time for this, but he also seemed sincere and in need of closure, so I suggested something I hoped would suit us both. "We should bury it tonight at Ethel's." That would buy me the time I needed to pack at least, and hopefully it would make him feel better about this whole episode, too.

"Great idea, Angela," Octo-Cat said with one of his hard-earned smiles.

I glowed in the light of his rare and wonderful praise. He was a diva, sure, but it did feel good to make him happy, especially considering that most of the time every little thing I did disappointed him greatly.

"*Tonight,*" he shouted merrily. "That also gives me time to work on what I'll say." He then trotted off, leaving me to tidy the mess and prepare it for burial.

Ugh. As glad as I was that he felt better, I'd planned to talk to him about Lou Harlow's murder and the strange cats she'd left behind.

Well, that would just have to wait.

Why was my to do list only getting longer the harder I worked today?

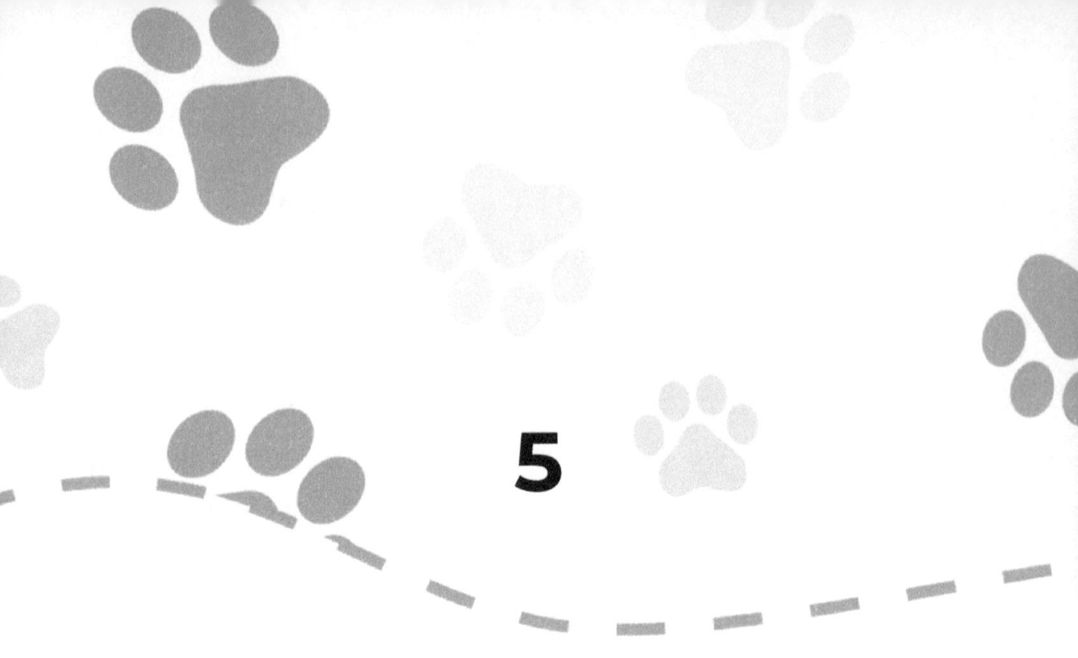

5

All of Octo-Cat's previous sorrow evaporated the moment we pulled into the long, winding driveway of Fulton Manor.

"Home!" he yowled, even being so brave as to detach his claws from my thigh so he could prop himself up and look out the window. "Oh, it feels so good to be home!"

I parked and opened my driver's side door, and he immediately jumped over me to get to the ground outside. "Home!" he continued to cry as he rolled back and forth in the grass like a crazy kitty.

I was just about to ask him to rein it in when he raced up the porch steps and through his specialty cat door, which slid open in response to a special signal his collar emitted. All this time I'd never replaced his collar and he'd never asked me to. He probably always knew we'd end up here someday. After all, he'd engineered the entire thing.

Octo-Cat had clearly found a way to keep himself occupied.

Meanwhile, the movers were still packing things up at my old rental, which gave me a little bit of time alone with my new mansion now.

A mansion! And it belonged to me!

Ridiculous.

But, okay, also super cool.

My eyes moved up the three stories all the way to the turret rising up beyond the far side of the roof. I'd already decided to make my bedroom there in the tippity top tower just like some kind of weirdo modern-day princess. Nan had claimed the master bedroom, which had belonged to Ethel before she died. It was also where she had died, and I just felt icky about being in the same house, let alone the very same bedroom.

Nan simply laughed and said, "Oh, sweetie pie. Death is a part of life." I figured at her advanced age, it must not bother her as much as it did me. Personally, I hoped I never reached the point in life where I was comfortable sleeping in the same spot a dead body had lain only months before.

It was eerie enough moving into a house that had served as the scene of a murder. In fact, I was still working on coming to terms with it. By now, I felt pretty sure my first electric bill would be many hundreds of dollars, seeing as I planned to sleep with every single light on until I no longer felt afraid of my own house.

Had it been my choice, I'd never have picked a dwelling so grand. But Octo-Cat had insisted upon it. Even Mr. Fulton—my former boss—seemed happy to be unloading the house quickly, even at a substantial loss to himself and the other heirs.

As I watched Octo-Cat run back and forth through the cat door, moaning with delight each and every time, I really did have to admit the place suited him. So what if he was a common housecat? Looks could be deceiving, and his heart was definitely bourgeois to the max.

I left him to his merriment and grabbed one of the lighter boxes from my trunk. Inside, a thin veil of dust clung to almost every possible surface. I probably should have cleaned it out before moving in, but I didn't exactly have the cash to hire someone. Besides, the move had happened so suddenly, I barely had time to pack, let alone do much of anything else.

We'd get to it. Eventually.

Just add it to the bottom of my never-ending to do list. Or maybe somewhere in the middle.

My goal was to have the place at least livable before Nan joined us at the end of the month. She needed more time to pack up the entire life she'd lived in Blueberry Bay as well as all her mementos from her time on Broadway.

I understood that, so I didn't tell her how the thought of sleeping in this giant place alone frightened me to the very core. I had Octo-Cat, who may or may not protect me in the event of danger. A fifty-fifty shot was still better than having zero help, if the need for it were to suddenly occur.

Another unsettling thing?

Fulton Manor and Harlow Manor next door had almost the exact same blueprint. Although they were both built well before the rise of the McMansion, I guess somebody had liked the first so much, they'd decided to build a second almost exactly like it.

Somehow, I found myself drifting toward the grand staircase time and again. It looked so much like the one next door that it made me shudder each time I passed. I was like a deranged moth drawn right into the middle of the flame. *Burn, baby, burn.*

"What's wrong with you?" my cat asked, eyeing me wearily after his ten-millionth time through the cat door.

I shrugged. "Just a bit weirded out by the murder next door."

He stopped dead in his tracks, not even putting his front left paw all the way down as he stared at me. "Wait, *what?* Somebody killed that nice old lady? When?"

Oh, that was right. We hadn't gotten the chance to talk yet, given the entire teacup episode. "This morning," I told him, watching him carefully to see how he'd react once he had more information. "Or, probably last night, actually."

He gasped and stomped his paw down onto the hardwood floor. "And you didn't tell me?"

"There was that whole thing with the teacup, and I… I'm sorry." I apologized, knowing that it was the most surefire way to avoid an altercation. Octo-Cat loved fighting and hated losing, which meant I was constantly on the bum end of *that* deal.

He shook his head in dismay and stared at me for an uncomfortably long time before trotting up a few stairs and positioning himself just so. "Go on. Tell me now," he demanded. "I need to know exactly what happened."

I felt nervous under the spotlight of his scrutinous gaze but did as I was told. For as much as he was supposed to be my pet, it really felt as if I were the one who'd been trained. "The senator was killed. Someone pushed her down the staircase," I explained.

"The staircase!" Octo-Cat exclaimed, lifting one paw and then the other while he stared at the stoop beneath him.

I nodded dumbly, unable to form words just then.

"Jacques and Jillianne," he somehow managed to hiss between clenched teeth. "I'll skin them alive, those good for nothings." He jogged down the steps and was just about to dart out the cat door again before I stopped him.

"Wait!" I cried. "You know Jacques and Jillianne?" I felt so stupid every time I said their Frenchified names. Why did cats need such fancy names? Octo-Cat was bad enough with his eight names, but at least all of them were in English. Wait. They were, right? It was honestly kind of hard to remember, thus his new and improved—and much, much shorter—moniker.

He sighed but kept his back to me. His tiny kitty shoulders heaved with the weight of his obvious disappointment in me. "Of course I know them. We used to live next door and—will you look at that?—now we do again."

"Are you friends?" I asked eagerly, running a half circle around him so that we were once again face to face.

He looked like he was about to sneeze. He didn't. Instead, he said, "With those weirdos? No way."

"I mean, they look a little different, but that's not a reason to—"

"It's not their looks, Angela. It's the way they talk." He growled at me, much like the big hairless cat had that morning.

I wasn't sure what game we were playing here, but I hated to be left out. I shook my head and scowled at him. "You're not sounding any less racist here. Or is it breedist? Whatever the case, not a shining moment from you."

He simply chuckled. "Oh, you'll see what I mean. Give it some time. Shouldn't take too long."

He trotted up a few steps and then turned back to me, something I couldn't quite interpret shining in his eyes. "By the way," he said as if a sudden thought had just occurred to him.

"Death by staircase? Yeah, classic cat move."

"What do you—?" I started.

He cut me off with a villainous laugh he liked to trot out whenever he wanted to be particularly theatrical. Apparently, this was one of those blessed times.

"I mean," he said, between manic gasps for air. "Jacques and Jillianne killed your senator. The cats are guilty. Case closed." He sulked slowly away, still laughing to himself.

I took two giant steps back, feeling like I'd just looked into the void and saw my death play out before my very eyes. Whatever happened next, I'd make sure to watch my step when it came to the grand staircase I'd once considered the crowning feature of my new home.

Octo-Cat's laughter echoed through the halls. Why was this so funny to him? Why was he still laughing, and about this?

Apparently, he and my mom shared the same morbid fascination with the senator's death. Too bad they both talked to me instead of each other.

It's just his way, I reminded myself. *He likes being the center of attention. He'd never actually hurt you.*

But then I thought of all those little old cat ladies who died in the city only to be devoured by their most beloved pets and shuddered again...

Well, at least I knew Octo-Cat would only eat Fancy Feast.

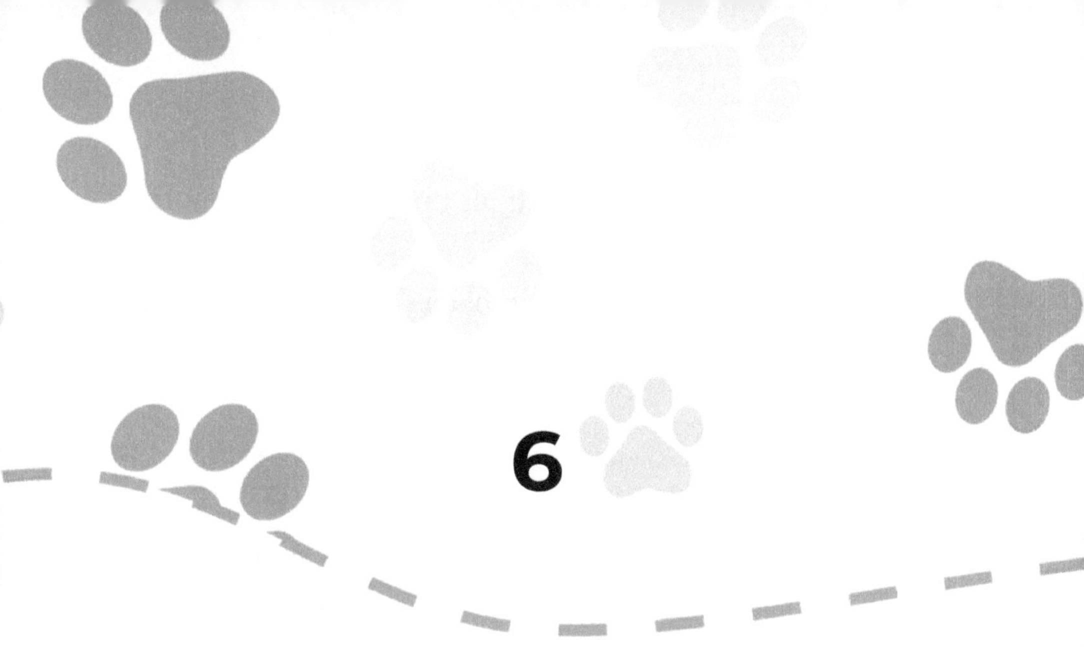

6

Even though I needed to take some items upstairs, I decided to stick to the main level of the house while the movers hauled all my heaviest belongings in through the front door. I'd need just a little bit more time to come to grips with what Octo-Cat had just revealed about feline-on-human homicide and the preferred method for it.

Here I hadn't even known such a horror existed. *Silly me.*

Truth be told, I hadn't brought much from my old place, and so my preliminary unpacking was quick. Since I still felt queasy every time I passed by the staircase, I decided to head outside and take a walk around the property.

Gorgeous, intricately kept flowerbeds surrounded the house on three sides, and the back opened up to a lovely two-tiered deck, complete with a fire pit and twin porch swings. Farther out, a thick forest rimmed the property, giving it all the privacy you could want and more.

Okay, so half my week would probably now be spent on yard maintenance going forward, but even I had to admit it would be time well spent.

A soft rumble in the distance along with a flash of red between the trees caught my eye, and I tromped through the grass to check it out. Apparently, if I angled my head just right, I could see straight through to the late senator's yard. A bright red sports car had just pulled up the drive, and it was one I recognized instantly. After all, there were only two fancy red sports cars in all of Glendale; Nan drove one while Thompson owned the other.

I watched in horror as my boss, the senior partner at our law firm, Mr. Richard Thompson, clambered out of his car and up the steps toward the house. Uncharacteristically, he came without the briefcase that was usually attached to him like a boxy extension of his left limb. He also appeared nervous as he loosened his tie and glanced around the estate to see if anyone else was nearby. The police had mostly cleared out by then—or at least taken their get-together elsewhere. And, thank goodness, he didn't know to search for me on the other side of the forest.

I remained rooted to the spot as Officer Bouchard stepped out of the house and strode forward to greet Mr. Thompson. His badge reflected the sunshine like a polished nickel. "Richard, can I help you with something?"

I craned my neck to try to make out Mr. Thompson's expression, but a low-hanging branch blocked my view.

"I heard the news," Thompson said. His deep voice projected through the forest. "Thought I'd stop by to pay my respects."

Officer Bouchard jogged down the steps and motioned for the other man to follow. "I'm sure you don't need me to tell you that this isn't the appropriate time or place."

"I know," my boss agreed. He seemed unsure of what to do with his hands. "It was just so… so unexpected."

The policeman sighed and raised one of his arms high to run a hand through his hair. "Yeah, we're all pretty beat up about this one. It doesn't change the rules, though."

They exchanged a few quiet words that got lost before they reached my ears, and then Mr. Thompson climbed back into his car and left.

"What was *that* about?" Octo-Cat asked, choosing that exact moment to rub up against my leg and giving me the fright of my life.

"I have no idea," I told him honestly, still very much suspicious as to how both me and my firm at large now became tangled up in every single murder around town. Granted, there weren't any murders until Ethel Fulton earlier this year—or at least none that I knew about.

"I hope somebody without any pets moves in next," he informed me with a bored yawn as we both stared vacantly through the trees.

This surprised me enough to risk a glance toward him. It's not like anything was happening at Harlow Manor anymore. Even Officer Bouchard had disappeared from view now.

"Don't you like other cats?" I asked him.

"In *my* territory?" He made a sarcastic *psshaw* noise. "I'd much rather *not* share, if given the choice. This is my land. These are my trees to climb, and in their branches? Those are my birds to devour... or at least deliver to the foot of your bed when you've been a good human."

I shuddered at the memory of his most recent *gift*. "I guess I'll make sure not to be a good human then."

He nipped at the blades of grass in front of his paws, swallowed a few bites, and then snickered. "Just for that, now my puke will be green."

"Um, okay," I said with a shrug. Honestly, his punishments often weren't much worse than his rewards, and this one seemed especially tame.

"It will throw off your whole day," he explained with a smirk. His laughter became sinister, and I knew he'd gone full-on into evil genius mode. The only problem with that is our definitions of the word *genius* varied substantially.

When he stopped laughing, he took a deep breath and glanced up at me. "You don't get it, do you?" he said with a frustrated groan that was also part growl.

I shook my head, just as Officer Bouchard popped into view outside of the Harlow place. Why was he there? What was he doing?

"You'll have to clean up green puke," my cat explained between laughs that seemed to be losing their steam. "Normally, you start your day by cleaning up brown puke. You see? It will make everything different right from the start of your day. You won't be able to stand it!"

"You got me," I said with a resigned sigh. It would be better for us both if he thought he'd found a new means of punishing me. He derived such great pleasure from trying out new training techniques, that I didn't have the heart to correct his misunderstandings when it came to what did and didn't work for disciplining humans.

"Got it out of your system now?" I asked, turning back to study him with a skeptical smile.

"For now," he answered. "But just you wait until tomorrow morning!"

"Okay, great." I glanced back toward Officer Bouchard's immovable form and my curiosity continued to grow. Who would kill a four term senator when she was so liked by her constituents? Why did the police find it necessary to guard the crime scene? And what, if anything, did her weird, hairless cats have to do with it all?

"Hey, are you busy right now?" I asked my cat when I realized he might be able to sneak through the woods for a closer look.

He just turned his nose up and said, "Yes," then turned around with his tail also held high in the air, flashing me an unnecessary view of his kitty butt.

"Well, thanks for that," I shouted after him.

With one more glance though the trees, I decided to give it a rest. At least for now. Maybe the cops had already identified the culprit and that's why they were guarding the scene. Even if I had an official title now as part of Mom's impromptu branding session this morning, I was still inexperienced and new at this.

The police were the experts, and I had to trust them to do their jobs right. Even as I thought those words, however, I knew it would only be a matter of time before I found myself creeping through those trees to investigate the scene of the murder firsthand.

7

Night was fast approaching by the time the movers left. They not only helped me move my meager belongings in, but they also stayed to help reorganize the existing furniture within the manor and to pack some of the unneeded pieces into their truck for a quick stop off to the local charity shop.

Okay, maybe not so quick, considering they ended up moving more out than they moved in. But I definitely wasn't keeping the bed Ethel had died in, or any of her bedroom set for that matter. I didn't care that Nan was just fine repurposing the furniture for her own use. It creeped me out and I refused to keep any part of it in my home. It was already bad enough that Octo-Cat absolutely refused to part with the formal dining room set that had hosted the poisonous dinner party. I did not need to top that off with my Nan sleeping in some other old lady's death bed.

"I'm glad they're finally gone," Octo-Cat said, standing with his forepaws on the low window frame as he watched the moving truck pull away. "They smelled bad, like human body odor. *Blech.*"

I rolled my eyes, but luckily he was too distracted to notice. "That's probably because they were moving heavy things for us the better part of the afternoon."

"Still gross. I have a very delicate olfactory operation up here," he said, twitching his nose demonstratively. Well, I couldn't really argue with him on that point.

"Are you good?" I asked, hoping he would go easy on me, though I half expected him to make me move his belongings from one place to another all night long until he came up with the winning arrangement.

"I'm good," he answered. His complacency gave me a wicked shock to the system. Would living here be like living with a different, less demanding cat? One could only hope.

"I'm ready for the funeral when you are," he said, plopping his butt on the worn oriental rug and staring up at me with large, probing eyes.

The teacup—right. "Okay, I'll go get the box," I said, trying to remember if I'd left it in the car or tucked it away somewhere in the kitchen.

Octo-Cat raced ahead and blocked my path. "I said when you're ready."

"I am ready. We can do it now." *Aww,* he was being so sweet to consider my needs for a change. Maybe the loss of his teacup made him value the friends he had left. Maybe we really had reached a turning point in our relationship.

He shook his head and took on a condescending tone. "No, Angela. You are *not.* I wasn't going to say anything, because I assumed you already knew, but..." He paused to take a deep, dramatic breath. "You smell like human body odor, too."

...Or maybe nothing had changed at all.

I threw a hand on each hip and stared down at him. "So what? You want me to take a shower first?"

"Not want," he corrected, studying his paw nonchalantly. "Require."

I so badly wanted to call this whole ridiculous teacup funeral off, but instead I turned on my heel and headed toward the bathroom. Man, he really did have me trained.

As much as it irritated me to be told what to do by my cat, the hot water did soothe my aching muscles, and I felt more like myself after slipping into my favorite jeans and rejoining Octo-Cat downstairs.

"Ready!" I trilled, going once more to retrieve the teacup.

His furry form appeared at the top of the stairs, giving me quite the fright in the process. "No," he said simply. "This will not do."

"What's wrong now?" I asked, tapping my foot impatiently. That was one bit of body language he understood well since he often did the same thing by flicking his tail.

"Isn't it customary for humans to wear black when attending a funeral?" He tilted his head to the side as if it pained him to have to explain such a simple concept to me. After all, I was supposed to be the human expert around here.

"Yeah, but—"

He held up a paw to silence me. "That's what I thought. So, chop chop, you."

I sighed but went to find the dress I had worn to Ethel's funeral a few months back, anyway. At this point my annoyance was such that my cat was lucky we weren't headed to *his* funeral.

He's grieving. He's grieving, I reminded myself over and over again. But the truth was, he could be having the best day of his life and would still treat me this way. Most people had a sense of cats' haughtiness and entitlement but didn't know how deep it ran due to their inability to hold a conversation with their beloved animal overlords the way I could. Still, no matter how much he complained, Octo-Cat did forgive me for most of my flaws, so I did my best to put up with his.

The next time I came back down those stairs, I clung tightly to the handrail in case the tabby's agitation matched my own.

Octo-Cat gave me a purr of approval as he took in my black maxi dress and swept back hair. "Finally. Now come," he trotted through his electronic cat door and waited on the porch for me to join him. Once outside, I grabbed the tiny makeshift coffin—which had once been the box for a pair of flipflops I'd purchased from the discount shoe store—from my car's glove box and followed him to the side of the house.

He stopped at the end of a retaining wall that had beautiful pink azaleas spilling over the sides. "I chose this spot," the cat informed me, "because these remind me of the pretty little flowers that once lined our dearly departed teacup."

When I squinted at the flowers and then down at the remains of the Lenox dishware in my hands, I realized that he was absolutely right. It was really quite sweet that he'd put so much thought into this. I wondered if he'd be so discerning when planning my farewell, should he outlive me. A morbid thought, it was true, but with all the murders around here lately, it was also a valid one.

"Should I go get a shovel?" I asked when he made no move to dig into the soft earth.

"That would be for the best, Angela." He bowed his head reverently. Was he praying? If so, what deity did cats pray to? Did he have the same God as me? And how did one send off a soulless object to the great beyond? So many questions when, honestly, I'd always just assumed my cat worshiped himself and expected me to join his strange religion as well.

I left him to his… *whatever he was doing.* There would be time for questions later. Now I had to respect the strange ritual I didn't quite understand but knew enough to see it was of vital importance to him.

Luckily, it didn't take me long to find a small hand shovel among the supplies in Ethel's gardening shed. As I jogged back to the scene of our interment, I wondered if Ethel had ever tended to the landscaping herself or if she'd always hired it out. I also wondered how long it would take for me to learn the specific care for each of the many types of plants that lined the property. Hopefully not so long that I killed some of them in my ineptitude. I really didn't want to have any more funerals for inanimate objects. Sure, plants were technically living, but I still didn't think they deserved to have funerals in their honor. Obviously, the teacup was a special case; I hoped this was obvious to my cat as well.

Returning to him, I settled onto my knees and began to dig in the spot Octo-Cat had pointed out. While I did this, he stood by and started a lengthy eulogy about the life and times of his friend teacup.

"It always gave me water when I was thirsty," he moaned. I decided not to point out that this was because he refused to drink from any other vessel.

"And unlike it's brother," Octo-Cat continued. "It was never contaminated by letting a fly into my Evian." His voice quivered as he continued, "No, sirree. It kept the water in and the flies out, just like a good teacup should do. I'll miss you, teacup. Breakfast just won't be the same without you. Nor will my dinner."

I worked very hard to keep my face straight, and thank goodness for that, because he turned toward me in complete seriousness and said, "Now it's your turn to say a few words."

Well, shoot. Why hadn't I prepared anything? I should've seen this coming from miles away. Still at a loss, I said the first thing that came to mind, hoping it would please him. "It was a good teacup. Pretty. Matched the others in its set."

"It did! It did!" Octo-Cat cried, and when he drew quiet again, I heard the unmistakable sound of a crash on the other side of the woods.

"What was that?" I whispered to my tabby.

He stood quietly, staring down into the open grave I'd dug for the teacup and its coffin.

"Did you hear that crash?" I asked again, more frantically this time. What if the murderer was back? What if he was coming for us and we were just sitting right out in the open, unmoving, not even looking?

My palms began to sweat. Thank goodness I was no longer holding onto the teacup, because I'd have dropped it to a second death.

Octo-Cat kept his eyes cast downward, still serious, still reverent, completely unmoved by my fear. "I think we're just about done here," he said sorrowfully. "Angela, will you please shovel in the dirt?"

I nodded and carefully pushed the dirt around the shoe box as Octo-Cat sang a mournful song with no words, only mews. It would have been beautiful, if I wasn't worried that it was leading a killer straight to us. Luckily, he closed his eyes as he sang, which enabled me to glance over my shoulder and keep an eye on the woods.

It took about five minutes to finish his wordless song. Our weird ritual now finished to his apparent satisfaction, he bowed his head one more time and said, "Okay, time to go play detective," then ran head-long into the woods.

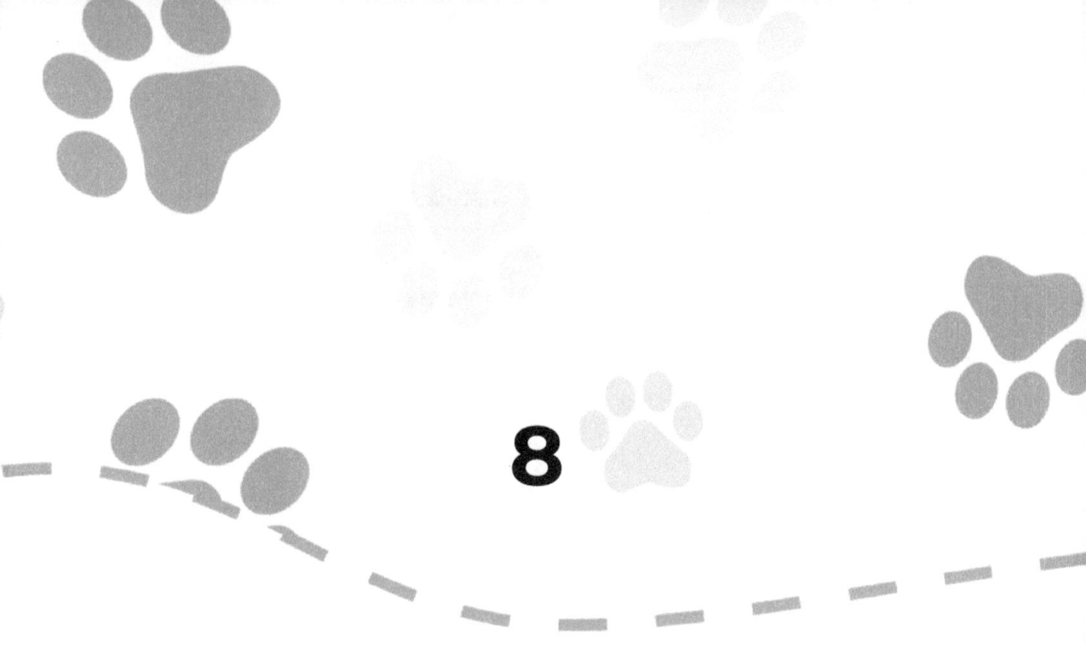

8

I could scarcely keep up as Octo-Cat tore his way through the dense forest. Branches slapped into my chest as I wove my way deeper and deeper. The woods that joined the two properties didn't run more than fifty feet wide at the most, but with no clear path to guide me through, they felt much deeper and darker than they had by the light of the afternoon.

Even treading carefully, I managed to snag my foot on a knotted root, which sent me careening face forward into the dirt. Of course, I'd needlessly been wearing open-toed dress shoes for the teacup funeral, which made for a particularly painful toe-stubbing experience.

I moaned and rolled over onto my side, clutching my poor injured toes and I searched the darkness for Octo-Cat. He'd probably made it all the way to Harlow manor by now, which meant I was alone in the creepy forest, sporting an injury that would make it difficult to escape quickly should trouble come calling.

An ominous crunch sounded a few yards away as something took slow, deliberate steps toward me over the bed of dried leaves that clung to the forest floor like a thick carpet.

Please don't be a wolf. Please don't be a wolf, I begged inwardly. Would wolves be brave enough to come so near a residential area? I had no idea, but the forest that linked our houses stretched far and long throughout the posh neighborhood. It was totally possible that some bigger animals had made their homes nearby and had now spotted me as an easy post-supper snack.

"Hello?" I called into the darkness, because it felt more terrifying to remain silent. Perhaps Officer Bouchard was still standing guard at Harlow Manor and would come running into the forest to rescue me. Hopefully he'd be at least a touch more careful than I had been.

The crunching leaves silenced, leaving me alone with the eerie howl of the wind sweeping through the trees. Well, I was never ever coming out here at night again. Nope, wouldn't do it, no matter how curious something made me.

And tonight seemed like a really good time to start my "no woods at night" rule, just as soon as I could get out of here.

I shifted onto my back and pulled myself to a seated position. Everything hurt, and I'd definitely be needing another shower. Thankfully, nothing appeared to be broken, so I pressed my already dirty hands deeper into the dirt and pushed myself to a standing position. My injured side had a hard time taking the weight, so I hobbled like a zombie, moving very slowly through the growth.

I'd only made it a few feet when the crunching started up again.

I wanted to run but knew attempting to move faster with my injury would only lead to another wipeout. So, I plodded slowly along with some unknown animal following in close pursuit. I'd reached the halfway point between the senator's house and mine when I heard Octo-Cat shout, "Oh, if you're looking for trouble, you've found it, all right!"

"Octo-Cat?" I called, turning behind me to search the trees for his tiny striped body. I'd never been so happy to hear his demanding, little voice in all my life.

Unfortunately, it wasn't him I found standing before me now. Rather, twin pairs of yellow-green eyes blinked into view, moving closer and closer until we were only a few feet away from each other. The white spots on the smaller cat made him easier to pick out, but the large black Sphynx remained mostly shrouded in the shadows, save for those large, glowing eyes.

Octo-Cat broke through the tangled limbs of the forest a few seconds later and looked me up and down. "What happened to you?"

"I fell," I said flatly, unwilling to take my eyes off our two strange visitors. Although, I supposed these woods belonged to them as much as it did us.

"Did they trip you?" He put himself between me and the other cats and growled, making me feel slightly safer and a lot more loved.

"I don't think so," I said, searching the forest floor for the nasty root that had caused my fall but coming up short in the expanding darkness.

"Well, I wouldn't put it past them," he mumbled.

The larger Sphynx stepped forward and let out a string of deep meows.

"Oh, jeez, not this again," my cat hissed in response.

"What did he say?" I asked, hobbling over to the nearest tree and extending a hand to rest on its trunk so that I wouldn't be stuck standing on one foot for this entire exchange.

As much as he'd hated working with the traumatized Yorkie on our last case, he seemed even angrier about having to speak to the Sphynxes. Octo-Cat took a deep breath before translating. "He said, '*at night the owl sounds in such a way our curiosity compounds.*'"

Well, that hadn't been what I expected. "Um, what?" I asked, shifting my weight to give even more of it to the tree.

"Not what," Octo-Cat corrected with a heavy sigh. *"Who?"*

"Huh?" I brought my free hand up to scratch at my head, completely baffled now.

He sighed again. "Remember how I told you I don't like their kind? *This* is why. It's not because they look funny. It's because they talk funny. Everything they say comes out as a riddle. It's why they're called Sphynx cats. Get it now?"

"You mean like the mythical creature that guarded the secrets of the gods?" I found it both crazy and fascinating that an old story I barely remembered actually had bearing on our modern world.

"Oh, it wasn't as selfless as that," Octo-Cat spoke as if he'd personally known the Sphinx of ancient Greek mythology. "It was a nasty demon, tormenting everyone just because it could." He spat toward our two hairless visitors and raised the hairs on his back menacingly.

"Wow," I said, hardly above a whisper.

Octo-Cat turned back toward me, somehow even more agitated than before. "So now you can see why I wasn't too keen to go chatting these guys up. The big one is Jillianne, by the way, and the little one is Jacques."

"I know you're a little uncomfortable right now," I said placatingly. It didn't escape me that each of the three cats had four good, strong legs, and I only had one. Despite his frustration, at least Octo-Cat had stayed by my side. "But we could really use their help," I continued. "Could you please just tell them that I'm their new neighbor and that I'm thrilled to meet them?"

"You know the ancient Sphinx enjoyed killing people, too?" Octo-Cat licked his paw while talking, perhaps because he didn't like sitting in the dirty forest, or perhaps to show off that he had fur while our two conversants did not.

After a little back and forth, he informed me, "They say, and I quote, '*Whether written on note or banner or mat, this is our greeting, to human from cat.*'"

"Ha, they're saying welcome!" I cried, having far more fun now than my poor, long-suffering cat. "How do they come up with those so fast? They must be geniuses."

Octo-Cat growled. Once again, it seemed, our definitions differed. "I don't have to sit here and take this, you know. If you want my help, you'll refrain from encouraging their unwieldy behavior."

I thought he'd said they always talked like this, but correcting him now would just send him scampering off toward home, and I still had so much more I needed to find out from our two hairless wonders.

"Can you ask them if they know who killed their owner, please?" I said instead.

Octo-Cat kept his eyes firmly on mine, a challenge. "This is getting old real fast, so I suggest you think over each question carefully, because I am definitely not doing this all night," he warned.

"Fine, fine," I groused. "Now, tell me, what did they say?"

He pressed his ears back against his skull and shook his head. "Yeah, you're enjoying this way too much, but I'm telling you right now, we are *not* adopting them."

I was just about to yell at Octo-Cat again, when he delivered the next riddle in a bored monotone. *"What we say to confirm, even if it makes one squirm."*

"Yes!" I shouted gleefully. "That means yes, right? They know!" This case really could be open and shut, seeing as we had two key witnesses right here and more than happy to talk to us.

Octo-Cat let out a dreadful groan, then turned tail and disappeared between the tree branches.

"Hey, wait!" I cried, slowly attempting to follow after him. I hoped the Sphynxes would follow, too. I was dying to ask them the next question. It would be the only one we needed to find the murderer—oddly my question would be the same as the answer to their first riddle: *Who?* As in, who killed the senator? How was Octo-Cat not getting this?

"They know who killed the senator," I shouted after him. "Now you just have to ask one more question and we'll have solved this one in record time!"

I couldn't see him anywhere. Had he really just run off and abandoned me? And here I was starting to think he cared. Well, two could play the punishment game, and I suspected I'd have a much easier time annoying him than he had bugging me.

"Oh, Octo-Cat!" I called in one last ditch attempt to lure him in with kindness. "Where are you?"

Nothing. Even the wind had stopped howling through the trees.

Well, this was just great. He'd run off and left me injured and alone in a scary forest. Unless...

I turned around to search for the Sphynxes behind me, but instead bumped into a large, barrel-shaped chest. A human chest.

I didn't even bother to look at his face as I twisted around and made an attempt to run. Hurt foot or not, I needed to get back to the relative safety of my house. Needed to get out of these twisted woods now. My very life might just depend on it.

I'd only made it a single step, when he grabbed my arms and pulled me back into his chest.

"Hey, what are you—?" I yelled as I struggled to get away.

He brought one sweaty hand up and clamped it over my mouth before I could finish my cry for help.

Well, this was it. This was how I died—not on the stairs but lost in the woods just a couple dozen feet away from my new palatial home.

This was not turning out to be a very good moving day.

Not at all.

9

This was it. Fight or flight. Preferably both.

I'd been detained by a murderer before. I'd been pitched into the wharf and left for dead. I could survive this. Summoning all my strength, I bit down on the fleshy palm that covered my mouth.

Yes! That did it.

My attacker cried out in pain. He pulled away at once, clutching his injured hand. "Ouch, what'd you do that for?" his voice came out a bit high-pitched for a man—nasally, too.

"Hey, you're the one who attacked me!" I corrected, studying his red face and matching red flannel pajama pants. He was far less scary now that I got a good look at him, but it didn't change the fact that he could easily overpower me with his size and strength.

"Who are you?" I demanded. "What are you doing in my woods?"

He didn't need to know I'd only just moved in that afternoon. In fact, I'd probably be safer if he didn't.

At least he had the decency to look properly chastised. Still clutching his wounded hand, he rushed in with an explanation. "I heard talking, so I came out to see what was going on, and then you ran straight into me."

I scoffed and crossed my arms over my chest. It must be nice to be a man, to be able to wander into the dark woods with no worries for your safety beyond the normal serial killer with a chainsaw type of thing. Then again, I often found myself charging into dangerous situations with little more than my temperamental tabby to back me up. I guess that meant I couldn't judge him too harshly. "That still doesn't tell me who you are."

"I'm Matt Harlow," he said, thrusting his uninjured hand toward me in greeting.

"I bit the first. Do you really want to trust me with the second?" I asked, widening my eyes in challenge just like my cat so often did to me. I wouldn't feel safe until we got out of the forest. I was at way too much of a disadvantage here in the dark unknown with a much larger man before me and an injury slowing me down.

Matt jolted back and offered up a nervous laugh. At least he was scared, too. "Good point," he said. "So you're okay, right?"

"I'm fine," I said, even as the throbbing in my toes intensified.

"That's all I needed to know." He lifted his arm in a swift wave, then turned back in the direction he came from. "Have a good night."

I stood watching him go until he ducked out of eyesight, then continued my journey back toward home. So that was Matt Harlow, the senator's next of kin. Had we met under different circumstances, I could have prodded him for information, see what he knew. As it was, though, I'd much prefer to wait for the light of day and a reliable cell signal before possibly accusing him of murder.

Okay, so he seemed like a nice enough guy—tall, chubby, not unlike a teddy bear, but that didn't change the fact that his inclination upon meeting me had been to grab hold of me and cover my mouth. That was way creepier than those hair-lacking, riddle-smacking cats would ever be.

"I'm home," I called when at last I trudged through the door. I'm not sure why I even bothered announcing myself when clearly my feline roommate wasn't too bothered about my safety.

Octo-Cat intelligently remained hidden. Otherwise, I definitely would have given him a stern talking to about abandoning me in the woods right when the Sphynxes were about to reveal something crucial to our case. Well, if he wanted to hide from me, he could go to bed without dinner for all I cared.

I stomped through the house just to make sure he knew how angry I was with him. On my third pass through the open floor plan of the lower level, I stopped off at the kitchen to plop a fresh serving of Fancy Feast into Octo-Cat's bowl. As much as I wanted to teach him a lesson, I also didn't want to have to deal with an entire night's worth of his yowling.

But I got my jab in anyway, because I served him his least favorite flavor—the chicken we had only because it was part of the multi-pack I got from our local warehouse club store. Normally I saved up several dozen, then dropped them off as a donation for the local animal shelter, but I figured it would be okay to use one for a very necessary revenge.

Not satisfied, I marched up the stairs to my tower bedroom and wedged the door shut behind me. The cable company would be coming by tomorrow to connect the Internet, so for now I had to depend on my phone's mobile connection to surf the web before bedtime. Although the pages loaded painfully slow due to our proximity to the woods, I wanted to do some quick research into the senator's recent activity to see if anything jumped out as a possible clue to her murder.

While I was at it, I looked up Matt Harlow, too. From what I could tell, he was just a normal middle-aged guy from the city who'd recently gotten divorced and worked a job in sales. Nothing jumped out at me as serial killerish, but it was possible he'd only killed once to date, provided that Lou's untimely demise could be pegged squarely on her son's shoulders.

Honestly, I was stumped here.

An impatient scratching sounded outside my door.

"Go away!" I called, not wanting to deal with my diva cat just then.

Octo-Cat murmured a few soft words to himself that I couldn't discern, although it sounded like he was having some sort of argument. "I'm sorry!" he called to me after a slight bit of hesitation.

I was so shocked I dropped my phone onto the bed beside me. I don't think I'd ever heard that particular combination of words cross his lips. *"You'll be sorry,"* sure, but never a genuine, heartfelt apology.

I smiled to myself, ready to milk this moment for all it was worth. Just like Octo-Cat, I had to get my victories somehow. "What was that?" I asked, pretending I hadn't heard.

Whether he was here to demand a better flavor of Fancy Feast or because he genuinely felt bad, I didn't know. At least it was something, though.

When his voice came out strained, I could tell this moment was punishment enough. "You know what I said. You're just—*aargh!* I'm sorry, all right? I'm sorry!"

I raced toward the door as if in slow motion. Honestly, the moment wasn't that different from all those times the heroine runs in slow motion through a field of bright flowers to reach her hero. Yes, I loved my cat, and this moment was special to me, so don't judge.

Swinging the door open, I smiled down at him and said, "I forgive you."

"Great," he said with a sly smile. "By the way, there's some nice green puke waiting for you at the bottom of the stairs." He trotted away, swinging his hips triumphantly. Honestly, I couldn't even remember what the green puke punishment was about, but I had bigger fish to fry.

Leaving my door open in case he wanted to come back for some apology cuddles, I snuggled back on my bed and returned to my research on the late senator and her next of kin.

First I read all the news articles pertaining to her from this past month. That bored me out of my mind, so I shifted my focus to what I personally knew already.

With the notes app on my phone open and ready, I typed in everything I'd discovered so far:

Served four terms, likely to be reelected.

Died by falling down the stairs.

Bottom stair smashed in.

Mom asked to investigate for the news.

Icky gut feeling at the crime scene.

Two Sphynx cats from breeder in France.

Officer Bouchard stood guard outside for the better part of the day.

Mr. Thompson came to visit and was turned away.

Next of kin is Matt Harlow. He ran into me in the woods and covered my mouth when I tried to scream.

There, that was everything so far, right? If I considered everyone mentioned in the list that meant my first round of suspects included Officer Bouchard, Matt Harlow, Mr. Thompson, my mom, and some cat breeder in France. And, oh yeah, also her two cats. I should have probably added any person who was rumored to be running for the senator's seat in the next mid-term election, too. We were still more than two years away, which made me think a political opponent was rather unlikely.

That led me back to another very important question: how did the senator know Mr. Thompson? Sure, I could just ask him the next time

I showed up at the firm for work, but would he be willing to tell me the truth or just send me further astray?

I Googled for close to an hour, searching for any connection between Harlow and Thompson, but came up short. Since I was still off work for the remainder of the week, I decided to call in a favor from a friend.

"Hello?" Charles, the junior partner at our firm and my former crush, answered in a hushed whisper.

"Charles, I need a favor," I told him.

"I'm at the movies with Breanne. Just a sec." I heard some angry groans from his fellow movie goers, then a minute later his voice came back loud and strong. "In the lobby now. What's up?"

"The senator was murdered today," I told him in case he didn't already know.

But he did. Of course he did. "They haven't ruled out the fact it could have been an accident," he corrected.

"But *I* have," I said, and he knew better than to argue. "Anyway, interesting fact: Thompson showed up this afternoon and tried to gain entry to the house, but the cops turned him away."

"That's weird. Wait, how do you know that?"

"I live next door now. Remember?" I answered matter-of-factly.

"You just can't keep away from a good mystery, can you, Russo?" he said with a laugh, even though we were talking about a murder here. It made my heart melt for him a little all over again. Seeing as he was spoken for, though, I swallowed back that particular feeling and returned my focus to the facts before us.

"Can you look into Thompson for me?" I asked. "Find out how he knew the senator? Why he showed up today?"

"Will do," he said. "That all?"

"Yeah, get back to your date, lover boy." I hoped he couldn't detect the sarcasm in my voice. Whatever the case, he quickly ended the call, leaving me alone in my giant house once again—and possibly with a murderer next door.

Maybe I could convince Nan to move in early? Then I would have a temperamental cat and a feisty old lady to protect me, should trouble come calling.

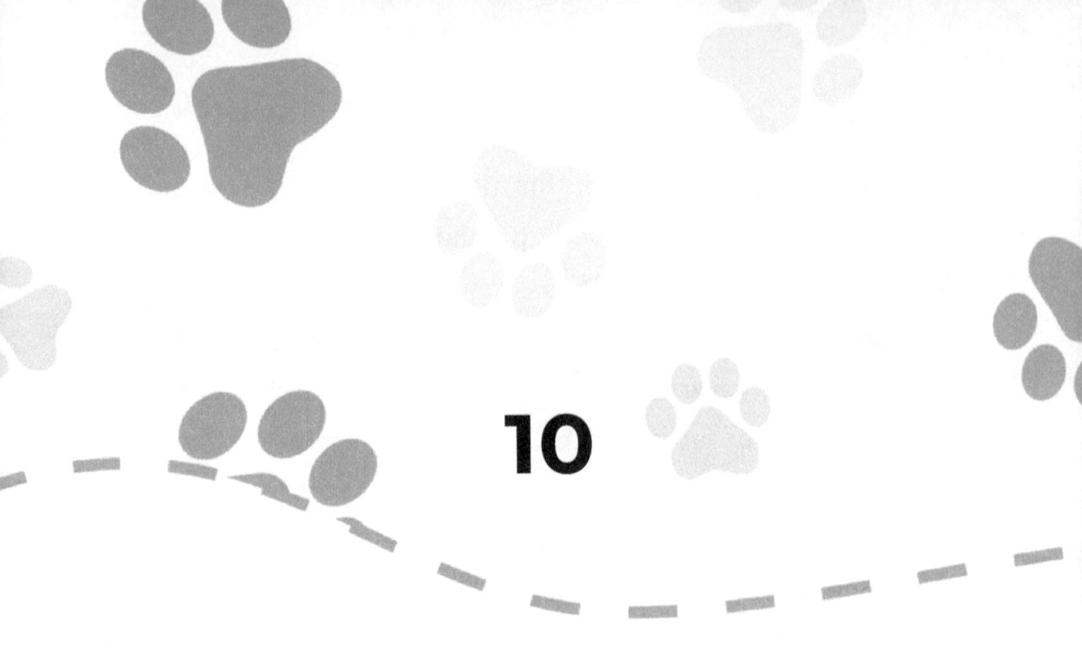

10

Despite another couple hours spent researching the late senator's life, history, and political stances, I didn't feel any closer to solving her murder the next morning. Sure, it could have been a big inheritance grab as had been the case with Ethel Fulton's murder, but somehow I doubted it.

As frightening as I'd found him last night, her polite and pudgy Midwesterner son didn't strike me as a killer—just a bit socially inept. Still, I couldn't rule him out completely. Otherwise I'd be left primarily with the two cats and possibly my boss as suspects.

Hopefully Charles would be able to find out what I needed to know about Thompson by the end of the day. I'd been there for him when nobody else was willing to support his "unwinnable" double homicide case. Against all odds, we won that time, and I knew we could win again. There was no case attached, but we at least owed the world the truth about Lou Harlow's death.

After a quick breakfast of dry Cheerios, I pulled back my hair and threw on a bold retro sundress, then climbed into my car. I wanted to solve this thing as quick as possible—not just for the senator, not just for the world at large, but for myself, too. Sleep had not come easily last night, and I doubted it would again until I knew I was safe in my new home.

"Where do you think you're going?" Octo-Cat demanded, jumping on top of my hood and staring daggers at me straight through the windshield.

"Next door," I informed him. I wasn't risking those woods again, whether or not the sun was now shining brightly. "Now get off my car so I can start the engine."

"I'm coming, too," he said, then sprinted toward the forest. Not surprising in the least. He had his preferred method of travel, and I had mine.

I navigated down my long, twisting driveway, down a small stretch of road, and then back up Harlow manor's long, twisting driveway. Yeah, once my poor foot made a full recovery, it probably would be faster to traipse through the woods, but sometimes fast wasn't the most important part of getting somewhere.

Like when it came to solving a mystery.

I'd learned that my first time out of the gate. There I'd gone, galloping toward that finish line without even taking the proper time to prepare myself for the race. And it had nearly gotten me killed.

Come to think of it, I'd put myself in mortal danger as part of solving my second case, too. This time I'd be real glad if bringing Harlow's murderer to justice didn't involve any flirtations with death on my part. It would certainly make me feel more professional if I could solve a crime without endangering *anyone's* life in the process.

Maybe today would be my big day—an important turning point for Ms. Pet Whisperer P.I. I chuckled at the notion, but admittedly my Mom's nickname had started to grow on me.

When I pulled up to the Harlow estate, I was surprised to see no police cars or sports cars in sight. Instead, a rusty old truck sat parked just before the main entrance. The door hung wide open, but I couldn't see anyone inside—not even the esoteric cats that I knew for a fact still lived here.

"I'm here!" Octo-Cat's muffled cry broke through the woods. "And I come bearing gifts," he added as he appeared carrying a dead rodent in his mouth.

"Gross," I said, already accepting that tomorrow morning's cat puke would be extra disgusting.

"Is someone there?" a deep voice called from within the house.

I hung back near my car and waited for the speaker to emerge onto the porch. When he did, I squealed for joy and ran forward to throw my arms around him. "Brock! It's so good to see you out in the wild." I hoped he wasn't offended by my choice of words, but it felt better to not directly mention that the last couple of times I'd seen him he'd been in either court or prison.

"Angie, right?" he asked, returning my giant grin. "Thanks for helping with my case."

Oops. Of course, he didn't know me as well as I knew him. I'd spent the better part of an entire week obsessing over his case, whereas he'd only ever seen me for brief periods in the middle of what had to be the most stressful time of his life.

"Hey, any time," I said with a playful fist bump against his shoulder.

"Well, hopefully never again," Brock corrected with a laugh. "But I appreciate the sentiment."

He looked good. Real good. His long, dark hair had been cut into a shorter style with just enough length left to it that someone could run her fingers through it.

What? Me? *No.* My last crush had ended horribly—with him dating someone else. And here dear Brock could scarcely remember my name. I didn't need to go fantasizing about the romantic possibilities between us.

Then again, his smile came easy and genuine. I couldn't believe that vile red-headed realtor was his twin sister. Other than their shared last name, they had almost nothing in common. At least not that I could see.

Brock motioned for me to join him in the house, then crouched back down in front of the stairs and returned to work.

Those pants. That shirt. His muscles. And the way he handled that hammer... *Gah.*

It seemed my crush on Charles Longfellow, III, was all but forgotten. Falsely accused or not, I wondered if Nan would approve of me dating an ex con. Heck, she'd probably find it even more exciting than I did.

No, no, no. Bad Angie! I didn't have time to date—or even to really think about dating—when there was a murderer on the loose.

"So they hired you to fix the stairs?" I asked, just so that I had something coherent to say.

His dark, sparkling eyes were so pretty as he turned to study me. "Sure did," he said. "And I'm grateful for it, too. Even though I was acquitted, a lot of people around here still feel weird about hiring me."

"Oh, I could think of a few things for you to do." I grew hypnotized by the swell of his muscles beneath his jeans once more. Wait, had I said that aloud?

"What's that?" he asked, turning to me and running a forearm across his head.

"Uhh," I stumbled here, honestly unable to remember what I'd been thinking. Then it hit me. As handsome as I found the man standing before me, this wasn't about him. It was about my own personal kryptonite—coffee. Suddenly, I remembered that I hadn't had any caffeine before coming over. No wonder my brain was applesauce. I needed to be way more careful about that going forward.

Pinching the inside of my arm to reinvigorate my senses, I finally smiled and said, "I have some jobs around my new place if you have the time. I live right next door, actually."

He stood and glanced toward my house as if he could somehow see it through the solid stone walls of Harlow manor. "Yeah, I'd love that."

Octo-Cat appeared in the doorway with traces of fresh blood on his furry face, but the carcass of his mid-morning snack thankfully nowhere to be seen. "No wonder you don't have a boyfriend," he muttered as he set to grooming himself.

Oh my gosh, my game was so bad even my cat could tell. Not a great start to my day. Not at all.

Octo-Cat's rude arrival reminded me that I had come for a very specific reason, and that did not include flirting with the help. "Actually, I just stopped by to see Matt Harlow. Is he here?"

Brock fished through a container filled with nails until he found the ones he wanted. "Nope, he left almost as soon as I got here. Will reading," he explained, keeping his focus now on his work. "Want me to tell him you stopped by?"

"Sure, thanks." With nothing else to do here, I turned back toward the door, shooting Octo-Cat a dirty look as I passed by him. He still claimed that all humans looked the same, but he had about a ninety percent success rate when it came to discerning a person's gender. I wondered if the Sphynxes had the same shortcomings he did. If they'd seen the killer but wouldn't be able to identify him.

"Oh, wait. There was something I forgot," Brock called after me.

I turned around so fast, I practically spun in a full circle. My dress twirled around me like some kind of old-timey movie, and Brock chuckled.

"I just wanted to let you know that we have an official offer on your nan's house. Looks like your new roomie will be joining you in no time."

Oh, yeah. He and his sister were the ones in charge of selling Nan's house. The world did exist outside the two of us and my rude kitty commentator.

"Thanks," I told him. "That is good news."

I walked slowly back to my car, careful not to put too much

weight on my injured foot. Now that Nan had a buyer for her house, she could join me much sooner than we'd originally anticipated.

I had zero shame in admitting that I was a scared little girl who needed her grandmother to tuck her in at night. At least until Glendale's newest murderer was caught and reprimanded. Maybe I could invite her over today to celebrate her pending sale and beg her to stay the night.

When she found out I had a mystery right next door, I knew she wouldn't be able to resist.

11

Sure enough, Nan agreed to stop by later that afternoon to *get the goods* on our newest investigation—her words, not mine. Maybe I should have called my mom instead, seeing as she was already involved. But Nan had been a ready and willing partner the last time around and I liked her less direct approach when it came to questioning witnesses.

Had Mom not built a career for herself in journalism, I have no doubt that she could have made a fantastic prison guard. Nan, on the other hand, was an actress through and through. Even though her time on Broadway had ended almost fifty years ago, she still liked to don costumes and dive straight into whatever new character we needed to aid our investigations.

Me? I guess I was the brains behind our little operation. Whatever it was. Right now, we were still just impromptu vigilante detectives with a knack for finding both clues and trouble. Of course, if my mom had her way, I'd soon be hanging out my *Private Investigator for Hire* sign on the front lawn.

Nan was the actress, the good cop. Mom was the dogged reporter, aka bad cop, and I was the one who did all the research and then charged straight into battle without any regard to my own personal safety.

So maybe I wasn't really the brains, after all.

I unpacked some more boxes as I thought this over—as if any of it mattered, as if I were writing a novel or casting a TV show about our exploits. That would be the day! And it would be one both Mom and Nan loved. For now, I just wanted to get my clothes all hung and organized in my new closet.

I'd chosen the smallest bedroom in the entire manor not just because I loved the idea of living in a tower, but also because it felt more like home. Despite her flair for the dramatic, Nan had raised me to be humble and to find happiness right where I sat, and as such, the whole owning a mansion thing would definitely take some getting used to.

I let out a frustrated sigh when less than half of my wardrobe fit in the tiny tower closet. It may have been comprised mostly of thrift store and charity shop finds, but I loved every single article of clothing I owned and was loathe to part with any of it. They just didn't make clothes like they used to in the eighties and nineties. True, I'd hardly been alive during those decades, but it didn't mean that I couldn't adore the bold pops of color and fun patterns in the here and now.

"Who pooped in your litter box?" Octo-Cat asked, choosing that exact moment to creep out from underneath my bed. I hadn't even known he was there, the sneak.

"You have some really weird sayings," I told him with a frown before returning to the much bigger problem at hand. "And my clothes don't all fit in the closet."

"First of all, so do you." Octo-Cat sucked in a deep breath as he ventured into the closet to check things out. Coming back, he said, "And second, I really don't see why you humans need so many outfits, but you do realize we have six bedrooms in this house, right? Six! That's one more than the number of lives I have left, which seems more than enough to me. Just choose one of the other rooms and put your stuff in there."

I shook my head, wondering if I should ask more about how he'd lost his first four lives and what exactly that even meant. As far as I knew, I only had one life to live—only one to lose. That's why, even though our sleuthing was exciting, it could also prove to be very dangerous.

"C'mon," Octo-Cat said with a breathy exhale. "I think I know the perfect room for this, if you'll follow me."

I kept hold of the stack of hangers in my hands as I followed him down the spiral staircase and across the second floor of our new home. Well, new for me, at least. My cat had easily settled back in as master of this domain. I'd never seen him this at ease in my old rental, but then again, it seemed this particular tabby was born for greater things and more extravagant surroundings.

"This one," he said, stopping outside a closed door at the end of the hallway and pawing at the light streaming from beneath.

I opened it up and gasped, dropping my pile of hangers to the ground in a clattering mess. Somehow I'd forgotten about this room entirely. Sure, I'd toured the house a couple times before signing on the dotted line, but back then I was still enamored of the general luxuriousness that I had a hard time noticing the finer details.

And, oh, this room was fine.

First of all, it had a big window seat like the ones I'd coveted at Harlow Manor. The gorgeous piece of architecture stretched at least six feet long, which meant I could even nap there if I wanted. Heavy blackout curtains flanked it on either side. They must have been closed the other times I'd seen this place; that must have been why I didn't remember it. I liked that explanation much better than choosing to believe that I had either overlooked or forgotten such major details.

From the vaulted ceiling hung an antique crystal chandelier, which caught the sunlight and cast tiny rainbows all around the room. Most of the bulbs had burned out, but that didn't lessen its opulence one bit. The honey hardwood floors were scratched up but still sturdy. It wouldn't take too much work to sand them down and polish when I had the cash and the time—or maybe just the sexy local handyman—to do so.

"So, will this work as your new closet?" Octo-Cat said, hopping up into the window seat and taking a quick look outside before turning back to me. "It's small, so I figured you'd like it."

"Closet?" I gasped again. "No way! This is going to be my new library."

I'm pretty sure tears had formed in my eyes and were falling down my face and soaking my t-shirt, but I simply did not care. Octo-Cat could make fun of me all he wanted, but I'd finally found true, unreserved excitement when it came to our new digs.

How could I feel any other way, considering I now slept in a tower like Rapunzel and would have my own personal library like Belle? I'd stepped into a living fairytale. Sure, it turned into the Haunted Mansion ride when the lights went out, but... but...

Now I had my own personal library!

A loud rap sounded on the door downstairs, bringing our special moment to an end. Had it not, I could have stood there all day, sketching out plans for what the vacant room would one day soon become.

"Do we not have a doorbell?" I asked Octo-Cat, begrudgingly shutting the door behind me and heading toward the stairs to the first floor.

He shrugged and raced away to find out who had come calling.

As loathe as I was to step out of this beautiful daydream, I figured it might be Nan and she did not like to be kept waiting.

"Hello?" a nasal, masculine voice called.

A second series of knocks sounded, a bit more urgent this time.

Instantly, I recognized Matt Harlow as I spied his familiar shape through the stained-glass panes on either side of the front door. I flung the door open and stood blocking the inside. True, I had paid him a visit earlier that day, but I was still incredibly nervous around him—and nervous is exactly how I would remain until I could fully clear him as the killer.

"Hi," he said, tucking one hand in his pocket and using the other to offer me a friendly wave. I wondered if that was the same one I'd bitten the night before. "You stopped by earlier?"

I felt in my pocket to make sure I had my phone on me as an added security measure, then stepped back and gestured for him to come inside. "Would you like to join me for some tea?" I asked, seeing as it was the neighborly thing to do.

Octo-Cat ran across the foyer, making terrible, ear-splitting noises. "Too soon! Too soon!" he cried.

"Is your cat all right?" Matt asked, craning his neck to get a better view.

I shrugged. "Eh, he'll be fine. Tea?"

"Sure, thank you." A genuine smile stretched right across Matt's face, and for the first time I saw the resemblance he bore to his late mother.

I led him to the formal living room and motioned for him to sit on the old Victorian couch trimmed in dark cherry wood. There were lots of different woods throughout the house, and I wasn't sure whether that was the result of poor planning or a decades-old decorating style I didn't quite understand. Halfway to the kitchen, I turned back, sensing I had the perfect opening to ask Matt a couple very important questions.

"You have cats, too. Right?" I hoped my eagerness to discuss the Sphynxes wasn't too obvious. Provided Matt wasn't the murderer, I would need him on my side.

He steepled his fingers before him. It seemed he was unsure of what to do with himself while he sat in my house. "Me? No, but my mom has always had them ever since I can remember."

"What's going to happen to the two that are there now?" I asked casually.

He shrugged and tried to get comfortable on the overly firm sofa. "I'm not sure," he admitted. "They've been hiding from me ever since I arrived. I thought maybe I could take them back home and give them to my kids, that way they'd be my ex-wife's problem instead of mine. But I worry those two might give my kids nightmares like the ones I had growing up."

"Nightmares? Why?" I asked, even though I already understood. Anything to keep him talking.

"Have you ever seen a hairless cat?" he asked with a shudder. "It looks like their brains are on the outside."

I laughed, and so did he. The description was pretty accurate. Even still, I'd begun to like Jacques and Jillianne now that I'd gotten the chance to talk with them a bit. Sure, they were a bit different, but they were also really stinking cool. "You mentioned having nightmares growing up. Have you always been afraid of cats?"

He cleared his throat and coughed into his fist. "I am not afraid of cats. I used to like them, but then Mom met that breeder in France and since then it's only been the finest purebred Sphynxes for her."

It seemed I had an opportunity here, one that seemed so fortuitous I hadn't thought it could ever happen. "If you wanted me to look after them while you decide what to do with them, I'd be more than happy to help out," I offered with an ingratiating smile.

"*What?*" Octo-Cat demanded, running back through the room and jumping up onto the couch beside Matt. "You can't be serious! There is no way I'll allow—"

"Sure," Matt said, interrupting my feline's tirade even though he didn't know it. "That would be great. That is, if you don't mind."

"Oh, I don't mind at all," I said with a huge smile, enjoying the expression of horror on my tabby's face.

"Traitor," Octo-Cat muttered under his breath.

Matt reached out to pet Octo-Cat but was summarily clawed by my very cranky kitty. "Ouch," he cried. "And that was my good hand, too."

The cat hissed and ran to hide in another room, shouting kitty curses at the top of his lungs.

"Sorry," I said, feeling a swell of embarrassment. I hoped he'd still trust me to watch his mother's cats after seeing how crazily the one under my care behaved.

"So, how about that tea?" I asked, scurrying away to the kitchen before he had a chance to refuse. This would give me a few private moments to plan my questions. If I asked the right ones, I just might find the missing pieces I needed to solve Lou Harlow's murder once and for all.

12

I brought Matt a cup of plain Earl Grey tea—no cream, no sugar, no good, really. It would have to do, though, seeing as I hadn't had time to go to the store since moving in yesterday afternoon. Honestly, it was kind of a miracle that I even had this.

"Thanks," he said with a friendly smile, accepting the warm mug and holding it between his hands. "Look, about last night, I just wanted to apologize for... Well, I'm sure you remember."

"Water under the bridge." I waved off his apology, even though I was happy it had been given. I needed to keep him on my side if I were to learn what he knew about his mom's murder.

"You're just being so hospitable and then offering to take the cats, too. I feel really bad about how I acted. It's just..." He sighed heavily and turned the mug around in his hands so that the artwork faced me. It was my *crazy cat lady* mug. Nan had gotten it to celebrate my official adoption of Octo-Cat a few months back, and it had quickly become my favorite.

Matt sighed and cast his eyes toward the floor. "It may not be the manliest thing to admit, but I was terrified."

"It's understandable," I assured him. "After all, someone did just kill your mother."

"Exactly!" Matt lifted the tea to his lips, took a small sip, then set it on the coffee table. There weren't any coasters, but the old piece of furniture already had lots of wear, so I figured this wasn't a problem I needed to worry about at this precise moment. "I'm staying in her house, too. Granted, it was my house growing up, but it just gives me the creeps."

"My thoughts exactly." I reached forward to offer him a fist bump on the subject of staying in creepy houses. He didn't seem to know what to do with it, so we shook hands instead.

"So, you grew up around here?" I asked, taking a sip from my own mug. I couldn't stand tea without at least two spoonfuls of sugar mixed in, so I'd secretly filled mine with plain hot water. At least this way I could accompany Matt, make my questions seem more like a conversation than an interrogation.

"Not around here." He stopped and shook his head. "*Here.* Right next door."

"If you don't mind my asking, why did you leave?" I was really pleased with how things were going so far. Matt was opening up to me without even the slightest hesitation. How much more would he be willing to tell me before he reached the bottom of that tea cup?

"Love." Matt snorted and rolled his eyes. "Lot of good that did me."

I winced sympathetically. Even though I'd never been in anything more than puppy love, I felt for the recent divorcee. Everything must have still been so fresh and new, and now he'd lost his mother on top of it all. "So, why don't you come back? I'm assuming your mother left the house to you."

"She did, but I don't know." He drummed his fingers on the side of his mug and frowned. "It would be hard to live there without constantly thinking of her."

"Was she a good mom?" I asked before taking a casual sip from my mug of hot water.

If Matt thought my questions were coming too fast and close together, he made no indication of it. Rather, he seemed happy to share, or at least happy to have someone to talk to. The poor guy.

"She was the best," he said with a nostalgic sigh. "Everything you read about her in the papers is true, by the way. She really had the kindest heart. Even before she got elected, she was always volunteering somewhere. In fact, we spent more of our Christmases serving up hot meals at the soup kitchen, then opening gifts at home."

"That's incredible. I'm sure a lot of people will miss her dearly. I know I will." I already knew this about her, of course, but hearing it from her son's lips made me that much angrier that someone had brought her life to an early and violent end.

Matt's eyes lit up with true warmth. "Did you know her well?"

I smiled. "Well, I voted for her every time I was able, and I could always tell she believed the things she said. It was refreshing."

Matt picked his tea up and took a long, slow sip. "I have no idea who would want to hurt her," he said, shaking his head. "It just doesn't make any sense."

"It could have been an accident," I pointed out, even though I didn't believe it myself.

"Maybe," he conceded.

We sat in silence for a few moments. He didn't say anything else, but I could also tell he wasn't ready to go, so I asked another question.

"When I stopped by earlier, you were at the will reading. Did everything go okay there?" I thought back to the first and only will reading I'd attended. It was the same one where I'd nearly died at the hands of an old coffee maker, where I'd discovered my powers and met Octo-Cat for the first time. As far as my experience told me, will readings could be a real riot.

"It was fine," Matt answered passively. "No real surprises. I got the house. My kids both got trusts set up for when they turn eighteen. Most of the rest of it went toward a scholarship fund she'd talked about setting up for years but had never got the chance to follow through on."

"A scholarship? That's nice," I said, nodding along. "For students who want to study politics?"

Matt scoffed. "No way. Mom always hated politicians. Even more so after she became one. Said they were smart people with good intentions that got twisted along the way. But hers never did. God bless her soul."

"May I ask what the scholarship is for?" I asked, hoping it wasn't insensitive to track back after his tender words. "I mean, I'm thinking about going back to school, so maybe I'll apply for it." I wasn't really considering more school at the moment, but knowing me and my insatiable love of learning, it was really just a matter of time.

Matt glanced around my swanky manor house, his implication obvious—why would *you* need a scholarship? He didn't say that, though. Despite our rough start, I could tell he was kind, exactly the way his mama had raised him to be. "Biology. Or, more specifically, marine biology," he told me, and it was not the answer I'd expected.

Seeing the confusion on my face, he jumped in to explain. "I know, it seems weird for a senator, right? But back in the 70's, she'd just had me and my dad wanted her to stay at home to raise me. I guess that never suited her and she divorced him eventually, but before she did, she became involved with the new *Save the Whales* movement. It gave her that first taste of political activism, and she was hooked."

He paused and took another sip of Earl Grey before continuing. "It's why she stayed in that big house by herself all these years. She didn't want to leave the ocean and all it meant to her. I guess I take after her a little bit myself because I made sure to get a place that overlooks Lake Michigan back in Chicago. Even now, I can't imagine looking out my window and seeing anything other than water."

"So, she wants to continue saving the whales through her scholarship fund," I summarized with a dreamy smile. "That's beautiful."

Another knock sounded at the front door, this one fast and light.

"Coming!" I yelled, jumping to my feet then squealing with happiness when I saw Nan through the stained glass.

"Okay, I'm here," she said as she stepped inside. She was wearing bright green galoshes and leggings patterned with rainbows. Up top, she wore an old T-shirt that had lost much of its original color from having gone through so many wash cycles. "Now catch me up on these riddle-speaking cats."

I turned toward Matt and made a funny face. "It's this book we're reading together," I explained quickly. Books really made the best excuses because few people would ask follow-up questions. It was sad but convenient nonetheless. "Anyway, this is my nan. Nan, this is Matt. Senator Harlow was his mother."

"Oh, you poor dear," Nan said, rushing over to sit beside him and pressing the back of her hand against his forehead. "How are you feeling?"

"Fine," Matt answered, though it sounded more like a question.

"I voted for your dear mama each and every time," Nan announced proudly. "They didn't come any better than her."

Matt raised his mug. "I'll drink to that."

I returned to my spot in the wingback chair across from them. "Matt was just telling me a bit more about his mom's legacy. Also, I've volunteered to watch the senator's cats while Matt gets the rest of the estate sorted out."

"One can never have too many opinions or too many cats," Nan said with a nod and a chuckle. Neither of these seemed true to me, but I let it pass.

Matt took another long drink of tea, then set his empty cup back on the coffee table. "I should probably be going," he said, rising to a stand. "Thank you again for the hospitality and the kind words about my mom."

Nan stood, too, and gave him a warm hug. She looked so tiny wrapped around his big, bear-like form. Even so, I could tell he appreciated the gesture.

After Nan let him go, I got up and followed Matt to the door. "Let me know when you want me to come by for the cats," I said as we lingered at the doorway.

"Oh, right," he said in a way that suggested he'd already forgotten —or was pretending to have forgotten after Octo-Cat's little hissy fit from earlier. "Are you sure it isn't too much of an imposition?"

"I'm sure," I said, perhaps too quickly. The truth was I needed those cats. They held the key to busting this murder mystery wide open, and I really wanted to know what they would say. "In fact, maybe I should just come with you now? Give them some time to settle in before nightfall."

I couldn't risk him changing his mind, and now that I had Nan here, she could help keep Octo-Cat in a good enough mood to actually be useful. Even though I was supposedly his best friend, he clearly preferred her company to mine. I tried not to let that hurt my feelings.

Matt's brows pinched together as he studied me. "Are you sure you're sure?"

"The more, the merrier!" Nan said, slinging an arm around each of our waists and pulling us closer. "Now let's go get our guests."

Matt didn't say anything more as the three of us exited onto the porch. I searched around but didn't see any extra vehicles—other than Nan's souped up sports coupe—which meant Matt must have chosen to walk through the woods to pay me a visit.

And, even though he'd been a perfectly lovely companion for afternoon tea, this realization did not sit well with me. If he felt comfortable traipsing through the woods after our mutual scare last night, might he be willing to come through them again by the cloak of night?

Maybe I wasn't as safe as I'd hoped after all.

13

At the Harlow manor, Matt begged off to take a call, leaving Nana and I to locate and load up the two Sphynx cats. Despite our best efforts to be quick, it still took nearly an hour for us to find Jacques and Jillianne, catch them, and then get them back to my house. Apparently they were every bit as adept at hiding as they were at telling riddles. So that we wouldn't risk them slinking off again, Nan and I carried them straight up to the room I had dubbed my future library and closed the door tightly before letting them out of their carriers.

I'd also brought Octo-Cat in to join us, and I had the fresh scratches to prove how very *not* thrilled he was to be there.

"I object!" he cried, hurling himself at the closed door in protest.

"Oh, hush, or I'll give you something to object about." I had no idea what that might be, but luckily my mostly empty threat worked.

"C'mere, my sweet kitty!" Nan cooed, tapping her fingers on the hardwood floor where we both sat with our legs crossed.

Octo-Cat hated being called *kitty* but he loved Nan, so he traipsed over and climbed into her lap. She immediately fussed over him and began to scratch that special spot right beneath his chin. I could see the rage melt right out of him. Thank goodness.

"Let's make this quick," he said, eyeing me with obvious disappointment. Luckily I was used to his theatrics and his disappointment, so this didn't thwart my plans in the least.

The two Sphynx cats had retreated to the far corner of the room and sat shivering near the central cooling vent. They looked so miserable that I almost felt bad confining them here. Still, they had intel that we needed, and they were the ones who'd chosen to sit right beside the cold air pouring into the room.

The little one let out a croaky meow, and Octo-Cat sighed. Like he'd suggested, I'd do my best to make this as quick and painless as possible. If not for him, then at least for our two visitors.

"Let's go," Nan said, her eyes sparkling with excitement. "I can't wait to solve some riddles." I'd already told her everything she needed to know on the phone that morning, and now she was primed and ready to see some action.

"Okay." I focused my gaze on Octo-Cat, who did not return the eye contact. "Octo-Cat," I said again to get his attention. "If you want this to be quick, you have to pay attention."

He turned toward me with ears back and tail poofed. "Fine. What do you want me to ask the two hairless wonders?"

"Ask them who killed their owner," I said with the same impatient attitude I'd perfected as a teen.

Nan giggled gleefully, and Octo-Cat remained seated on her lap as he shouted toward the Sphynxes.

They remained in their dark corner, almost as if they'd been glued there. It took much longer for his back and forth with them than it had with our former terrier witness, and I'll admit I started to get a bit bored as the minutes passed by without any further answers.

Then, suddenly, Octo-Cat snapped his eyes toward mine, his whiskers twitched, and he did not look happy. "I knew it!" he cried. "You thought I was being breedist or whatever, but my first instincts were absolutely right."

"What do you mean?" I asked, rubbing my hands on my legs to awaken the sleepy nerve endings.

Nan glanced down at Octo-Cat with the dearest admiration as he revealed, "*They* killed the senator."

"Oh, c'mon!" I shouted. Was he really coming back to me with *this?*

He remained steadfast in his insistence of their guilt. "No, really. They just admitted it."

"Yeah? Then tell me what they said," I demanded, wishing I didn't have to rely on him to be my translator when there was a clear bias at play here.

"It would be a whole lot easier if you'd just take me at my word, you know? But fine." He sighed then recited back their latest riddle. "'*Excuse us while we provide this breakthrough, for the guilt lies with the ones you see before you.*'"

He was right, of course. The answer was obvious, but…

"That's not even really a riddle," I said glumly. "It's just a rhyme."

"Good gravy. They just gave you a confession, and it's pretty direct as far as their type goes. What more do you need?"

"Ask again in another way," I demanded, then whispered to Nan to fill her in while Octo-Cat talked with the Sphynxes some more.

Another several minutes passed before Octo-Cat addressed me again. "Well, Angela. They said, *'You didn't believe us the first time, but you already know who committed the crime.'*"

Octo-Cat thumped his tail hard against Nan's leg, and she abruptly stopped petting him. "Good enough for you now?" he demanded with wide eyes.

"Not quite," I answered to his great dissatisfaction. "They say we already know, but I have a whole list of suspects. It could be Mr. Thompson or Matt or even Officer Bouchard."

"Or it could be the two freakazoids who literally just confessed to murder," he spat, shooting them a cold look, which he followed up with a hiss.

"What do you think, Nan?" I asked after relaying the latest clue.

"Phooey," she moaned, rubbing her temples in little circles. "I was never very good at riddles. Either of you could be right with your interpretations."

I chewed on my bottom lip while thinking about what to do next. "Okay, how about this?" I said, waiting for Octo-Cat's attention to snap back to me. "Ask them how they killed her. Not how she died, how *they* killed her."

"We already know that," he said, condescension dripping from each syllable.

I shook my fist at him and growled, which was enough to get him to cooperate for a little bit longer.

When he returned to me with their message, he stated it plainly with no commentary. "'*Up it goes and at the same time down, it is here that the answer's found.*'"

"Stairs," I said, recognizing a version of this riddle from my school days. "Okay, so that was *where*. I still need to know *how*."

He batted a paw in my direction. "You're insufferable. You know that?"

I could tell his patience hung on by a single frayed thread—mine did, too—but we weren't done yet. "Oh my gosh, please just ask them already!" I exploded. I'd wrongly assumed that his fondness for the senator would make him more cooperative this time around. Then again, this whole time he'd been certain that he'd already single-handedly solved the case. Who needed facts and testimonies when you have an ego the size of our entire home state?

Octo-Cat groaned and said, "You owe me. You owe me *so big* for this."

"Bigger than the mansion you requested after that last favor?" I shot back, refusing to be bested by a cat… again.

He rolled his eyes but revealed the Sphinxes' next riddle despite his protests. "'*Sure of foot and light of heart, this is how she fell apart.*'"

"Now I feel like they're just volleying my question back at me. This is going to take forever," I whined, resettling myself on the uncomfortable floor. I couldn't wait to fill this room with comfortable furniture and wall-to-wall shelves of books. I would have sat in the window seat for this exercise had Nan not settled on the floor first. Seeing as I was more than forty-five years younger than her, I shouldn't have been having this hard a time.

She reached forward and put her hand on my knee. "Honey dear, if you trust your cat, just let him do all the talking. It seems that might be easier for everyone involved."

If I trusted him. That was a huge *if.* Colossal.

Octo-Cat had clearly made up his mind before he'd heard even a single detail about Harlow's death. But still, I couldn't deny that the Sphynxes did seem to be confessing to the crime in their own special round-about way.

"You're right," I told Nan with a small smile, and then to Octo-Cat, "You don't need to translate for me. Just talk with them and then catch me up later."

He eyed me wearily, then hopped out of Nan's lap and joined our two hairless witnesses in the corner. After several minutes of mixed meows, he trotted back and took up his spot in Nan's lap once more.

"They did it. They killed her by tripping her when she was on the stairs. They are sorry and say they feel really bad about it. As much as I despise them, it doesn't seem like they did it on purpose, but who knows?"

"Thanks," I murmured. I felt a little better, seeing as he'd conceded one point. Earlier he had been certain that they murdered their own in cold blood. Now he was saying that they did it accidentally. Could this whole investigation really been all for naught? Were my instincts that wrong? I was supposed to be getting better with each case, not worse.

Just then, the phone in my pocket buzzed. I fished it out and read the new text message from Mom that popped up on my screen:

Police ruled H's death an accident. I'm coming over.

Well, that answered that.

I passed my phone to Nan so she could see the message, too.

"You don't really believe that, dear," she informed me, setting Octo-Cat to the side so she could push herself up from the floor in one smooth, fluid movement.

I struggled to a stand with far less grace. "I don't know what to believe any more," I admitted. The last couple days had passed in a dizzying whirl, from moving to snooping and everything in between. Both my mind and my body were exhausted. Was it possible I was seeing clues where none existed?

One look at Nan told me she hadn't given up on this yet.

And that was enough for me to keep going, too.

14

Mom arrived about ten minutes later. That was the thing with small towns like Glendale—it never took long to get where you were going. I was a bit removed from the main village action, now that I lived on the swanky East side, but everything remained incredibly close and the traffic was generally light.

Nan pranced through the foyer to let her in, a fact which Mom did not seem happy about.

"Angie?" she asked, charging into the living room where she found me sitting with my smart phone. "What's she doing here?"

Not her politest moment, but my mom and Nan also preferred each other in small doses. Apparently personality types in my family skipped a generation, so if I ever had a daughter of my own, I'd find myself with a little girl who was both too garrulous and too ambitious for her own good. Nan and I had gotten the weirdo gene, and that suited me just fine.

"We were discussing the senator's death," I answered, hating the way the corners of my mother's mouth dipped even further.

"I thought we were working on the case together?" she said, her usual confidence strained. She glanced back toward the door as if debating whether she should make a run for it.

"We were," I said gently, hating that I'd hurt her feelings yet again. "I mean, we are, but..."

Nan breezed past Mom and plopped down onto the couch. "Oh, come off it now, Laura Jean. We're all in this together. Right?" She patted the seat beside her and motioned for Mom to join us.

"Right," I said, offering my mom a quick hug to lift her spirits. "Besides Nan hasn't been here long. Right?"

"Right," Nan answered with a wink that I doubt my mother missed. *Sigh.*

"Well," Mom said, shaking her head and tilting it to either side—a nervous tic she'd picked up during my toddler years, or so I'd heard. "As long as I'm still part of the club, I have some news to share."

She reached into her purse and pulled out a notepad. "First off, the death was ruled an accident. They think she may have had too much to drink at a charity fundraiser and then tripped and fell down the stairs."

Tripped over her cats, I thought, but didn't say anything. I still wasn't ready to talk to Octo-Cat in front of my mom and didn't want to invite questions that would require either doing so or telling her *no* when her feelings were already very clearly hurt.

"The next of kin came in last night," Mom continued. "Matthew Harlow, a divorced salesman from Chicago."

I nodded along mutely.

"The county has assigned a police detail to guard the place whenever he's not at home," Mom continued.

"A police detail. Why?" I remembered seeing Officer Bouchard there yesterday afternoon and how unsettling I'd found it. Nobody had been there this morning, though, when I stopped by. Well, except for Brock the handyman.

She set her notepad down and fixed her eyes on me. "Because the senator was such a prominent person in the area, they're worried that people might come by to loot or take souvenirs. It certainly doesn't help that she has one of the nicest homes in all of Glendale."

Mom widened her eyes at me. *And so do you,* her body language yelled loud and clear.

"So, what now?" I asked, that familiar sense of disappointment creeping up on me again. I should have been happy that the death was solved, but something still didn't feel right. "Case closed?"

"Ha!" Mom shouted. "Hardly! They can call it an accident all they want, but I know something fishy is going on here."

I grinned and gave Mom a high five. I was so glad we agreed on this vital point.

"And when the cops won't do their duty, it becomes the reporter's responsibility to find the truth. Right, dear?" Nan said with a placating smile.

"Right," Mom said, although she seemed less sure of herself now.

"I agree," I said, grabbing my phone and handing it to Mom.

"These are my notes. Granted, I have a few things to add after talking with Matt this afternoon."

"You met Matt? Without me?" Mom shook her head and kept her focus on the phone, but I could tell it really hurt her feelings.

"I'm sorry, Mom." And I meant it. I needed to try harder, now that the two of us had started spending more time together, now that we shared this interest. "It wasn't exactly planned."

"She ran into him in the forest last night," Nan said, leaning forward and clasping her hands together.

"Nan," I cried. "Would you please just stop helping?"

I caught my mom up on all that she had missed in the past day and a half. "Sorry for not calling sooner. It's just been one thing after the next," I said when I'd finished.

"Thanks for filling me in," she said a bit too cordially for my liking. "But I should probably be off. Bye, Mom," she told Nan, who remained seated in her chair as I walked my mother to the door and said goodbye.

"Why do you do that?" I asked my grandmother when I returned. "You know it bugs her."

"That's why I do it," Nan said with a chuckle.

I placed both hands on my hips and stared down at her.

"What? She does the same thing to you!" Nan insisted, and she was right about that.

"Maybe let's all work a little harder on getting along." I fell back into my chair with a sigh. "I mean, we're all grown-ups here."

"As you wish."

"Great." Now, that Nan was properly chastised, this brought us to our next matter at hand. "So, will you please stay the night?"

A naughty expression crossed Nan's face as she laughed and asked. "To protect you from the monsters under your bed?"

I just glared at her, refusing to play these games. "You know why."

"I do," she said, nodding thoughtfully and appearing completely somber as she did. "I just had to get one last jab out of my system. I promise I'll play nice from now on."

"And you'll stay?" I asked, making no attempt to hide how important this was to me.

Nan nodded. "I'll stay."

I let out a giant sigh of relief just as Octo-Cat returned from wherever he'd been during my mother's visit. I assumed this was because he still hadn't forgiven her for the teacup incident yesterday.

"Um, hello there. Hi. What are we going to do about the two murderers you invited to live with us?" he demanded, nodding his head toward the upstairs.

"Oh, Jacques and Jillianne!" I cried. "I guess I should let them out of the library now. *Huh?*"

He took several steps back and squinted angrily, not unlike the expression I'd expect him to make if I ever dared punish him by spritzing him with a water bottle. That is something I would never in a million years do, though—especially now that I knew he could murder me with ease, should the inclination arise.

"Absolutely not," he said emphatically.

"But you said it was an accident," I reminded him, making slow work of rising to my poor, tired feet.

Octo-Cat flicked his tail so crazily that it looked like one of those giant, wavy armed blow up guys outside of an auto dealership. "Yeah, and do you want them accidentally killing you? You only have one life, right?"

"Okay, you have a point." I'd give him that. As much as I felt for the two Sphynxes, I really didn't feel like dying today.

Nan watched with amusement as my cat and I talked, even though she only understood one side of the conversation. "If those two Sphynxes are staying in there, we should probably take them food and water. And a kitty box," she added.

"Good point." They were our guests. The least I could do was make them a bit more comfortable. "Octo-Cat, where did we put your spare litter box?"

"Oh, no. No way. No how. You have absolutely got to be kidding me. You give them my litter box, and I'll make extra sure I use your bed for all my kitty business going forward." Well, that wasn't what I wanted, but it also felt wholly unnecessary to need to head to the store to buy new supplies when we had everything we needed right here.

I sighed and asked a question I was almost certain I would regret. "What do you want me to do?"

"I want you to send them home. I don't like having them here." He remained tense, standing between me and the stairs.

"But don't you want to find out who killed the senator?" I asked, taking several steps closer.

"Uh, hello? We know who killed the senator."

I thought about this. Perhaps there was still a way I could get through to him. "Then shouldn't we keep them locked up until they can... um, stand trial?" I was reaching, I knew. I had no idea what animals normally did to mete out justice, but I knew Octo-Cat was a big fan of legal television shows. Hopefully appealing to his fondness for all things crime and punishment would convince him to start seeing things my way.

"Oh, Angela, you're absolutely right," he ground out, as if this possibility shocked him to the core. "I'll go stand guard."

"He's going to keep watch," I explained to Nan, wondering how I'd just managed to add kitty prison warden to my resume and if it would ever even come in handy.

Well, at least Octo-Cat was occupied.

For now.

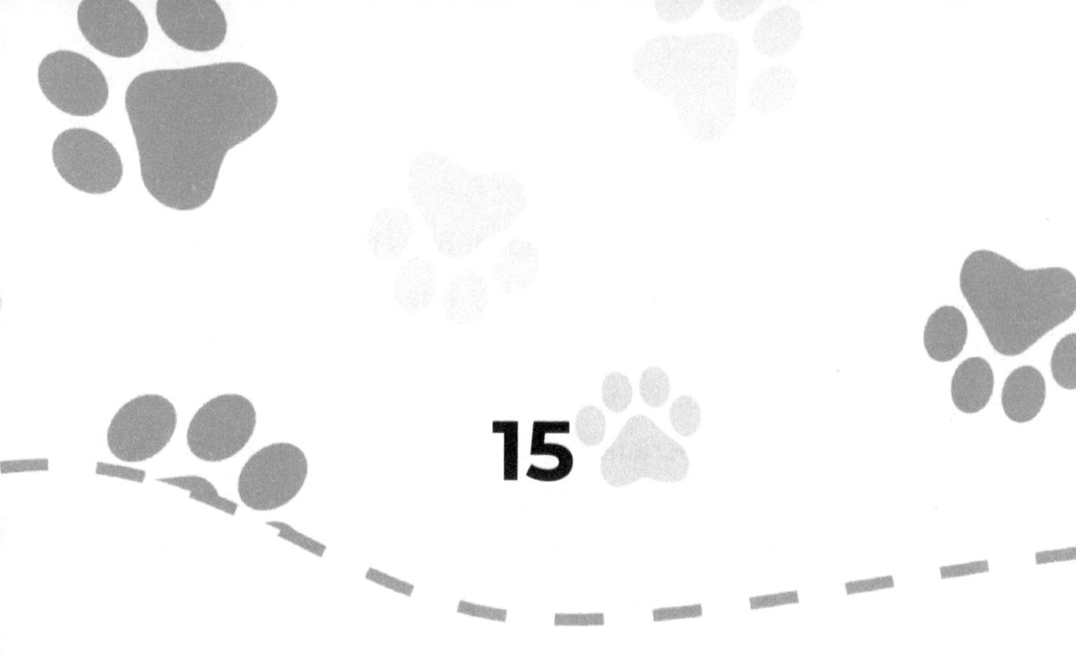

15

I slept better with Nan staying the night. I still locked the door to my tower, but at least we were making progress in turning the giant manor house into a home. Soon my boxes would all be unpacked, Nan would officially move in with all the colorful old knick knacks that reminded me of growing up, and we'd hopefully catch Harlow's killer, too.

Lately, that was the stuff of dreams—or at least my deranged ones.

Feeling wonderfully rested, I awoke the next morning to the most glorious smell in all of human history.

Coffee!

Taking the stairs two at a time, I bolted toward the kitchen. There, I found my dear, sweet, beautiful Nan standing with a polka-dotted apron tied around her teeny waist and a giant, steaming pot of coffee in her hand.

"Good morning," she trilled.

I'd have given her the hug to end all hugs if I wasn't worried that doing so might spill the coffee. In my huge rush to get everything moved in time, I hadn't even thought of what having Nan as my roommate would mean. So what if I was terrified of coffee makers after my near death experience? I still longed for that delicious, life-giving brew, and now, thanks to Nan, I would actually have it.

"Thank you, thank you, thank you," I cried as she grabbed my freshly washed *crazy cat lady* mug and poured me a cup. "Where'd we get the coffee maker, anyway?" I asked, after that first glorious sip of heaven on my tongue.

"I brought it with me," she explained, bending down to check on whatever she had in the oven. I hadn't initially smelled anything over the intoxicating aroma of the coffee, but now that I'd adjusted a bit, the scent of banana bread became unmistakable.

"You're still afraid of coffee makers, right?" Nan turned back to me with a bright smile. She'd always been a morning person. Me, not so much.

I nodded anyway, too deliriously happy to be embarrassed as I took another gratifying sip.

"Well, then I guess I'll just have to be in charge of breakfast from here on out," she declared as she continued to move about the kitchen like she owned the place. I guess, in a way, she now did.

"Hey," I said after I'd consumed enough caffeine to perk up my brain. "Where did you sleep last night?" I'd had Ethel's old bedroom set hauled away, and Nan hadn't officially moved in yet, which meant her bedroom set wasn't here yet, either.

"I roomed with our two hairless visitors," she said her eyes aglow as she squeezed my bicep. "That window seat was so comfy."

"Nan," I scolded. "You're not supposed to sleep there."

She brushed off my concern by waving a dish towel in my direction. "I slept perfectly well, thank you."

"Regardless, I should probably call someone to at least get your bed moved here." I drained the rest of my coffee as I thought.

Seeing I'd finished, Nan immediately plucked the mug from my hands and topped it off.

"Oh, I could ask Brock," I realized as my brain continued to wake up. "He's already planning to come by today to offer me some quotes on a few rennos around here. I'm sure he'd be happy to haul whatever you need over in that truck of his."

Suddenly, I remembered another thing we hadn't yet discussed. "When I ran into him yesterday, he said you had an offer on your house?"

Nan gloated at this news. "That's right. And I bet you'll never guess who."

Normally I didn't like guessing games, but I was still so happy from the coffee that I became a willing participant. "Mom and Dad?"

"*Ha!* Like they'd ever leave their place by the bay. Guess again." She wiped at the counter distractedly as she watched me try to puzzle out an answer.

"Is it somebody I went to school with?" I guessed. I couldn't think of anyone I knew in town who was looking for a new place, so I was completely stumped here.

Nan smiled and shook her head. "Nope, but it is someone we both know. Someone who's quite handsome."

I leaned back against the counter, mug still in hand. *"Hmm."* Nan was a shameless flirt and found half our town handsome by my most recent tally. I knew her latest crush was on the much younger Officer Bouchard, but he didn't strike me as the type to appreciate a retro, cozy Cape Cod in a landlocked neighborhood.

Unable to control her excitement anymore, Nan burst out with her big reveal. "Why, it's our very own Charles!"

I laughed at her joke, but Nan just kept staring at me with that earnest look in her eyes. "Wait. You're serious?" I squeaked.

She bobbed her head enthusiastically and did a happy, little twirl. "Dead serious. He said it was time he put down some roots now that he'd made partner."

"Nan, that's wonderful!" I cried, dancing with her now. "Since we're all friends, you may even be able to visit your old house from time to time."

"Oh, I'm counting on it," she said, her eyes glinting with untold mischief as she transitioned into a fast foxtrot that I had no hopes of replicating. "A happy ending for everyone."

A gentle rap sounded on the front door, drawing both of our attention.

"I'll get it," I told Nan, placing a hand on her shoulder as she stilled her movements. "You stay with the banana bread. I want a piece as soon as it's out of the oven."

"Roger that," she said, offering me a salute for reasons I didn't understand. Then again, if I understood even half of Nan's schemes, I counted it a good day. So far we were off to a great start.

I padded toward the foyer with bare feet, messy bed head, and a half-full mug of coffee. When I spied who was on the other side of the stained-glass windows, my heart screeched to a stop. Okay, not really, but it may as well have, given the absolute shock and horror I felt in that moment.

Brock saw me before I was able to duck out of view and gave a friendly wave. There would be no retreating now. *Oh, poop.*

I turned my back and wiped the sleep from my eyes, then put on my best closed-mouth smile and opened the door. "Good morning."

"I hope it's not too early," he said, looking me up and down as he assessed my hot pink pajama pants and spaghetti string tank top.

"Nope, you're right on time. Come on in. Nan!" I called back toward the kitchen. "Brock's here and we're going upstairs."

"Okay, boss!" she shouted back.

Brock frowned and pressed his hand to the stair bannister, stopping in place. "Yeah, about that... Could you please not call me Brock anymore?"

This surprised me so much I forgot about my desire to keep my mouth closed until I'd had the chance to brush. "What? Why not? Isn't it your name?"

He sucked air through his teeth before saying, "It is, but that name is so associated with the trial now, I kind of cringe every time I hear it."

That definitely made sense. The man had been accused of a double homicide, and for months everyone in Glendale was convinced of his guilt. I didn't blame him for wanting some way to mark a fresh start.

"Oh, of course. What should I call you instead?" I asked with another closed-mouth smile.

He let out a giant sigh of relief. "How about Cal? Short for Calhoun, so it's still my name, but it's not tainted like the longer version."

"You've got it, Cal," I said, then made a dorky, little clicking noise and pointed my finger at him like a fake gun. Really not cool.

He seemed to find it endearing, though, because he laughed. "Thank you, Ang."

We headed upstairs to the room that served as both my future home library and the makeshift kitty prison. Octo-Cat stood stationed outside the door, appearing as if he hadn't slept a wink all night. That would be like eschewing sleep for several days, had he been human. I shuddered to think at just how cranky he would be until our Sphynx visitors were released—or at least transferred to another prison.

"Go get some sleep, you," I told him in a cutesy voice, the kind a normal cat owner might use when talking to a normal cat.

He yawned and stumbled off.

After entering carefully to make sure no Sphynxes escaped in the process, I turned to Brock and explained, "This is my favorite room in the whole house. I want to build shelves right onto the walls, spruce up the floors, add some more lighting, and turn it into a library. What do you think?"

"This is the perfect place for that," he said, turning in a slow circle in the center of the room. "Hey, aren't those the senator's cats?" he asked upon spotting Jacques and Jillianne shivering in their favorite icy corner.

"It's a long story," I said, moving back toward the door. "Could you maybe grab some measurements for me real quick? I'll be back in five."

Once he agreed, I latched the door behind me and then raced to the bathroom to run a brush through my hair and a toothbrush through my mouth. I also splashed some cold water on my face, but decided doing anything more would probably be overkill.

"It shouldn't be too much for me to do the work you're looking for," Brock—oops, *Cal*—said when I returned. He'd been standing by the window seat that looked out onto the beautifully landscaped backyard. You could just barely see the ocean beyond the tips of the trees, and it was a lovely sight to behold.

"That's great," I said, joining him at the window and feeling a little shiver of excitement overtake me. Even with caffeine rushing through my system, I still found myself a bit tongue-tied with this gorgeous man so near. "How much, and when can you get started?"

Cal told me a figure that made me a little sick to my stomach until he explained that this would include the custom-built shelving I needed to line my walls. After that, it seemed like a steal. I couldn't believe that this prince would be building me my fantasy library.

Dreams really did come true.

We shook on it, and then he said, "It's early enough that I can actually get started today. Like I said, not a lot of folks are lining up to hire me, given my recent history."

"You've got yourself a deal, Cal Calhoun," I said with a huge smile, thrilled that we'd be spending more time together. Partially because he'd be nearby in case of danger, and partially because I most definitely had the hots for him now. "Nan and I will both be around unpacking some boxes today. Just holler if you need anything."

"Will do."

"Oh, and Cal?" I had to keep saying his new name to get used to it. The more I said it, the more I liked it. It was uncomplicated and appealing, just like the man himself.

"Yeah?" He removed the measuring tape he'd brought with him and let its long yellow tongue snap back into place.

"Do mind the Sphynxes. They're slippery little buggers," I said, parroting the words Officer Bouchard had said to me just a couple days ago.

And with that, I slipped out of the room and ran up to my tower to find the perfect outfit for casually running into my new crush later that day.

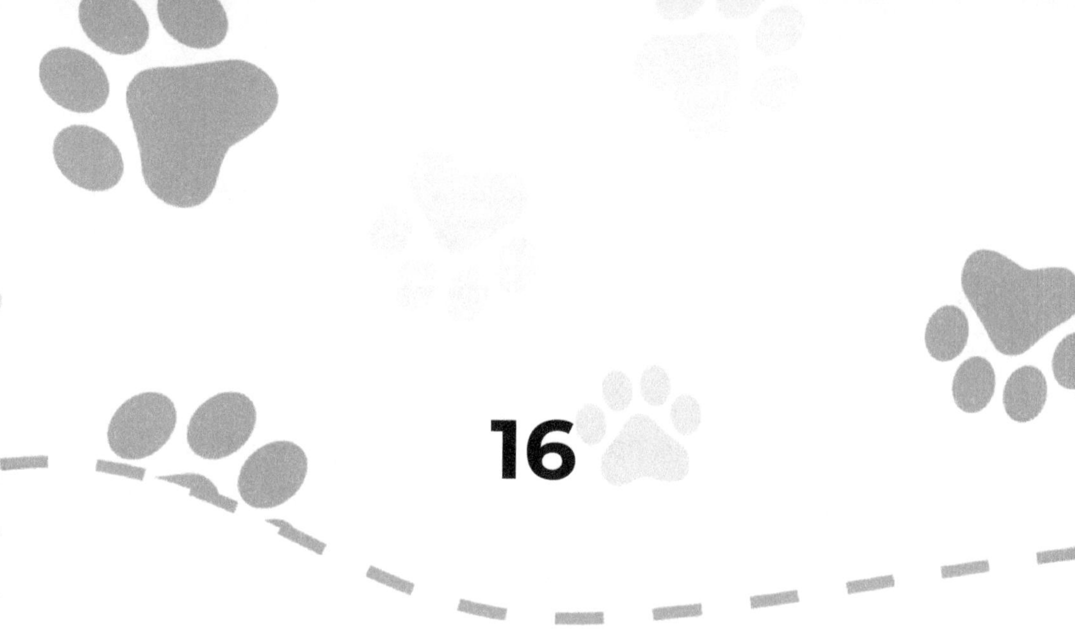

16

My phone started ringing aggressively while I was mid-shampoo. I shut the water off, grabbed my towel, and jumped out just in time to catch Charles before his call got routed to voicemail for a second time.

"Hello?" I asked, dripping onto the cold tile floor. I pushed open the old window with a creak. At least that would let some warmth in here.

"Angie, it's me," Charles said as if he somehow didn't know that caller ID existed and was standard on all phones these days.

"What's up?" I asked, hugging my towel tighter around myself. Of course we'd be having this conversation while I was wet and naked. Knowing my luck, I'd slip on one of the many puddles forming below me, hit my head, get knocked unconscious, and then Brock—I mean, Cal—would have to bust through the door to save me. Maybe I'd even wake up with a second secret super power while I was at it.

Okay, now I was wet, naked, and in a panic. I carefully lowered myself to sit on the edge of the tub while Charles explained the reason for his call. At least, if I fell from here, I'd have a shorter way to go before hitting the floor.

"Sorry I didn't call back yesterday." I heard the unmistakable sound of a door shutting on his end of the call. He paused before explaining further, "Thompson took a couple days off for bereavement."

"For the senator?" I asked, not expecting this news about my workaholic boss.

"Yup," he said, sounding every bit as surprised as I felt. "Apparently the two of them were closer than any of us knew."

I gasped, almost losing my balance and scrambling not to fall. "Were they having an affair?"

"Oh, c'mon," Charles ground out. "Thompson and Harlow, really?"

"Well, anything's possible," I mumbled defensively.

"That's not what was going on," he said with obvious irritation.

That didn't stop me from continuing my line of questioning. He had information, and I needed to know it sooner rather than later. "Then what was?" I demanded.

"Get this," Charles said, and I could just picture him smiling as he paced around his office. He so loved revealing shocking twists, the smoking gun. I wondered if that was what we had here now. "Harlow was planning on stepping down. She was grooming Thompson to run for election as her hand-picked successor."

"Thompson?" I exclaimed. "But he's awful with people." Not

only did he insist on calling everyone by their last names, but he often openly criticized me and the other people at the firm. I knew it was all to protect our stellar reputation, but still. The thought of him as an elected politician representing my state made my stomach churn.

"Maybe," Charles said, apparently unwilling to badmouth the senior partner the way I was. "But there's no denying he's smart and, believe it or not, he and Harlow share a lot of the same political views, too."

"Like what?" I cried, still unable to believe what he'd just revealed.

"They've been friends for a long time. In fact, they met more than thirty-five years ago when they were both doing grassroots work for the *Save the Whales* movement. Thompson said those were some of the best years of his life."

There was that *Save the Whales* thing again. Could it be important? Important enough to cost the good senator her life? And, if so, did that mean Thompson might be targeted next?

"Charles?" I said, knowing I could trust him with this. "Do you think the senator might have been murdered for something to do with her environmental activism?"

"Then or now?" he countered, and I could tell that big, beautiful brain of his was already thinking hard.

"Either," I said. "Is there anything you know that could give some insight into why somebody might have wanted her dead?"

He sighed. "You know the police ruled her death an accident."

"Yeah, but I doubt you buy that, either."

"It *is* suspicious." He thought for a moment before saying more. "How closely do you follow national politics?"

"Not very," I admitted. "I did some Googling on the senator and any recent pieces mentioning her, but nothing jumped out at me."

He chuckled. "Well, here's a quick recap. Last week it was announced that a major oil company had petitioned to put in an access pipeline. It's a new proposal, but people are worried about it. Most of it would run right through our state, even cutting off the corner of one of our national parks."

That sounded awful. I loved my home state for its natural beauty and proximity to the ocean just as much as the senator had. Some giant oil operation would take part of that away, and for what?

"I can see why the senator wouldn't have wanted that, given her deep love for the environment," I told Charles.

"It's still got a while before it goes to vote, but Big Oil is lobbying hard to make it a reality. Their argument is that it would create jobs and bring us another much-needed local energy source, thus lessening our dependence on foreign oil." He explained everything pedantically without a hint of how he felt about the proposal. Seeing as he was a recent transplant from California, I found myself wondering whether Charles sided with Big Oil or the national parks. I knew where I stood.

"But the senator wouldn't have been okay with the destruction of one of our national parks, I take it."

"She definitely wouldn't have been, though it's only about five-thousand acres and the pipeline proposal includes building a new protected park farther upstate." Was he playing devil's advocate for the sake of argument, or did he truly believe the pipeline was anything other than a disaster waiting to happen?

I grew frustrated and let out a massive groan. "What's the point of protecting it, though, if anyone with enough money can destroy it on a whim?"

"I see what you're saying, Angie. I do." Charles sighed and paused for a moment. "But you have to understand, our checks and balances are put in place for a reason, and they work, too. It's not a whim. If the pipeline is going to get approved, a majority of the senate needs to vote in its favor. And, as you know, Harlow was just one out of a hundred."

I ran my fingers over the soft edges of the towel. My skin was quickly moving toward dry as this conversation carried on, but my hair was still a shampoo-y mess. "So then why would the murderer single out Harlow?" I asked.

Charles's voice grew quieter, leading me to believe someone might be passing outside his door and that, for whatever his reasons, he wanted to keep this conversation private. "Let me once again remind you that we don't know whether there was any foul play involved, but if there was, then there'd be a lot of reasons one might single out Harlow."

Oh, this was getting good. Maybe Charles had the smoking gun after all. "Such as?" I asked, my curiosity reaching a fever pitch.

"For one, as one of the two senators representing the state where the proposed pipeline would be built, her opinions hold a little more sway," he started, paused, then raised his voice back to its normal volume. "Add to that the fact she was a mostly conservative politician who could be pretty much guaranteed to vote with the Democrats on any issue that even touches the environment. With a split senate like we have, she could very well end up the deciding vote when the issue goes to vote. Or at least, she could have been."

A knock sounded on the other end of the line.

"Just a sec!" Charles shouted, then said to me, "I need to go."

"Thanks, Charles," I said. "This has been hugely helpful and given me lots to think about."

"Angie, wait." He paused. When he spoke again, his voice sounded lower and far more serious than before. "Please be careful. If you're right and there's some huge political conspiracy underfoot, then you could find yourself next on the hitman's list. Let it go. I'm begging you. Let the authorities deal with whatever did or didn't happen. Okay?"

"Okay," I said agreeably, crossing my fingers just in case. I didn't want to worry Charles, but at the same time, I was so close to having this thing solved it just didn't make sense to back out now. "Thanks for the call. Bye."

I hung up before he could offer any further argument, finished my shower, got dressed, and went to find Nan.

With any luck, we'd have this case wrapped by nightfall.

And maybe for once, luck might actually be on my side.

17

For the better part of that afternoon, I thought about all the locals who might benefit from that proposed pipeline. How much did one need to get out of the situation to consider murder a viable option?

I suppose someone unemployed could want a job bad enough to take such drastic measures, especially if he had a family to provide for. But the proposal was still very new, which meant the news hadn't stretched too far about what could be coming our way. Even though I didn't follow current events as much as I probably should, I still learned about most major stories via my various social media accounts.

This one hadn't made the rounds yet. At least not within my network.

Harlow's murderer had to be somebody on the inside. Someone who paid close attention to the news, or made it even.

Pondering this further, I put a call in to my mom. Unfortunately, it went straight to voicemail. *Boo.*

I spent some quiet time researching on my laptop but continually came up short. I'd talk to Nan about my conversation with Charles soon, but she had a hard time keeping quiet when she got excited. Her voice would echo like crazy through this giant house, and with Cal still here working in the library, our talk would just have to wait.

After another hour passed, I tried calling Mom again. She would never give up on a story before it reached its satisfying conclusion and, seeing as she was the one who reported the news, she most definitely would know more about the pipeline and even its possible beneficiaries.

Still no luck. *Grr.* She must have her phone turned off, which was almost never the case with her. Maybe she and Dad had decided to catch a matinee at the new movie theater the next town over.

Agitated and unable to sit and wait any longer, I decided to go see how things were going in the library. Maybe I could find a nice way to send Cal home early so that I could talk my recent finding over with Nan.

"Knock, knock," I called before pushing my way inside.

The room had grown chilly, and I wrapped my arms around myself as I stepped into the library. Glendale had reached that special time of year where the days were sunny and warm, but both morning and evening temperatures dipped uncomfortably low. The library's large bay window hung open, its sheer drapery fluttering inward.

Cal wasn't there, and neither were the two Sphynxes.

Oh no. This was not good at all.

I raced down the stairs, searching for somebody, anybody.

Cal stood outside, loading up his truck. "I'll be back tomorrow if that's okay," he said before taking in my panicked expression. "Uh, is that not okay?"

"Did you leave the window open up there?" I demanded. My voice came out crazed and shrill, which I hated. "The cats are gone."

He pushed the door on his truck bed up and gave me a pained look. "Shoot. I'm sorry. Let me help you find them."

Not able to wait any longer, I raced around the perimeter of my yard, hoping to find our two missing house guests while Cal searched closer to the house. He must have informed Nan at some point, because she came outside to help, too.

"I didn't leave the window open," he said when our paths crossed again. "I did open it briefly to air out some of the dust, but I kept my eyes on the cats the whole time. When I shut it again, they were still in the room."

"I believe you," I said, but that didn't lessen my worry any. What would Matt say when he found out the cats I'd begged to babysit were now runaways? Whether or not he wanted to keep them, he most definitely would not be pleased that I'd managed to lose one of the last reminders of his mother.

I peered into the forest uneasily. Would I have to brave those woods again? Would Octo-Cat be willing to help? And just where was he anyway?

I spotted a little red sports car in front of the Harlow place. It seemed Thompson was over for a visit with Matt. Hopefully that would keep him occupied long enough for me to safely recover the missing cats. We looked for another half hour, but by that time, dusk had begun to settle in.

"I'm really sorry again," Cal said when we still hadn't made any progress. "Is it still okay for me to come back tomorrow?"

"Of course. And seriously, don't worry about it. I know this wasn't your fault," I assured him.

He nodded grimly, then ambled over to his truck and sputtered off.

"I'm going to go start on supper," Nan announced, giving me a sympathetic pat on the shoulder. "Don't worry, dear. I'm sure they'll show up soon."

I worried my lip while taking another loop around the property. Why were these Sphynxes so good at hiding? And why wasn't Octo-Cat here to help?

Giving up at last, I trudged up the stairs and went to investigate the upper floors of the house. Maybe they hadn't gotten outside at all. It was possible they were just tucked into some other cold corner, shivering with abandon. Seriously, what was up with their desire to be cold all the time?

The house itself had dropped a few degrees since my last pass through. Much to my chagrin, I found that I'd left the bathroom window wide open following my chat with Charles. I eased it shut again, finally deciding I'd earned a break. I could search again later with fresh eyes. First, I just needed to sit a while.

As I approached the stairs, a shadow shifted at the end of the hallway. I squinted for a closer look, wondering if at last I'd found the Sphynxes, and just as I was about to give up the search, too. Unfortunately, it wasn't the cats—just my poor, overworked imagination. Keeping my eyes on the beautiful stained-glass windows in the foyer below, I stepped down and directly onto Octo-Cat, who hadn't been there even a second earlier when I'd glanced down to ensure I had a clear path.

He let out a terrible, twisted yowl, and I quickly adjusted my weight to avoid hurting him any further. This adjustment caused me to lose my balance and tumble down several steps before catching myself halfway down.

"You tried to kill me!" I shouted, clutching my throbbing head. I'd hit it—I'd hit *everything*—on the way down. "You really tried to kill me!"

Octo-Cat widened his eyes in horror. "It was an accident," he insisted, hobbling down for a closer look. I could tell he was hurting, too, but he'd live.

Me? I'd almost been murdered by my cat, and I had no idea why.

Nan came rushing in. "Angie, goodness! Is everything all right?"

"Octo-Cat tried to kill me," I screamed again. How could this be real?

"No, Angela, no!" he continued, not even flicking his tail or making any of his usual irritated gestures. "It was an accident. There was a shiny red dot. I didn't mean to—"

Suddenly, the front door burst open. My mom stood there, backlit by the setting sun, her hair wild with twigs sticking out of it at odd angles. "Get in the car now!" she told me. "Mom, your keys!" she told Nan.

"I didn't do it! I didn't do it!" Octo-Cat cried, but I could deal with him later. I ran down the steps as fast as I could and hopped in the passenger's side seat of Nan's sexy red sports coupe.

"What's happening?" I cried as Mom joined me and jammed the keys in the ignition.

The engine roared to life and she pushed the car into high gear, creating a giant cloud of dust behind us. We took off so fast, the momentum whipped me back against the seat hard. My head began to throb again, but the physical pain was nothing next to the morbid curiosity I had for whatever came next.

"Mom!" I shouted, holding on tight to the dashboard as we flew down my driveway and turned onto the road ahead. "What is happening?"

"I saw who tried to kill you," she said, and for the first time I noticed she was panting with exhaustion. "I was in the woods and came running the second I saw him slip out of your window. He killed Harlow, and now he was trying to kill you. My little girl! If I catch him before the cops do, he's dead."

"Mom!" I screamed again just to ensure I could be heard over the roar of the engine. She made another sharp turn, and Nan's hot little ride fishtailed onto the main road that ran through Glendale. "Who? Who tried to kill me?"

She gripped the steering wheel so tight her knuckles turned white, but she only gunned the gas pedal even harder. We crossed the train tracks, and Mom practically lost control of the vehicle. Still, we were moving forward at speeds faster than any car should even be able to drive.

"C'mon, c'mon," she muttered, her jaw set in a determined line.

Sirens wailed behind us, and I recognized one of the county patrol cars as it pulled up behind us and quickly gained speed.

"Mom!" I cried. I still didn't know what was happening, but it felt like I'd been saved by one murder plot only to wind up right in another one. "Stop! The police are behind us!"

"Good," she said, taking another deep breath as she accelerated even faster. The speedometer edged dangerously close to the one-hundred and sixty miles per hour mark. How was this possible? Why were we even doing this?

Panic gripped me hard as we continued our wild ride. Oh my gosh, someone had tried to kill me, and now I was going to die at the hands of my mother's crazy driving!

"Where would he go?" Mom shouted at me. "Where would he go next?"

"Who?" I screamed again. I still didn't understand anything.

"Your boss," she ground out, changing lanes with abandon. "Richard Thompson."

18

My mind reeled while my body slammed against the car door and my seatbelt dug into my chest. Did my mom really think that my boss had tried to kill me? That couldn't be possible. Octo-Cat had tripped me. I'd never even seen Thompson that day.

"Mom," I said, hyperventilating. "I'm not sure what you saw, but Thompson was never at my house."

"Yes, he was," she shouted, taking another sharp turn.

We were going toward the law firm, I realized then. The cop car stayed right on our tail. I turned back and saw Officer Raines's determined face as she pursued us. She and Mom had already gotten off on the wrong foot, and this impromptu high-speed chase pretty much ensured they'd never be on friendly terms, no matter what happened next.

"I don't know how he got in," Mom continued. "But he climbed out through the window."

"When?" I pleaded, still not understanding. How could any of this be real?

"About two minutes before I made it to your door," she said, slowing slightly as we passed by the law firm. Thompson's car was not there.

That timing Mom reported lined up pretty well with my fall, but...

"There weren't any cars. I didn't see or hear anyone leave before us," I insisted. Even if Thompson had somehow managed to get in and out of my house without being detected, he hadn't gone anywhere in that little red sports car of his. The irony didn't escape me that the pursuant and the pursuer had the exact same type of vehicle. What a chase this would have been, had Thompson actually been a part of it.

"Of course," Mom yelled, twisting the car in an action movie-like U-turn. "He's still on foot! We have to get back! Your nan!"

Fear gripped every fiber of my being as I thought of my poor, vulnerable grandmother all alone with a killer. She was tough, but that was all attitude. If he came at her physically, she wouldn't stand a chance.

The sirens whooped behind us. "Pull your vehicle to the side of the road," Officer Raines commanded over the loud speaker.

"C'mon, Mom," I said, still clutching tight to the dashboard. "Get us back to Nan!"

I had no idea where my mom had acquired her wicked stunt driving skills, but she got us back to the manor house in record time, which was saying a lot considering how quickly we'd initially peeled away.

As soon as the car skidded to a stop, I jumped out and raced toward the house, stumbling on the porch stairs as I went. "Nan!" I cried. "Please be okay!"

Nan appeared in the open doorway wearing her polka-dotted apron and drying her hands on a dish towel. "Of course I'm all right, dear. Just finishing up dinner. Did you and your mother have fun on that high-speed chase of yours?"

I hugged her tight but was quickly pulled back by one very angry Officer Raines. Somehow, she already had Mom cuffed and face down in the dirt. "Stop!" I screamed. "We aren't the bad guys!"

Officer Raines slapped a pair of cuffs on me anyway and began to cite my Miranda Rights.

Mom struggled on the ground. "He's still here somewhere. He tried to kill my daughter!"

The lady cop did not seem amused. "Likely story," she mumbled.

But Nan poked her hard on the shoulder, causing us all to gasp. "You listen here, missy! If my daughter says there's a killer on the loose, then you better believe there's a killer loose. So what if she went a little over the speed limit? Is that as bad as having a murderer on the loose?"

Officer Raines laughed sarcastically. "*A little!* Try one hundred and twelve at least."

"I had to get your attention somehow," Mom groaned, trying desperately to flip herself over.

"Well, you got it," the officer said, grinding her hand into my shoulder as she forced me down the porch steps. "My attention and a one-way trip straight to county jail."

No, no, no. This was all wrong. I hadn't had time to finish putting together the clues to figure out why Thompson would want to murder Harlow and then me. But I trusted my mom. If she said she saw him, then he was probably still here somewhere.

"Thompson!" I shouted, trying and failing to get away from my captor. "We know you're out there."

"Stop deflecting," the officer spat. Why wouldn't she just listen to us? If she hauled Mom and me away, then Nan would be in definite danger and Thompson would most likely never be brought to justice.

Officer Raines pushed me toward her cruiser with Nan hitting her every step of the way. "You let my granddaughter go!"

This was all going very wrong very fast. There was only one person left to turn to now. Well, not person exactly...

"Octo-Cat!" I screamed, craning my neck over my shoulder to glance back toward the house. "Help us!"

Right on cue, my dear, sweet tabby came running through his special electronic door flap and looked up at me with shaking eyes. "Angela, I'd never, ever hurt you."

"I know," I said tenderly, which was difficult considering I was still in police custody. "Help us. Help us catch Thompson. He's the killer, not the cats."

Officer Raines regarded me with a piteous look. "*You* might be able to get off on an insanity plea," she said, and clearly this dissatisfied her greatly.

Octo-Cat ran into the yard and started shouting at the top of his lungs. We all watched as he cried, "Jacques! Jillianne! Now is the time! Let us bring your human's killer to justice! Do as cats do! Do it now!"

I don't know whether he actually knew where they'd been hiding, but a moment later a terrible growl sounded on the roof, followed by a hiss, and...

Thompson staggered into view, away from the spot he'd been hiding in behind the turret. *My turret!*

"There he is!" I shouted to Officer Raines, twisting violently to force her to look.

"Sir," the cop shouted, spotting him at once. "Why are you trespassing here?"

"Oh, um," My boss sputtered, running hands over his suit jacket. His face had fresh blood dripping down the side, and I instantly recognized the work of one ticked-off kitty—maybe two.

Thompson reached beneath his jacket, then pulled out a gleaming pistol. For the third time within a span of fifteen minutes, I was at risk of dying. What a day this was.

"Sir! Drop the weapon!" Officer Raines yelled, pushing me to the ground presumably for my safety.

Octo-Cat sprinted over to me and began to lick the dirt away from my cheek with his sandpaper tongue. "I'm so sorry, Angela. To think, I was used like that. I would never hurt you. You're my human, and I love you."

"I know," I said, wishing I wasn't cuffed so that I could stroke his soft, fluffy head. "I love you, too."

A terrible scream ripped us apart. I looked just in time to see

Thompson hit the ground. His leg twisted at an unseemly angle following his two-story fall, and he cried out in tremendous pain.

Rolling onto my side, I looked up and saw the previously missing Jacques and Jillianne sitting at the edge of the roof licking their hairless paws happily. And suddenly it all clicked into place. I still didn't know why he'd done it, but Thompson had used the Sphynxes to trip the senator the same way he'd used Octo-Cat to trip me, the intelligent jerk. No wonder the poor, distraught cats had confessed to the crime.

Octo-Cat glanced toward Jacques and Jillianne on the roof and cried in delight. "They did as cats do!" he enthused, rushing toward Thompson's prostrate form.

What happened next wasn't pretty. He walked right onto Thompson's back and popped a squat. A wet spot quickly darkened the light suit jacket, and the unmistakable smell of ammonia mixed with the fresh evening air..

"That's for trying to kill my human!" he yelled, proceeding to scratch Thompson with his hind legs in a fury.

Nan laughed and clapped her hands together. Honestly, I'd have done the same if I wasn't cuffed at that particular moment. "Wonderful," she squealed.

"Officer Raines," I mumbled, my face squashed to the ground. "That man broke into my house and tried to kill me. We're pretty sure he's also the one who killed Senator Harlow and tried to make it look like an accident."

Thompson just moaned in agony.

"You're lucky a fall like that didn't snap your neck," the policewoman said, taking the cuffs off me and my mom, then going over to snap a pair on Thompson. "Or maybe not, seeing as you're going to have a lot of explaining to do once we get you to the station."

She forced him onto his feet, and he cried out in pain again.

"Serves you right!" Nan shouted as Officer Raines stuffed him in the back of her cruiser and fled into the night.

So, now that we knew whodunnit, it was time to figure out why...

19

Mom, Nan, and I gathered around the formal dining table, the same table that had been used to serve the poisonous meal that caused the late owner of this estate to lose her life. I tried not to think about that too much, though, as I dug into the delicious and hard-earned meal before me.

Despite our posh surroundings, we were eating tuna noodle casserole with a Vienna sausage and breadcrumb topping.

"I can't believe Mr. Thompson killed his friend. I can't believe he tried to kill *me*," I said, shaking my head sadly.

Octo-Cat sat beside me slurping a fresh dish of cream. He lifted his head, burped, and smiled at me unapologetically. It was amazing how quickly things reverted to normal around here.

"Well, you said he wasn't a very good boss," Nan pointed out, stabbing a mini sausage and taking a bite out of it, extreme bliss apparent on her face.

"Not a good boss and murderer seem miles apart to me," Mom pointed out. She'd found an old bottle of pinot noir in the cellar and was now taking generous sips from an overfull wine glass.

"You solved it," I said, giving her my best, most daughterly smile. "You're the one who figured everything out. *How?*"

She hesitated for a moment, took another drink, and then said, "Well, it wasn't easy, but I knew when the death had been ruled an accident that it just couldn't be the truth. Since you and Nan seemed to have formed your own investigative club, I decided to stake out the forest and watch. It's what any good journalist in my position would do."

"And then you saw Thompson creeping around," I provided.

"Yes. It was especially suspicious when I saw him climbing out of a second-story window. Invited guests just don't do that." She took another slow sip and sighed. "I still don't know why, though."

"Harlow was planning to retire. She was grooming him for her spot," I revealed. "Charles told me earlier today."

"Hey, you never told me that!" Nan protested, setting her fork down and pressing a napkin to her lips.

"I didn't tell either of you. I didn't get the chance."

"So, it seems," Mom said, rubbing her finger around the top of her wine glass as she spoke. "That Charles tipped off Thompson, which is why he came sneaking around here."

"Charles would never put me in danger," I argued, dread pooling in my stomach once again.

"Not knowingly," Nan agreed. "Do you think he was tricked?"

"It was my fault," I mumbled, seeing now what had happened. "I asked Charles to talk to him about why he'd visited the crime scene on day one."

"And that conversation was enough for him to know that you were on to him," Nan said with a scowl. "I never did much care for that man."

"You also never met him," I pointed out, loving how ready and willing both my mom and my nan were to come to my defense.

"They were friends," Mom said after a few silent moments passed. "He killed a friend. For what, power?"

"I honestly don't know," I said. "Maybe Officers Raines and Bouchard will be able to get it out of him, though."

"I really hope we've seen the last murder in Glendale for many years to come," Nan added with a sigh.

"I don't," Mom said, raising her glass. When Nan and I both turned to her aghast, she said, "What? It makes for good news."

"I'm with her," Octo-Cat said from his spot beside me. "I've never had this much fun in all my lives."

We finished supper and mom went home. I realized too late that Cal hadn't gotten the chance to deliver Nan's bed, but she seemed nonplussed by this.

"I like sleeping in the window seat," she said. "It's like an adventure."

I rolled my eyes but headed to bed all the same.

Octo-Cat followed a few paces behind me. "Angela?" he asked. "Are we okay?"

We both got into my bed, and I stroked his back. "Of course we're okay. It wasn't your fault."

He hung his head and moved out of my reach. "I should have tried harder. I should have helped more with the Sphynxes."

"Yes, you should have," I agreed, unwilling to waver on this one specific truth. "But we can't change the past. Only try to do better tomorrow."

Octo-Cat purred and rolled onto his back. "You may pet my belly now," he informed me.

I hesitated with my fingers hanging about an inch from his furry underside. "Do you promise not to bite me?"

"I promise not to bite you ever again," he said. Well, that was an empty promise, if I'd ever heard one. No matter how euphoric and in love with me he felt now, tomorrow would come and I'd no doubt find myself on his bad side once more. I didn't doubt his intentions, though.

For tonight, I decided to relax a little and let myself enjoy his unexpected kindness. I petted him for a while longer, until my phone buzzed beside us.

"Just a sec," I said, shifting the call to speaker. "Hello?"

"It's Charles," my friend said, out of breath.

A huge smile stretched across my face. "I know."

"I'll leave you to your boyfriend," Octo-Cat announced, trotting out of my room and off into some other part of the house. I was happy Charles couldn't understand him, especially since he was still very much in a relationship with Breanne Calhoun and I still didn't know what would come of my new crush on her twin brother, Cal.

"I heard what happened with Thompson," he said. His voice cracked, and it sounded as if he might be crying. "The police came by to question me tonight. They thought since I was his partner, I might have been involved."

"They know you weren't, right?" I ground out, absolutely unwilling to let Charles take the fall for this. He was only involved in the first place because I asked for his help.

"It's my fault he came after you." His voice cracked again. "If anything had happened to you, Angie—"

"Stop. Nothing happened. I'm fine. What about you? Did the police clear you yet?"

"Not officially, but I'm sure it's just a matter of time."

"I'm still trying to figure out why Thompson would have killed his friend." I began chewing on my thumbnails again. Luckily, Charles couldn't see my disgusting habit and Mom wasn't here to swat me over it.

"I don't think he meant to," Charles answered. "My guess is he just wanted to hurt her enough to get her to step down early so he could take her place."

"But why?"

"Hopefully he'll confess whatever his motives were, but I'm willing to guess he and Harlow disagreed when it came to the proposed pipeline. They both loved the environment, but Thompson may have been more willing to bend his ethics for the right price."

"That's awful," I spat, then wiped my mouth with the back side of my arm.

"Yeah, it is," Charles agreed. "But you promise you're okay?"

"I promise," I assured him. "Hey, I hear congrats are in order. You bought Nan's house."

He laughed. “Oh, that. Yeah, I have fond memories of our time working the Calhoun case there together.”

“Good night, Charles,” I said with a huge smile on my face. Maybe I still had a chance with Charles after all.

“You done?” Octo-Cat asked, standing just outside the open door.

“Yeah. Do I get more cuddles now?” I asked, patting the bed beside me.

He glowered at me. “Angela, not in front of company!” He stepped aside to reveal Jacques and Jillianne who also stood waiting in the hall. They couldn’t understand me like Octo-Cat could, but apparently that was beside the point.

“Sorry,” I mumbled and sat up in bed. “C’mon in.”

All three cats entered and found comfy spots on top of my comforter.

I waited for Octo-Cat to explain what was going on, and after a short awkward silence, he did. “I know you still have questions about what happened, so I went and found these two and brought them here for you.”

“But you hate the Sphynxes,” I whispered, covering my mouth just in case they could somehow read my lips.

Octo-Cat shrugged. “They’re annoying, but also kind of cool. Did you see the way they knocked that guy right off the roof? It was awesome.”

I laughed and reached forward to touch the small Sphynx, Jacques. His bare skin was surprisingly soft—not slippery and cold like I expected.

Jillianne came forward to request pets, too, but Octo-Cat hopped onto my lap and meowed a warning. "Paws off my human!" he shouted.

I just laughed again. I loved when Octo-Cat took pride in our relationship. Since he had no problem insulting me freely, I knew his compliments also came straight from the heart.

"Okay," he said once they'd both retreated to the end of the bed. "What do you want to know?"

"You mentioned a red dot when you—I mean, when I fell. Did they see a red dot, too?"

The cats exchanged meows back and forth, and for once I just sat back and enjoyed the spectacle. A few minutes later, Octo-Cat had his report. "Yes, a shiny red dot. The laser pointer."

"If you know it's a laser pointer, then why do you chase it?" I asked him.

He turned toward the Sphynxes, but I interrupted. "No, I'm asking you that."

"It's not a decision we make to chase the shiny red dot," he told me gravely. "Some things just are. Like how the sun rises, the rooster crows, the cat also chases the shiny red dot."

"Who's talking in riddles now?" I asked with a smirk. "That was incredibly poetic."

He rolled his eyes. "Do you want me to help you or not?"

"Yes, please." I gave him an apologetic pat on the head. "Would you please ask why they always sat in that cold corner?"

"Oh, I already know that, too," Octo-Cat said. "They were punishing themselves."

"Punishing themselves?" I asked, feeling so sorry for those poor hairless kitties.

He nodded. "Cats love warmth, and these guys need it even more than the rest of us. They felt so bad about killing their human, they decided to punish themselves for it."

"Do they know it's not their fault?"

He shook his head. "I'm not sure. I tried explaining it to them, but they're still pretty upset."

"Aww, poor things," I cooed, shifting myself to the end of the bed so I could pet them again.

"Angela, we are not keeping them," Octo-Cat warned.

"That's okay," I said with a smile, giving him another soothing pet. "I already have the perfect cat, and besides, I think I already know the perfect person to take them in."

20

It's been a couple weeks since Nan, Octo-Cat, and I moved into our new home, and now it really does feel like home. The best part—well, other than us all being together, of course—is the new home library Cal made just for me. I moved my desk in there and now spend hours, reading, researching, or just browsing social media. I try to stay better informed about current events now that current events almost got me killed.

Mom couldn't be prouder.

My former boss, Mr. Thompson, pled guilty to manslaughter. As Charles had suspected, he never meant to kill the late senator Lou Harlow—just rough her up a bit. He confessed to tampering with the stairs and slipping something into her drink at the charity fundraiser that night. And, yes, he'd used her own cats against her. By means of a shiny red dot, Jacques and Jillianne ended up becoming a deadly murder weapon. Thompson had meant for the entire thing to look like an accident, but he hadn't counted on me and my team of super sleuths getting involved.

He claims he hadn't tried to kill *me,* either—only give me a fright—but I was not buying it. He didn't need to convince me, though. He didn't really need to convince anyone, because he'd already been disbarred and would never ever get the chance to serve in the Senate. Now it was merely a question of how much jail time he would get. I hoped it would be a lot.

Jacques and Jillianne finally seem to have forgiven themselves, and though they missed their former owner dearly, they now have a really good cat dad. It wasn't Matt who adopted them both, but rather Charles Longfellow, III. I knew he'd been lonely ever since Yo-Yo the Yorkie moved out and, seeing as he was putting down roots, two kitty roommates seemed the perfect way to make a house a home.

He didn't even find them creepy. I guess being from California meant he could handle a lot of weird things without so much as batting an eye.

The senator's son, Matt, decided to stay in Blueberry Bay, too. He said he wanted to continue his mother's legacy and is currently battling his ex for summer custody of their two kids. He hopes to give them the kind of dreamy, ocean-side childhood he had growing up. He makes a nice neighbor now that I'm not afraid of him anymore, although he does plan on selling and moving into some place smaller so he has more money to contribute to the Lou Harlow Scholarship Fund.

The late senator left her mark on Washington, too. While Matt was sorting through her things, he found a mostly finished proposal for a new wind turbine farm, right here in the great state of Maine. She hadn't gotten the chance to present it to her Senate committee yet, but Matt is making sure it gets into the right hands.

So, everything's getting wrapped up nicely. Not exactly with a bow, but… you take what you can get.

Now we just had one major matter left to handle, and that would happen today. My new doorbell chimed, playing a cute old-timey jingle that Nan picked out from the huge list of options.

"Coming!" I cried racing down the stairs and flinging open the door.

Mom looked nervous, but I wasn't. I gave her a tight squeeze and then led her up to my new library.

She gasped at the big reveal. "Oh, Angie. It's a dream."

I motioned for her to take a seat at the window. I'd already opened it wide to let the balmy spring air circulate through the room. This room was no longer a prison, but rather a sanctuary.

"It is," I agreed with a blissful sigh. "But that's not why I invited you here today."

"Oh?" Mom folded her hands in her lap and waited.

"There's someone I want you to meet. *Octo-Cat!*" I hollered, and seconds later my kitty partner in crime came running to join us.

Mom laughed. "I already know Octo-Cat," she said, reaching out to stroke his soft, striped head.

I smiled and shook my head. "Not like I do. Do you want to talk to him?"

Her brows pinched together, and her eyes darted from me to Octo-Cat and back again. "How?"

"Through me." I put my hand on top of hers, and her eyes lit up with true mirth.

"Really?"

"Really." I squeezed her hands and let go.

Mom couldn't hide her excitement even if she'd tried. "I have so many questions! How does it work? Can you understand other animals, too? Can he understand me? How does the coffee maker factor into all of this?"

I laughed again. Mom's face fell, but I wrapped an arm around her to show her that it was okay.

"Those are all good questions," I said. "Let's take them one at a time."

WHAT TO READ NEXT

Ever since Angie Russo woke up from a near fatal run-in with a coffee maker, she's been able to talk to—and even worse, understand—one very spoiled tabby named Octavius.

This collection includes *Dog-Eared Delinquent, The Cat Caper,* and *Chihuahua Conspiracy.* Read along as Angie discovers the source of her strange power... and promptly forgets it again. Add in an unwanted blast from Octo-Cat's past and a trouble-making new fur baby, toss on your favorite deerstalker cap, and let's go sleuthing!

The *Pet Whisperer P.I.: Books 4-6 Special Collection* is now available.

Get your copy so that you can keep reading this series today!

SNEAK PEEK

DOG-EARED DELINQUENT

Hi, I'm Angie Russo, and my life is way harder than you'd expect for someone who lives in an old East Coast mansion. Well, it's not really my house— more like my cat's. After all, it's his trust fund that pays the bills.

It may seem like I've won the lottery but think again. Times are tricky when you have a talking cat bossing you around day-in and day-out.

Yeah, I said it.

My cat can talk.

As in, we communicate, have conversations, understand each other. I'm not sure how or why our strange connection works, only that it does. And as much as I wished I knew more, sometimes you just have to accept things at face value. It all happened so fast, too. I went to work unable to talk to animals, got zapped by a faulty coffee maker, got knocked unconscious, and when I woke up again—*bada bing, bada boom!*—now I'm talking kitty.

I've decided to think of it as a stroke of fate, because it really does feel like Octo-Cat and I were meant to find each other. In the past six months alone, we've worked together to solve three separate murder investigations. I guess that's why I'm considering my mom's advice and officially looking into starting a business. She's dubbed me Pet Whisperer P.I.—not because I want anyone else to know about my strange abilities, but because we needed some kind of excuse for me to take Octo-Cat around on my sleuthing calls.

After all, I wouldn't be much of a Sherlock without my Watson. Okay, *I'm* probably the Watson in our relationship. If you've ever been owned by a cat, then you should understand.

Regardless, I'll be the first to admit that my whole life changed for the better once Octo-Cat became a part of it. Before then, I was just drifting from one thing to the next. I'd already racked up seven associate degrees, due to my unwillingness to commit to any one major long enough to secure a bachelor's.

I guess you could say nothing ever felt quite like the perfect fit, but I kept trying anyway. I knew that somewhere out there my dream job was waiting... even if I didn't quite know what it was yet.

You see, greatness kind of runs in my family, and for the longest time I'd worried that particular trait had skipped right past me without a second thought.

My nan had followed her dreams to become a Broadway star back in her glory days, and my mom was the most respected news anchor in all of Blueberry Bay. My dad lived his dream, too, by doing the sports report on the same channel that featured Mom.

Now at last, after so much yearning, so much searching, wishing, and praying, I've found the career path that fits me like a glove—and that's private investigating. So what if I'm not getting paid for it yet? I probably could if I threw everything I had at getting my P.I. business up and off the ground.

But I'm scared of letting down the good people of Longfellow, Peters, & Associates. Oh, that's right. My favorite frenemy Bethany is the newest partner, and I am so proud of her. Between her and Charles, I know the firm is in the best possible hands, but quitting to pursue self-employment?

That's downright terrifying.

True, I'm only part-time at the moment, but the twenty hours per week I put in are really well spent. I know I'm making a difference, and yet...

Aargh. I've never had this much trouble quitting a job before. Why can't I just hand in my two weeks' notice and say, "See ya around?"

Maybe part of me still longs for the chance to see where Charles and I could take our relationship, provided he's willing to ditch his annoying realtor girlfriend. Or maybe I don't want to leave Bethany behind when we've worked so hard to overcome our differences.

It's also likely that I'm afraid of spending all day and all night at home with my crabby tabby for company. Nan lives with us now, too, but Octo-Cat reserves all his whining just for me. I mean, I guess it makes sense, seeing as I'm the one who understands him.

At the end of the day, life sometimes requires hard decisions.

Historically, I'm not so great at making them.

If I just give it a few more weeks, maybe the right answer will fall into my lap. Yeah, I like that idea.

Until that happens, though, I'll just continue to wait and pray I get the courage to ask for what I really need. First, I'll have to make sure it's actually what I want, and then...

Watch out, world! I'm Angie Russo, and I'm coming for you.

* * *

"I come bearing muffins!" I cried as I bounded into the firm ten minutes late that morning. I still had a hard time calculating my new commute, but I hoped that Nan's homemade baked goods would more than make up for my tardiness.

"Ahem," somebody cleared his throat from the desk near the door. *My* desk.

I whipped around so fast, I fumbled my beautiful basket of muffins and dropped them straight onto the floor. All of Nan's hard work was ruined in an instant. It was a good thing she enjoyed baking so much and probably already had another fresh batch ready and waiting at home.

"Let me help you," the stranger said, rushing over to offer assistance I most definitely didn't need. I watched him from the corner of my eye, still refusing to acknowledge this interloper's presence. From what I could discern, he was tall and gangly, with white-blond hair and thick, emo glasses.

"Oh, good," Bethany said, clasping her hands together as she strode toward us both with a smile. "You've met Peter."

"Peter?" I asked with a frown as the new guy stuck his hand out toward me in greeting. Looking at him straight on now, I saw he wore his dress shirt open with a t-shirt underneath that read *Awake? Yes. Ready to do this? Ha, ha, ha!* Charming. The disturbing top half was paired with wrinkly cargo khakis on bottom. Fulton and Thompson *never* would have let this fly in their days. Yeah, I knew the firm was mostly better off without them, but still couldn't we at least try to look like professionals here?

"You're Angie, right?" Peter asked, grabbing one of the muffins that had touched the floor and shoving it into his mouth with wide eyes. *"Mmm,"* he said pointing at it. "So good."

I disliked this guy more and more by the moment, but Bethany seemed so excited to introduce us that I forced a smile and shook his hand despite my better judgement.

"Peter's our new intern," she explained. "He's going to help you manage your workload."

"I don't need help managing my workload," I shot back, recoiling from Peter's grasp when he wouldn't let my hand go after the normal, polite period of time for a greeting.

Bethany frowned. "Not exactly true. It's been harder for all of us since you switched to part-time, but it's okay, because Peter is the perfect person to step in and smooth things out."

Yeah, me going part-time was the problem, and not the revolving door of partners we'd seen so far this year.

"What exactly are his qualifications?" I asked, regarding him coldly.

Peter popped the remains of that precious blueberry muffin into his mouth and mumbled, "I'm her cousin, and I work for minimum wage."

Bethany shot him a dirty look, finally showing me that he bugged her, too. That at least made me feel a little better about all this. "Really, Peter. You need to stop being so liberal about sharing your salary."

"Sorry," he muttered with a shrug that suggested he really couldn't care less about it.

Why was he here? I may not be the best paralegal in the world, but I was miles better than this guy. He probably didn't even have his degree. This was all wrong. I couldn't quite say why exactly, only that I hated everything about this Peter guy.

"Wait," I said, realizing something. "Your name is Peter Peters? You sound like a super hero."

"Or a super villain," he countered with another shrug and a strange, new smile.

"Anyway," Bethany said, glancing at her feet to make sure no errant muffin crumbs had attached themselves to her shiny patent pumps. "This is Peter's first day, which is why I asked him to come in a bit early. Can you help get him set up? Show him the ropes?"

"What kind of ropes?" I demanded. I didn't normally start my work day by playing babysitter to some annoying nepotistic hire.

No, right now, I was supposed to be in Bethany's office while she safely brewed me a cup of delicious, life-saving coffee. There was no way I'd touch another coffee maker as long as I lived, but I still enjoyed the extra jolt it gave me when someone else was willing to brave the brew master.

"Just the stuff you normally do," Bethany answered with a dismissive gesture, already turning to take her leave. "If either of you need me, I'll be in my office. I have client meetings most of the morning, but should be free around lunch time."

"Okay, bye," I said, turning to my new charge, resigned that I would have pretty much the worst work half-day ever.

He smiled after his cousin. "Too-da-loo!" he called, waggling his fingers, then turned to me. "Okay, so I'm ready to learn how to be you when I grow up," he announced.

He did not just say that!

Well, so much for turning in my notice. There was no way I could leave the firm with this bumbling oaf of a paralegal. If only we could cue a makeover montage in real life. I'd choose one of my favorite upbeat 80's pop jams, spend a few minutes reforming him, then call it done and move on. Real life never worked fast enough.

"Let's go set up your email," I said with a sigh, leading him back to my desk that we now seemed to be expected to share.

"Cool, cool. And when do I get my company-issued iPhone?" He bobbed his head, following after me like a lost little duckling.

"What? Why would we give you an iPhone?"

"Uh, hello. FaceTime." He twisted his hands and formed a rectangle about the size of a smartphone then looked at me through the gap.

And just like that, he went from simply irritating to downright terrifying. FaceTime was the same app I used to call my cat from work. Our senior partner, Charles, had found out when he was still brand new to the firm and bribed me to help him defend a client. Was it just a coincidence that this Peter Peters had alluded to it now?

Or did he know something that could get us both into very big trouble?

Oh, I did not like this. I did not like it one bit.

***Dog-Eared Delinquent* is available as part of the *Pet Whisperer P.I.: Books 4-6 Special Collection*.**

Get your copy so that you can keep reading this series today!

ABOUT MOLLY FITZ

While *USA Today bestselling* author Molly Fitz can't technically talk to animals, she and her three feline writing assistants have deep and very animated conversations as they navigate their days.

She lives with her child and their own private zoo somewhere in the wilds of Alaska. Molly will occasionally venture out for good food, great coffee, or to meet new animal friends.

Learn more about Molly and her books, and be sure to sign up for her newsletter at **www.MollyMysteries.com**.

ALSO BY MOLLY FITZ

Learn more about Molly's collected works, so that you can decide which book you'd like to read next...

PET WHISPERER P.I.

Angie Russo just partnered up with Blueberry Bay's first ever talking cat detective. Along with his ragtag gang of human and animal helpers, Octo-Cat is determined to save the day... so long as it doesn't interfere with his schedule.

Start with book 1, ***Kitty Confidential***.

MERLIN'S MAGICAL MYSTERIES

Gracie Springs is not a witch... but her cat is. Now she must help to keep his secret or risk spending the rest of her life in some magical prison. Too bad trouble seems to find them at every turn!

Start with book 1, ***Merlin Takes a Familiar***.

PARANORMAL TEMP AGENCY

Tawny Bigford's simple life takes a turn for the magical when she stumbles upon her landlady's murder and is recruited by a talking black cat named Fluffikins to take over the deceased's role as the official Town Witch for Beech Grove, Georgia.

Start with book 1, ***Witch for Hire***.

THE MYSTERIES OF MOONLIGHT MANOR (WITH TRIXIE SILVERTALE)

Sydney Coleman has it all—until she doesn't. No sooner does she launch her bed and breakfast, than a trio of ghosts turn up oppose her at every turn. They insist she solve the murder of their mistress, but Sydney is desperate for cash. If she can't book some guests fast, her haunted mansion is utterly doomed.

Start with book 1, ***Moonlight & Mischief***.

CONNECT WITH MOLLY

Sign up for my newsletter and get a special digital prize pack for joining, including an exclusive story, *Meowy Christmas Mayhem*, fun quiz, and lots of cat pictures!

Sign up: **MollyMysteries.com/subscribe**

Now, if you ever wished you could converse with cats, here's your opportunity! This is me officially inviting you into my whacky inner world as part of my Cozy Kitty Book Club.

For those who just can't get enough of my zany cat characters and their hapless humans, this book club will provide new content to devour and the chance to get to know my best author friends.

From exclusive stories, behind-the-scenes trivia to never-before-released bonus content, and monthly giveaways, there's a lot to love about the Cozy Kitty Book Club. Join today to find out what we're reading next!

Join: **MollyMysteries.com/club**

www.ingramcontent.com/pod-product-compliance
Lightning Source LLC
Chambersburg PA
CBHW020717310726
48979CB00004B/949

* 9 7 8 1 6 4 4 5 1 5 2 9 7 *